ALL NIGHTMARE LONG

ALL NIGHTMARE LONG

Tim Lebbon

Introduction by Sarah Pinborough

FIRST EDITION

ISBN
978-1-78636-851-5
978-1-78636-852-2 (signed edition)

Design and layout by Alligator Tree Graphics.
Printed in England by T. J. Books.

PS Publishing Ltd
Grosvenor House
1 New Road
Hornsea, HU18 1PG
England

editor@pspublishing.co.uk
www.pspublishing.co.uk

CONTENTS

CONTENTS

ALL NIGHTMARE LONG

I have known Tim Lebbon for over twenty years now. That's a mind-blowing amount of time and yet it has passed in the blink of an eye. One minute you're the young guns of the genre and the next you're the old guard and wondering what the hell *TikTok* is and how are people using it to sell books.

Tim and I started out together really, he was a couple of years ahead in publishing terms, and I still call him *Bruv* because he was like a big brother to me back around 2003/4 when I was starting out. He told me which cons to go to, he introduced me to people, we drank and smoked (he didn't do triathlons then—*as an aside, reader, I had to look up how to spell that word!*) and talked about conquering the world and creeping people out with our stories.

Twenty something years on, we still have those conversations. Tim is still as ambitious and fired up as he was when I first met him in person, in a pub in Wales, at his launch for *The Nature of Balance*. He's still as excited about work, as driven, as relentless as he was then. But has he changed? Sure. Everyone does. We get older.

More knots in the wood. Time has more meaning now. We've seen more changes in the world, the people around us, the lives we live.

Tim's writing has changed too. I was a fan of his early work and I'm still a fan now, especially of his short form writing. Tim has a real knack with novellas and short stories that I'm quite envious of, and he clearly loves writing them.

How can I describe this collection? I guess, *grown up*, springs to mind. I remember reading Stephen King's *Hearts in Atlantis* when it came out and loving it but thinking, *this is grown up Stephen King*, and I had the same feeling reading the stories in this collection. Tim's grown up.

Are the stories still creepy? Oh yes, of course. *Clown's Kiss* in particular absolutely terrified me with its quietly building dread. Tim Lebbon can do creepy all day—or night—long. But now his tales are not about the jump scares or potential boogey-men under the bed. These are stories that *chill*, I feel. Like reading an M.R James short story before bed and thinking, that wasn't too bad, and then staring at the ceiling in the dark as your skin prickles with the after-effects. That's how I felt reading these. And so of course I read them before bed and let my skin prickle.

But I found that the after-effects weren't just the prickling of my skin. They're rich these stories, thick with things learned through the passing of time. The ache of loss. The pain of mourning—mourning of a person, a place, a time gone by, a person we once were. The ghosts that walk with the living who grow closer as we age. The loss of things we realise we may never have, that in the flush of youth seemed so close within grasp. This is a grown-up collection and it deals with grown up themes. These stories have been written by a man in the decade between his forties and fifties— the move from young to middle-aged—and Tim has clearly mined the seam of emotions that comes in that decade when curating this collection.

The titles of the stories he's chosen reflect these themes too —*Relics, Skin & Bone, In the Dust, May the end be Good*— the phrases ache with a sense of the inevitable march of time and how we change with its heavy footsteps.

There is nothing complacent and middle-aged here. Thoughtful, skilled and crafted, yes. I would even say *elevated*. All that drive and energy that Tim had when I first met him is still there in these stories, but now they're written with a defter hand. With more experience behind them. With more life and loss bound into the words.

Yes, we're older. Yes, we're more weighed down with the problems of life and the ticking of the clock than we were when we first met all those years ago. But for Tim at least, nothing in his storytelling has slowed. He's maturing like a fine wine. His tales are richer and deeper and more full-bodied. So, pour yourself a glass and take a seat. Sip this book or down it in one, whichever way is your preference, you're in for a heady experience.

And it will last *All Nightmare Long*.

Sarah Pinborough

For Dad
1931–2021

ACKNOWLEDGEMENTS

A big thanks to all the editors who first bought or commissioned the stories contained in this collection. And huge hugs to all the very great friends I've made through writing—too numerous to mention without the risk of missing some out, but you know who you are. Honestly, there are no better people on the planet, and I feel blessed.

Eternal gratitude to my lovely wife Tracey, and kids Ellie and Dan. Yeah, okay, they're 23 and 18 now, but I still get to call them kids for a while yet. My family kept me grounded during the pandemic and lockdown, because honestly, having the mind and imagination of a horror writer is not advisable during such a world-changing event. But exercising with my family in the garden, racing each other around a local 5k route, cocktail parties at home, all helped keep things on an even keel.

Thanks to my agents and friends Michael Prevett, Ed Hughes and Caspian Dennis, and especially the splendid and incomparable Howard Morhaim, for whom I still maintain a red phone.

Finally, a huge thanks to Pete, Nicky and the rest of the PS Publishing crew. It's always a delight working with you, and here's to many more.

IN STONE

S everal weeks following the death of a close friend, I started walking alone at night. I was having trouble sleeping, and I think it was a way of trying to reclaim that time for myself. Instead of lying in the darkness remembering Nigel, feeling regret that we'd let the time between meetings stretch further each year, I took to the streets. There was nothing worse than staring at the ceiling and seeing all the bad parts of my life mapped there in cracks, spider webs and the trails of a paint brush. I thought perhaps walking in the dark might help me really think.

On the fifth night of wandering the streets, I saw the woman.

I was close to the centre of town. It was raining, and the few working streetlights cast speckled, splashed patterns across the pavement, giving the impression that nothing was still in the silent night. Over the past hour I'd seen several people. One was a night worker—a nurse or fireman, perhaps—hurrying along the street wearing a backpack and with a definite destination in mind. A couple were youths, so drunk that they could barely walk or talk. One was a homeless woman I'd seen before. Two dogs accompanied her like shadows, and she muttered to herself too quietly for me to hear.

They all saw me. The worker veered around me slightly, the youths muttered and giggled, and the homeless woman's dogs paused and sniffed in my direction.

But the new woman didn't look or act like everyone else. At three or four in the morning, anyone left out in the streets wanted to be alone. Closeness was avoided, and other than perhaps a curt nod, no contact was made. It was as if darkness brought out mysteries and hidden stories in people and made them solid, and that suited me just fine. I wasn't out there to speak to anyone else; I was attempting to talk to myself.

There was something about her that immediately caught my attention. Walking in a world of her own, she followed no obvious route through the heavy rain, moving back and forth across the silent main street, sometimes walking on the pavement and sometimes the road. The weather did not appear to concern her. Even though it was summer, the rain was cool and the night cooler, but she walked without a coat or jacket of any kind. She wore loose trousers and a vest top, and I really shouldn't have followed her.

But Nigel told me to. It was his voice I heard in my head saying, *Wonder what she's up to?* He had always been curious and interested in other people, the one most likely to get chatting to strangers if we went for a drink. Last time I'd seen him he'd been more garrulous than ever, and I wondered if that was a way of hiding his deeper problems and fears. He could say so much, but still didn't know how to ask for help.

The woman drifted from the main street to a narrower road between shops, and I followed. I held back a little—I had no wish to frighten or trouble her—but tried to make sure I kept her in sight. The rain was falling heavier now, and I had to throw up my hood to shield my eyes and face. The side street was not lit. Rain blanketed the night, making everything even darker and giving a constant shimmer to reality. Her movements were nebulous and fluid, slipping in and out of the darkness like a porpoise dancing through waves.

To my left and right, large spaces opened up. These were the service yards of big shops, covered delivery and storage areas that I barely noticed if walking these streets during the day. Now, they were pitch-black burrows where anything might exist, and I was pleased when the woman passed them by.

As she neared a smaller street, she paused. I also stopped, tucking in close to a wall. I suddenly felt uncomfortable following her. I was no threat, but no one else would believe that. If people saw me stalking the woman, they might think the worst. If she saw me, I might frighten her.

I was about to turn and walk back the way I'd come when something gave me pause.

The street ahead was a place I knew well, home to a series of smaller, independent shops, a couple of nice pubs, and a few restaurants. Nigel and I had eaten and drunk there, and I'd walked that way more times than I could recall. In the stormy night, it glowed with reflected neon from shop windows. A rush of memories washed over me, and I gasped.

The woman seemed to hear. She tilted her head slightly, then walked out into this narrower road. I followed. I had the sudden sense that I was witnessing something secret. I felt like an intruder, emerging from my safe, warm home to stroll dark streets I knew nothing about.

During the day, this place was a bustling centre of commerce and fun. Now it was a whole new world.

By the time I moved out onto the street, the woman had paused beside a series of bronze sculptures on plinths. They'd been placed fifteen years before as part of the millennium celebrations, and I hardly ever noticed them. Seeing them at night, flowing with water that shimmered and reflected weak light, gave them a strange form of life.

The woman was staring past the sculptures and into the mouth of a narrow alley. I knew the place. It was a dead-end passageway between a fast-food joint and a newsagents. I'd stumbled down there once years ago, drunk, a young woman holding onto my arm as if I could be more stable than her. I had vague memories of what we'd done. Shambolic, clumsy sex amongst split bags of refuse and broken bottles did not make me particularly proud, and I'd only ever spoken of that moment with Nigel.

As I wondered what her interest might be in that grubby place, and just what it was about her that troubled me, she began to take off her clothes.

I caught my breath and pulled back around the corner. I felt unaccountably guilty witnessing the woman's shedding of clothing, even though she was doing it in the middle of the street. Her shoes came off first, then her vest and trousers. Naked, she stretched her arms to the air and let the rain run across her body. She might have been beautiful.

Rain flowed into my eyes. I wiped them and looked again. There was something wrong.

The woman was moving past the bronze statues and heading towards the entrance to the alley. Her motion seemed strange. She drifted rather than walked, limbs swinging slightly out of time, her movements not quite human. Her pale skin grew darker. Her hair became a more solid cap around her head. She slowed before the alley—hesitant, or relishing the moment—then stepped into its shadows.

As she passed out of sight, I had the very real sense that she was no longer there.

I ran into the night.

"And you ran all the way home?"

"Yeah."

"Dude. You. Running."

I laughed. "Who'd have thunk it?"

Ashley licked her finger and used it to pick up cake crumbs from her plate. Finger still in her mouth, she caught my attention and raised an eyebrow. I rolled my eyes. Ash had been my best friend since we were both babies, and although I couldn't help but acknowledge her beauty, I'd never been drawn to her in that way.

"Still not sleeping?" she asked.

"No. Not well at all."

"Hence the walking at night."

I nodded.

"You're very, very weird."

We both sipped at our coffees, comfortable in our silence. The café around was filled with conversation and soft music, merging into a background noise that kept our own chat private.

"Maybe she was a prostitute."

"No."

"You're sure?"

I nodded.

"So you'd recognise one?" She had that cheeky glint in her eyes, and I couldn't help but smile. Ashley called herself shallow, but I knew that wasn't true at all. She was simply someone who knew how to regulate her depths. She'd been a levelling force in my life forever, and never more than since Nigel stepped from that ledge.

"It's only around the corner," I said. "Will you come with me?"

"And search for the mysterious vanishing woman? You bet!"

We left the café. It had stopped raining and the town was alive with lunchtime buzz. Ash and I met for lunch at least once each week, working within ten minutes of each other making it easy. I dreaded her leaving to work elsewhere. She'd mentioned it once or twice, and I knew that she'd had a couple of interviews. It was only a matter of time. Ash was not someone that life held back, and the world was calling.

"It will get easier," she said, hooking her arm through mine as we walked.

"Yeah, I know."

"Wish I'd known him better."

I nodded. Felt a lump in my throat and swallowed it down. "Me too."

As we approached the place where I'd seen the woman earlier that morning, I heard the cheerful shouts and laughter of a group of school kids. They were maybe nine or ten, posing around the bronze statues as teachers took photos. They probably shouldn't have been up on the plinths, but no one would tell them to get down. Who would intrude in such excitement and joy?

I headed past the statues and children, aiming for the alley between the newsagents and the fast-food joint, which was doing a busy trade. People queued out the door. A young woman emerged from the alley, wearing an apron with the takeaway's name emblazoned across the front. She offered us a quick smile, then pushed past the queue and back into the shop. I felt a release of tension from my shoulders, a relaxing in my gut. Ash must have felt it too.

"See?" she said. "No gruesome murders."

I turned to her and nodded, and then something caught my eye. A litter bin stood beside a bench close to the statues, and splayed across its lip was a dirtied white vest.

"Oh," I said. I blinked, remembering the woman lifting the vest up over her head.

"What?" Ash asked.

I pointed at the vest. "Why wouldn't she dress again afterwards?" After what, I did not say, or even wish to consider. She must have walked home naked. If she had walked home at all.

I headed for the alley, and Ash came with me. It smelled of piss. No surprise there. But it also smelled of rain, fresh and sharp, even though it had stopped raining well before I'd finished running home eight hours before.

"Delightful," Ash said. She stepped over a pool of vomit on the ground.

It was unremarkable, a narrow alley with a dead end thirty feet in, dirty rendered wall on one side, old bare brick on the other. A couple of metal doorways were set into the walls, without handles and looking as if they'd been locked for decades. There were a few black bin bags, one of them split and gnawed at by night creatures—cats, rats, foxes. A pile of dog crap held a smeared shoe print. A dead rat festered against the blank end wall.

"She didn't come out again," I said.

"Not while you were watching."

"But her clothes."

Ash shrugged.

I walked the length of the alley, fearing what I might see, eager to make sure there was nothing there. I shifted a couple of rubbish bags with my foot, releasing a foul stink that made me gag.

"Jesus, what a wonderful smell you've found!" Ash said.

I covered my mouth with the collar of my coat and went in deeper, shoving bags aside with my feet. Old wrappers spilled, slick with rotting food. Things crawled in there, dark and wet, reminding me of the nude woman flowing with rainwater, silvery, flexing and shifting like something inhuman. I bent down to look closer and saw a nest of slugs, leaving trails like slow echoes and pulsing like something's insides.

"Weird," Ash said. She was looking at a spread of brickwork close to the ground, a few feet from the end of the alley. I went to her and stood close, our coats brushing. She grabbed my hand.

"What?"

"Don't know," she said. She shivered. "Let's go."

"Hang on." I crouched, leaning in closer, trying not to block out precious light so that I could see what she'd seen.

"Come on. Let's go."

"What *is* that?" I asked. But neither of us could answer.

The bricks were old and crumbling, covered with black moss, joints clotted with decades of filth. This wall had never seen sunlight, and perpetual shadow had driven darkness into the brick faces and the mortar in between. Across a spread of brickwork, something protruded. It looked like a swathe of dark pink pustules, solid-looking rather than soft, dry and dusty even though the brickwork around them was damp. I reached out to touch, but Ash grabbed my arm.

"What if it's poisonous?" she asked.

"It's just the bricks," I said. "Frost-blown, maybe. They've deformed over time." I reached out again, but didn't quite touch. Something held me back. Something about the shape of the feature, the way it swept up from the ground and spanned several courses of bricks.

It looked like an arm reaching from the ground, embedded in the wall and only just protruding. At its end, a clenched fist of brick-work protruded more than elsewhere, cracked and threatening to disintegrate at any moment.

I wondered what that fist might hold.

Ash grabbed my coat and pulled me upright, shoving me before her along the alley and back into the street. "It should be cleaned," she said. But she didn't enter the fast-food shop or the newsagents to share this opinion with them. Instead, she headed back to work.

I stood there for a while looking at the discarded clothing in the litter bin. It was slowly being buried beneath lunchtime refuse— coffee cups, crisp bags, sandwich wrappers. Soon it would be completely out of sight. Forgotten.

I wondered where the woman had gone.

"I'm sorry," Ash said. She'd called me after work, on the way to her boyfriend's place.

"For what?" I was in the park, beyond which lay the old terraced house where I lived. It was raining again, and a few umbrellas and coats hid anonymous people as they took various paths home.

"I just . . . that place at lunchtime felt a bit odd. Didn't it?"

"Yeah." But I couldn't quite verbalise how the alley had felt strange. *Like somewhere else*, I might have said. The idea crossed my mind that I'd seen a ghost, but I had never believed in them. I was a rationalist, an atheist, and until Nigel's death I'd been happy and comfortable with that. Since he'd taken his own life, I had been struggling. Not for him, because he was gone now, flickering out from a wonderful, expansive consciousness to nothing in the space of a pavement impact. But for me. All that was left of Nigel was in my mind, and the minds of those who loved him. That didn't seem much to leave behind.

I thought of those weird shapes across the rotting brickwork, blown clay in the shape of a rising, clasping arm and hand.

"Max says hi."

"Hi, Max."

"See you soon. And don't go wandering tonight. Weather forecast is awful, and you need sleep."

"Damn right. Bottle of wine, then bed, like a good boy."

"Good boy." Ash hung up, leaving me alone in the park with the rain, and the puddles, and the memory of a time me, Nigel and a few others came here to play football when we were kids. I thought I heard his laugh. But it was someone else, and I started walking again before whoever was laughing caught up with me.

Wind roared around my house and made the roof creak, rain hammered against the closed windows, and next door's dog barked, waiting for them to come home. I tried to sleep for a while, but failed miserably. The brief buzz I'd had from the bottle of wine was gone, melted away into the darkness of my bedroom. I lay awake for a while staring into the shadows.

Then I got up, dressed, slipped on my raincoat that was still wet from walking home from work, and went out into the night.

It was almost two in the morning.

I walked into the city. I lived in a suburb, but it was only fifteen minutes through the park, past the hospital and into town. All that time I saw no other pedestrians, and only a few cars. Some of them were police vehicles, and one slowed when it passed me, a pale face peering from the window obscured and made fluid by rain impacting the glass. I stared back, hiding nothing. The car moved on.

I was heading along the main street, intending to visit that alley again. There had been something strange about the woman, but I found that I was not afraid. I had no idea why. Maybe it had been

Ash's strange, repulsed reaction to that feature on the wall, and my realisation that I was less troubled than her.

The weather was atrocious. Wind howled along the town's main thoroughfares like a beast unleashed, revelling in the fact that there was no one there to view its nighttime cavortings. It whistled through the slats of fixed benches, rattled shutters on jewellers' shops, and flung litter into piles in doorways and against wet walls. Rain lashed almost horizontally, spiking into my face and against my front, the coat hardly any barrier at all.

I leaned into the wind and rain, working my way through the town, and the night was alive around me.

I saw a few people. It was earlier than I usually chose to walk, and a couple of the later clubs had only kicked out an hour or so before. A few drunks huddled against the weather and tried to remember where they lived. Some were in pairs, more alone. I also saw the homeless woman with the dogs. The hounds looked my way, but I don't think they growled, or if they did the wind carried the sound away. Maybe they were growing used to me.

There's a part of town where five roads converge. People call it a square, though it isn't really. It's disordered and accidental, the same as most people who pass through from midnight onwards. That night it was a wilder place, and as I approached along the main street I had to stop and stare. The square seemed primeval. Great cliffs of brick, stone and glass rose up on all sides, channelling torrents of wind and rain that met in the middle as if in battle. A tornado of litter and rain twisted back and forth, throwing off its contents and sucking more in. The sound was staggering, the effect intimidating. I could see shop windows flexing beneath the onslaught, as if the buildings themselves were breathing great, slow, considered breaths.

I stood there for a while just watching, and then as if carried like shreds of refuse on the storm, memories of Nigel came in.

We cross the square, arms around each other's shoulders. It's a Saturday afternoon and we've been in the pub all day, ostensibly to watch a big rugby match, though neither of us is really into sport.

The atmosphere was electric, the pub a sea of shirts of two colours, good-natured banter fuelled by beer turning into hearty singing, and much friendly mockery of the losing team. It's been refreshing and upbeat, and Nigel has said that tribal warfare has never been so much fun. We're going to buy food. We head down one of the narrower streets—

—and Nigel reels from the blow, staggering back into a doorway as the big, thick thug storms after him. I've never been so afraid in my life. But that's Nigel getting picked on for no reason. We simply walked the wrong way and met the wrong nutter. He's drunk, that's obvious, and though I'm not one to judge by first appearances, he looks like he likes a fight.

He launches another punch at Nigel, then I'm piling into the bastard from behind, shoving him forward as hard as I can into the shop window. Glass cracks. He half-turns to glare at me, murder in his eyes and blood running from a cut in his forehead. Nigel lands a punch on his nose, a pile-driving crunch that we'll talk about for years to come—

—we're following two girls who have been smiling at us all afternoon. We're too old to stay at home, too young to hit the pubs, so town is our afternoon playground, and today feels special. Nigel is the good looking one, and both girls have been eyeing him. I'll become used to playing second fiddle to my friend.

I sighed, and my breath was lost to the storm like so many memories. His death still hit me like this, and I wasn't sure I'd ever grow used to it.

Buffeted by high winds, soaked to the skin, I decided to make my way home.

The shape started across the square just as I took my first step. It was a man, perhaps late fifties, long grey hair swirling around his head and coat flapping in the wind. Yet none of his movements seemed quite right. His hair moved a little too slowly, like flexing wire on a stop-motion mannequin instead of real hair. His coat seemed to shift and wave in slow motion. He paced across the square with a definite destination in mind.

He looked just like the woman I'd seen the night before. Out of place, removed from his turbulent surroundings, walking his own path through a city that seemed unable to contain him.

I followed.

Walking across the square, emerging from the shelter of the buildings, I submitted myself to the full force of the storm. It was as if with every step I took, the storm focussed all of its attention on me, driving along streets and roads and smashing together at that violent junction. I staggered left and right, arms spread for balance, the hood of my coat alternately filling with wind and acting like a sail, then flattening against my scalp like a second skin. I forged on, head down, thinking of arctic explorers fighting against harsh gales to reach their goal. Rain stung my face. I could hardly see anything, squinting at the ground just ahead of me to see where I was going. I crossed the paved area, then a road, and then finally I felt the storm lessen as I neared another building. Hugging myself to its shelter, I looked ahead and saw the man. He was barely visible, a hundred metres ahead and already passing into the night. Winds whipped around him. Rain hammered down, dancing sworls in weak streetlights.

Between one blink and the next, the man was gone.

I strode ahead, moving fast to try and catch up. The storm screamed at me, threatening or warning. I paid no heed. I needed to see the man again, follow him, try to talk with him. I walked back and forth along the street, passing closed shops and cafés, and saw nothing. I ventured into doorways in case he had fallen and was hidden beneath piles of wind-blown litter. When I faced a narrow arcade, I pressed against the metal grille securing its entrance and tried to see deeper.

The night seemed even darker in there, and more still. The shadows were heavy. Watching, I also felt watched.

I took a couple of steps back. My breath was stolen by the wind. Glass smashed in the distance. A car alarm erupted somewhere out of sight, and part of a large advertising hoarding bounced along the road towards the square, shedding parts of itself as it went.

Even if the arcade was not locked up, I would not have wanted to go that way.

I hurried back through the square and started towards home. I saw a couple of other people, and they avoided me as surely as I avoided them.

I slept for three hours that night, naked and cold in my bed with wet clothes piled beside me. Dawn woke me. The man haunted my dreams even as I lay in bed awake, still walking, grey hair and coat shifting to some force other than the storm.

Morning brought relative calm. As I ate breakfast I watched the news, and saw that the storm had wreaked havoc across the country. Damage was in the millions. Miraculously, no one had died.

I chewed cereal that tasted like cardboard and thought about that.

No one had died.

It was a Saturday, and as I followed my previous night's route into town, the streets soon started to bustle with cheerful shoppers, gangs of kids laughing and joking, and people all with somewhere to go.

I had somewhere to go as well. The square was a very different place from just a few hours before, full of people and life, none of them aware of the shattering storm that had existed there so recently. The storm was a dangerous animal, come and gone again, and it had visited with almost no one knowing.

Across the square and along the street where the man had disappeared, I expected to see his discarded coat slowly being buried in a litter bin or draped over the back of a bench. There was nothing.

The arcade was open. Home to a café, a clothes shop, a candle shop and a second-hand bookseller, it wasn't somewhere I ventured frequently. In daylight, it looked less threatening. I stepped inside. A waft of perfumed air hit me from the candle shop, followed by the scent of frying bacon. It felt safe and warm.

I tripped, stumbled, almost fell, and a youth reached out and grabbed my arm to stop me hitting the ground.

"You all right, mate?"

"Yes," I said, startled. "Thanks."

"No worries. They should fix that." He nodded vaguely at my feet then went on his way, headphones in and thumb stroking his phone.

I looked down. The mosaic floor covering was humped as if pushed up by something from below. Yellow paint had been sprayed across the area some time ago, either a warning to beware or an indication of somewhere that needed to be fixed. No one had fixed it. The paint was faded and chipped, worn away by thousands of feet.

"Hey!" I called after the kid. "You know what happened here?" But he had his headphones in and was already leaving the arcade.

I frowned and moved sideways, shifting my perspective of the raised area. The mosaic tiles weren't only pushed up a little from below, forming the dangerous swelling that I'd tripped on. There was something in their clay shapes.

It looked like a face.

I gasped, closed my eyes, turned away and leaned against a wall. When I opened my eyes again I was looking through a window at an old man sitting inside the café, nursing a mug of tea. He stared at me, and past me, then looked down at his phone.

I glanced down at the ground again.

It *might* have been a face. The curve of one cheek, forehead, the hollow of an eye socket, and splayed out behind it was a flow of irregularities in the old tiles that resembled long, grey hair.

"Oh, God," I said. I wanted to grab someone and ask them if they saw what I saw. But if they didn't, what then? What could I say, ask, believe?

I took a photo of the raised area then hurried away, because there was someone I could ask. Ash was my leveller. She would hear me out.

As it turned out, Ash had already phoned that morning and left a message on my landline.

"Hey. Give me a call. Got some news."

I made some coffee first. Every step towards home had calmed my panic, and I was feeling more and more foolish over what I thought I'd seen. As I waited for the coffee to brew, every second that passed seemed to bring me closer to normality once more. Looking at my phone helped. The photo I'd taken showed nothing amiss, other than a slightly misshaped area in the arcade floor. However I viewed it, whether I zoomed in or not, there was no face.

But that's right, I thought. *Because it's daytime. They only come out at night.*

The idea came from nowhere, and was chilling.

The phone rang as I was pouring coffee. I jumped and spilled some, cursed, snapped up the phone.

"Hey, it's me," Ash said. "Fancy a coffee?"

"I just made one."

"Right. Can I come over?"

"Er . . . why?" It wasn't often that Ash and I saw each other on the weekends. She was usually doing stuff with Max, and I was busy with the football club, or meeting friends, or travelling down to Devon to visit my family. Dad would grumble and talk about politics. Mum would ask if I'd met a nice girl yet.

"Max and I are moving away. I got that job in Wales. I heard yesterday."

"Oh. Wow."

"You okay?"

"Yeah, sure. Of course. Delighted for you!"

Ash was silent for a while. "You go walking last night?"

"No." Once uttered, I couldn't take back the lie. I wasn't sure why. Maybe because Ash had already started to move away, and to include her in my troubles would be selfish. She'd wanted this for a long time. That didn't mean I had to be happy, but I could still be pleased for her.

"So I can come over, tell you all about it?"

"Come on over."

"I'll bring cake."

"You know me so well."

"The city eats people," she said. She took a bite of cake as if to illustrate the fact. "We're communal animals, but we're not meant to be somewhere with so many other people. Why do you think places like London feel so impersonal? Live in a small village, a hamlet, know almost everyone there, that's when you're happiest. Here . . . it's like we've created a monster and we're feeding it every day."

Her comments hit me hard. They sounded like her trying to defend her decision to leave for somewhere more rural, and that wasn't like Ash—she was always headstrong and positive. Maybe she was worried about me.

"You think that's why Nigel did what he did?"

Ash raised her eyebrows, as if she'd never even considered it.

"I think Nigel was a sensitive soul. Life was too much for him, and living in the city didn't help at all. But no, he had his own real problems, only aggravated by being here. What I mean is . . . people disappear. One day they're here, the next they're gone, and it's as if they've vanished into nothing. Know what I mean? The city eats them, spits nothing out, and eventually they're just forgotten."

"That's pretty depressing."

"I don't want to disappear," she said.

"You never could. You're too . . . wonderful." I grinned, bashful at the compliment. But she saw how serious I was, because she didn't take the piss.

"You should leave too." She tapped her engagement ring against her mug.

"I'm . . . not sure I could."

"Really? You love this place so much?"

I shook my head. No, I didn't love the city at all. I just couldn't imagine anywhere else feeling like home.

We chatted some more, then talked about her leaving party which she'd be throwing in a couple 'of weeks' time. She wanted me to DJ there. I said I was honoured, and I'd only do it if I could throw in some AC/DC. She hated them, but relented.

As she finished her cake I thought of the city eating people, and the outline of a face in broken tiles, and the bubbled surface of blown bricks in the shape of an arm with clenched fist.

Now that I had an idea of what to look for, I saw the city in a whole new light.

That Sunday afternoon I walked. There were plenty of people around because many of the shops remained open, and the place felt relatively safe. But as time passed by, and I saw more, that sense of safety began to evaporate.

By the end of the afternoon I felt like a meal in the jaws of a beast.

I saw distortion in an old swimming pool's caged-over window, and if I looked at just the right angle I could make out the shadow of a naked torso in the imperfect glass.

At the base of an old hotel's side wall, where access chutes into the basement had been concreted over, two knotted protuberances might have been hands with fingers broken off. Clasping for air forever, the stumpy remains of digits pointing accusingly at everyone left alive.

The stepped marble plinth of a war memorial had been damaged by vehicle impacts and the effects of frost, but there was another imperfection in its structure that became obvious to me now. The curve of a back, ribs plain to those who could see, one shoulder blade arched as if the buried subject were swimming against its solid surroundings.

Finally I decided to go to the place where Nigel had died. I had only been there once since his death, and facing the reality of the scene had been too disturbing. Now, there was more I had to see.

I would go at night. I dreaded what I might find.

It was three in the morning, and the homeless woman was there with her dogs once more. The creatures glanced at me, then as I started to approach they pulled on their leashes, one whining, the other snarling.

"I haven't got anything!" the woman said. The fear in her voice was awful.

"I'm no harm," I said. "I just want to—"

"What are you doing here at three in the morning, then?" she snapped.

"What are you?"

She didn't answer this. Instead, she tugged on the leads and settled her dogs. We were outside a pub, long-since closed for the night, and she leaned against some handrailing that delineated its outdoor smoking area.

"I'm walking because someone I know died," I said. "A friend. And I want to know . . . " *Whether the city took him*, I wanted to say, but I wasn't sure how that might sound. "I'm going to see . . . "

"Plenty wrong with the city at night," the woman said. "During the day, people keep it alive. Probably best you go home."

"But I've seen you before. You're always walking."

"I know where not to go."

"How?"

"Experience." She muttered something else under her breath. I couldn't see her face properly, and I didn't want to go any closer in case that looked threatening. Perhaps she was talking to her dogs.

"I'm going to the old station building," I said. I hoped that might encourage some comment, positive or negative.

"Hmm."

"Should I?" I asked.

I saw her silhouette shrug. "You should just go home." She started walking away and the dogs followed. When I tried to trail after her the animals turned and growled, both of them this time. I slowed, then stopped.

"Why?" I asked, expecting no reply.

"Make a habit of this and the city will notice you." Then she was gone, keeping to the middle of the street and avoiding the deep shadows beside buildings.

The night was quiet and still, no storms, no rain, and on the way through town I saw several other walkers. I wasn't sure who or what they were. I did not follow them. I was also careful to keep my distance, partly because they scared me, but also because they deserved their privacy and peace.

I carried on towards the old station building. It was six storeys high, converted into an office block a decade before, and Nigel had worked in an advertising agency on the second floor. That morning he'd taken the stairs, walked past the door exiting the staircase into his studio, and continued to the top. The maintenance door into the plant room on the roof should have been locked, but he'd planned his morning enough to make sure he had a key.

Once out on the roof, no one knew what he had seen, said or done. There was no note. Three people in the street below had seen him step up onto the parapet. Without hesitation he had walked out into nothing.

Where he'd hit the ground there was a raised planting bed at the refurbished building's entrance. He'd struck its wall, breaking his back. I went there now, a torch in my hand, dread in my heart.

At every moment I expected to see Nigel walking somewhere ahead of me. The echo of a man taken by the city and clasped to its dark, concrete heart, out of place and no longer of this world. But I was alone.

I searched for half an hour—the brick paved area around the entrance, the planter wall, the soil and shrubs of the planter itself. But I found no sign of Nigel. As every minute passed by my sense of apprehension lifted some more.

He's not here. The city didn't get him. It didn't eat him.

People had seen him jump, and perhaps that made a difference.

He hadn't died alone with only the cold concrete for company. His body hadn't lain there for hours or days afterwards, night crawling across him, darkness coalescing around him. Even dead, Nigel had remained in the human world, because his suicide was born of it.

Though still sad at his death, I felt relieved that he had escaped something worse.

My mood buoyed, I started for home as dawn peered across the built-up skyline. Yet something was different. The skyline I saw looked slightly out of skew, as if new buildings had risen during the night and others had been taken down. The silence remained, broken only by cautious footsteps echoing from unknown walls. Occasional strangers avoided each other's glances. But there was now something else that I had never noticed before. In the silence that hung over the city, a terrible intelligence held its breath.

As I reached home, I feared that the city had noticed me at last.

TRICK OF THE LIGHT

I t was the longest drive she had ever made on her own, and she so wanted the house to feel like home. But when she turned up the short driveway from the narrow country road, and the place revealed itself behind a riot of trees and bushes, Penny stopped the car and looked down into her lap.

"Oh, Peter," she said.

"That's okay," Peter says. "I'm here with you. You're a brave little rose, and you'll always be safe with me."

Penny's hands were clasping together. She forced them apart and reached for the ignition, silencing the car's grumble. It, like her, had never come so far.

She looked up slowly at the house, trembling with a subdued fear of elsewhere that had been with her forever, but a little excited too. This was her taking control. Her heart hurried, her stomach felt low and heavy, and she thought perhaps she might never be able to move her legs again. The mass of the house drew her with a strange gravity. For Peter's memory, and the short time she had left, she so wanted to understand.

She had bought it because of its uniqueness. While it had a traditional-enough lower two levels—tall bay windows, stone walls, an inset oak front door, sandstone quoins—a tower rose a further two storeys, ending in a small circular room with a conical roof and dark windows. The estate agent had told her that an old boss of the coal mines had used the tower to oversee work in the valleys. The mines were long gone and the valleys changed beyond recognition, but Penny quite liked the grounding of this story. It gave the building a solid history, and that was good. Mystery had always troubled her.

Beyond photographs, this was her first time seeing the house. Her first time being here, in her new home. She knew that Peter would have been impressed.

"I think you'll like it here," she said, and as she reached for the door handle, a movement caught her eye. She leaned forward and looked up at the tower's upper windows. Squinting against sunlight glaring from the windscreen, holding up one hand, she saw the smudge of a face pressed against the glass.

"Oh!" Penny gasped. She leaned left and right, trying to change her angle of sight through the windscreen, but the face remained. It was pale and blurred by dust. Too far away to discern expression or features, she had the impression that the mouth was open.

Shouting, perhaps.

Penny shoved the car door open and stood, shoes crunching on the gravel driveway, fully expecting the face to have vanished as she emerged from the vehicle's warm protection. But it was still there.

"Ah, Mrs Summers," a voice said. A tall, thin man emerged from the front porch, and though she had not met him, she recognised her solicitor's smooth manner and gentle voice. "Is there . . . ?" He rushed to her, his concern almost comical.

Dust, she thought. The shape was much less solid now.

"Hello, Mr Gough." She only glanced at him as she held out her hand, and he shook her hand whilst looking up at the tower.

"A problem?" he asked. "Broken windows? A bird's nest in the aerial?"

"No," Penny said. *I did not see a face at the window.* "No problem. Just a trick of the light."

Mr Gough's affected concern vanished instantly, and his smile and smoothness returned. "It is a beautiful sunny day, isn't it?"

Penny did not reply. She approached her new home, and already she could hear the phone inside ringing.

Peter moves his food around the plate. Pork chops, boiled potatoes, carrots, cauliflower. He's eaten some of the meat, and picks at where shreds are trapped between his teeth.

"Fuck's sake," he mutters.

"Peter, *please* don't talk like that," Penny says. Sometimes she thinks outright anger would be better, but Peter rarely loses his temper.

"It's just . . . " He trails off, and she knows what he has to say.

"It doesn't appeal to me," she says. "The heat, for one. Flies, midges, the diseases they carry. The toilets out there, and you know me and my stomach. And the sun is so strong. I burn just *thinking* about going out in the sun." It makes her sad, this gulf of ambition between them. It has always been present, but where there were once bridges of love and mutual respect, they have petrified as they both aged.

"Fuck's sake," he says again.

Peter gets up and leaves the room. She hears him storming upstairs, opening and closing cupboards, and when he comes down again he is wearing his hiking boots, trousers, and a fleece.

"Where are you going?"

"Somewhere else," he says. The gentle way he closes the front door is worse than a slam.

"I *worry* about you," Belinda said.

"I'm fine."

"Mum, you don't sound fine."

"It was a long drive, that's all, dear. And you know me, I haven't driven that long in . . . " *Ever*, Penny thought. *I'm further from home than I've ever been.* She felt suddenly sick, and sat gently on the second stair.

Take a rest, Peter says, tough voice soothing. *Take the weight off.*

A shadow filled the doorway and Mr Summers paused, as if waiting for her permission. She waved without looking, and the shadow entered her house.

"So. The house?" Belinda asked.

"Beautiful. He'll love it." There was an awkward silence.

"Russ and I will bring Flynn down for a visit next weekend. See if you're settled all right, look around. Russ says to make a list of any jobs that need doing."

"I still won't have it that he's dead," Penny said. "You know that."

"Mum, it's been over seven years. He's been declared—"

"I don't care what some strangers declare about my husband. I'd know if he was dead, and I say he isn't. He's . . . gone somewhere else, that's all."

"What, for a long walk?"

"Bindy."

"Sorry, Mum. But don't talk as if you and Dad had some kind of special bond. We both know that isn't really true."

"It'll be lovely to see Flynn," Penny said. "The garden's big enough to kick his football around. And can you ask Russ to bring some stuff for cleaning windows?"

"I will, Mum." Belinda's voice was heavy with concern and frustration, but Penny was here now. She had made the break. Left her own home, bought somewhere unusual, twelve miles from the nearest town and without bringing her TV with her. The furniture was coming the following day, but she had been careful to bring particular things herself—walking boots, a coat, a map. She loved the symbolism in that.

"It's not much, dear," Penny said. "I know that. It's not Cancun, or China, or an Antarctic cruise, or the Northern Lights, or any of those things he always wanted to do with me. But it's something. It's a small step on a longer journey. He'd be very surprised by me and . . . proud, I think." She glanced up at Mr Gough, listening and trying to appear distracted. And then she looked around the large hallway, three doors leading off into new rooms, timber floor scuffed, ceiling lined with old beams. "He'll love it here."

"Okay, Mum. Just . . . call me if you need anything. Will you do that?"

"Of course. Give my love to Russ and little Flynn."

"Love you, Mum. Really."

Belinda hung up first, and Penny could tell that her daughter was starting to cry. She hated hearing that. Which was why she had yet to tell Bindy that she was dying.

"Would you like a tour?" Mr Gough said.

Penny shook her head. "Just the keys, please."

"But you really should look at the tower, it's a remarkable feature, makes the house—"

"Really, I'm fine. Very tired." Penny stood, wincing at the pain in her hips from the long drive. Her bones ached from the other thing.

"Okay, then," the solicitor said. Smile painted on, now. He handed her a bunch of keys, then a smaller set. "Spares." He glanced around. "Lovely old place. You're very lucky, Mrs Summers."

As he turned to leave, a sense of such profound terror and isolation struck Penny that she slumped back against the stair bannister, grabbing hold as the house swam around her. She tried to call out, but her mouth was too dry. *Help me!* she thought, feeling a great weight of foreboding bearing down upon her. *Up there, there's something above, a terrible thing that is pressing down on me now I'm inside. Dusty windows, a trick of the light, but I can hear it up there, I can almost smell it, and I wish I was back in my garden with the roses and rhododendrons.*

Then the feeling started to filter away, and she knew that this was an important moment. She could give in to the terror and run. Or she could remain in her new, temporary home.

There, there, Peter says, his rough working-man's fingers stroking her cheek with infinite care and softness. *Come on, my little rose. Don't be afraid. You never have to be afraid when you're with me.* He has not spoken to her like this since they were in their twenties, madly in love and obsessed only with each other. *I'll never let you be hurt.*

"Thank you, Mr Gough," she whispered. The departing solicitor waved a hand without turning around, indicating that he must have heard. As he climbed into his Jeep, he glanced back at the house just once.

Not at Penny. At the tower. His constant smile had vanished.

She gave herself a tour of the house and wondered what she had done.

Belinda and Russ had been stunned when she reached a decision to sell the family home. But they had become increasingly supportive as Penny stuck to her guns and insisted that this was just what she wanted. "Maybe your father is right and I *am* just stuck in my ways," she said, and the worry niggled at her that this was hardly a big step. Moving from the home she had shared with Peter for forty years, out into the country, to a hamlet where fewer than a hundred people lived, the house Grade II listed and an architectural oddity that occasionally attracted visitors . . . it was nothing, really. The sort of change some people welcomed every couple of years of their lives.

But to Penny, it was the world.

The house was incredibly quiet. So much so that as she strolled through its corridors and rooms, she heard a high, lonely aircraft passing over the landscape outside. *You'll never get me on one of those*, she'd said to Peter when he suggested a simple flight to the Channel Islands to get her used to flying.

Penny opened the back door and paused, head tilted. She smiled. "One step at a time." The garden was wild and overgrown, awaiting her attention. She probably wouldn't have time to do much with it, and that made her sad. But she would make her mark.

The rooms inside were not decorated to her taste, but neither were they worn enough to require immediate redecoration. There was oak flooring throughout and she would have to get used to that, being more at home with patterned carpets. The house smelled unusual, and the sounds were strange—creaks, groans, taps—and she had no real sense of its shape and the space it occupied. It was nowhere near home, and she felt something like an intruder.

When the furniture and boxes arrive tomorrow everything will change, she thought. Everything she owned was packed in a lorry somewhere right now, ready to be transported across the country and deposited in this strange place. In her old house, her belongings had been a network of memories and safety, creating an environment she knew. Packed away, they were just luggage. *Home is where you are*, she'd said to Peter once, but he'd scoffed and gone into a quiet sulk. Later, he'd said, *You're rarely where I am.*

"Everything I have will be here, apart from him," Penny said. Her voice was loud. A bird sang somewhere in the garden, as if in response.

A steady *tap, tap, tap* came from somewhere that did not feel like part of the house.

Penny walked from the kitchen to the hallway, unconsciously matching the rhythm with her own footsteps. She paused at the staircase, one hand on the bannister, looking up. The sound was more distant than the bedrooms or bathroom on the first floor. More hollow, and sadder. She knew the sound. Peter, sat in his armchair with a glass of whiskey in one hand and his eyes distant, while she sat on the sofa and watched the next episode of some TV series she was already losing interest in, and his foot would tap against the wooden leg of his chair. Just a gentle impact, as if he were ticking away the seconds of his life. She would hear, but had never, ever said anything. He was always like this after an argument—a screwed up travel brochure beside his chair, and a dead dream floating in his glass.

He would usually go anyway, but never with his wife.

Tap, tap, tap . . .

"Peter," Penny breathed. The noise ceased. She held her breath.

Keys in hand, Penny walked slowly upstairs. Each tread had its own feel and sound, and probably its own memories.

Spooking yourself, Peter says. *You always worry too much, my rose.*

Penny reached the landing and stood before the doorway that led to the tower. She had not looked inside on her first walk around the house. Had passed it by, truth be told, because it had felt like the last place she wanted to see. *Too dusty up there*, she'd thought, and she decided that was the one place she'd send Russ when he and Belinda came over the following weekend. Up into the tower, to clean those windows and see what else was there.

"Silly," she said. She reached for the door.

"You're just stuck here," Peter says. "Don't you see that?"

"But I like it here."

"You used to enjoy travelling. All those weekends we spent down in Cornwall when we were courting. The tour of Scotland in the motor home. Don't you want to do all that again? Don't you ever think about how time just . . . "

It always goes the same way.

So Peter packs a bag and leaves. He says he is going hiking for a weekend in the Lake District, but he never comes back. His body is never found.

Penny persistently insists that Peter is still alive somewhere, and that drives a rift between her and her daughter. Because there was never any tension between Belinda and her father, and if he *is* still alive, she says, he would contact her.

"No," Penny says whenever the subject is brought up. "He's not gone. Not Peter. He's out there somewhere, waiting for me to join him. And one day, I will."

Belinda never believed that she would. In truth, neither did Penny. But discovering that she only had months to live had changed something fundamental about the way she viewed the world. Before, she had felt safe and secure in her own small bubble of existence. Now, she already sensed that everything else was moving on. Leaving her behind. She was a dead woman walking, and she had one more chance.

She paused with her hand on the door handle. It was metal, round, and vaguely warm, as if someone gripped it on the other side. It was only a tower, and a room. Perhaps there was a chair up there, and she could sit and look out over the landscape, watch the sun set over a hillside instead of her neighbours' rooftops for the first time in—

Tap, tap, tap.

The sound was closer. Beyond the door, up whatever staircase might have been built within the tower. Peter, tapping his foot impatiently against a chair's leg.

Penny gripped the handle tighter, but was suddenly convinced that there was someone directly on the other side of the door, holding the handle, ear pressed to the wood, smiling expectantly as they awaited her decision.

My little rose, Peter says, *sometimes you're so scared of the smallest things, so fragile and sensitive. It's a hard world, hardy and impartial. But I'll look after you.*

She let go of the handle and took two steps back until she nudged the landing balustrade. The tapping had stopped, but the silence was worse.

"Stupid woman!" she berated herself, and she started singing to fill the space. Still singing, she searched through the set of keys until she found one for the tower door. She locked it, then paused, listening for movement on the other side. But there was none.

"Of course not," she said. "Just an empty room, and dust."

Hungry, thirsty, a little angry with herself for being so easily scared, Penny went down to the kitchen and switched on the kettle. She'd brought everything she needed to make tea and cook a simple meal, but as the kettle boiled she opened the back door to the wild garden once more.

She walked outside, fiddled with the keyring until she had removed the key to the tower door. She threw it as far as she could, turning away so that she did not see where it landed.

"There," she said. "That settles it. The house is way big enough for me anyway." She entered the house again, not once looking up.

And not looking up meant that she felt watched.

Penny ate her fried egg sandwich. She'd speckled it with cayenne pepper, because Peter used to like that, and so spent the next half an hour sipping milk from the bottle and trying to lick the burn from her lips. And she tried to make sense of the house around her as the light outside changed.

She missed her little three-bedroomed home. She had always known where she was in that house in relation to every other room. Her awareness had filled the entire place, when Peter was there with her and, later, when he was gone. It had been more than a home, and sometimes she'd forgotten where she ended and the house began.

Now, the new house hung around her like something waiting to pounce. There was no sense of equilibrium. The first floor felt as though it sought to crush the ground floor. The kitchen was too large, crowding out the dining room, storage room, and pushing into the corner of the quirky living room. Penny felt vaguely dizzy, as if every part of the house was constantly moving, just slightly. Even when she closed her eyes and hung onto the table, the feeling persisted.

And above it all, the tower.

Maybe Belinda was right. Maybe he *was* lying out there somewhere, gone to bones and dust. And he'd have died alone, perhaps with a broken leg or a heart attack, under lonely skies without Penny there with him.

Don't be soft, Penny, Peter says, and she looked around, certain that she actually heard those words spoken. The natural direction for her to look was up. *I'm fine. You know I am. Fine now that you've made the break, and taken the risk. And how does it feel, my rose? How does it feel?*

"I'm not sure yet," Penny said. Even the way her words echoed was unfamiliar. "I'm a little bit afraid."

Don't be, my darling, Peter says. Penny had not heard such love in his voice for many years.

Dusk approached. In the valley, it was a wild time. The breeze increased, rustling the trees along the edge of Penny's new garden. Dogs barked from somewhere far off. Birds flitted overhead, and sitting on a stone bench outside, Penny watched them circling the tower. None seemed to land. She could not blame them. There was something so intrinsically wrong there, but she was doing her best to steer her attention away from its upright bulk. To give in to the tower would be to admit defeat.

"I might just as well go home," she said. The overgrown garden dampened her voice, and her words quickly faded to memory.

She walked around the garden with a glass of wine. She never usually drank wine except on Friday evenings, and then only a glass or two after eight o'clock. Now it was Tuesday, barely six-thirty, and she loved the feel of the glass in her hand, the fruity taste of wine on her lips.

The garden was larger than she had thought at first. Either that, or the boundaries were poorly marked and she was strolling across open hillside. She always felt the bulk of the house to her left, but most of her attention was directed downwards, at the twisted vegetation, long grass, and exposed tree roots that sought to trip her. She stepped over and around obstructions, and thought per-haps tomorrow she would walk further into the hills. There was a famous trail up on the ridge, so Mr Gough had told her. Popular with walkers. Peter had been a walker.

"I was a sitter," she said to the garden. "A not-doer. A nothing. A . . . waste of space." She hated the term, because Peter had used

it referring to her on more than one occasion. "Waste of space."
She looked across at the house, the looming tower, and realised
that she now stood in its stretching shadow. The sun touched the
hillside beyond, and cast a palette of reds and oranges around the
tower's stark lines. The glazed room was exposed to the sunset.
There was a solid shadow within, as if a shape was standing in the
centre of the room. And Penny wondered what would change were
she to suddenly disappear, and what would fill the space she had
left behind.

She began to cry. It was dislocation and fear, but also a growing
sense that time had passed her by. She had never, ever thought like
this before, even when Peter had angrily insisted that he only had
one life, and he would not fritter it away waiting for her.

Don't be sad, Peter says. His voice is stronger than the breeze,
brighter than the sunset, and more meant for her than the hushing
trees and calling birds. *You've done well, my sweet rose. You know
not to waste any more time, or time will waste you.*

"Are you coming back to me?" she asked.

You think I ever left?

Penny stares up at the tower room, convinced that she will see
movement there, or a face, or a sign that this new home is more
than just her own. But still it exudes a weight of wrongness, as if
the tower and room had been built onto the house long after it had
first been constructed.

"I'm not going there," she said. "The house is plenty big enough
without me ever having to go there." No one replies, and she sees
that her glass is empty. She does not even remember drinking the
wine.

Back in the kitchen, the bottle is empty as well. Penny sits on an
old stool and rests her arms on the worktops, her head on her arms.
Her bones are full of aches, reminders of mortality. She closes her
eyes.

Tap, tap, tap . . .

"You never call me your little rose anymore," she says.

"Huh."

"What does that mean?"

Peter looks across at her from the driver's seat. They are stuck in traffic on the way home from the supermarket. She bought food, he bought a CD and a book about Eastern European cuisine and a cheap one-man tent light enough to carry on a hike or a bike. "That was a long time ago," he says.

"So much just fades away," Penny says sadly.

"Huh." The car pulls forward some more, and Penny watches her husband driving. He remains silent, stern. She wishes he would just throw her a glance, a smile, a cheeky, *My rose never fades*. But the rot has set in years before, and now they are simply awaiting dead-heading.

She opened her eyes to darkness, and a cruel throbbing against her skull. The house sat around her, quiet, still, and she felt that it was observing her pained waking. The weight of above pressed down against her, almost crushing her into the stool and worktop. How could the tower have not tumbled long before now? How could it stand, so heavy and dense? Even though she could no longer hear the tapping sound, she could feel it through her hands and feet. Transmitted through the body of the house like a secret message from one room to another. *All about me*, she thought, and she slipped from the stool to the kitchen floor. She unrolled the sleeping mat and sleeping bag, climbed in, ignoring the pressure on her bladder, the need for a drink of water, the fear of what else might be sharing the floor with her in the darkness. She had not been this drunk in decades, but today she welcomed it. Her world swayed. She was protected by numbness, and still feeling that *tap, tap, tap* touching delicately against the flagstone floor, she was pulled back into the dark.

Dawn, and she had dreamed of Peter sitting upright on a chair in the room at the top of the tower. There was no other furniture. Just Peter, seven years older than when she had last seen him, walking boots and trousers and waterproof jacket still on, day pack propped by his side with the flask open and cup of steaming coffee, sandwich box balanced on one knee. *So you came?* he asked, not sounding surprised. He had always known that Penny, his rose, would follow.

"I have to see," Penny said. She glanced around the kitchen until she saw the set of keys, remembered throwing the tower key outside. Then she recalled the spares Mr Gough had given her. She emptied her bag and snatched up the keyring.

Her head pulsed with each stair she climbed. Her heartbeat matched her footfalls, reverberating through the house. She wondered whether her presence here would become an echo for whoever might own the building after her.

At the door to the tower, she touched the handle again. It was cool. It took a few moments to find the key that fitted the lock, and as she tried she looked around the landing, at all those closed doors. She had been into each room yesterday, but did not own any of them.

The key turned, and the lock tumbled open.

"Are you there?" she asked, expecting the *tap, tap, tap*. But there was nothing. She pushed the door open.

The circular staircase was made of cast iron and probably worth a small fortune. It did not make a sound as she climbed. She passed two windows out onto her garden, but it felt as though she was looking onto a world she had never visited. She saw places she had been, recognising none of them.

The stairs ended on a narrow landing with a single door. It was dusty and cobwebbed. She touched the door handle and it was warm, but she did not wait to think about why. She tried it, then unlocked it with another key, wondering only vaguely why the tower room should be locked away behind two doors.

"Open the door, my little rose," she said, imagining the words on her husband's lips, and she turned the handle. Peter was waiting for her inside, and soon she would hear his voice again.

As Penny pushed the door open she saw something flash across the small room beyond, dashing for cover, terrified of being seen. She gasped, hand pressed to her chest. Her heart beat the *tap, tap, tap* she no longer heard, and as it transferred through her other hand to the door, she saw a smear of light quivering in the room's opposite corner. A window-shaped reflection, brought to life by her fear. She shoved the door a little more, and the reflection disappeared.

She entered the room. There was nothing there. The dusty windows caught the sun's early light and filtered it, casting dust-shadows against the floor and one wall.

The door was closing behind her, and Penny turned to see herself in the mirror hung on the back of the door. Through the haze of old dust covering the glass, she looked nebulous, almost not there.

Also not there, Peter. There was no chair, no husband. The room contained old, old dust, and stale air, heavy with the aromas of age and seclusion.

"I'm here," she said. "I'm here!" Louder. Dust floated down from the ceiling and flitted in pale sunbeams, like tiny flies startled at her presence.

A broken wooden blind hung down across one window, and one end tapped gently against the panelled wall. There were no broken panes, no breeze. Penny closed her eyes and felt a slight dizziness not connected to her hangover. The tower moved, or the world. Now that she was here it did not matter which.

Penny began to understand. She had not come here to die. Neither had she come to try and make amends to her absent husband, or to prove to herself that she was not as he had always portrayed her. She had come because this was another place where she belonged. This empty, barren room was her home, not the house down below. And there was no way she could leave here again, because every-where else felt so terrible, threatening, and a million miles away.

She pressed her face to a glass pane. At least with dust on the windows, she was shielded from some of the distance.

Soon, she would lock the door, prise a window open a crack, and drop the keys outside. Belinda and her family were not visiting for ten days, so there was plenty of time. Because Penny's was the face at the window. And she was a trick of the light.

CLOWN'S KISS

The house had been vacant for some time. Small, run-down, some might even say ramshackle, it clung to the side of my own home like a wretched Siamese twin. An oddity in the street—Isaac had once commented to me that he was amazed how such a place could exist in Wellington Pond—it was rarely the subject of discussion amongst the villagers, and I never once saw anyone glance at it as they passed by. It had always struck me as strange that a house that size, in a village this small, could simply be forgotten. But then I was coming to realise that there were many strange things about village life that would take me two lifetimes to learn.

The old lady had been a hundred and one when she died, two years before I moved in. She'd remained undiscovered for three weeks before the postman noticed a maggot crawling from the letter flap. They say she'd been trying to open the front door when she slipped and fell. Heart attack, maybe. Or just old age. How can old age be a cause of death? I've always wondered that, but it's not the sort of thing you want to ask old people. And being old myself, not the sort of thing I really wish to dwell upon. So she died, and no one came to put the place up for sale, but neither did anyone move in. A complex web of legalities seemed to stymie any investigation into ownership, and so it had simply become the dead old lady's home, ignored and then forgotten.

At least, that's what I'd been told.

She used to employ a gardener, so they said, and he hadn't returned since her death. The grass had grown knee-high, the rambling roses had erupted from arches, frames and trellises to probe inquisitively towards the property's boundaries, and the herb garden had gone mad. Mint grew everywhere, and sometimes when the wind was right my own garden was filled with a delicious, warm herby aroma that always made my mouth water. But it made me feel queasy, too.

It was a strange place. Not spooky or disturbing, or weird-strange. Just so *not there*. Like the inevitability of death, next door's existence crept up on me and surprised me into silence from time to time, and those days would always carry a shadow until sundown.

The day I saw the clowns, I was cleaning the upstairs windows. I was doing it from the inside, because I didn't trust myself up a ladder anymore, and between wipes I saw a flicker of colour. I squinted, thinking perhaps the sun had struck the glass just right and thrown a rainbow across my eyes.

There was something strikingly biological about the colours in the clowns' outfits, as if they had spilled from inside something living—pinks and purples, the red of blood, the yellow of bruising. There were four of them working their way through the neighbouring garden. Their movements seemed exaggerated, limbs lifting and falling again as if feigning stalking. And something about them *was* predatory. They must have climbed the high wall that bounded the bottom of the garden, and I wondered whether anyone had seen them on the riverbank beyond, dog walkers or joggers or people out for a casual stroll.

But even then I was sure that no one had seen these clowns before. There was something new about them. Not fresh, but unseen. It was as if they had only recently blinked into existence, and I was the first to view their splash of garish colour across the wilderness that next door had become.

I'd never found clowns funny, even when I was a kid. They never scared me, but I'd always regarded them as just a little bit ridiculous. The best clowns for me were always those who never needed to augment their humour with funny faces or ridiculous outfits. These four surprised me more than anything, and I watched until they disappeared from view close to next door's back wall. Though not one of them glanced up, I had the feeling that they all knew I was there.

I pressed close to the window to see more, but my breath misted the glass, and the angle was all wrong. So I just stood there for a while, staring down at the calming, ordered patterns of my own garden before looking next door again.

Those four paths, trampled into the tall grasses and brambles and occasional ferns, looked like the fingers of a giant hand.

"There are clowns next door," I said, and my words misted the window once more. I wiped the glass, dropped the cloth, and went downstairs to the phone.

"Dad, it's like when you were shouting about seeing a tiger in Asda's. You spooked the hell out of the checkout girl, and you're lucky they didn't call the law."

"I did see a tiger," I said.

"Yeah, a bloke in fancy dress advertising some Indian soup, or something."

"Chinese."

"Eh?"

"The soup. It was Chinese. Sick joke, all about tiger penis soup, or something, and . . . "

"Right. So these clowns, maybe they're . . . I dunno, a publicity stunt, or something."

"In Wellington Pond."

Isaac remained silent. I knew what my son thought of the place

I'd chosen to live. Since my dear wife had died a few years before, he'd told me that I'd gone soft in the head and softer in the heart. But I'd always been proud of the choices I'd made. *Nothing ever happens in the Pond*, he'd say, as if that was a bad thing.

"I know what I saw," I said.

"But no one's lived there for years. Since before you moved in, you told me."

"That's what the villagers told me." I found myself sinking into the same sad shadow that always enveloped me when I talked to Isaac. We'd always been close as father and son, but since his mother's death I had the impression he'd been counting down the years to my own departure as well. Maybe it was unfair of me, but I was certain I caught an underlying impatience in his voice sometimes. I knew he was busy with his wife and their high-flying careers.

Maybe it *was* just me imagining things.

"Well, perhaps the circus is in town," he said, chuckling. "You remember that time you took me?"

"No," I said, suddenly panicked because I could *not* remember. I could have sworn then that he and I had never been to the circus together. And even as he reminisced—the trapeze, the fire-eater, the clowns and the incredible jugglers—the memories remained elusive.

"You don't remember?"

"Oh, of course," I said, but no, I still didn't. And Isaac knew that.

"Right. Okay, Dad, gotta go. Mandy's cooking for some friends tonight, I promised I'd make a mousse for dessert."

"Chocolate or vanilla?"

"Bye, Dad."

"Bye."

I put the phone in its base and stared at it for a while. It would not ring again until Monday, when my friend Patrick would call to see if I was going to the pub for lunch that day, which I always, always did.

"I saw the clowns," I said, and the silence neither mocked, nor heard. I was the sole listener, and had been ever since Mary had died.

Sometimes five years felt like forever.

I went out into the garden. It was my work of art, and I often spent more of my waking hours outside than in. Mary and I had always loved gardening, and the several times we had moved house together had found us cutting back bushes, demolishing old sheds, and digging and planting vegetable patches before painting wood-work and stripping wallpaper inside. That had changed a little when Isaac came along, but not much. We'd always made sure that his room was well-kept, but as far as we were concerned our living space was our garden. *You're closer to things out here*, Mary had always said, and though I'd never asked exactly what she meant, I thought I understood. Now, it was in the garden where I felt closest to Mary.

I passed the patio area outside the back door, breathing in the heady aromas of heavily scented roses and honeysuckle. Following a winding path that led through the heart of a wild area—given over to long grasses, creeping heathers, and a gorgeous array of wild flowers—I took pleasure in seeing birds bustling around the many feeders I had hung about the garden, and noted a few borders that needed weeding and turning over. That would be a task for after lunch. Mary had usually done the weeding, and I was still adapting to doing it myself.

This was my garden, not Mary's. She had never even seen it. But I knew that she was here with me in every touch of plant or soil.

I approached the high fence between properties, and for the first time ever I was aware of the solidity of the garden next door. It had a weight to it, as if all those overgrown shrubs, trees, and grasses could exert a gravity upon my more ordered plot.

"I saw clowns," I whispered, remembering a flash-image of the four of them converging on the house next door. And when I breathed in I smelled fresh meat. Their colours, like insides turned out.

I shivered. Paused, with one hand resting against a heavy wooden bench to hold myself upright. Then I tried to smile at my old man's foolishness.

Something screamed.

I froze, in my sunlit garden with flowers painting a palette of beauty, bees droning, birds flitting between branches and feeders, waiting for the noise to repeat and looking around for any signs that it had happened at all. The birds still sang, unfazed by whatever the sound had been. The garden lay unchanged. My heart alone reacted, thudding at the memory of the piercing cry, an unreliable witness.

Listening to the garden sounds, I wondered whether I'd heard the scream at all. From elsewhere in the village came traffic noise, the barking of a dog, and the distant voices of people chatting. No one else seemed to have heard.

I was waiting for the scream again. It did not come, and slowly I relaxed. It could have been a cat, or the screech of brakes from somewhere, or perhaps a dog's pained yelp as it cut its paw or sprained a leg.

I looked at the fence I had been edging towards. It was almost six feet high, too tall for me to look over but not high enough to hide the evidence of next door's abandonment. A willow extended probing branches, a rambling rose hung across the top of the fence for a third the length of my plot, and other plants draped over and through the close-boarded slats. It was a slow invasion, and I spent some time each week trimming and clipping, halting the advance.

"I should take a look," I said. "Pull the bench a bit closer to stand on, peek over, see what's going on." I started dragging the bench, blood thumping in my ears as I struggled to lift it. I wasn't as young as I used to be. But when I'd moved it close enough to climb on and hold the top of the fence, I paused and stood back.

It looked all wrong. It *felt* wrong, seeing the bench there. It was out of place.

"No, no," I said, shaking my head, worrying at my sleeves with my fingertips as I felt sweat breaking out across my forehead. "No, it doesn't belong there." But instead of pulling the bench away I turned and hurried back up the garden, tripping on the patio and almost falling in through the French doors. I closed them behind me.

I felt no more settled inside my house than outside, so I put the kettle on and heard Mary's voice echoing from the past. *A cup of tea helps anything.*

"Is there a circus nearby?"

"Why would you ask that?" Kevin the shopkeeper replied, his hand holding my ten-pound note halfway to the till. He became motionless, staring, his held breath inviting my response.

"Well . . . " I frowned and shook my head. "Just wondering. Thought I heard circus music."

He counted out my change and deposited my tenner. He seemed suddenly unsettled, distant, and for the big friendly man this was unusual.

Kevin had been one of the first people I met when I moved to Wellington Pond. Following the removal truck into the village—frightened at the fact that it carried my whole life, and most of the evidence of my existence—I'd stopped at the corner shop to buy a bottle of wine. Kevin had been sitting behind the counter drinking coffee, and his open smile for a stranger had immediately warmed me to him. He was friendly, helpful, welcoming, and had not appeared at all cliquey, as Isaac had warned me most villagers were. My son hadn't wanted me to move out of London mainly, I think, because it would be more inconvenient for him to pay his duty visits to me out here.

Born and brought up in the village, Kevin had said only good things about its inhabitants. He had sent me on my way with a free bottle of wine as a "welcome to the Pond", and our friendship was instant.

Now, he frowned as he handed me my change, and barely caught my eye.

"Not that I'm interested," I said, smiling. "Never bothered with them when I was a kid, and when they stopped using dangerous animals, I became even less interested. It's the threat of bloody death that made the lion tamers entertaining, you think?"

Kevin shrugged, his massive stomach moving beneath his tee shirt.

"And I gave up the high wire just before I moved here."

Kevin tried on a smile, but it was not his usual.

"Don't worry," I said, smiling. "I'm just clowning around."

It was so quick, so fleeting, that I almost missed the flash of fear in his eyes. Then he turned away and started coughing, one hand on the counter and the other pressed to his mouth. Since that first time we'd met, Kevin had seemed to be growing larger by the month, and now watching his body quiver and shake as he coughed was strangely fascinating.

"You okay, Kevin?"

Kevin did not look at me again. He took a deep breath, staring down at his feet as he waited for the coughing to subside.

I left the shop and stood outside for a while, watching several cars passing by and waving to the people I knew. They smiled at me—Beryl the cake maker, Charles the taxi driver, Bernard the self-proclaimed village problem solver—and some deep part of me wondered if they all carried secrets.

Back at home, I unpacked the rice I'd bought from Kevin's and started on my jambalaya. Mary had never liked what she called 'dirty foreign food', so since she'd gone I had been virtually living on Chinese, Indian, Italian, Mexican and Cajun food, and I could not remember the last time I'd roasted meat and boiled vegetables. Isaac was worried, saying that I wasn't watching my diet well enough, and that he'd lost one parent and didn't want to lose another, and I think that might have been the only time I ever really swore at him. *For fuck's sake, Isaac, I'm almost eighty years old, and I want to live a little before I die.* He'd shut up, and I think my comment upset him a lot. But it was an incident that had faded away without ever being mentioned again.

I stirred, and tasted, and all the while I had one eye on the French doors. I usually kept them open as much as possible, whatever the weather, enjoying the contact with the outside. But now it unsettled me. As I moved the frying pan off the heat to let the food settle for a while, I became more and more angry.

"Bastards!" I whispered, needing to say it but afraid that they'd hear. "Whoever they are . . . *bastards!*" I strode through the door and down to the bottom of the garden, standing on the triangular decking area with hands on hips and staring back at the neighbouring house. There was little to be seen that I hadn't seen before, and nothing significant had changed. The windows looked the same, blank and dark. The sagging gutter had perhaps dropped another couple of inches. It was simply the house that had always been the dilapidated negative of my own, but when I blinked there was something else.

A splash of grotesque colour.

I returned indoors and ate, slowly and quietly. Listening. Hearing nothing.

They waited until midnight before screaming again.

The cry startled me from a deep, terrible dream that I forgot instantly upon waking. It left me with a sense of imminent panic, my heart pounding and blood pulsing at my ears, and for a few seconds I thought I had plummeted into a bottomless sleep, and that the vanished nightmare was reality.

I sat up in bed and took in several deep breaths, and the scream came again. *Mating foxes*, I thought, but the night was too dark and loaded, and I'd heard foxes mating before. Their screams sounded terribly pained and childlike, and these screams were neither.

Not children.

"And that's not pain," I whispered. I tried to recall the noise, analyse it, playing it over in my memory as I sought to identify just what it had been trying to tell me. I moved to the window and opened it wider, gasping at the soft cool breeze that swept beneath my loose pyjamas. The moon was almost full and hidden behind light clouds, its diffused light silvering open areas of garden and deepening shadows beneath trees and bushes. Next door's garden was dark. Heavy shadows pulsed there, as if the night had a heartbeat.

"It was laughter," I said. A breeze ruffled across my garden and set plants swaying, as if agitated by my words. "Something was laughing."

But what laughed like that? And why?

I slammed the window closed, seeking familiarity in my bedroom. I knew the furniture, the shape of the room, the smells and sounds, and I tunnelled back into my lonely bed, my refuge. I lay there for some time but something kept me awake. A shadow I was staring at, a shape on the wall.

After a while I turned the lamp on and saw a spread of dampness at the junction of wall and ceiling. It was the wall I shared with next door.

I turned off the light and rolled over so that I was facing the other way. Tomorrow I would try to find out more.

It was only a house.

But when I stood on the pavement in front of my house and looked at next door's front fence, the rusted gate, the overgrown garden, and the façade that presented a face that most villagers seemed reluctant to see, I saw something that set my skin crawling, and which gave the day no more comfort and safety than the previous night.

Above the house's tilting, broken front porch roof, a faint smile was pressed into the moss-greened render, consisting of a spread of pale red funghi, dried like a bloody lipstick kiss, and whichever angle I viewed it from, it remained.

I was sure I had never seen it before. But at the same time I could not recall ever standing there and staring at the house.

"Clown's kiss," I said. A horn tooted along the street and I looked that way, startled, to see Jill McGovern driving towards me. She was waving cheerfully, and I tried to temper my expression to appear calm and content rather than scared and uncertain. Jill was a villager through and through, and had been one of the first to welcome me as one of their own. Even though I was not. Even though, as Isaac continually told me, I never would be.

"Jill," I said as she drew up beside me and wound down her window. "I saw clowns in next door's garden. There's laughing, and a mark or something on the house's front wall."

"Oh, I don't know anything about all that," she said, waving my words away like annoying flies. "Can you give me a hand setting up some tables at the village hall for the fête tomorrow?" She was a nice woman, but totally self-obsessed. She would listen, nod and laugh when I spoke, but I was not sure she actually heard anything.

I took another look at the house—

The clowns' house, that's what it is now.

—and for a moment, at a dusty upstairs window that hadn't seen a cloth in years, the insinuation of a fleshy face drew back into the shadows. I blinked and took a deep breath.

"Didn't you hear me?" I asked.

"Only Harry is busy setting up a bottle stall, and one of his tables collapsed and he lost some bottles, so I don't really want to ask him."

The house was still and silent. I sighed. "Of course, Jill." At least it would get me away from here for a while, and the idea of company was pleasing.

I eased myself into her passenger seat and she started talking. As she drove, I tuned out.

We passed a few houses on the left and right, flitted through the shadow of the railway bridge, and then the road curved sharply around the high church wall and entered the village square. Between the bakery and the scruffy garage where old Max stood pumping diesel, a small thatched house sat back slightly from the square. I could not recall ever noticing it before. Its front garden had gone wild, and one of its upstairs windows had been smashed by a tree limb that had grown right into the house. Its thatch was holed.

"That place," I said.

"What?"

"There, next to the garage. Who lives there?"

Jill slowed the car, then sped up again, leaving the square down a winding lane that led between two orchards.

"Old Max, I keep telling him to slow down, take a break and sit back a little. He's eighty-nine, you know? His mother lived until she was a hundred-and-one, father, I don't know, some say he ran away years ago, but Max won't talk about it."

"And you won't talk about that house with the smashed window and broken thatch. No one can live there, surely? So what's the story?"

"The story?" Jill sounded suddenly glum, and the silence after she had spoken was loaded. With sadness, I thought. Or perhaps something else.

"Something's going on," I said, and it was as much to myself as Jill.

She slammed on the brakes. Her little car slewed across the country lane, bumping as the wheels slid sideways over the badly maintained surface. I braced myself against the dashboard, tensing, wondering why she had braked and waiting for the impact of metal against the stone wall. But Jill stared calmly from her window as the car came to a halt.

"Leave," she whispered. The car was still rocking, creaking on its springs, and I could not be sure of what she said. Not one hundred percent certain. But I shook my head, and she turned to look at me as if she had seen a ghost.

"I can't," I said. "This is my home now. I've *made* it my home, and you've helped me do that, Jill. You and lots of others. I've felt welcomed into Wellington Pond, and I love the village now probably as much as anyone. Why should I leave?"

She held onto the steering wheel and looked straight through the windscreen, and for a moment I thought she was going to talk about tables at the village fête again, and Max's age, and Harry's smashed bottles. But instead, she remained silent.

"I know what I saw, so who are they?" I asked.

She did not respond.

"Well, fuck them," I said.

Jill blinked rapidly, wiping grim reality from her eyes like irritating dust. Then she started the car again and sighed heavily, smiled, and as we pulled off she told me how she and her boyfriend used to scrump apples from those orchards and make home-made cider.

I sat back in the seat feeling more isolated than ever before. Back in the city after Mary had gone, I had felt alone surrounded by millions of people. Such an impersonal place. So lonely. Now, the community I had come to call home was taking on the same feeling.

As we approached the village hall and I saw the bustle of the car park and playing fields, I vowed that today would see the end of things. I'd visit the house next door and find out what those weird people were up to.

We parked, I stood from the car, knees popping and my back taking a few seconds to straighten. I hated growing old. My mind was still middle-aged, but my body betrayed me. Jill marched off to order someone around, and I leaned on the open car door and looked out past the hall.

Across the playing fields, where a gang of kids kicked a football around and a teenaged couple lay close together beneath an old oak, was a house I had never noticed before. Half of its roof had caved in. Its fences were slumped down beneath the weight of rampant roses. Windows were dark and foreboding.

I held my breath, then slowly let it out. *I'm just seeing what I want to see,* I thought. If you're looking for a white Ford you suddenly see a hundred of them, and wonder why there are so many.

Yes. That was it.

I followed Jill into the hall and started moving tables around. And all the time I did my best to deny the red smear I'd seen on one high gable wall of the house. I had no desire to go close enough to know the grin.

After a couple of hours setting tables for the following day's fête—a couple of hours during which I heard as much gossip about the butcher's lesbian daughter, the threat of parking charges in the village car park, and Mr Robinson's hedge as I could stand—I decided to walk home. All that time I'd spent dragging tables and unstacking chairs I had been avoiding the subject of strange clowns and empty houses, and so naturally that was all I'd thought about. So now that my good deed for the day was done, I decided that there was something else I could do.

Open my eyes. Make up my own mind about whether or not anything mattered.

Leave, I thought she'd said. But perhaps she had merely whispered a word I could never know.

I deliberately chose an off-road route, afraid that if I stuck to the road I'd be offered a lift by any well-meaning villager passing by. I didn't *want* a lift, obliged to sit and converse with someone else. I wanted to walk. I wanted to be on my own.

I climbed over the stile beside the village hall and cut across the fields. At first I considered crossing directly back towards the village and passing closer to that other abandoned house. But something about it repulsed me. I kept glancing over my shoulder as I walked, and it was only when an overgrown hedgerow shielded the building from view that I started to relax.

It was a warm, still evening. Flies and bees buzzed, birds flitted and sang, and the dipping sun seemed reluctant to leave. My feet swished through the long grass, kicking up showers of seeds that caught the sunlight. I felt a sneeze grow and fade again. My eyes watered.

There's nothing there, I thought, and looking around I could not believe that anywhere even close to here could be dark, bruised, corrupted and tainted with mad laughter. This was a *good* place, and it carried its shadows well.

The village was quiet, the meadows even quieter, and after another field and a couple of sweet-smelling orchards I entered the village close to the old abattoir. The building was long-since abandoned, but there was nothing that troubled me about it. It was a comfortable dilapidation like my own old age, not a forced decay. There had been talk of turning it into a café for summer visitors. I'd always thought that a little grotesque. I preferred it boarded up and silent, a memorial to the many thousands of creatures that had cried their last inside.

I wended my way behind the small new estate they'd built just the year before, and past there, behind the overgrown corner of another orchard, I found one more house that I had no memory of seeing. This was larger than the other two. Though I had walked this path several times before, it was entirely possible that I had simply never looked that way. I moved back and forth along the old wooden fence. Trees shielded the house from view, but I could tell that it was empty. An upstairs window was smashed. Ivy smothered a couple of downstairs windows. Some roof tiles were missing, tufty plants grew from the guttering like a green fringe, and the overgrown garden seemed on the verge of possessing the building for its own. I could not see any clownish smile, or kiss, or any other mark, but that did not mean it was not there.

But tempted though I was, I could not make myself go closer to investigate. I tried to convince myself that it was because the fence was too rickety to climb, the undergrowth grown too dense to push my way through without snagging my clothes or skin on thorns.

In truth, I was scared.

Leaning against the fence, observing the house through a narrow gap and with leaves disturbing my view, the flash of dirty colour was almost too brief to register.

I gasped and stepped back, closing my eyes and turning away. Too tired, too worried. Maybe too old. I shook my head, but knew that I had to turn around again.

The broken upstairs window seemed to pulse with a forceful, rotten rainbow as a face came close and moved back again, close, back. The third time it retreated from the window it stayed away.

I hurried home, trying to rationalise. *It was a shadow thrown by trees. A skin of wallpaper inside the old house flickering in the breeze.*

But no tree grew that close to the house, and the evening was calm and still.

"This is just *stupid*," I said. Grasshoppers scratched their agreement. The buzz of bees echoed my words. I resolved to discover what was happening here. A village like Wellington Pond always had one deserted house, a place that kids could believe was haunted, adults could think was used by kids for drinking or screwing, and which would spend years and years slowly rotting down towards the ground, until some developer bought the plot and demolished the house and built something new. One house, yes, that was a given. But I had seen four today, since my eyes had been opened wider and my suspicions had sharpened my senses. Four, without really searching at all.

Four clowns had arrived next door.

It wasn't often that I spoke with Isaac twice in a day. Sometimes we went a week or two without talking, and that was fine, he had a busy life and I couldn't expect him to worry about me morning, noon and night. But as soon as I entered my house I picked up the phone and sat in my living room, looking out across my front garden and nursing the phone in my lap. I'd brought his number up on speed dial and my thumb hovered over the green button.

My son might still be in work. He worked long hours. My call would be an annoyance, nothing more. Even when he had all the time in the world, I only really heard impatience and boredom in his voice.

"This is for me to sort out," I said.

I stood and marched through to the kitchen, opening the back door and stepping out onto the patio. The sun was setting now, and the air had that heavy feeling that only a warm summer evening can carry.

My garden was no longer my own. The shape was mine, the

spread of plants, the wild parts attracting butterflies and bees and birds, the tended borders now eruptions of colour. But there was something else going on that I had never planned. The colours were just a little too deep and rich, too wet. The reds were too thick, the yellows too stark.

It's the light. It's later than I'd thought, darker, the shadows are spreading and making everything seem heavier . . .

But try as I might, I could not convince myself that all was well. Flowers hung heavier than they should, stalks stretching, as if made of sculpted flesh instead of delicate petals. Towards the rear of the garden, I saw a rose bush dripping into damp soil.

My heart started beating harder and faster, skipping a few beats every now and then, fluttering like a trapped bird attempting to flee. I backed towards the doors and stepped inside. The shadowy kitchen was cooler than the garden and more like home.

I watched shadows fall, a glass of cold milk from the fridge in my hand. I was shaking. More than once I spilled milk and it splashed across my shoes, speckling the flagstone flooring. But as the darkness grew, I felt better. It hid the garden away.

Sitting at the small dining table in the kitchen where I was so used to eating dinner for one, I looked at the phone again. I still didn't like wireless phones. I'd preferred it in the old days, when you had to go to where the phone was kept to speak. Mary and I had bought an old church pew from an antique shop and kept it under our stairs, and that had been our phone seat. She'd made cushions for those longer phone calls. When Isaac had gone to university we had often sat there together, our heads pressed close so that we could both hear our son's excited voice.

I suddenly wanted to hear my son. I dialled, expecting the answer phone again, but instead Isaac said, "Dad."

"I'm really worried, Isaac."

A sigh. "What about?"

"Well . . . " I couldn't really tell him, could I? The clowns I'd seen moving in next door, the fallen houses with red smears that reminded me of a clown's made-up mouth, the laughter that might or might not have been dreams. The dampness on my walls, spreading, consuming, that had not been there days before.

"Dad?"

"My garden looks overgrown."

"Don't beat yourself up about that. You're just a bit older than you were, that's all. So what if a few weeds take hold?"

"It's not that," I said softly, but I couldn't find a way to tell him exactly *what* it was. I'd weeded and tended the garden earlier that day, and the day before, and most days before that. In the summer especially I was out there for much of the time, and several friends had commented that mine was the best kept garden in the village. High praise for someone who, in the little time he had left, would never really be accepted as a true villager.

I couldn't tell him just how wild the place had become.

"I'll pop up on Saturday, Dad."

I was standing by the French doors looking out. Things seemed to be moving out there, even as the darkness swallowed them. I'd never known that plants could laugh.

"Dad? Saturday? Can't stay long, we've got a meal thing in the afternoon, but I'll come up and give you a hand in the garden. Dad? That okay?"

"Yes, thank you, son."

"Cool. See you soon."

I dropped the phone onto the kitchen worktop. "Dinner, then bed," I said. "Tomorrow's a whole new day." That had been Mary's favourite saying. Only once had she ever been wrong.

I stood in my open front doorway and looked out towards the street. It was mostly quiet. I could hear subdued voices in the distance, and smell the scent of barbecue, and the idea that others were gathered and having fun made me feel even more alone.

I'd had the idea to go to the White Horse to see if there was anyone there I could speak to. I wanted to ask about the house next door and the old woman who'd owned it. The villagers had said that she'd died in there, but now I couldn't remember exactly who it was who had told me.

And I wanted to ask about the other houses I'd seen. Those tumbled, old, overgrown places, hidden in plain sight across the village, ignored and passed by as if ignorance could hide them even deeper. It must have worked. If I *had* seen any of them before today, I'd not registered them at all.

I closed my eyes and thought of the village square. Even though I had only seen it that afternoon, I could not see the thatched cottage in my mind's eye. I saw Old Max pumping petrol in the little garage, the grocer's on the corner, the bed & breakfast place set back slightly from the square, the bakery, the stream that cut the square in half, bridged in four places for road and paths. I saw the red phone box set against the tall wall bounding the church yard, the church itself proud and grey in the shadow of ancient oaks, the attractive houses lining the road that passed by across the square's eastern edge. But I could not see that abandoned house. I knew it was there, I could imagine what it should look like. But the painting on my mind needed changing.

I opened my eyes again, and suddenly the thought of going out into the darkness held no allure. If that house was so troublesome for me to remember, then what if I approached someone and they . . . ?

They'll look right through me.

I shivered. It was a horrible idea. A ridiculous idea, too, because Wellington Pond had taken me willingly to its bosom, the villagers welcoming me not as a stranger but as a villager-to-be. But it felt like a cooler, more sinister place now. In the darkness there was not only the village, settling down for the night; the barbecuers, chatting softly and laughing gently as stars speckled the summer sky. There was also deception. There were places that should not be, and in those places, *things* that should not be.

I closed the front door and threw the bolt. Even though this place had only been my home for several years, it still felt like my castle. Mary had never been here, but I carried her memories rich and full in my mind. She would never be cast aside, ignored, forgotten.

"It'll all be fine," I said, and my voice echoed comfortably from furniture and walls that I knew so well. "Tomorrow's a whole new day."

I watched TV all evening without seeing anything, then went up to prepare for bed. In the bathroom I switched on the light and saw my ghostly visage peering at me in the big mirror above the sink. I gasped, shocked, and wiped the mirror free of condensation. It did no good. I still looked pale and wan, as if a fine dust had settled over my eyes.

Or my face.

I wiped a hand across my skin, but the greyness remained, pale, corpselike. My skin felt slick and greasy.

Washing and cleaning my teeth, I hummed a tune to help me forget the things I had seen and heard. It was an old Chas and Dave song, one which Mary and I had once danced to in a London boozer many moons ago. It had become *our* song.

Trying to imagine the singers' cheery faces, I saw only leery clowns. Closing my eyes brought them into sharper view. Opening my eyes, I saw only myself. Greyer than ever. Puffy around the eyes, red across the nose and around the mouth.

Changing.

Retreating to bed—the one safe place in any home, from a child pulling covers up over its eyes against the darkness, to an old man like me seeking sleep to escape reality—I reached over to turn off the lamp. Only then did I notice the area of dampness on the wall and ceiling. It had spread since earlier that day. It had bloomed, too, like a bruise finding colour after its initial, angry darkness. Purples and reds, oranges and yellows, and the plaster wall and ceiling had taken on the pitted, textured appearance of old skin.

I debated whether to turn out the light, but decided that the darkness would be worse.

There was no sleep for me. Only a twitchy wakefulness.

I heard creeping in the attic above my head, creaks too regular and purposeful to be caused by the house settling or mice skipping across attic boards. Something kissed wetly, a sound like moist lips opening and closing again, opening and closing, and the damp seeped across the ceiling and down the walls. It flowed, like a mix of melted wax finding its own shape.

"Isaac," I said, shaking. "Mary." But they were both far away from me now. I tried to move but I was frozen, trapped in my bed by the illusion of safety. The pure, deceitful illusion.

Distant laughter droned in, dulled by heavy walls and heavier shadows. And then another cackling burst from much, much closer, above me beyond the ceiling. Less than eight feet away. It rose and fell, and beneath the mad laugh I heard the insistent scraping of sharp, coloured nails.

My whole house creaked and groaned as it settled into its fate. Glass cracked somewhere downstairs. Floorboards warped. A door buckled in its distorting frame.

I tried to shout for help, but an altogether different sound came from my mouth. It was answered from the house next door.

The ceiling began to sag and crack as something forced its way through from above.

Reaching for the phone that I'd brought to bed with me for the first time ever, I wanted to call Isaac. But I was worried that he would hear only maniacal laughter. And I was afraid that although four clowns had arrived one late summer's afternoon, five would leave.

RELICS

"I know where you can buy a dragon's cock."

I tried to hide my surprise. Not because I believed him, but because he'd never before shown any inclination to speak. I'd been aware of Fat Frederick for over six years, and I thought it might have been the first time he'd even looked at me. Until now, I'd been less than a shadow.

"What would I want with a dragon's cock?" I asked. I remained cool, taking deep swigs of the harsh chemical they passed off as single malt in the Slaughterhouse Bar. Nice name. Hide in pure sight. I'd heard rumours of four people who'd been carried from here in bags. The fifth I'd seen with my own eyes.

He seated himself next to me. I heard the stool creak and groan above the music, the chatter of patrons, the clink of bottles and smash of dropped glasses. In the far corner, two men were planning something criminal over a table awash with spilled beer. One had a patch over his left eye, the other sported a long, pointed beard coiled with razor blades. A scruffy man sat on his own at another table, rolling a flick-knife between his knuckles like a drummer with a stick. Three women tended a fourth, blood speckling her shoulder and face. Courtesy of the flick-knife, perhaps. In the darkest corner, a man squatted beneath a table with his face buried between a woman's thighs, neck muscles straining. She smoked a crack pipe and stared at the ceiling as if completely unaware.

Classy joint.

"Well, there's the obvious use, first of all," Fat Freddie said. "It's only a shard, a splinter, but a dragon has the biggest cock in the animal kingdom."

"Dragons aren't real."

"And then there are more . . . arcane uses," he continued as if he hadn't heard me. "Soaked in gin, it makes for an effective food spice. Meaty and hot. Dried and ground up, dropped in a lover's drink, it aids libido. Keep the dose low, though. Dangerous." He tapped his greasy nose with a chubby finger, a gesture I found quite sickening. "Toxic cum."

I took another swig of drain cleaner. Slammed the glass down. The bartender glanced my way and I nodded once. I'd been nurturing an image down here for a long time, and couldn't afford to let it slip. It was hard enough being a woman in a world like this. Image was everything.

"You like our Scotch?" Freddie asked, surprised.

"No. Why are you talking to me?"

He feigned offence, and then something about him changed. It was chilling. All pretence at civility and good humour melted away, and I was suddenly sitting beside one of the most dangerous crime lords in London.

"Angelica Golden," he said. "You know why I'm talking to you. You *did* it so I'd talk to you."

"Did what?" I asked, but then I saw his expression—that slack, heavy face, eyes dead as if they reflected his many victims' final moments—and I wished I hadn't. Lying to Fat Freddie was stupid.

"You've been coming to the Slaughterhouse for a long time. You never cause trouble. You ask questions sometimes, but I allow that. It's a bar, and questions are why people like you come to places like this. But certain questions draw my attention. I wouldn't be who I am if they didn't."

He signalled the barman. The gesture was so subtle that I wasn't sure I'd seen it at all. Next moment there was a bottle of Laphroaig and two glasses on the bar before us. Fat Frederick scooped up the bottle and both glasses in one huge hand and slid from his stool with surprising grace.

A flush of fear washed through me. *Have I gone too far?* I wondered. I watched for different signals he might give others in the Slaughterhouse—a blink to kill me, a nod to drag me out back and cut off my hands.

"Come on," he said. "Let's go and talk about the relics."

Walking away from the Slaughterhouse, the world suddenly seemed so much larger.

I'd always known that there was more to the world than meets the eye. Even more so since losing Vince. When he vanished the streets grew darker and my mind opened to things that caused most people to glance away. The average person has a filter that they don't even know about. Especially here in London, where a thousand sights can hide one uncomfortable truth. It's easy to walk the streets and ignore the things that should not be, because the human mind is designed that way.

Dipping myself beneath the general ebb and flow of city life, I'd heard many rumours of stranger things. The pub basement in Holborn where a vampire from the twelfth century was buried beneath a foot of concrete and ten feet of compacted soil. Sometimes there was a heaviness to the air in that place, so it was said, a texture during those short, irregular moments when the entombed vampire's mind approached consciousness.

The unfinished tunnel in the Underground, where construction had been halted because no one would work that route. The sense of threat and terror was far too great.

And not only buried things. There were places in London hidden from common view, folds in the city negotiable only by those ready and willing to open their minds a little wider. Some of these places I had visited myself. They were usually curious, perhaps troubling, with their sense of otherness and their colourful and strange people.

Sometimes they were frightening.

I'd never actually *seen* anything. Not really. Much as I'd searched—because the collection of arcana had been Vince's domain, and the gathering of strange tales had obsessed him for those last couple of years before he vanished—all I'd ever found were hints and reflections. Like fading dreams, those deeper truths I sought kept themselves hidden one degree past the corner of my eye.

But then there were those places and things that Fat Frederick had just told me about. And there was the box he had opened for me.

I sat on the Tube carriage, rocking slowly back and forth, good whiskey swilling in my stomach and warming my bones, and I never once came close to nodding off. Perhaps I would never sleep again.

"It's how I make my way in life," he'd said. "Everything else is just . . . " He'd waved at the air, dismissing everything I knew about him with one wave of his hand. The bars and brothels, the drugs and murders, the payments to police and local councils disguised as charity.

"Why are you showing me this?" I'd asked.

And then the bombshell. "Because I want to find Vince as much as you do."

The thing in the wooden crate.

"It's the one relic I'll never sell. How can I?" He'd sounded almost dreamy then, and for a few moments I regarded Fat Frederick as an equal. A man capable of innocent fascination and joy, rather than the brutal, cynical killer I knew him to be.

I closed my eyes and remembered the angel, curled up in that box as if waiting to be born. But it was long-dead. Childlike body petrified, wings curled around its papery torso, feathers still whole but greyed with dust. Its face . . .

I could not remember whether I had even seen its face. Maybe I had shut it from my mind. Or perhaps I had been too terrified to look.

When I opened my eyes again, the two men sitting opposite were looking at me. One of them half-smiled and glanced away, the other stared over my shoulder through the window into the fleeting darkness. I wondered what they saw.

I got off at the next stop even though it was not mine. The platform was busy at this time of night, and I was pleased at that. The bustling people kept shadows on the move. I went with the flow and stood on the escalator taking us towards the surface, and all the way up I felt someone watching me.

It's only natural, I thought. *Now that I know, I can feel the weight of the unknown city around me.*

Out from the Underground, away from the warm, spicy stench of fuel and dust and hidden depths, I stood on London's rainy streets and let the crowds pass me by. For a moment I had the impression that they parted around me and I stood there like a rock in a stream, and I wondered whether knowing more of the hidden world had made me a part of it. But then a teenager nudged my arm and apologised, a man stepped on my foot, and I negotiated my way across the pavement to lean on the railing beside the road.

I looked up into the sky and watched the illuminated rain falling down towards me. It held me in its damp embrace.

Vince knew, Fat Frederick had said. *Sometimes I think he knew more than me.* Still looking down at that dead, ancient angel he kept in an old oaken box, he gave me the name of someone I should see.

Everyone leaves part of themselves behind.

That evening I sat in my apartment and looked at what I had of Vince. Photographs, scribbled notes, concert ticket stubs, memories in image and print that formed the ephemera of six years together. I spread everything around me on the floor while I drank a bottle of

Merlot, but there was no sense of Vince being there with me. I tried putting on some Radiohead, his favourite band, but though the words and music edged some way towards making those memories richer, there was still something lacking. A pair of his shoes smelled only of old shoes. I ran my hands across the inside of one of his favourite jackets, but felt nothing but cotton and leather.

All the while, the woman's name sang to me from earlier that day. *Mary Rock will answer your questions*, Fat Frederick had said, and I could only wonder why he had never been to her himself.

Head fuzzy from the wine, still unsettled by what I had seen earlier that day, I decided to venture back out into the night. My search for Vince had been ongoing since the day he vanished three years before, but only now did I feel one step closer. Perhaps speaking to Mary Rock would take me closer still.

It was raining even heavier than before. I shrugged myself deep into my coat and clasped the phone in my pocket. It was almost two in the morning, and though London never slept, it did give way to a dark community that rarely saw daylight. I had never questioned why a phone could give me a sense of safety, but it did. Perhaps because it was a route to the outside world.

Taxis buzzed the streets, looking for trade. Other cars kerb-crawled, occupants shrouded by night. The rain enclosed me, but I kept my head up and my eyes open, searching for any shadows that moved the wrong way. I knew how to protect myself, but that didn't mean that I relished the chance to use that knowledge.

It was a two mile walk to the address that Fat Frederick had given me, and I decided to do it all on foot. A taxi seemed too impersonal. I would use the time to clear my head, and to think through what had happened and how things had settled where they were now. I had always felt like a piece of flotsam bobbing on the whims of London's tides, and after tonight that sensation was even stronger.

The city watched my progress with calm, satisfied eyes.

I often daydreamed about feeling Vince's gaze upon me. I was convinced that he was still alive, though there was no evidence at all to support that. His friends, his sister Mel, his mother living in

Australia, had all long-since given up hope. That said more about them than Vince, although there was no doubting his troubled history and the terrible way he'd treated his family in the past. But I loved him now as much as I did that night he vanished, and I wanted him back.

Just popping down Asbo's for a bottle of wine, he'd called. Asbo was what we called the local Asda's supermarket on account of its general clientele. I was in the bath and had heard him opening the front door, and I'd shouted, *Get some Jelly Babies.* Those were the last words I said to him.

The bath was cold by the time I'd started to worry.

I moved along a street that bustled during the day but which was now all but silent. Restaurants and bars were closed up, some of them glowing faintly from low-level lighting. A few still sported neon signs in their windows. Some had doors protected by grilles or heavy metal rollers, others chanced their luck. Rain splashed on the pavement and made the reflections of streetlights come alive. It swilled along the gutters, pooling around drains blocked with litter and dog shit. A car sat on flattened tyres. A homeless man huddled in a doorway beneath torn cardboard boxes. I could just see his shoes, and for a shocking instant I imagined them attached to something horned, scaled, inhuman.

I slowed my pace and a growl came from beneath the boxes. I hoped it was his dog.

I hurried on, taking the phone from my pocket and glancing at the locked screen. It had become habit, almost a nervous twitch. I still expected to see a message from Vince waiting for me one day.

Three shadows moved towards me along the pavement. They were talking, animated, at ease with the dark. I moved to the edge of the pavement, my coat brushing against parked vehicles. The men's voices lowered only a little as we passed, and one of them said, "Evening."

I nodded and moved on, glancing back several times to make sure they had not stopped and were staring back at me, ready to give chase.

Damn it, Angie! I thought. I was never usually this nervous. And I hated the fact that the more I found out, the more scared I became. This was my city. I'd lived here my whole life, and I'd always suspected it had strange depths and hidden secrets. Knowing that for sure should not change the way I was.

But the angel, its papery skin, dusty feathers . . .

"It's all just old dead things!" I said, my voice startling me. I hadn't realised how quiet it was.

I entered a residential area. The streets were darker and even more deserted. I saw a couple of city foxes trotting across the road ahead of me, and the sight of them gave me comfort. They were jittery creatures, and if there was anything at all wrong with the night they would be in hiding.

There were a few lights on in houses. Some were upstairs, some down. I passed one window where the curtains were wide open and a man sat watching TV with the lights on. He held a can of beer in one hand and ate from a takeaway carton with the other. I watched for a moment, then turned away. He was in his own world, as was I.

I paused a little longer outside another bay window, looking across the small front garden at the gap between curtains. The lighting inside was more subdued, but I could still see the couple fucking. The man sat on the sofa and the woman rode him with her back to me, leaning forward so they could kiss, offering me a frank look at that glimmering, wet place where they joined. She pounded onto him as if angry. His hands grasped her buttocks.

I had not made love to anyone since Vince had disappeared. I suddenly felt like an intruder, spying on this couple as they indulged in something so private and intimate. Perhaps the city was watching me like this all the time.

It took an hour to reach Mary Rock's address. I was surprised when I arrived, and I had to check a couple of times that I'd come to the right place. I programmed the postcode into my phone and it confirmed that I was on the correct street.

The houses were large, probably a million pounds-plus, but there was a uniformity to them that surprised me. Detached, the eight houses along the street differed only in the designs of their gardens and the choices of window dressings. I'd expected a supplier of relics, someone who dealt with Fat Frederick, to live somewhere more distinct, and at the same time hidden away. An old warehouse in the docklands, perhaps, converted to open-plan apartments and with hidden basements. Or a deconsecrated church, converted into living accommodation.

Now that I was here, I wasn't sure what to do. It was four in the morning. The rain had lessened, and soon dawn would sheen the east. There were already more vehicles on the roads than there had been before. The city was stirring.

My uncertainty was settled when the front door of the house opened and a tall, thin woman walked along the path that curved across the front garden. She was black, graceful, perhaps fifty years old, and she walked with her hands in her pockets. So casual. Reaching the low front gate, she pulled it open without a sound.

"Angelica," she said. "Frederick told me to expect you. You look cold. Please, come in, I've already put some coffee on."

Mary Rock seemed so normal.

That should have made me turn and run.

Inside, the house was warm and pleasant, well-appointed and with a homely feel. Its ground floor was taken up with an open hallway from which a wide staircase curved upwards, a comfortable living room smelling of scented candles, and a couple of other rooms I did not see.

"Please, take a seat," Mary said, pointing at a wide leather sofa. "I'll pop through to get coffee. How do you take it?"

"White, no sugar. Did Vince sit here?" I was looking at the sofa. I could imagine him there, and in my mind's eye he was grinning up at me with that I've-done-something-stupid lopsided smile of his that I hated to love.

"Oh yes, many times," she said. I watched her pass through a set of double doors. She wore jeans and a heavy jumper, walked bare-foot, and carried herself with an alluring grace. She almost seemed to float.

I followed, deciding not to sit.

The doors opened into a big kitchen with a dining area attached. Half of the kitchen was given over to a comfortable corner sofa, the rest was all chrome and shine, modern and expensive. I saw machines whose function I didn't even know. Mary had a proper coffee machine, and she worked it as I watched.

"Oh, okay," she said, noticing me. "We'll be going downstairs, anyway."

"Downstairs?"

"You came to see, didn't you?"

She didn't ask *what* I had come to see, nor did she give a clue. But I nodded mutely, watching as she made coffee and steamed milk. Our fingers brushed as I took the mug from her, and she was staring into my eyes.

"Vince was such a nice young man," she said. "So proper and . . . old-fashioned."

I snorted. "Really?"

"That's who I saw," she said, smiling and shrugging. "Everyone is different away from home. Come on. Are you ready?"

I don't know, I thought, suddenly panicked. *Am I ready? For what? What is she going to show me? Fat Frederick took me to see a dead angel, but she . . .*

She was royalty to Fat Frederick's butler. It wasn't the house or the obvious wealth, because that could be feigned. It was in her manner and the way she bore herself. There was a weight to her gaze that had nothing to do with money, and everything to do with knowledge.

I was suddenly more afraid of this woman than I had been of anyone in my life.

"Yes," I said. "I'm ready."

I followed her through the kitchen, past the sofa and into a lobby area. A door led into the garden, and another seemed to be a closet. She opened the third, smaller door, flicked a switch on the wall, and beyond her I saw a stone staircase leading down.

"Vince was one of my best hunters," she said, holding the door open. A waft of secret smells breathed up from the basements.

"Is," I said.

"I'm sorry?"

"*Is* one of your best. He's not dead."

"Oh." She tilted her head. "It's sweet that you believe that." She started down the staircase, and I followed.

A sense of time immediately enfolded me—the must of ages in my nose, dense shadows that seemed heavy and ancient. If the house above us was relatively new and pristine, this basement area was altogether older. The past hid down here, and I was an intruder.

"So he hunted for relics for you?" I asked. "The things that Fat Frederick deals in?"

"Oh, did he show you his angel?"

"Yes," I breathed.

"Bless him." She spoke like a mother talking about her child.

"It was . . . amazing."

"It's dead."

I was watching my footing on the stone steps. They were worn concave by centuries of use, and the idea of who had walked here before filled the air with ghosts.

"Dead?"

"Through here." The lighting was poor, spread weakly from a couple of bare bulbs swathed in dust and spider webbing. She walked ahead of me and I had to hurry to keep up. I had the sudden sense that I could get lost down there, and the thought of wandering in the darkness, hands held out before me, sent a chill down my back.

"Aren't all the relics from dead things? That's what they are, surely. Fossils. All that's left of . . . " I trailed off.

"Do you really think that?"

"I . . . " I wasn't sure what I thought.

"It's dark in here," she said. "It prefers it like that. Follow me, I'll give you something to help you see."

Mary Rock took my hand. It was unexpected and intimate, and I squeezed without even thinking about it. She squeezed back, this woman who might have been the most dangerous person I'd ever met, giving me comfort.

Darkness breathed us in as she closed a door. And there was something in there with us.

Mary held something against my face. "Put them on," she whispered. "Keep your eyes closed, and only open them when I say."

Glasses. Goggles of some sort. She let go and I used both hands to secure the strap around the back of my head, keeping my eyes closed as instructed. My heart thumped. I could smell something strange, a living scent that was unlike anything I had ever smelled before.

I wanted to turn and run, flee that place and keep running all day and night, out of London and into the countryside where perhaps I might find somewhere to hide, shed everything I was discovering, and live out my days in blissful ignorance.

"Open your eyes," Mary Rock whispered. She had a voice demanding to be obeyed.

I looked, and saw, and my whole world grew wider and darker than I had ever believed possible.

"My retirement," Mary Rock said beside me. "My future. One day I'll figure out how to kill it, and then . . . I'll start to harvest."

Thin limbs, as if from malnutrition, but I thought not.

"Vince was one of those who helped bring it in."

An elongated head, large eyes, elfin ears.

"In fact, he tracked it down. Ealing. Down beneath the city."

The worn stubs of broken wings.

"There's a whole world down there. Sometimes I fear that's where he's gone."

A fairy, I thought. *She has a fairy down here, alive, breathing, giving off warmth and a stench like . . . . like . . .*

"I have to leave," I said, and that was when the manacled, chained, wretched thing lifted its head and looked right at me.

I was surprised she let me go. Walking toward the front door, Mary Rock now at my back, I expected the impact at any moment. A heavy object against my skull, a blade between my shoulder blades.

"I want Vince back," she said as I reached the front door.

"So do I." My voice shook. Everything I knew had been shaken. The world beyond the door was a wider, stranger place.

"If anyone can find him, it's you."

I turned, she smiled, but it did not touch her eyes. Coolness came off her in waves. I thought back to when she had squeezed my hand, but could not recall feeling any warmth at all.

I opened the front door and stepped out of her house backwards, still looking at her, trying to find something else to say. But what else *could* I say?

You have a fairy prisoner in your basement.

By the time I reached the street I was running.

Something followed me home.

The streets were busier now, and it was almost seven in the morning. Residential streets hummed with passing cars, early morning deliveries, and children hustling towards their pre-school clubs. With so many people on the streets, I did not feel any safer.

As I walked, I tried to connect Vince with the amazing things I had found out, tried to imagine him hunting things like that creature in Mary Rock's basement through the shadowy places and forgotten buildings of this great, mysterious city. And as I remembered his warmth, his love, the look in his eye as he came in from one of his supposed late-night rehearsal sessions with his band—

Something brushed past me, just out of sight. I span around, ready to face anything, and instead there was only empty pavement. I was in front of a café filled with people having an early morning fry-up and tea, and several of them sitting at a window table stared at me. No one smiled.

I hurried on. I could feel attention upon me, a prickling on my neck, a cool tingle down my back. Traffic growled and tooted, people shouted, motorcycles grumbled, and in all that noise I still heard one whispered word:

Angie.

Only Vince called me Angie, and only when he wanted to piss me off. My name was Angelica, and that was what I liked.

I turned a full circle again, scanning the street and looking up to the rooftops. A shape shivered behind a window, shaking rapidly just out of sight. A shadow flitted from one roof to another, leaping along a ridge with the sun behind it. Looking into the rising sun, shielding my eyes, I could not quite make out what it was.

Maybe because of what I knew, I could sense so much more.

Or perhaps whatever was out there *knew* that I knew, and that was why it followed me. Stalking. Hunting. Letting me know that with the knowledge I now carried I might never be alone again.

I raised my hand for a taxi. It slowed, then sped up again as if the driver didn't like the look of me.

I glanced in a shop window to see if I was crying or bloodied, and standing behind me I saw the reflection of a face I knew.

I turned quickly, gasping, "Vince!" and ready to embrace the man I loved. He'd lied to me for the six years of our relationship, but I was more than ready to forgive him. He had deceived me, perhaps believing that I was nowhere near ready to know what he knew. I'd prove him wrong. I'd tell him about Fat Frederick's dead angel and Mary Rock's barely-living fairy, and Vince would see my manic, ecstatic acceptance of this greater new world.

But the man standing behind me was not Vince. I didn't know who he was, or what, but he stood so close that I would have smelled his breath, if he had any.

He examined me. I have never been so thoroughly analysed. He tilted his head to one side and looked me up and down, and I could feel his gaze brushing my heart.

"Don't hurt me," I whispered. All awareness of my surroundings was gone. I had no thought of help. Somewhere very far away I could hear traffic and see the vague, ghostly shapes of passing pedestrians, but in reality there was only him and me. His face was . . . forgettable. Even as I blinked I lost track, and saw him anew each time my eyes reopened. "Please don't hurt me."

He grinned. I was certain I would not forget that, even as his face faded from memory. I would never forget so many teeth.

Then the man leaned forward and smelled me, filling himself with my scent, before turning and losing himself in the crowd.

I did not even see him go.

I ran, like a scared little girl in a fairytale, all the way home.

The thing that sniffed me is still out there, and it knows me. I cannot let it scare me off.

I'm going to find Vince. My determination grows, and a desperate, deep part of me wishes he'd shared this part of his life so that we could have lived it together. That's a big part of the reason I want to be with him once more. Because I love him, yes.

But also because I want us to share the adventure.

SOLE SURVIVORS

That final image caused me to recall the most terrifying seven hours of my life. It was his eyes. He didn't look as though he'd spent nineteen days trapped underground in the mine, slowly starving, suffocating, breaking nails scratching desperately at rock-falls while he waited for the rescue teams to drill adjacent tunnels, avoiding flash floods, swallowed in the darkness when batteries finally ran out and the deep, endless black closed in at last. His face resembled that of a survivor, true. He had sunken cheeks and coal filth so ingrained I doubted he'd ever look clean again. But not his eyes. They were bright, gleaming.

Just like hers.

Thirty men and women had been trapped in the coal mine. It was a privately run business, the last working mine in South Wales, bravely hanging on to traditions and processes slaughtered by the Conservative government in the seventies and eighties. An explosion caused a cave-in, and the first few days were spent trying to establish whether there was even anyone left alive. They were almost quarter of a mile below the surface, and because the main shaft was still unstable, a hole was drilled directly down into the affected area. A fibre-optic cable was fed down, and those first haunting images of pale, desperate faces suddenly filled with hope went around the world.

There were fifteen survivors huddled there, praying for rescue.

Live coverage of the rescue attempt followed. Relatives of the fifteen were tracked down and interviewed, the engineers involved in the rescue operation becoming minor celebrities. I heard through a friend of a friend—these were the circles I moved in, after all—that the chief engineer had already signed an exclusive newspaper deal even before the main rescue shaft first broke through.

Food and drink was lowered. A doctor went down. Nineteen days after the disaster, news flashed around the world that the first of the fifteen trapped miners was being brought up.

One by one they pulled them out of the mine. It was covered live, with a global audience estimated, at its height, of almost a billion. I suppose good news has value after all. And even though I'm a jaded old fuck, I must admit even I shed a couple of tears.

It was the faces of the men and women as they came up. Like they'd been born again and were seeing the sky for the first time, the sun, the fluffy white clouds and the hundreds of family and friends who had been camped out at the pit head for two weeks.

The fifteenth miner surfaced. It was the ultimate feel-good story, cruel fate avoided and the Grim Reaper denied his full harvest. Celebrations at the rescue camp were exuberant and wild, and a famous image was born of a filthy, soot-covered woman holding her husband tight to her and laughing over his shoulder.

But it didn't stop there.

They brought up a sixteenth survivor, a man, and everything seemed to change.

It was his eyes. Filled not with wonder and joy, but humour. As if he was laughing at us all.

Just like Jemima.

In October of 2012, three years ago, a train from London Paddington to Swansea derailed close to Bristol Parkway station. Someone had left a car on the line and then fled. There was CCTV footage, and a couple of witnesses, but no one was ever caught. There were whispers of terrorism, but general consensus settled on the notion that it was an idiotic prank gone wrong. Perhaps they'd intended moving the car before the train came along, or perhaps it had stalled during a dare.

I was sitting in the third carriage, working on a piece commissioned by a national triathlon magazine. I'd interviewed four ex-forces personnel who'd lost limbs in Iraq and Afghanistan and had then gone on to compete in an Ironman triathlon. I was proofing the piece and checking out some of the photos that had been commissioned, making sure my article sat well with them.

I'd been conscious of the woman across the narrow table from me for some time. An elderly lady, she'd tried catching my eye several times. I hated being rude. She wanted a conversation, that was all, and sometimes on train journeys I sought the same myself. More than one commission had come from casual chats with people at airports, train stations or in pubs or restaurants. But I had to get the article finished. I tried to keep to myself, but she was insistent.

"Looks very fascinating," she said at last, nodding down at my tablet.

I sighed and sat back. She was right. It had been an inspiring job, because more often than not I was interviewing murderers and those left behind to grieve, politicians who could never give a straight answer, and the victims of disasters.

Three seconds later, before I could respond, we became victims ourselves.

The train juddered at first, then before I had a chance to think it jarred and shook so hard that I slammed forward against the table. Pain flared, a rib broke. The world seemed to lurch and then turn, and I slid sideways wondering why I was puking, I was never travel sick, I was so used to travelling that—

My tablet and the woman's cup of scalding coffee flipped from the table and struck my shoulder and face. The tablet bruised my collarbone, the coffee burnt my left cheek and neck. I was moving by then, lifted up from the seat to crack my head on the overhead luggage rack. The woman bounced up and down again in front of me, and I thought, *I don't remember her wearing red.*

Everything turned and twisted, glass shattered, metal crumpled, plastic tore and scraped and slashed, and I rolled, battered and mixed in with the wreckage, both mechanical and human.

When the train came to a standstill and everything fell still, the silence made me want to scream.

I didn't lose consciousness. I have no idea why, because the pain from my ribs was exquisite. My head throbbed and my face was wet with blood. For a while I thought it was my own. Then I saw the woman above me, crushed between a table upright and a concertinaed seat. Her face was turned away from me, though it shouldn't have been, and I remember spending a long time debating whether this was a good or bad thing. If her head hadn't been twisted far around, I would have been forced to look into her dead gaze for those long, lonely hours between crash and rescue. It was the distorted version of a human body I had for company. Everything was wrong about the dead woman. No one was supposed to look like that. No one should have bled so much.

After a while the bleeding stopped. I found that I had one free hand, and I was able to wipe most of the mess from my face. But I couldn't help swallowing some of it. Warm, sticky, I gagged and tried not to vomit again. Unable to turn my head, I hated the idea of choking on my own puke.

I lost track of time. Once, the wreckage moved with a jolt, and I thought someone was shifting it or cutting through to get me. But it must have been the wreck settling.

I tried to shout, but my mouth wasn't working properly. Terror and pain had stolen my voice.

Hours passed. Trapped by a shattered train, I was constantly in fear of being crushed to death, or burning, or dying from my wounds. I couldn't tell how badly I was hurt. Someone else was screaming, and that went on for what felt like forever.

They took me out eventually, as the sun was setting and I was starting to shiver uncontrollably. I'd been trapped for seven hours and had pissed myself. The dead woman's blood had dried like a mask across my face, stiff and cloying.

They cheered when they brought me out, and I even managed to sit up a little and smile before the pain in my chest drove me down again. As they carried me on a stretcher towards a waiting ambulance, I saw a woman being helped out from the wreckage just ten feet from where I'd lain for so long. She was smiling, a soft, satisfied smile that disturbed me the moment I saw it. She did not have a scratch on her.

I'd learn later that her name was Jemima. That first moment I laid eyes on her I knew I would have to interview her.

I discovered more details later, when I was being checked over in hospital. Even though the train had been slowing on its approach to Bristol Parkway, once the engine derailed it ploughed on for almost quarter of a mile. Three carriages and the rear engine became detached, the remaining four rolled. Scores of people were injured. Hundreds poured from the wrecked train, helping hundreds more in acts of heroism that were talked about for weeks and months after.

By lunchtime, thirteen bodies had been recovered, and six people were confirmed still missing, including me.

At the end of the afternoon, when the crushed wreckage of the most badly damaged carriage had been sifted through, four more bodies were found. What was miraculous was the people found alive.

Three of them.

I was given a commission by the *Guardian*. I'd worked for them many times before, and I was friendly with the commissioning editor. She told me that Jemima had granted only one interview, and that I was the one.

It was an exclusive. That made me even more nervous than I already was.

Because there was something wrong. I didn't understand why the media and public couldn't see that. Was it just me? As well as the Woman Who Never Was, as someone on TV news had named Jemima—and we only had her assurance that that was her real name—she was also being called Miracle Girl. The girl part was pushing it, because she was easily forty years old. As for the miracle . . . I don't know where that came from, but it didn't seem to suit the circumstances at all.

Miracle implied survival against the odds.

Jemima had not survived. She had been born.

I met her in a hotel suite in central Bristol. They'd let her stay there free for several days, because it was good publicity for the hotel and she had claimed nowhere else to stay. She was drinking coffee when I entered her room, black and strong, unsweetened. She would have three cups during our short interview.

"So you're the one I can talk to," she said as I entered. Other than her, the room was deserted. I'd expected a publicist at least, clinging to her like some sort of fleshy parasite. But there was no one. The room was vast and silent, cooler than it should have been. I shivered as I crossed a desert of cream carpet to the chair set opposite her.

"I understand I'm the one you *asked* to talk to," I said. I shrugged the bag from my shoulder, winced at the pain, delved inside, brought out a notebook and pen, a digital recorder, my phone, put the bag down, picked it up again, all under the dawning realisation that I didn't want to look at her. I was afraid that her eyes would be the same as when I'd seen them several days before.

They were. When I finally sat, cringing once again at my bound ribs, she pinned me there with them. Cool, a stunning light blue, they exuded humour. Her smile was more of a smirk. She sipped at her coffee, hardly putting the cup down before bringing it to her mouth again. She watched me through the steam.

"How are you feeling?" she asked.

"I'm okay. Broken rib, bumps and bruises. Lucky."

"Lucky you were in a terrible train crash?"

"I'm lucky I didn't die. And you?"

She waved the question away. I knew there was nothing wrong with her. *Without a scratch*, the headlines had read. It hardly seemed possible.

"Ready?" she asked.

"Yes. Of course. Why did you ask for me?"

"It had to be someone."

"You seem quite well considering what you've been through."

"Been through?"

"The crash. Being trapped for seven hours with two bodies for company."

"Oh, yes," she said, sipping more coffee. She seemed to enjoy every mouthful as if it was the first.

"Can I ask you a few questions?"

"Sure."

"What's your name?"

"Jemima Chadbourn. My middle name's Susan, but I've never used that, never liked it."

"Where were you born?"

"Hillingdon hospital, London. July 17th, nineteen-seventy-five."

"Where do you live?"

"Here and there." Her smile was constant now, her eyes boring into me. I'd chosen to use the recorder, but wished I had been taking notes as well. I craved those few seconds now and then looking down at my notebook.

"Where were you travelling on the day of the train crash?"

"Swansea. I'd never been there."

"So it was a pleasure trip?"

"Pleasure?" she asked.

I caught my breath. Something about her expression had changed, from amused to sultry, and she inspired an instant reaction in me. I glanced away, confused and unsettled.

"Everything's a pleasure," she said.

I checked the recorder. The back of my neck prickled, my balls tingled. A cool rush passed through my body, back and forth like a rapid tide.

"There's no record of you on the train," I said.

"I bought a ticket on the day, not online."

"No record of your birth at that hospital. No birth certificate, no National Insurance number. No passport. I can't find you anywhere."

"Yet here I am." She shrugged, one of the most human gestures she'd made, and drained her cup. "People should keep better records. Coffee?" She stood and walked to the coffee machine in the corner, and I had a chance to assess her without her stare distracting me. She was tall and slim, athletic, quite beautiful, and possessed of an easy grace.

"What about your family?" I asked. "Aren't they concerned for you? How come you're staying here?"

"You can't choose your family," she said without turning around. She was pouring more coffee, and something about her manner when she did so disturbed me. It was as if she lost just a little control as the caffeine flowed, and the scents rose around her. I'd spoken with enough junkies and obsessives to see signs of cravings and addictions, but this wasn't quite that.

"What about friends?" I asked.

Jemima came back to her seat with two mugs of coffee. "Oh, I have friends," she said.

I blinked. Looked away. Checked the recorder.

"You weren't supposed to be on that train," I said. "You survived, yet it seems you came from nowhere."

"Nowhere?" she asked, sitting and leaning forward, suddenly interested. "You've been there?" Then she sat back chuckling to herself.

"I don't know why you want me here," I said. "I can't write an interview from this. I need to know about you. A bit of history, something of interest."

Jemima drank her coffee. "Isn't it enough that I survived?"

"Did you?" I asked. For the first time, the only time, there was a flicker of something in her eyes other than that underlying humour, the constant subtle mockery. I can't say that I annoyed her. But perhaps I struck a chord.

"I'll give you a quote," she said. "Maybe you can build something around that."

"I doubt it," I said.

She laughed, scratching at her cheek, brushing hair over one ear. She looked me up and down. I could not perceive what her interest might be.

"Well?" I asked.

"I'm not the only sole survivor," she said.

The interview was over then, and minutes later I was out of the hotel and down on the street, frowning as I turned over what she'd said. I tried to make sense of it. She hadn't been the sole survivor. There were others.

It wasn't until the coal mine disaster that I had an inkling of what she'd meant.

I thought of Jemima as my train passed the point where the derailing disaster had occurred. There was a memorial close beside the line— I'd seen it on the news when it was unveiled, but had not been able to force myself to attend the ceremony—but we passed it in a flash, little more than a blur. I wondered what the point was of having it there if no one could see it. Such physical memorials were for the benefit of the living, surely? The survivors? The dead would not care.

Three days after I met her, Jemima vanished. She'd still been staying in the hotel, and she'd been seen that morning at break-fast. It had not taken long for the hotel staff to start feeling uncomfortable around her. *It's like she doesn't really see us*, one of the hotel's waiters said in an online interview when news of her disappearance appeared. *It's not that she's aloof. We have plenty of aloof people staying here. It just felt like we were nothing to her. Ants to an elephant.*

The train passed through the Severn tunnel. I swallowed and my ears popped. A woman across the aisle from me tutted when her phone connection broke. She'd been on it since Paddington, speaking loudly about her boyfriend and his new tattoo and his weekend away with his mates to watch football while she was left at home and should she really be buying a place with him and blah blah. I'd given her a few stern looks but they washed around her, unseen, unfelt. I wondered what she saw of the real world. I wondered how she would react if the real world confronted her. She'd be a gopher in a snake's eyes.

The man's name was Terry Welford. I could find no trace of him before the mining disaster. He'd been brought up as a survivor, but I didn't think he was anything of the sort. I wasn't sure what he was, so I was going to South Wales to conduct some interviews. To begin with, I wanted to speak to some of the people who had been trapped down there with him.

I had no exclusives this time, because the stories were already being told. Newspapers and magazines, TV programmes, there were even rumours of a couple of sizeable book deals being inked just days after the rescue. I was hoping that my credentials would get me past some of the publicity people who'd swarmed to the survivors, and if that didn't work, I'd inveigle my way closer in other ways. Thirty years as a reporter had taught me a few tricks, and a lot about human nature. I knew it wasn't only the allure of cold hard cash that drove people to tell their stories. Sometimes, they just wanted someone to believe them.

On the train I read many of the tales, filtering them, assessing which of the survivors I should be talking to. There were three who had yet to tell their stories. These were probably the ones awaiting payment for big exclusives or book deals. A few others had been in the press and on TV, and one was even rumoured to be appearing in a reality TV show soon. There were four who'd only been interviewed once or twice, and I could see why. Their pictures showed people touched and troubled by their experience, not beaming joyfully into the camera with sun on their faces.

One of them looked haunted.

As the Welsh countryside opened up around me, I went about finding this man's address.

I could still see the skeleton of the old mining town hidden beneath decades of new development.

"And up there, at the head of an old mine, that's where they've built a load of new shops," Angie said. "There's a Costa there, and though the town council is resisting MacDonald's, it's only a matter of time." She was a local who had offered to show me around, and a representative of the private company that owned the mine. Public Relations Executive was her job title. I suspected it was a position created on the day of the explosion and cave-in, but she was nice enough, and she seemed open and honest. She kept telling me what a miracle the rescue had been, as if the constant use of the word in the media was still a few utterances from saturation point. "They've hidden the slag heaps beneath forests and landscaping, and made museums and tourist attractions of the old mine workings. I suppose it could have been worse."

"How's that?"

We were walking along the main street of the little valley town. There had been significant investment in this place. New housing crept up the hillsides, shop fronts had been upgraded, a couple of streets had been pedestrianised. I wondered how much of this new investment was generated by the mine, but it was a question I held off from asking. I had no wish to sound sceptical. It was a good thing they were doing here, a co-operative arrangement between local families and businesses to keep their population in employment. How profitable that employment might be, and for how long, was a sensitive subject, especially right now. I wasn't here to write a social piece. I might not be here to write anything at all. This was all to do with personal curiosity. My own story.

"Other places have been left to die," she said. "At least here you can see the valley's history, even if it is hidden beneath the surface veneer."

"So where is Terry Welford staying?"

"You really want to interview him?" Her voice became guarded for the first time.

"Yes. He's the mystery, isn't he?"

We paused close to a small park. Children played on swings and a climbing frame, while adults stood around the edges chatting. The whole town had a strange feel after the disaster and rescue, although most of the media trucks had already moved on to the next story.

"No mystery really," she said.

"You know him, then?"

Angie frowned. "Well . . . yes. No."

"Yes or no?"

"Oh look, there's Max!" She waved to a man approaching along the road, grabbed my arm, urged me towards him. Max was one of the survivors, and in seconds he'd agreed to talk to me about what had happened. We wandered along the street towards a local café. Angie sat us outside at a pavement table. I guessed it was meant to look Parisienne, but it was still a picnic table on a pavement in a Welsh mining town. There was something nice about the owner's attempts, almost innocent. I was hoping that Angie would go inside to buy drinks, but she sat with us while I started asking him questions. All the usual ones . . . How do you feel? What was it like? Will you go underground again? What did you drink? How did you all help each other down there?

Max was a good interviewee, polite and erudite, and I could tell that he'd answered these same questions in the same way a dozen times before. He enjoyed telling his story, though, and I found myself swept along. For a while I even forgot that I was a reporter, and a strange look from Angie urged me to continue making notes as Max talked.

When she finally stood and nipped into the café to buy us some drinks and cakes, I asked my real question.

"Who is Terry Welford?"

Max frowned and looked away.

"What's the problem?" I asked, instantly cursing myself for coming across as aggressive. Angie might only be a minute or two, and I had the strong sense that the only time I'd get anything meaningful from Max was when he was alone. He suddenly seemed vulnerable. I felt sorry for him, because he'd lost friends and been through a terrible ordeal. But I needed to know more.

"No problem," he said. "Just . . . " He trailed off and waved to someone as they drove along the street. He didn't smile. I guessed everyone knew everyone here, and Max's new-found celebrity status probably meant little in this close-knit town.

I was something of a fool. I realised it then, sitting across from this man who had been swallowed by the earth for almost nineteen days. He and his mates must have been convinced they were going to die, either from starvation, thirst, suffocation, crushing, or driven mad by the encroaching darkness as the batteries in their lamps began to fail. It would have been a horrific way to confront your own demise, a slow death without the touch of loved ones to guide you through, or the comfort of knowing it came at a reasonable time. And here I was confronting the whole event as a news story. Max had waved to that driver not because he was a survivor, but because he was a fellow resident of this town. He wasn't a news story. He was a man with a life rediscovered, welcomed back into the arms of loved ones who had been so sure they might never see him again, alive or dead.

I'd done a little research. As well as the fifteen missing presumed dead from this recent disaster, there were bodies beneath these rolling valleys from many decades before, crushed or trapped in places too dangerous to ever venture again.

"I'm sorry," I said. "I don't mean to sound pushy."

"'Course you do," he said. "You all do. What happened to me isn't good enough, is it? Because it ended too well. Good news isn't news."

"Viewing figures prove otherwise," I said.

"How many of those were watching in case we were brought up in body bags?"

I had no reply.

"One reporter, two days ago, asked me how the experience had affected my sex life with my wife. Can you believe that?"

I raised an eyebrow because yes, I could. There were certain papers and news sources that looked for the base line in everything.

"Look, I know you've told your story a hundred times," I said. "And to be honest, I don't want to tell the same story again. I've spoken to a lot of people like you, decent people. I know that pretty soon you're just going to want to get on with things, and the sight of another strange car in the town or an outside broadcast van will make you spit."

"You've come to find out about the stranger," he whispered.

I clammed up. I had a whole little speech ready to continue about media intrusion and the rights of a private life, but he stopped me there and then.

"The stranger," I said, nodding. "Terry Welford."

"If that's even his name."

Angie came out of the café then, carrying a tray bearing three mugs of tea and a plate of Welsh cakes. "I bought two each, don't know if you even like them but Jean makes such nice cake." She sat down beside Max and glanced across at me, pausing only slightly when she sensed the atmosphere between us. "Everything okay?" she asked.

"Everything's fine," I said. And although I probed and asked some more questions, Max grew subdued and unresponsive. Angie apologised, muttered something about his traumatic experience and how tired he still was. I saw the truth. When the two of them stood to leave, and Angie dropped a tenner onto the table to pay our bill, Max glanced at me one more time, and I saw his fear.

Fear of the stranger.

The last person I had ever expected to see in that little Welsh mining community was Emilio Sanches. But there he was, across the street from me, walking along the pavement at a steady, unhurried pace. The school day had ended, and a flood of children in black and white flowed through the streets, ducking into shops and scampering along the narrow pavements. Cars crept along the road, drivers conscious of the flow of youth.

Sanches walked, his pace confident and consistent, with no sign of any collision. He didn't have to move aside for the children, and none of them seemed to notice him, even though he was going against the flow.

I tried to match his pace on the opposite pavement, but it was too crowded. In the end I stepped onto the road and moved quicker that way. I skirted parked cars, pausing now and then to let traffic pass. All the while I tried to keep my eyes on Sanches.

He shouldn't have been there. He *couldn't* have. But I had never doubted my own eyes, and I had seen him enough times on the news and in the papers to be sure. This was Sanches, and him being present sent a chill through me, and painted this town and valley in a very different light. Even though the sun still shone, this was suddenly a much darker place.

After the train crash and Jemima, I found two other instances of a mysterious survivor being pulled from the jaws of fate. They had been distant and remote, too far for me to travel on my meagre savings. Nevertheless, after the mining disaster and Terry Welford, they took on new meaning.

The first was a tower block fire in Chicago three years earlier. Seven people had been trapped on the top floor, unable to escape down two collapsed and fire-filled staircases, too high to be reached by ladder. Thirty-one people had died already, and everyone else had been evacuated. But these seven had been in the penthouse gym and the alarm on the top three floors had failed to sound.

In this age of instant news, images were immediately flashed around the world. The burning building became familiar on screens across the globe, as did the harried faces of the fire chiefs and rescue services as they devised plans to save the seven. Save the Seven even became a hashtag on Twitter, with over half a million suggestions as to how the rescue could be implemented. Days after the fire, the Chicago emergency services admitted that they'd had one person checking Twitter full-time in case any bright ideas surfaced.

Many photographs and film clips of the desperate survivors emerged. They all had mobile phones, and as well as using them to contact loved ones and speak to the rescue services, some of those trapped posted on their own social media pages. Several images became instantly famous. One was a selfie of all seven of them, huddled against the eastern windows with a view of the city behind them. Smoke hazed across the image. I didn't know whether to cry for them, or laugh at them. They'd even used a selfie stick.

With efforts to extinguish the flames failing, all focus shifted onto extracting the survivors from the doomed structure.

As the flames spread and the west glazed wall of the seventeen-storey building collapsed, a helicopter pilot braved the brutal updrafts, blinding smoke, and deadly billows of flames to hover above the roof. Firemen lowered themselves down, and in the space of twelve minutes all seven trapped workers were rescued.

They also brought up an eighth person. Her name was Mandy Taylor. She should not have been there.

After Jemima, I tracked down any information I could on Mandy Taylor. At the time the focus had been on the daring and very visible rescue, but even on the day there were some telling comments from the survivors. *She wasn't there*, one of them said when questioned about Taylor. *She'll be a shadow behind me forever*, another said. I saw one man afraid to look into the camera, as if worried he would see his own reflection, saying, *I never knew her, and wish I didn't now.*

She vanished the day after the rescue, and no one knew anything about her. Not why she was there, how she had made her way through the building's security, where she came from. No family could be traced. She had appeared on none of the survivors' photos during the fire. It was strange, though. They all remembered something of her, but only snippets, as if only the group might recall her as a whole.

Those few images of her, blurred and busy from the staging area of the rescue, were even more haunting when I returned to viewing them later. Being helped down from the helicopter, she was looking around with an enigmatic smile blurring her features. I knew that if I could see closer she would have bottomless, dead eyes.

The second instance involved Emilio Sanches. A plane had crashed in the Sierra Nevada mountains two years before the Chicago office fire, it was believed with no survivors. But Sanches was pulled alive from the wreckage. He was not on the flight manifest, possessed no identifying documents, and there was not a scratch on him. He should not have been there. Sceptics suggested he might have placed himself within the wreckage before anyone could reach the crash site, perhaps an attention seeker or a sick-minded individual looking for recompense from the airline. But those who arrived first said that was impossible. They had found him buried beneath shattered seats, burned sections of the fuselage, and body parts.

For two days he became something of a celebrity, all the more so because he refused to be interviewed about the crash by the media. He sought neither fame nor wealth as a result of the disaster. Cameras made do with footage of investigators going to and from the hospital where he was being kept, despite being uninjured. As time went on, these investigators' faces grew more stern.

When Sanches disappeared, new news came along to cover his mysterious trails.

Now here he was, in a small Welsh mining town. Emilio Sanches. As I tried to follow him along the street I had very little doubt it was the same man. I'd pored over the few distant images of him for hours on end, setting them side by side with pictures of Jemima and Mandy Taylor. Each shot had been taken in a similar circumstance—the survivor placid and calm in a group of bustling, hassled officials. With each of them, it looked as if they were somewhere else. Somewhere pleasant.

They had the look of people who knew more than they were letting on. It was their aloofness that I found so chilling.

He passed by a few shops without glancing into the display windows, seeming to know where he was going. He didn't look around to see whether he was being followed. Indeed, he paid little attention to his surroundings. Most people walking along a busy commercial street like this would notice shops or displays, read advertising posters and hoardings, catch sight of people who might interest them for one reason or another. Or if they didn't do that, it would be because their attention was swallowed by a mobile phone eighteen inches from their eyes. Sanches had no phone, nor any interest in his surroundings. Pedestrians parted around him. He might as well have been walking along a deserted, plain, anonymous street.

I jogged across the street, narrowly avoiding being mown down by a teenager on a mountain bike. He fired a curse my way, and I was worried that Sanches would hear and glance around. But just as sights seemed not to interest him, sounds also passed him by. A young girl screamed as she joshed with her friends. A couple of older boys sitting outside a bargain shop swore profusely, swigging from cans of cheap no-brand lager. A mother shouted at her child. A car horn blared, music thumped from the open window of a flat above a launderette, a couple of small dogs on leads barked and spat at a bigger hound staring them out from the passenger window of a passing car.

Emilio Sanches was oblivious to it all.

I hoped he was equally ignorant of me following him.

He turned a corner off the main street and I jogged to catch up, concerned that I would lose him. I needn't have worried. The street he was heading along was narrow, faced either side with terraced miners' houses, and it appeared deserted other than him. This increased the chance of him seeing me, but I could not risk losing him. As far as I was aware, no one had seen this man in over five years. After vanishing following the plane crash he had not been mentioned again in the media, and initial investigations on my part had brought up no evidence of him surfacing anywhere since. It was as if he existed only in that narrow time slot—involved in a disaster, rescued, fêted for a couple of days, and then gone.

I almost called out after him. Perhaps I was mistaken, and my journey here had brought memories of those other disasters to the surface. It would not have been the first time I'd imagined things. My ex-wife had frequently been forced to shake me awake from nightmares, and since our divorce I'd convinced myself that I had imagined her love for me. That was the only way I could cope with letting her go.

As I followed, less than fifty metres behind Sanches, I was aware of trying to quieten my footsteps. My heart seemed to be thumping too fast, too loud. My breathing was ragged, an old man's breath even though I was barely fifty. I'd often berated myself for my lack of fitness, a shame that had always manifested in an "I'll start tomorrow" outlook.

I slowed, then paused. There was no traffic noise.

There was no sound of any kind, other than my own frantic heartbeat and laboured breathing.

Ahead of me, Sanches pulled open a low timber gate and approached a front door. I heard the gate's hinge creak. I heard his gentle knock.

I glanced back towards the main street, less than a hundred metres behind me. I could see a couple of shops facing the street entrances, a bookmakers and a takeaway. Neither of them seemed to be open. There was no traffic passing by, no children rushing home from school. Nothing, no one.

"What the hell?" I whispered, and it sounded like a scream.

Tap . . . tap . . . tap . . .

I turned again at the sound, and Sanches was knocking on the door once more. He was also looking along the street at me.

For the first time since I'd set eyes on him, he was not smiling. Even from this distance I could tell that his eyes were black. Not just dark, or shaded, but the deep, impenetrable nothingness of infinity.

From this angle I could not see the door, but I knew that it had been opened, because the light around Sanches changed. It lessened, as if shadows flowed out from the house to meet him in defiance of the blazing sun.

Then he entered, the door snicked shut behind him, and I turned and ran, desperate to find noise and people and certain that I was lost forever.

That evening, after enjoying the company of people once more in the local pub and convincing myself I had simply witnessed a quiet, secluded street, I managed to speak to a couple of the other survivors from the mining disaster. There was a group of them in a pub helping to organise a memorial for those who had been lost. It was a subdued atmosphere, but not as sad as I might have expected. With the pain of losing friends came the initial delight in being rescued.

Guilt and depression would come later. I knew that, because I'd seen so many places like this before, and so many people. The thing about being a reporter was that most news was bad news. That was the nature of things.

The survivors did not seem keen to talk, and with both of them, the mention of Terry Welford inspired a strange response.

"Him? Strange guy."

"Was he always that way?"

"Always?" The woman frowned and stared into the distance.

"Did you know him before?"

"Yeah, sure. I knew him from . . . . We went to church together, he used to sit . . . "

The second survivor was far less vague.

"Don't you fucking mention him to me again. He wasn't down there. He shouldn't be up here."

"What do you mean, he wasn't down there?"

"Fuck off. Just fuck off. Go and pick over someone else's corpses. We've got dead people here, they're the one that matter."

"But how did Welford—"

"Fuck *off*!"

The shout quietened the pub, and in that loaded atmosphere I was the stranger who drew the stares. As I left, I did not feel threatened. I quite liked the fact that they could all see me. I felt like one of them, even though I had no idea how a community like this really worked. They were hard people in a way, but close and solid. Dependable. I came from the big city where you could live next door to someone for ten years without sharing a single word with them.

I wandered the streets for a while, then just as I was heading back to my bed and breakfast I bumped into Max. He was on his own and the worse for wear, pissing in the doorway of an abandoned shop. I felt bad for taking advantage, but I stopped to engage with him.

Three minutes later, Max was stumbling away and I had the address of where Terry Welford was staying.

I recognised the street immediately. Pausing at the end, still on the town's main shopping street, I tried to swallow down the unreasonable fear ebbing around me. There were lights on in the little houses, casting a weak glow across the road that barely added to the pale illumination from the two working streetlamps. But a heavy darkness still seemed to sit down there, drawing me in with a terrible gravity. I resisted. I leaned against the wall of a corner shop and felt the day's heat radiating out from the stonework, a memory of fine weather and sunlight.

Closing my eyes, my mouth ran dry.

I hadn't touched a drop of booze since Jane left me ten years before. I wasn't sure why. Part of me had wanted to live the cliché, a troubled investigative journalist falling into a pit of alcoholic despair when his wife left him, using drink as a crutch to hobble from one story to the next, taking shadowy meetings in London boozers where exclusives were bought for a wad of cash and a few shots of harsh whiskey. But when Jane went, it had spurred me to clean up my act. It had been the kick in the head I'd needed. For a while I'd believed that she would see what I was doing and come around, return to me, and I craved that to happen because I loved her truly, madly, deeply. I still believed that she loved me too. Trouble was, she loved the new man more.

We remained in touch. I stayed off the drink, enjoying the new sober me even if it didn't necessarily lead to a newfound fitness and zest for life. Perhaps I was the new cliché, noughties man made good. I'd even tried writing a piece about the whole experience. But I was so used to dissecting other people's lives that my own seemed immune to my scalpel-sharp writing.

Right then, in the heart of that town subsumed beneath sadness at its loss and joy at the survivors' rescue, I'd have given anything for a drink.

"This is what I came here for," I said. My voice was not as loud as it had seemed earlier that day, when I had followed Emilio Sanches down this road. In fact the place seemed much more alive than it had then. TVs flickered behind drawn curtains, and I could hear a dirge of voices, music and jingles through windows left open on this warm evening. I shouldn't have been afraid. If anything, I should have been excited, because I sensed I was close to the heart of a story no one else had perceived. If I researched and wrote this right, it might make my name. I remembered my constant joke to Jane: For thirty years I've been trying to be an overnight success.

I started down the street, slowly, expecting at any moment the background buzz of reality to slip away. A car passed along the main road behind me, souped up and blasting bad music. I was glad for it. I even hummed along for a while, trying to find sense in bass and drum.

As I approached the door to the small house, I had no idea what I intended to do. I'd made no plans, and the thought of knocking made me shiver. Then I noticed the alley that ran between this house and the next, a narrow corridor with the building continuing overhead. It must have offered access to the rear yards or gardens, the space pitch black at this time of night. I pulled out my phone and flicked on the torch.

Something skittered out of view, making me jump. A cat. Maybe a big rat. But it was gone now, and as I moved into the alley the phone torch lit all the way through to the end.

It only took me fifteen seconds to creep through the alley to the narrow space beyond. Wooden fences and gates stood to my left and right, six feet tall to offer some scant privacy to the small back gardens.

As I reached for the gate on my left, the silence struck home.

I gasped and froze, tilting my head in an effort to hear something. Anything. No traffic noise, no chatter of TVs from neighbouring houses, no voices. No creatures slunk in the darkness. In the distance to my right I could see the hills rising steeply towards the old closed mines, now a site given over to commerce and tourism. There were no lights up there.

The sky was dark and clear, stars flickering in the summer evening heat. I tried to make out any blinking plane trails but there were none. Perhaps this place was not on any flight path.

I knew I should run. I'd known for a while that something was very wrong here. Perhaps it was from that first moment when they'd pulled me from the train wreck and I'd seen Jemima, unmarked, emerging from the same ruin where so many had died with a smile on her face.

But I had come too far to turn back. I'd always sought mysteries, and even when writing about mundane things I'd often imagined uncovering something amazing.

I touched the gate and pushed. It remained closed. There was a small latch, and before taking hold I switched off my phone torch. The latch moved soundlessly and the gate drifted open, allowing me access to the small rear yard.

There was enough starlight to make out a few details. It was a sparse space with nothing to indicate it was used by whoever owned the house. No patio furniture, no plants, no washing line or bins or recycling bags. It was bare but for a couple of rusted bikes and the remains of an old greenhouse, glass long gone and timber frame warped and rotting.

There was a light on in the house, silvery and flickering. I guessed it came from a TV. I could still hear nothing, and each footstep across that yard sounded like a grinding, scraping impact. I held my breath but that only made my heart beat louder. My clothing seemed to rub loudly as I moved.

Close to the back door I paused and glanced at the window to the right. A curtain was drawn, but there was a narrow gap between curtain and wall through which the pale light flitted. I leaned close to the gap to see if I could peer inside.

The door opened. I gasped and stumbled back, tripping over my own ankle and going sprawling, hands held out to break my fall. I cried out as I fell, and the shape in the doorway seemed to repeat the sound.

Terry Welford looked down at me. He wore the same sardonic smile. He scared me more than ever before.

He held out his hand. "Come on," he said.

I stood shakily, knowing I should turn and flee, but knowing also that I couldn't even if I wanted to.

They were all there.

Emilio Sanches leaned against the wall opposite the living room door. He seemed to be examining his nails, but his eyes were on me. Mandy Taylor was sprawled on a sofa. Jemima sat in an armchair nursing a big coffee mug in her lap. She nodded a greeting.

"Who are you?" I asked.

"You know our names," Welford said.

"No. I really don't think I do."

"You're just in time for the decision," Jemima said. "You should feel honoured."

Under the collective gaze of all four people, I felt only terror. My legs were weak, stomach turning. *They all know more than me*, I thought, and it's difficult to describe how dreadful that understanding was. It was as if I was a child again thrown into a room full of adults, people who would *always* know more than me, no matter how much I learned. I was nothing to them. An ant to an elephant.

"Shall I?" Jemima asked.

There was a pause and I felt something pass between them all. Sanches glanced around, hand still close to his face. Mandy Taylor sat up a little, tucking her legs in. She was staring at me. Not smiling.

"I'll leave," I said. "I'll go now and I won't come back."

"It's a little too late for that," Jemima said. "And I know you. I got to know you during those hours in the wreck, when you were choking on that dead woman's blood and pissing yourself. I know that this is what you always wanted."

"No," I said. "I just want to leave. Whoever you are—"

"Let's finish up here," Mandy Taylor said. She sounded impatient.

"Here we are, then," Jemima said. She aimed a remote control at the TV and it flickered into life.

I wasn't really surprised at what I saw. Coverage of the train wreck from a bird's eye view, ambulances and fire engines and police cars scattered around, bodies covered beside the line awaiting collection. *I'm in there somewhere*, I thought, and it was a strange concept, as if I'd died and was looking down on myself.

Next, the burning building in Chicago. Windows burst outward under the pressure. Flames billowed, jets of water cast ineffectual spray across lower levels. Someone jumped, hair on fire.

"Oh, good show," Welford said. I didn't dare look at him.

The plane crash, the passenger jet now a blackened scar across a wooded, hilly landscape. Some trees were still smouldering. Clothes were hanging from branches, a smashed suitcase speared on a protruding limb.

"Not very creative," Jemima said.

"I worked with what I had," Sanches said.

"You've got a lot to learn," Welford said. "Look."

I recognised the faces. I'd seen them so recently, some in real life. Blackened with coal dust, they grinned out at the camera as they were pulled up out of the darkness. A final shot lingered on the rescue camp after the ambulances had left, focussing on people still milling there, hugging, crying, knowing that their own loved ones were down in the darkness forever.

"It's all about the passion," Jemima said. "The pain. The endless hours."

"Over a hundred died in the crash," Sanches said.

"Yes, but instantly," Mandy Taylor said. She waved at the TV. "I refer you once again to the falling burning man."

"You're all monsters," I said, backing away towards the door. Welford was behind me. His hand pressed against my back and he was cold.

"We're artists," he said.

"Creators," Jemima said, glugging at her coffee.

I shrugged off Welford's hand and backed against a dresser against the wall. Plates shook.

"I don't understand," I said.

Jemima stood and stretched. "So do we have a winner?"

"I think you know," Sanches said, actually sounding sulky.

"Yay!" Jemima dropped the mug and threw her arms up. Coffee splashed across the floor. Her smile was wide and honest, delight obvious.

"I don't understand," I said again, because nothing I saw here and nothing I had come to know made any sense.

"You never will," Welford said. "You can go. Maybe you'll want to write about us. But if you don't want to become a disaster waiting to happen, it might be best to forget."

"I can't," I said.

"You can," Jemima said. She came towards me, her eyes suddenly gone from pale blue to a deep, endless black. They all came, infinity-eyed, moving slowly and cutting out the light, their shadows a weight that was heavier than any train wreck, their smiles sicker than spilled blood.

They found me in the garden of one of the town's pubs. I was cold, damp from the morning dew, but the two women could tell I hadn't been drinking. They offered to take me to hospital but I refused, told them I was fine. I just needed a shower and some food and then I'd be heading back to London.

After they'd gone, I didn't even stay that long.

But I hesitated with every step. What if my train ploughed into the back of another? What if I hired a car and it rolled on the motorway and crashed into a petrol station? I could walk, but a bus driver might see me, swerve, drive into a bridge parapet at forty miles an hour. Once back in London my Tube might catch fire, a taxi could puncture and mow down a dozen pedestrians, a gas explosion might rip the heart from a tower block.

Standing on the pavement shivering and terrified, feeling the ghost-touch of those who should be dead on my neck and seeing their cold, knowing smiles, I imagined every terrible way there was to die.

SKIN AND BONE

After sixty-two days in the cold, the desert, the unexplored landscape where words hardened into solid shapes and every breath might have frozen his soul, Kurt's wedding ring fell off. He only removed his glove for a moment, needing the more dextrous use of his bare fingers to unhook frozen gear from the sled. And for a few seconds he didn't even notice that the ring had slipped away. It was like that sometimes down here, as if the cold could slow brain functions in the same way that it thickened oil and paraffin, made every movement three times harder than it was the day before. He saw it drop from his finger and sink into the snow, but it was several heartbeats before he said, "Shit."

He'd thought that metal contracted in the cold. Enough, at least, to keep it on his finger. But he supposed his loss of weight from starvation and excessive effort had finally superseded the ratio of gold shrinkage.

"Shit. *Shit*!" He had the good sense to put his glove back on before digging into the snow.

"What the hell?" Marshall asked. They were the best of friends, closer than brothers, but they had experienced strange moments on this expedition when they hated each other.

"My wedding ring," Kurt said. "Bindy will kill me."

"I doubt she'll even care," Marshall said, and he continued the laborious effort to set up camp. The sky was clear right now, a startling blue streaked with fingertrails of cloud high up. But a bad storm was coming, and they had mere hours to prepare.

"Can't you help me?" Kurt asked.

"Why don't you just—!" Marshall shouted, loud, breath glistening in front of his face and then breathing to the ground as a million tiny diamonds. He sighed. "Sorry. Yeah. Sorry."

The cold played strange tricks on the men. On day seventeen, Kurt had seen a line of camels on the snowscape to the east, walking slowly up the rocky ridge from the ice fields. He'd insisted that they were there, and even after Marshall told him he was hallucinating— and Kurt acknowledged that—the camels were still visible, slow and lazy. On day thirty, Marshall swore that his dick had fallen off. He'd tried stripping his layers to find it, preserve it in ice so that the surgeons could reattach it after the expedition. Even exposed, his sad shrivelled member turning blue in its nest of frost-speckled hair, he'd made Kurt grab it to make sure it was still attached. On day forty-seven, a day before they reached the South Pole, Kurt and his sled had slipped into a shallow crevasse, and it had taken Marshall four hours to haul him out. By then Kurt was trying to scream, but the cold had swollen his throat and frozen his pain inside.

The cold ate into a person. The physical effects were obvious, but the psychological impact was more insidious. They had hardly shared a harsh word in the thirty years they'd known each other before this adventure, but on day fifty-three Kurt had threatened to fucking gut Marshall if he didn't finish every last drop of his soup.

Such things were laughed about afterwards. They were doing this through choice, and they knew that odd things would happen. That made it almost bearable.

"Here it is," Marshall said. "Stupid sod. Don't lose it again."

"Oh, mate," Kurt said taking the small gold ring from his friend. "Marshall, thanks."

"Stupid sod." Marshall went back to unpacking the tent and equipment from the sled. "Now let's get a shift on. I don't want to freeze to death today."

"How about tomorrow?"

"Nah, not then either."

Kurt smiled as he slipped the ring back on. "How about three days' time."

"Help me with this."

"How about a week next Thursday?"

"Fucking prick!"

They finished erecting the small tent, and while Marshall zipped himself inside to light the stove and start melting snow for cooking and drinking, Kurt set about tying down the camp. He hammered stakes into the ice and tied the two sleds to them. Then he banged in more stakes and made sure the tent was secure.

Hands pressed into the small of his back he stretched, leaning back and looking around. As always, it still felt like he was pulling that damn sled across the ice. It might be months before he *didn't* feel like he was pulling all that weight. But it was worth it.

The desolate Antarctic landscape was as beautiful as it was deadly, and he never felt more alive than when he was on some mad expedition or other with Marshall. And this was the maddest of all. It was one of the harshest places on Earth, and survival took every ounce of intelligence and strength, endurance and ruggedness. It was that more than anything that had brought them here. The rest of the world was an endless distance away, so remote that it felt like a dream. Here and now was all that mattered.

Marshall had probably been right about Bindy not caring if Kurt lost his wedding ring. They'd been drifting apart for years, and she'd effectively told him that "another fucking adventure" would cost him his wife. She wanted kids and security, a three-bed house and a Labrador. He wanted danger and challenges, the satisfaction of taking on the elements, the thrill of extremes. Jack London had written "the function of man is to live, not to exist". Kurt was living as well as he could.

He tried to care about Bindy but could not make it happen. It was too cold, the incoming storm too terrible, to care about anything other than surviving the next few days.

"Toilet break!" he called, and Marshall muttered something from inside the tent. Kurt knew that they could well be confined in there with each other for days once the storm hit. He'd relish this one last opportunity to take a dump in private.

He tramped past the sleds, making a final inspection to ensure their equipment was tied down securely, then made for a rocky outcropping to the east. He knew from experience that it was further away than it looked, and after a few minutes tramping across the ice he reached it. Breathing hard, he turned around to make sure the camp was still in sight. The sky was still mostly clear, the sun was dancing with the horizon, and the storm was several hours away.

Behind the sculpture of snow- and ice-speckled rock he found a tent.

Kurt gasped, breath stuck in his throat, his body refusing to react. Then he let out his held breath and took a step back.

"Bloody hell," he muttered. "Hey, Marshall." But Marshall was still inside their own tent across the snowfield. Maybe if Kurt shouted he'd hear, but . . .

But he didn't want to call out to his friend. Not yet. He wanted to see what he'd found.

The tent was old. Very old. Almost shapeless, he could only tell what it was from the struts protruding like the smashed ribcage of a dead giant. The old canvas was its skin, and the humped shapes its distorted insides.

Kurt's heart was hammering. He'd heard about occasional finds like this—explorers out on the ice discovering remnants of old camps, forgotten expeditions, sometimes even the sad remains of dead adventurers. But through all their adventures in Alaska, the Sahara, South America and Nepal, he'd never seen anything like this himself.

He moved closer. A gust of wind blew a haze of snow across the scene, and he winced as it grated the bare skin of his face. He should have worn his hooded coat and heavy face scarf, covered up. He was becoming clumsy, so many weeks into their journey that routines that could save their lives were too easy to let slip. It was the Antarctic summer, the cold a mere thirty degrees below. But frostbite could still strike, especially with the rising breeze adding to the chill factor.

He didn't have long.

The tent material looked many decades old. It was holed in places, and when he grabbed at it a chunk came off in his hand. He knelt and lowered his face close to the snow surface, trying to see beneath the fallen tent. Trying to see what might be inside.

"I should get Marshall," he muttered, words made ice and stolen by another gust of wind. They sprinkled on the rocks beyond the tent.

Maybe it had blown here from elsewhere. Perhaps it had been buried for many decades, and some of the recent, deeper thaws had brought it back to the surface. Or it could have been nestled here all along, covered with snow one year, exposed the next, a yearly cycle of burial and exposure.

He stood and turned away, emerging into the open again and ready to go and get Marshall. Then, looking back out across the ice fields towards camp, he blinked several times, trying to make sense of what he'd seen.

It was like trying to retrieve an old memory, not his most recent.

Something there, he thought, and he clambered back behind the rocks. *Something not part of the tent*. And there it was. He crouched down and tugged at a support spur. It snapped off and pulled a spread of canvas with it, and beneath there lay a leg. He worked quickly to uncover the body. The clothing confused him, so thin and slight for the harshness of even the best conditions this place might present. Then he realised that it was not clothing at all. The corpse was naked. It was leathery, weathered skin.

He worked faster, uncovering the whole form until he reached the corpse's head.

And he cried out in revulsion and shock, stepping back and catching his heel on something buried in the ice—a timber support, a rock, a bone—and sprawling onto his back, never once taking his eyes from that face.

The plainest face he had ever seen. A blank. He had seen dead people before, but never like this, never so *washed away*. It was like a person who was not quite finished. The face held the features of a normal human, but even in death there was something so vague, so incomplete, that Kurt could not tear his eyes away. He wanted to. He needed to. But like a child fascinated with a crushed rabbit by the side of a road, he could only stare.

The eyes were sunken pits. The nose was a bump, unremarkable, shapeless. There was hair but it had been styled by ice and time into a shapeless wig. Flat lips were drawn apart over yellowed teeth, the mouth a slit as if sliced by a knife.

The figure stared just over his shoulder.

Kurt stood again, slowly. His shock receded and his heartbeat lessened. It was only as he backed slowly away that he realised there was another shape next to the first, partially hidden beneath the rest of the old tent, yet just visible. Its face, flat and blank.

He turned and tried to run, but his clothing was too heavy and thick, his muscles too weakened by eight weeks on the ice. He sprawled into the snow. It stuck to his chilled skin, reaching cold fingers into his mouth and eyes. He stood again and ran on, feeling a warmth around his crotch. He'd pissed himself.

By the time he reached camp he was exhausted. Marshall was still inside the tent, and when Kurt opened the flaps and tumbled inside he received a torrent of curses.

He'd let out all the heat.

"Dickhead," Marshall said. "Get them off. Get them dry. We might have another few hours of peace before the storm hits."

"What does the forecast say?" Kurt asked. He still hadn't told Marshall about the old tent.

Marshall checked out the small laptop sitting on a warming plate to encourage the battery back to life. "Four days of freezing our bollocks off," he said. He said something else, too. A quip, a joke. But Kurt didn't hear.

He wanted to tell Marshall, but he could not. The longer he left it, the weirder it would sound. *Oh and by the way, I found two dead bodies that don't even look like real people.*

"Hey!" Marshall nudged him softly.

"Yeah."

"Get those clothes off, Kurt. You need to get warm."

"I'm fine, I'm okay."

"Like hell. You're no use to me dead. All skin and bone."

While Kurt undressed and huddled deep into his sleeping bag, the words circled in his mind, and he realised why they sounded so strange.

The bodies he'd found were more than skin and bone. If anything they'd resembled shop mannequins.

"I need to get back out there!" he said, trying to unzip the sleeping bag. "I need to make sure."

Marshall moved closer to him, one arm around his shoulder and the other offering a mug of hot tea. "Drink. All of it."

The fight went out of Kurt just like that, and he realised that he'd probably been seeing things. He hadn't taken his snow goggles with him, and had left himself open to the cold. It was harsher than he thought. It did stuff to the mind.

"Marsh, I'm cold."

"Yeah. One guy I heard about on his last trip down here, he got so cold that his brain fluid froze. When they thawed him out he'd been reset as a six-year-old. All he wanted to do was get home and watch Power Rangers."

"You're so full of shit."

"You know it."

They drank hot tea together. Marshall rehydrated some spiced lentil and steak soup, and they hugged the warm mugs, spooning food into their eager mouths. They made small talk until the storm hit several hours later.

Then they hunkered down, listening to the wind, imagining the inches of snow being piled up and blown around them with every hour that passed.

They'll be smothered, Kurt thought, and the idea pleased him. *When we next get out of the tent they'll be gone, and it'll be like they never were.*

In places like this, the dead should stay buried.

Huddled into their sleeping bags, they listened to the storm. They didn't talk very much. They sat either side of the stove, reaching out occasionally to adjust the gas up or down. Wet clothes hung around them. The small tent stank of sweat and piss from the drying gear, but they were more than used to that. It was the odour of exploration, and they had been in a place like this together many times before.

Boredom rarely touched Kurt. He thought of his childhood dreams and how far he had come. And he thought of Bindy, waiting for him back home if he was lucky, gone if he was not. That was another strange thing about existing in such an extreme environment—right now, back home didn't seem to matter. London was as far away as the moon, and only the here and now was important.

A couple of hours into the storm, Marshall started brewing more tea. Kurt watched the blue flames kissing the pot, eyes drooping, blinking slower and slower, and then the pot and flames were gone.

The dead bodies appeared in their place. The storm was raging, scouring the landscape with ice fingers and teeth of frost, but around Kurt there was a circle of calm and peace. He approached the old, rotting tent and the things it might once have protected. They were moving. He could see that from far away, and though he had no wish to go closer his feet took him, tramping through fresh snow, ignoring the high winds and piercing cold that should be killing his exposed extremities. *No no no*, he thought as he walked closer, because the shape he'd uncovered seemed to be sitting up, turning its blank expression and empty eyes his way, leaning to the side ready to stand, shifting and quivering as if seen through a heat-haze, not a cold so intense that the marrow in his bones was freezing.

No no no, he said again, and when he took in a breath to scream he tasted sweet steam.

"Here," Marshall said. "Kurt? You awake?"

Kurt's eyes snapped open. He looked around the cramped tent and nodded, leaning to his left ready to sit up. "Yeah, fine. Nodded off." *And saw* them, he thought. *And I saw them moving out there in the storm!*

"What's up mate?"

"Up?"

"You're acting weird."

Kurt took a grateful sip of the tea. It burnt his split lips but he relished the pain.

"Well . . . " He sipped some more and sighed, making a decision. "I saw something out in the snow, over by the rock outcropping to the east. Couple of bodies."

"Yeah?" Marshall was interested, not shocked. They both knew how many people had died in this vast place, and how many of those had never been seen again. Marshall had climbed Everest several years ago, and often told Kurt about the bodies he'd seen up there. He said they weren't spooky or sad, just lonely. They'd died doing what they loved.

"But they were weird," Kurt said. "They didn't look . . . normal. Human. It was like they were mannequins, or something. You know, unfinished."

"Could've been really old," Marshall said. "Cold can do weird things to a body. Cold, dry air dries the corpses out, leeches all the fluids from them."

"But their faces," Kurt said, blinking and seeing that face staring at him. "Their eyes."

"Should've told me!" Marshall said. The revelation seemed to have cheered him up. "When the storm's passed we'll go and check them out together."

No way, Kurt thought, but he didn't say that. He didn't want to sound scared.

They finished their tea. The storm roared on. Neither of them spoke again for some time.

Kurt thought of Bindy, turning his loose wedding ring and trying to care.

The tent grew darker as snow piled up outside. Kurt kept the stove burning, and the air remained musty and heavy. He didn't mind. He was so used to the burning touch of cold on his skin that it was good to feel something else. And he knew it would be over soon. The storm would pass, they would dig themselves out, and their journey home would continue.

They'd leave those things behind.

Marshall mumbled in his sleep. He shifted, kicked his feet in the tight sleeping bag, then shouted. Kurt sat up and stared, not used to his friend making such a noise. He was always such a deep sleeper, and Kurt had always been jealous of just how quickly he managed to fall asleep. Clear conscience, Marshall would say. Now he twitched and moved, and when he kicked again he came dangerously close to knocking over the stove burning between them. It had a cover, and if tipped over there was an auto shut-off. But it was still a risk.

"Marsh?" His voice sounded thick and heavy, as if the warmer air held it longer. It was strange not seeing his breath condense. Moisture dripped from his beard. "Marsh?"

Marshall rolled onto his back again, kicking his feet in the sleeping bag. Its hood had twisted and fallen to half-obscure his face, and in the poor light Kurt couldn't make out whether his eyes were open or closed.

"Marshall!" He spoke louder, fighting against a gust of wind that roared around their tent.

Marshall stiffened, grew still, then started breathing easier. Bad dreams.

Kurt settled again, and passed the time by assessing his body, alternately tensing and then relaxing muscles from his toes up to see where problems might lie. The first two toes on his right foot had gone almost two weeks ago—he knew they were darkened, stiff, and it was likely that he'd lose them. But the rest of his toes seemed fine. It was surprising that he hadn't suffered more.

They'd agreed that they would only call for rescue if one or both of their lives were in danger. Frostbite, weight loss, snow blindness, borderline starvation, these were acceptable risks for the adventure they had embarked upon. They'd spent two days at the Pole, recovering at the research station there, but they'd found themselves keen to continue, working their way back towards the coast where they'd be able to pronounce their expedition a success. They'd both lost a huge amount of weight, and when Kurt looked in a mirror inside one of the huts he'd let out a startled cry. He'd not recognised himself.

Marshall had laughed at that. "Few people who come here and do the sort of thing we're doing go home the same person." he'd said. "This place changes people. Got to accept that."

There was not far to go, now. But as Kurt sat wrapped in his sleeping bag, feeling how weakened he had become in his time on the ice, he was further from home than ever before. It wasn't just distance and time, but remoteness. They were deeper in the wilderness than they had ever been, and closer to the pure unknown.

Marshall muttered again. Incomprehensible words mostly, but then one phrase that stood out harsh and stark. "My eyes are mine!"

Kurt's blood ran cold. He leaned across and shook his friend, rolling him back and forth in his sleeping bag, but Marshall would not wake. He stiffened beneath Kurt's hand, went limp, stiffened again, and all the time he was whining and mumbling wretchedly.

Kurt sat back, watching his friend dream and fighting a sudden, overwhelming desire to close his own eyes. He blinked slowly. It was dark in there.

Wind groaned around the tent, the storm given voice. He held his breath, but doing so meant he heard Marshall's haunted mumblings clearer.

Breathing deeply, tiredness swept over him again.

What's wrong with me? Why can't I stay awake?

But there was plenty wrong with him, and he knew it. Exhaustion, both physical and mental. Weakness caused by calorie deficiency. Aching bones, pulled muscles, torn ligaments, shoulders and back rubbed raw by the sled straps. The excesses he had been subjecting his body to for almost ten weeks, the intense cold, the endless hours of pulling and shoving, hacking routes through ice ridges to advance three miles in a day, climbing and slipping, falling and standing again because to stay down was to die. *Everything* was wrong with him, but he could not sleep.

He did not wish to find the dreams his friend was having right now.

"I should never have told you about them," he muttered. He unzipped the sleeping bag and started pulling on his wet clothes. They were slightly warmed by the air inside the tent, at least. But he knew that would not last.

He'd freeze in minutes outside, but he couldn't stay in here.

The landscape was transformed. The horizon had been dragged into dozens of feet instead of miles. The wide sky was hiding, the rolls in the land were swallowed by the snow, and all tracks and prints he and Marshall had laid down had been consumed.

He hugged his coat tight, pulled the heavy scarf over his mouth and nose, made sure his snow goggles were well fitted, and started out to the east. He tied the end of a cord to one of the tent uprights and played it out behind him as he went. It was his way back.

Kurt leaned into the wind, head down as he pushed onward. He seemed to get there quicker than before. Perhaps he'd drifted away while walking, mind wandering somewhere warmer and safer, but he could not remember where.

At first he thought they'd gone. *It can't have snowed that much!* he thought, struggling to fight down the excitement. Gone and buried again, they would be out of sight, out of mind. He could return to the tent and wake Marshall. He'd tell him that everything was all right. Then they'd wait for the storm to pass and make the final drive for the coast.

But then he saw a shape ahead between swirls of snow, tucked behind another ridge of rock, and he knew that he was in the wrong place.

Wind had raised a flap of the tent, uncovering the two bodies underneath. The storm whined between rocks, wind so harsh that it was stripping old snow and ice from the corpses rather than allowing new snow to settle. Against every instinct he went close, because he had to see.

One of the bodies had been turned onto its side, the arm beneath it propping it up, head dipped. Could the wind have done that? Perhaps fresh exposure to the elements had contracted dried tendons, or the frozen ground beneath the body had shrugged, lifted? The other corpse still lay on its back but its face had changed. It was fuller, not so death-like. Its lips were thicker, nose more sculpted.

Its eyes were open.

They stared unblinking as flakes kissed them and were lifted away by the wind.

Kurt needed to run but he stumbled forward instead, dropping to his knees and lifting off his goggles so that he could see for sure. The blankness had gone from these bodies. They looked like death-sculptures close to completion, rather than rough, lifeless forms.

He wanted to destroy them. If he'd brought a knife or an ice axe he'd have set about them, smashing and hacking them into pieces that were nowhere near human, and held no resemblance to . . .

But could he really move that close?

"It's all in my head," Kurt said, and the storm rose as if to swallow his words. A corner of the old tent flapped, and he squinted, looking closer, wondering how canvas could be networked with shapes that looked like old, dried veins.

Its poles might have been bone.

He backed away, then turned and ran for the camp, pulling hand over hand on the cord as if to haul himself and the tent together. In a blinding surge of snow he tripped and was enveloped, cool dark digits fingering into gaps in his clothing, his ears, leaking through poorly fitting snow goggles. He struggled to stand with one hand, the other still clasped tight around the cord. If he let go of that he would be lost, and then he'd die out here on his own. Perhaps Marshall would find him when the storm settled. Or maybe he'd be discovered in a hundred years by exhausted, terrified explorers.

He stood and moved on, his focus on the cord that was his lifeline.

Inside the tent Kurt hurriedly zipped up, throwing off his coat and crawling into his cold sleeping bag. He turned up the stove and broke a couple of chemical warmers. Their effect was vastly lessened through overuse, but they still took the chill from his hands.

"Not sure," he said, shivering. "Not sure what that was. Not certain . . . certain what I . . . I saw. Marsh? I dunno. But I think those bodies are moving." He looked sideways at the man lying motionless in his sleeping bag. "Marsh?"

Marsh whined. It began so low and quiet that at first Kurt thought it was the wind. But the noise rose, growing louder, harsher. As it became a scream Kurt screamed himself, trying to drown that terrible sound in his own fearful cry. But his own voice faded while Marshall's went on and on, and he reached out to shake his friend awake.

He would not wake. His eyes were wide, his mouth open, and when Kurt unzipped his bag he saw his friend's hands clawed in front of him as if grasping something unseen.

Marshall took in a long, ragged breath and started screaming again. But the scream did not touch his face. There was no frown and no grimace, little of Marshall there at all. His wide eyes reflected nothing.

Kurt kicked himself away from his friend, hand striking the stove and knocking it on its side. He felt an ice-cold touch across his palm, and when he looked he saw the burn, already blistering and bubbling yet feeling like nothing. He waited for the pain to sink in but it was quiet, subsumed perhaps beneath Marshall's endless scream.

"Shut the fuck up!" Kurt shouted. He pulled his fist back ready to strike, but held back at the last moment. Something was so terribly wrong. If he had to hit someone or something it was not Marshall.

He felt so tired. Despite the noise his own eyes drooped, he felt reality drifting even further away than it already was, and he reached up and gripped his cheeks between fingers, pinching himself awake.

It did not feel like resurfacing.

His eyes drooped again and he grasped the tumbled stove, waiting for long seconds before the searing pain finally scorched in. He opened his mouth, but Marshall screamed for him. The pain did not last for long. It was as if someone else had been subjected to the burn.

Out in the snow . . . he thought, and the idea of going out there and falling asleep was so enticing that he found himself unzipping the tent again, crawling outside, and slumping down in the fresh snow. Wind howled, but it was the usual emotionless scream that this continent was more comfortable with.

Marshall's screaming seemed even louder out here, and even more shocking because he was out of sight. He competed with the wind and won.

It's them, Kurt thought. *Something about them, their stillness, their lifelessness, and he didn't even see them.*

He scrambled over to the sleds and unhooked one of the covers, throwing it back to reveal the tool rack. He snatched up a long-handled ice axe and turned into the storm once again. The cord was still attached, and he followed it towards where he had dropped it so recently.

Marshall doesn't have nightmares. He's strong. He just sleeps and walks. The nightmares are from somewhere else.

Just before he reached where the bodies should have been, he realised that Marshall's screaming had stopped.

Behind the sheltering rock, just visible as grey silhouettes through the dancing, wild snow, he saw the two bodies standing with arms by their sides.

It was his lifeline. His umbilical back to the tent, back to reality, the thin cord bubbled with icy droplets stiff in his hands, waving in the wind and snapping back and forth. If he let go and lost it he'd stumble into the nothingness. Lose himself and die. It didn't seem to matter, but each time he grabbed, the burns on his hands sang a short sweet song of agony. He grabbed hold of this, too, because it was real.

Maybe they were following him. Or perhaps they were lost as well.

Marshall remained silent, and crawling back through the tent entrance and inside, Kurt saw why. His friend was not there anymore.

In his place was something that looked little like his friend. The similarity was vague at best, a rough attempt at impersonation. The body in Marshall's sleeping bag was devoid of expression and anything that might make it human, yet it wore his clothes and hair, carried the old scar on his cheek and that scruffy, ginger beard. Other than that, he might have been carved from ice.

Kurt tried to shout, scream. His voice did not work. Maybe it was the cold, but he thought not. He was starting to feel more distant than ever before, not only from Bindy and home and everything beyond this place, but from himself. He was becoming a stranger.

But still he fled. There remained that part of him—a spark of hope amidst wretchedness—that grasped onto instinct and believed in survival. He burst from the tent and fell, scrambling to his feet, running in the direction he thought was away from them. He tripped again and went sprawling. The cold did not feel so cold anymore. The white was not so white. His senses seemed more remote, as if he were viewing his life through the wrong end of a telescope. He tried to call for his wife but no longer remembered her name.

He stood and ran. The storm swirled him around, sending him

staggering into ice ridges and falling into drifts. Wind roared in his ears, a voiceless scream.

In the distance, two shapes approached through the whirling snow. They seemed to pass through the storm as if they were apart from it, and though Kurt tried to turn and run, his legs folded and he fell to his knees. He tugged the ice axe from his belt and held it up, ready to swing it, throw it, wield it in anger and fear.

The figures drew closer. They were naked but did not seem to feel the cold. One was Marshall, but his eyes were expressionless, no recognition there.

But Kurt recognised himself.

The other figure stood before him, head slightly tilted as it regarded him with an emotionless gaze.

Kurt went to swing the axe but dropped it into the snow. He reached out with both hands to ward them off.

The figure that was him snatched off Kurt's glove, placed its thumb and forefinger around his wedding ring, and lifted it clear of his finger. There was no friction or resistance. It was as if he was no longer there at all.

The figure slipped on his ring, then the two of them turned their backs on Kurt and walked away into the storm, leaving him forever in the frozen white silence.

STRINGS

I wake in the early hours and hear scratching, and moaning, and the secretive whisper of something brushing along walls. When this happened before, Margot and Ray were still my friends and staying with me, and I believed their lovemaking to be the cause of the sounds. Trying to keep quiet for my sake, the height of passion took away their caution. The scrape of fingernails against a wall. The steady touch of bedding shifting somewhere beyond my room. Their groans, low and long as if such ecstasy could last forever.

This time, I know the noises aren't caused by them, because Margot and Ray left three days ago. I suspect I'll never see them again. They became worried about what we were attempting to do, though I think their fear is misplaced. I think they're cowards.

I lie awake and listen, trying to place the sounds and figure out their source. They seem to be originating from inside my head as well as without, as if dreams can have echoes. I suppose they can. All this has happened because of a dream I had so many years before, a fervent desire that inspired and invigorated the three of us to try things never before imagined. That's me: the dreamer. I was the driving force, the passion, though they were the ones with the knowledge. We all had to give something, and I was happy to be the guinea pig.

Another scratch. A deeper groan. I can't yet understand what the noises mean, but in that cool, motionless darkness I realise that the time will soon come when I do understand. They're clearer now than they were last time I heard them. Clearer, louder, and closer.

It's working, I think, and the one thing I cannot do is open my eyes. Even in the dark, I fear that I will see.

"Don't mind him," Margot said, "he's just being a prick." I saw the look she threw Ray when she said it, and the brief flicker of some complex expression on his face. Part of it was annoyance, part excitement. I knew some of what he was feeling. Margot and I had been engaged until three years before, and I understood more about her than he'd ever know.

That's what I liked to think, at least. In truth, I believed our work was tearing us apart even on the day I slipped the ring on her finger. Ray wasn't so invested. He was here, he was helping, but he wasn't touched by what we were trying to do. For him, this was all about money and fame, his future and not anyone else's.

"All I'm saying is, I think you need to be careful," he said. He took another long swig of red wine. He drank it from half-pint glasses, and he'd already put away a bottle during dinner. "Your vitals always look weird after a dose, and that effect is growing."

"Maybe the instruments are on the blink," I said. "I'm feeling fine."

"You sure?" Margot asked. She leaned forward in the armchair and touched my knee. Ray bristled at the contact, and I hoped I didn't display the satisfaction I felt at his discomfort.

"Yeah. Fine. Better than ever." I stood and paced the room. It was a big living room, far too large for just the three of us. Two sprawling

L-shaped sofas, three armchairs, a slew of floor cushions, a massive TV affixed to one wall, and a fireplace I could walk into and stand up straight. The place slept twenty people in eight bedrooms, but we'd needed somewhere this big for all our kit and instruments.

Besides, it was out of the way and hidden from prying eyes. Grand House had its own mile-long driveway and couldn't be seen from any neighbouring roads, yet the nearest town was an easy walk away.

"It can't go on like this," Ray said. "It's not fair to us. We agreed right from the beginning, if something's looking off, we pull back and reassess our methods."

"Nothing's looking off," I say.

"What the fuck do you know?" Ray snapped. He shook his head, sighed. I was used to him playing the "what do you know?" card. "Neil, I can't in all good conscience sit here and agree that nothing's wrong."

I leaned against the fireplace. I stared into the big mirror hanging above it, offering a wide vista of the room behind me. They were both staring back at me. Margot ran her finger around the top of her wine glass. I had a sudden, unbidden memory of making love with her, the noises she would make, and I looked away in case my eyes betrayed it.

Something whispered deep within the stones of the chimney stack. I froze, head to one side.

"Neil? Did you hear me?" Ray asked.

"Huh?"

"I said I think you should see a proper doctor. I'm not comfortable with this anymore. I never finished my training."

"You're an almost-doctor," I said. "This is an almost-experiment. So what are you afraid of? Losing me, and losing your payday?" I turned around, daring a reply from them both.

Ray sighed. Margot shrugged and said nothing. The walls whispered in agreement.

———————

I sat back in the recliner while Margot prepared the next shot of our strange elixir.

She was the genius of this team. She knew it, I knew it, and Ray sure as hell knew it, too. Her work in nanotech medicines should have propelled her into the higher echelons of twenty-first century scientific achievement. When she and I were together, before Ray came along and our plans grew, she'd talked about it often. I understood some of it, but not much. Perhaps that was why we grew apart.

"More magic juice," I said, wincing as the needle pricked my arm.

"It's not magic." She concentrated as she depressed the plunger, glancing up at the screen beside the chair and down again at the hypodermic. Ray sat in the next room monitoring my reactions to the injection, and there was a constantly open channel between us and him. I could hear him humming.

"When do you think it'll start working?"

Margot withdrew the needle and dabbed the bubble of blood. She bent my arm back and patted it, telling me I should keep it there. It wasn't as if I didn't know. She'd put a hundred needles in me over the past twenty days.

I hated it when she was like this, so immersed in her work that she hardly heard me talking. It was just about the only time she and I were alone now, even though Ray could see us on his screens and hear every word. She acted like I wasn't here.

"Margot," I said. She wheeled her chair back to a table and tapped at her laptop.

"Soon," she said. She didn't sound convinced. "Ten minutes and you can do the tests."

I lay back in the seat and tried to feel the new stew of nano-bots streaming through my blood. There was nothing, even though several times I'd convinced myself that I could feel them pulsing towards my brain, implanting themselves there, setting to work. Margot would smile indulgently, and Ray would tut and shake his head.

I wasn't stupid, but I wasn't them. I was only here because I'd once loved Margot, and started us along a path I could not quit.

Who wouldn't want to be a superhuman?

I listened and looked, and heard and saw nothing different.

And then Ray called me into another room, and he started running through the same test procedures we'd been using for weeks, and everything began to change.

In the morning I open the back door and stand once again on the threshold.

It's been three days since Ray and Margot left, and I have yet to go outside. The house is set in several acres of land on the shallow side of a valley. The landscape is beautiful and wild. I see the regular quilt-work of fields in the distance, but closer to the house there is woodland, expanses of heather and scrub, and a rocky slope leading up the valley's opposite side. There is no sound of humanity. Even occasional vehicles passing along the narrow country lane a mile away are mere whispers, their engine sounds swallowed by the stone wall and hedge bordering the road.

And yet I hear. I hear *more*. Between breaths, something else comes in. It's a distant whispering, scheming intelligences hidden in the sunlight, languages I cannot know riding the breeze across the countryside. On the day Margot and Ray left I tried to replicate what these strange noises were, and I saw Ray's face as he recorded my impersonations. He looked cold in a warm room. He looked chilled.

They are much louder when the back door is open.

I take one step outside. My foot crunches on the gravel path, and the whispers instantly fade away to nothing. Even the breeze drops, a held breath. I hear my own breathing, and it's not the comfort it should be.

I take another step and the whispering begins again, louder, closer. It's an agitated babble, an excited susurration. I back up immediately and slam the door closed, and through the heavy old wood I can hear those noises joining the breeze, shushing through the house's old eaves.

They sound disappointed.

I pace around the house, examining the detritus of our time here. I have been in limbo since they departed, trying to persuade myself that it's all part of the experiment, an intentional abandonment to help advance the progress we'd been trying to make. But I can't convince myself of that. I saw Margot's fear when she left, although she seemed averse to telling me. Ray couldn't even face me.

In one of the big house's downstairs bedrooms, the two single beds are pushed aside to make room for a table bearing all manner of recording equipment. At its centre is the simple digital dictaphone I used.

"You're hearing more," Margot said, and she was the most animated she'd been for several days.

"Well . . . "

"There's nothing here. Ray? Is there anything here?" Ray sat at a desk weighted down with audio equipment, spectrographs, and frequency modulators.

"There's always something here," Ray said. "You know that. The air's full of sound, we can only hear things in a narrow bandwidth. Above that, below, there's always more."

"Whole new worlds of sound!" Margot said, staring at me as if I was suddenly something new. "So describe it to us. Tell us what it is."

Whispers, I thought. I was troubled by what I was hearing.

"I'm not sure I can," I said.

"Mimic," Ray said. "Use a microphone and a recording device, listen, try to repeat the sounds you're hearing."

"Will that really work?" Margot asked.

"Surprisingly effective, sometimes."

Margot nodded and turned back to me. "We'll leave you alone. You listen, and record. We want to hear. I *need* to hear!"

I knew very well that if these experiments succeeded in opening my ranges of hearing and sight, Margot would be the next one to undertake the course of injections. I was pretty certain even then that Ray wanted nothing to do with it. When he was drunk he talked about fucking with nature, but the lure of crammed bank balances and fame was strong.

"I'm afraid," I whispered. Beyond the room, something responded to my whisper. It sounded amused.

"Afraid of what?" Margot asked.

I wasn't sure how I could tell her. It would have been like explaining fear of the colour red to a blind person.

"Here," she said, thrusting the dictaphone against my chest. "We'll wait in the kitchen."

Margot and Ray left me in that room, alone with the whispers. I listened for a while, head tilted, brain struggling to decipher sounds it was never built or meant to hear.

Then I turned on the machine.

Around midday I see the first of the shadows. I've been expecting it. In a way, the expectation has been worse than the reality. Margot would bemoan the fact that my vision seemed unchanged by the experiment.

Now, I wish she was here with me again.

I'm standing at the open back door in the cottage's kitchen. The garden is large and nicely landscaped, with a climbing frame for kids, a barbecue area, and several paved patios for seating. The sun blazes down. The valley is deserted, save for me and the whispers that conspire to draw me out.

I see the shape dancing beneath a tree.

I blink, frown, shield my eyes from the sun, and look again. It's like a smudge on my vision, a blot in my eye. The tree branches hang low, and although the air here is still, the branches move as if disturbed by a breeze. Birds take flight. Several dead leaves fall, or perhaps they're shed by a squirrel hidden away in the tree. It's too far away for me to make out clearly, but the dancing figure I saw has gone. Just branches. Shadows.

As I turn away the whispers come in again, louder and closer than ever before, and in their alien tongue I hear mockery at my disbelief.

I slam the door and run through the house, seeking the false solace of my room. On the way to the staircase I pass the small second kitchen where Margot kept her concoctions locked up in the fridge. I still haven't cleaned up the mess. She smashed every container, poured the fluid into the sink, splashed it up the walls. She followed it down with a gallon of bleach, and the stink still burns my nostrils.

Perhaps I'm lucky they didn't consider doing the same to me.

I reach my small bedroom and slam the door behind me, sitting on the edge of the bed and expecting the whispers to follow. They keep their distance. Even the silence is loaded now, and I imagine great things poised to shout so loud that their voices will crush me down.

I know I'll have to leave soon. If I want to retain my sanity, I need to make it to the nearest town and ask for help.

The thought of walking along country lanes and hearing them all around drives me almost to tears, and I curl up on the bed. Even though for now they are silent once more, I wish the voices would let me sleep.

"Hairy bastard."

"I can't help that. It's natural."

"Not for everyone. You're less evolved."

Margot rested her head on my chest. I could feel her heavy breath on my sweat-dampened chest, feel the dampness of her against my thigh. We'd made love twice, and I was already considering whether I could manage one more before we both fell asleep. She had that effect on me. It was love, but it was also a deep, passionate lust.

"Maybe you could evolve me a bigger cock."

"I wish." She propped herself up on her elbow and turned to look at me. "You have no idea, do you?"

"What do you mean?"

"How it works." I liked her when she was like this. Her cheeks and thighs ruddied from my stubble, long hair sweat-dampened against her forehead, pupils dilated, she was approximately fifteen times more intelligent than me, and I loved it. I knew a lot of men who'd shrivel beneath such intellect, metaphorically and literally, but I found it a massive turn-on. In truth I did understand a lot of what she said, just not to the depth and degrees that she did. Sometimes she lost me, and if that happened I'd go along for the sound of her voice, the denseness of her passion.

"I mean, we've essentially halted human evolution. There's no survival of the fittest anymore, not for humanity. Imagine if we had to hunt food in the dark, and those with better eyesight survived and procreated more? But we have supermarkets and food dumped on our doorsteps. What if bats carried a deadly plague, and we had to listen out for their high-frequency calls and hide from them? Those with that hearing ability would survive and pass it on to their offspring. But we're cosseted in our four walls. Given medicines to cure things that should really kill us. Weaklings are helped to survive, and—"

"Weaklings?"

She shrugged. "You know what I mean. There's no natural selection anymore. We're *all* selected. We've stopped evolving because we think ourselves already perfect."

"And we're not?"

She reached down and grabbed me. Grunted in disappointment. Arched an eyebrow.

"Give me time," I said.

"We should do it. We've talked about it long enough. I've tried the formula on mice, rats, apes."

"Apes? I don't know—"

"Ray said he'll help."

"Ray? He's a prick."

"I like him," she said. " And besides, he's the best tech guy I know. He's got more stolen equipment in his basement than NASA. Apple would pay for some of the shit he's designed and developed just to amuse himself."

"If they did, he'd have sold it to them."

She started squeezing, kneading. "Yeah, he's all about the money, but that doesn't mean he isn't brilliant."

"He's worth a fortune already. Why would he . . . do . . . this?"

Margot wasn't answering anymore. She was smiling. "I do believe you're ready to go again."

I smiled. "Survival of the fittest."

I haven't been injected for three days, but it seems that Margot's theories on dosage and continuity were wrong. She always believed that my body's natural defences would attack the alien compound, and that would necessitate introducing more on a daily basis. It targeted my hearing and sight, its pre-programmed purpose to open up my abilities, expand and broaden them. It worked on my sensory organs, nerve receptors, signal transference, and also the parts of my brain given to translating such information. An artificial evolution, she called it. In her eyes, she was allowing those two senses to achieve their full potential, but they would always revert. I would be given a glimpse at something greater, hear a wider spectrum of sound. The effect was never meant to be permanent.

She was so wrong. The abilities are expanding and strengthening, not fading away. I have never felt so alone, yet the more time goes by, the more I begin to understand that I am surrounded. The things that surround me, though . . . I have no wish to know them.

I have to leave this place. Perhaps closer to other people, the effect will wear off. Maybe I'll even find Margot and Ray again.

I'll try to tell them it was all a joke.

It was as if the whispers I heard—those guttural, harsh croakings of things mostly unseen, in languages we were never meant to hear—channelled themselves through me. That was the only explanation I could give. Left alone in that room, I did my best to relay the things I was hearing in my own voice. At first it was like singing someone else's song, and I felt quite ridiculous, trying to remember the sounds and cadences, the tones and feel of those strange voices. Speaking into the dictaphone, I sounded like a dog making strangling noises, or a child attempting to feign a deep voice.

Then something strange happened. As I spoke, I heard those real voices in my ears, muttering their strange tones as if coaching me. I continued for a couple of minutes, then hit 'stop' and dropped the dictaphone onto the table.

The voices receded, leaving behind the echo of a soft, knowing laugh. It took a while to fade, and even when Margot and Ray came back into the room, I could hear the dregs of those strange sounds.

"Done?" Margot asked.

I nodded down at the dictaphone. She picked it up and pocketed it.

"Mind if me and Ray . . . ?" She gestured at the door, then the two of them left me there without waiting for a reply.

What happened next was the first instant I began to comprehend just how fractured my relationship with myself had become, now that I was hearing and seeing more. I began to realise that I was not only hearing higher and deeper tones, or seeing a wider band of the spectrum. I was hearing *further*. Seeing *deeper*. Something about what they'd done to me had shifted my reality, or moved reality around me.

More things were making themselves known to me.

A couple of minutes later I heard their raised voices. Ray was crying, wretched, wrenching sobs torn from the heart of him. Margot was shouting, sounding both startled and vulnerable. I knew what they had heard, and a perverse part of me was glad. I didn't want to be the only one.

She stormed back into the room, kicking the door open as if ready to attack me, but then just standing there, staring, and it was the utter fear in her eyes—the fear of me—that upset me the most. She remained in the doorway, ready to run at any moment.

"What have we done?" she said.

That night they left. I thought perhaps they'd gone out to discuss the experiment, leaving the confines of the house, and that they'd return in a few hours. But they had abandoned me. I tried to follow, but couldn't. Each time I left the building, those voices assailed me more, singing terrible songs that would drive me mad if I heard them a moment longer. They sang and sang.

Trapped with myself, I was becoming a stranger.

I know now that I have no choice but to leave. They're getting closer. If I lie down I hear their whispers, starting far along a wide, empty corridor and then drawing closer, louder. It's only when I sit up that they dwindle away. I wonder what would happen if I didn't sit up.

It's dawn when I decide to leave. I stand inside the back door for a long while, peering through the side window and searching the landscape for shadows that are out of place. There are none that I can see, but even that disturbs me. It means that they're hiding.

I close my eyes and press my hands to my ears. *I wish I was the old me*, I think. *I wish I couldn't see and hear more. I wish Margot had never been so clever, and Ray so cynically brilliant.* In comparison I was merely their lab rat, and they've left me alone to suffer now that they've finished with me.

Now that they're afraid of what they've done.

I wish like all the best lab rats, they'd put me down.

Opening my eyes, taking my hands from my ears, I see and hear them as soon as I open the door.

They can't touch me, I think. *They won't hurt me.* It is fair reasoning, because I am seeing and hearing things that are always there. The experiments have changed me, not my surroundings, giving me the ability to perceive realities that humans aren't supposed to know. That does not mean that they will now hurt me.

Maybe they're pleased to be seen. Perhaps those whispers I hear are songs of joy.

I cross the gravelled area and approach the long driveway. In my determination to leave, my senses become unguarded, and the world opens up around me. Birdsong fills the air, and I hear the differing tones, the deeper meanings. A breeze rustles through the trees, carrying rumours from afar. Sunlight dapples the distant valley sides. Its journey is over, memories of deep space splashed like foam across a seashore. I see and hear new realities and despair at my inability to understand.

I am two hundred feet from the house and moving away. *This might work*, I think. *If I find them again, perhaps they'll see that their fear was misplaced.*

I pass through the gate that borders the property and out onto moorland, following the rough lane up towards the road. That's when the whispering begins.

A breeze first, then a more sibilant harshness, inside my head and beyond. My blood runs cold, my skin prickling with goosebumps, because I have never heard them sounding so angry. Yet I have done nothing wrong. If they dislike my new abilities, then let them come and tell me why. I cannot remain alone in that house forever.

I walk on, pressing my hands over my ears. That only serves to trap the voices inside. Their strange words echo around my mind, leaving a corrupt trace of themselves wherever they touch.

I see the first of the shadows as I round a corner in the road. It hunkers down in a field behind a hedge, defying the sun, pulsing like a living thing yet surely not. Surely.

I freeze, shifting from foot to foot as I try to make it out. It is difficult to discern properly. Whichever way I look, however much I shield my eyes, the shadow seeks to dazzle me with refracted sunlight. I move closer, and suddenly the whispering in my head changes from angry to mournful. Still tinged with darkness. Still alien.

I see Ray's body splayed on the ground beneath the shifting shadow. My breath is stolen from me. He's on his back, eyes open as if staring at the thing above him.

It is wan and grey, and other colours of dark infinity I cannot understand. It is connected to Ray in a dozen places by long, flexing limbs. It seems to be dead as well, although I'm not sure these things comply with any distinction between alive and dead.

Fifty feet beyond it, another shape sits beneath an old oak tree. It is a similar shape and colour. I don't want to see what lies beneath it, because I already know.

"No," I say. "Oh, no. No." My voice seems to stir the attention of other things more distant and still unseen, because the whispering gathers pace and volume. I'm driven back by the words, stumbling over my feet and sprawling in the lane. I scrabble backwards, keeping my eyes on the things I should not see as they pulse and whimper above the bodies of my two dead friends.

I turn and run back to the house, herded by screams and screeches, shoved by shadows when I dare to glance back. I realise with a terrible finality that these things do not want to be known.

And now, I'm the only one who still knows.

Back in the house with the doors shut and the curtains drawn, I stagger into the large living room and lean against the fireplace, head hung, tears spattering the old slate hearth.

Outside, they have gone quiet. They know they have me.

I look up into the big mirror and see movement, and for the briefest instant I think Ray and Margot have come back. Their deaths are a mistake, as is the experiment. I'll get over it. With their help I'll get better, and we'll move on without ever revealing what we did here.

Then I see the thing standing close. I can feel it behind me, exerting a terrible gravity on my life and my soul as they surely do to every man, woman and child. Dark strings lead from around and within me, rising like quivering tentacles and meeting eventually in that monstrous puppeteer's hands.

Though I close my eyes, I will always hear its dreadful, intimate voice.

STRANGE CURRENTS

Stephan didn't think he could sleep, not when to close his eyes might mean death. But he was startled awake when two sea birds dropped into the boat, landing heavily, slumping to the fibreglass deck, displaying all the signs of exhaustion and on the verge of death themselves. He thought back to the dreams he'd had during the sleep he should have never let claim him. Dark dreams, where the sea rose up in vast towering shadows, and the hidden depths were crowded. His eyes hurt. His skin was rough and sore, as if burnt beneath alien eyes. Perhaps he hadn't slept at all.

The two seagulls hobbled around the bow of the lifeboat. But their exhaustion was feigned, and when Stephan moved to catch them, they took flight. One of them flapped away across the waves and was soon lost to sight. The other circled a few times, *caw-cawing* laughter or a warning. Then it followed its cousin, and Stephan thought, *They must have come from land.*

The realisation should have galvanised him. But he found it hard to move, to summon enthusiasm, even hope. Seven days ago the lifeboat's entire encasing structure—support posts and rods, tarpaulin, fixing ropes—had been torn away when the craft capsized. It had been pure luck that Stephan's foot had caught in a trailing cord, the twine twisting around his ankle while he'd been buffeted and spun in the raging water. When the boat righted itself again he had gone with it, tearing the muscles in his calf and injuring his knee, but saving his life. He'd been left draped over the boat's side, staring down into the water at the dark, massive shape that seemed to fade away beneath him.

There had been no storm. Something had capsized the boat and caused the maelstrom, and he still thanked whatever luck had saved him that he had not been cast into the sea. The boat was tiny compared to what he had seen—

—A whale, that's what it was, surfacing to breathe and finding him in the way, or perhaps simply curious—

—but he was smaller. Baling water with a plastic container he'd managed to save, he had kept the cord wrapped around his lower leg for another day before finally freeing himself.

Fifteen days exposed to the whims of the North Atlantic weather. Luckily it was summer, otherwise he would have frozen to death long before the impending starvation, dehydration and sunburn would take him. Yet though the winds in the daytime scorched his skin, night breezes blew in cutting and cold. Stephan's will to survive was strong, but the reality of survival had been growing weaker.

Those birds came from somewhere.

Carefully, painfully, he knelt up and crawled the length of the boat. It was small, designed for a dozen people, and six inches of water swilled in the bottom. He'd stopped baling days ago. Most of the fixtures and fitting had been ripped away during the capsize, including his supply of drinking water, flares, and the small bag containing food he'd been clutching to his side. He often wondered where that bag was now. He thought it would probably float, as the knot he'd tied in the neck had been strong, the drawstring tight. The food was all in packets, not tins, and there was little in there to give enough weight to counteract the air caught in the bag.

Maybe it would float forever. Caught on the tides, nudged by the violent winds, his food bag would likely survive him, drifting across the North Atlantic past Greenland, Iceland, back towards Europe where most of its contents had originated. A ship might run it down and thrash it to pieces beneath its propellor. A sea creature might take it, swallowed whole and unnoticed by a whale or chewed apart by a shark.

Perhaps it would float out here until the world came to an end and humanity was no more. A lonely voyage lasting forever.

"Wake up, Stephan!" he shouted. Tried, at least. But his throat was dry and swollen, his lips split from sun and salt spray, and his cry consisted mostly of blood spat into the bottom of the boat, and a groan of pain.

One of the boat's four paddles was still clipped to the side, the metal fastenings bent by the force of the coverings being ripped off. He'd tried to loosen it soon after the capsize, found the task difficult, and left it. Now he needed the paddle more than ever. To follow the birds. To find land.

Perhaps he might even survive.

"Don't think about it," he whispered, and the high and lonesome sound of the constantly moving sea tried to swallow his words.

His hands were cracked and swollen, but he plucked at the oar's fastenings for an hour, until his fingernails were split and the tips bleeding. At last the paddle sprung free and he cried out in delight.

It was cold and heavy in his hands, but it felt like taking action.

The birds were long gone, but he had taken a bearing from the sun when they flew away. Allowing for the time since they had flown, he took another visual bearing, sat on one of the raised seats at the side of the boat, and started paddling.

After fifteen days every action hurt, every movement denied the stillness and supplication his body demanded of him. He had never been so hungry and thirsty, and several times over the past few days he'd thought he was going to die. Sitting there, leaning against one of the seats cast into the structure of the vessel, he'd felt darkness closing in.

Something always pulled him through. Sometimes it was his wife's voice, sweet Mandy beseeching him to survive. Once it was a memory of building a bonfire with the man who had adopted him and become his father, a time from his childhood long-since forgotten until now. And once it was something he could not identify. A strange sensation, a feeling of need and craving that reminded him of dreams he used to have when he was sick. He could not adequately describe them then, though they had been terrifying and made him scream himself awake. And he could not explain that feeling now. Only that it had saved him.

It was as if someone or something else wanted him to survive, and once he had surfaced from the darkness, that someone or something drew back once again, observing rather than intruding.

He shook his head. Foolish thoughts. He'd run the gamut of emotions since the ship had gone down, but now that he was taking action he promised never to be tempted by death again. Life was too precious. That preciousness had brought him here, in his attempt to discover where he had come from, who his true parents had been. His adoptive father had told him nothing of them, had refused to even speak of family. Only that they had brought him across the sea, abandoned him, and returned to some strange place.

He slapped the paddle into the water and pulled, slap and pull, and though he could not tell whether he was moving, or even in which direction, it felt like he was doing something positive at last.

The seascape was vast and unforgiving, the great swell bringing the horizon near and then drawing it out again, as if teasing him. The steady breeze sprayed salt water across his face and exposed arms and hands, making his raw wounds worse and offering a tantalising taste of water that would only make him sick. Sometimes he thought he saw land across the heads of the swells, but the next sight would reveal it to be simply another wave in the distance. He heard the echoing hiss of the waves' laughter as his hopes were dashed once again.

He pulled on the paddle. The boat was too big for him to move on his own, he knew that, it would have taken six people rowing to even hope to take charge of the vessel's direction. But he had to try. Mandy's voice convinced him of that. His father's face seen through the haze of bonfire smoke, the spit of knots in wood, the rich, sweet smell of burning branches from the evergreens growing around his grandparents' garden.

"The birds came from somewhere," he said again and again as he paddled. The words formed a chant, a song that the waves and wind sang along with him.

Something passed beneath the boat.

Stephan felt a pull on the oar as if a sudden, violent current was attempting to tug it from his hand. He held on tight and hauled the oar back into the boat. The sense of something huge passing beneath him was powerful, and he feared he was about to capsize again. The boat seemed gripped in a strong wake, drawing it up the face of an oncoming wave and down into the trough beyond. Stephan was powerless, and he waited for the moment when the thing below would rise up, break surface, show him secrets that had been hidden since the moment the ship had sunk.

But nothing happened, and the casual swell of the sea guided the boat once more.

Nothing had gripped the boat. Just the strange currents swirling here, flows of warm and cold water starting as a splash at the equator and taking on energy beyond measure by the time they made it this far north. Such was the way with the sea. Most people thought it was a silent mass, still and calm but for the waves texturing its surface. In reality the sea was a living thing, clasping the fixed continents in its smooth embrace and curling, twisting, abrading them over eons too vast for the human mind to contemplate.

Stephan had just gained a glimpse at that vastness. Rather than feeling awed, he was only scared.

He picked up the paddle to follow the birds once more.

If a distress signal had been sent, it had not been acted upon quickly enough to save him. If the lifeboat had a homing beacon, it had either failed or been washed overboard. He had seen plane trails several times since the sinking, but they were high in the stratosphere, passenger jets taking people across the wide ocean upon which they could not imagine such a story being played out.

He could remember little from that awful night, only that he had found himself in the lifeboat, darkness pressing heavy all around and the sea roaring and convulsing in a violence that terrified him to the core. Sea sickness had crippled him, curling him in a ball beneath the boat's flapping covering. Fear refused to let him go. It grasped him in its wet, salty grip, squeezing hard, forcing more puke when there was nothing left to bring up.

He was only a passenger out here.

"The birds came from *somewhere!*" he said again, but already he was doubting his knowledge. Were such birds native to the sea, or the land? Had he really read somewhere that seagulls were land based? Or could the species he had seen cruise above oceans for weeks on end, landing on boats or debris for a brief rest, sleeping on the wing?

He didn't know for sure, and such uncertainty angered him. He was ignorant, thrown into an alien environment with no clue how to survive.

Yet survive he had, and his wife's voice called him onward, and his father's face glimpsed through smoke.

An hour later, with Stephan still paddling, a shadow passed beneath the boat.

This time he was sure there was something there. He snatched the oar back on board and the surface of the sea rose, smoothing out as if an unimaginable bulk forced water up from the depths below. The surge was gentle rather than violent, carrying the lifeboat forwards and easing the way.

Against all instincts, Stephan leaned over the side of the boat and looked down. He saw only water, the surface now so smooth that his reflection looked back up at him, broken by ripples from the boat. He could not see any deeper.

Heart hammering with fear and a keen excitement, he had to fight against the urge to lean out further and plunge his face beneath the surface.

The surge ended as quickly as it had begun, dropping the boat into another valley between swelling waves, and he picked up the oar again. Just as he scrambled onto the plastic seat once more, he glimpsed something across the tips of the waves.

Land?

He gasped and dug the paddle in, trying to drive the boat towards the faint shadow he had seen. He feared he was hallucinating again, and that next time the boat was picked out of a trough he'd see a bank of dark clouds low to the horizon. But after splashing for what felt like eternity the boat rose again, bow first, until he was resting atop a giant swell.

"Yes!" he shouted. It was definitely land, a wide band of hills and beach on the horizon, lit by the afternoon sun and speckled with breakers. He must have been even closer than he realised if he could see *breakers*!

Stephan started paddling again, harder than before. He ignored the pain from his damaged hands, gritting his teeth against the sting of split lips and sunburn, and he started to believe he was going in the right direction. He *had* to believe that. No other outcome would be fair.

Mandy had died when the ship went down. She had still been in their cabin, miserable from sea sickness, and Stephan had gone on deck to smoke a cigarette. A jarring thud, a series of dull, inexplicable impacts below the waterline, and he had been flung over the handrail and into the sea, swimming frantically as the boat quickly sank beneath the waves. The only survivor.

Maybe the cabin had remained watertight for a while. Long enough for her to really think about what was happening and believe him dead. He hoped not.

Keep paddling, she said, her voice soft and imploring, though he could not see her face.

"I am," he said, tears blurring his vision. "I'm paddling as hard . . . "

From the corner of his eye he saw something break surface to starboard, emerging like the smooth grey remnants of an ancient wave unspent. By the time he'd turned to look it had vanished, leaving behind a curious speckling luminescence that rose and fell with the swell.

"Keep paddling, keep paddling," he said, hearing Mandy's voice whispering the words beneath his own.

As the sun dipped towards the land in the distance, so he drew closer. The sea's majestic swell lessened and the waves became rougher, breaking into white-tops and splashing into the boat. He should be baling, but then he would not be able to paddle. But if he kept paddling for too long, and the waves grew even worse, the boat would be swamped.

He was close enough now to start making out some detail. There was a small seaside town slouched along the dark strip of land, shadows striving for the sea from huddled rooftops, winding roads leading up from the shore and towards the hills much farther back. The hills were low, heavily wooded, seemingly immune to sunlight.

Something troubled him. Something about the town. He silently berated himself, concentrating on driving the paddle in, pulling, and again.

But the tide was taking him in anyway, so soon he stopped paddling and took a closer look.

A few lights had been lit in buildings close to the shore. They looked like beach huts of some kind, perhaps fishermen's huts, and the lights pulsed like oil lamps. Down the beach, closer to the breaking waves, a dark line of seaweed seemed to mark the dividing line between ocean and land.

"I'll cross that line," Stephan said. He'd been talking to himself for days, keeping himself company, and he suddenly started crying at the uncertainty of his situation. More unfair than his wife, drowning slowly in their cabin. More unfair than his adoptive father, taken by cancer. He did not feel saved.

A heavy weight passed beneath the boat once again, drawing it more rapidly towards shore. He squinted in the dusky light. There was something strange about the little town. Something darker than the dusk, because although the sun was still in the sky it seemed to avoid the buildings and streets of that place.

The dark line of seaweed on the sand was moving. It quivered and flexed like a giant snake, but then Stephan made out what it really was. Not seaweed at all. People. Hundreds of people, standing in line along the beach that fronted their little town, not quite far enough forward to let the foaming water touch their feet.

Hundreds of people, waiting for him.

You're going to be saved, Mandy said from somewhere deep in the ocean's depths, where perhaps even after all this time her cabin had yet to flood. The man who had adopted him, dead for years, nodded in agreement, his old face lost behind a veil of smoke that wasn't smoke at all, but salty spray thrown up by the strengthening wind blowing Stephan towards shore.

He reversed the paddle and started pushing it the other way. His lacerated hands bled into the water. His split lips pouted fiery pain at the sky. His paddling became more frantic as the town grew closer, and with that closeness came the unbearable, sickening realisation that after days adrift on the cruel ocean, this was the last place on Earth he wanted to be.

The sea carried him landward. Another mass passed beneath the boat and it lurched on, and the paddle was suddenly ripped from his hands, disappearing beneath the waves even though it was made of hollow plastic and designed to float.

Stephan knelt in the middle of the lifeboat, helpless in the face of his own fate. He suddenly had no wish to be saved. As he felt the boat's hull grinding against the first sandbank that signified the approach of land, he finally made out the staring, strange faces of those who waited. They had been expecting him, and he wondered whether he'd ever been on a ship at all. Perhaps he had always been out here being drawn, steadily and relentlessly, towards this terrible shore. Maybe he was being brought home.

A MAN WALKING HIS DOG

I was still shaking when I returned home, so I made myself a cup of tea and sat on the decking in my back garden, wishing I'd added a shot of something stronger but feeling too traumatised to go back in and find the whiskey. My regular seat on the timber bench welcomed me, knowing my shape and affording me some level of comfort. But I was still shivering, and not only from the deep winter chill. It's not every day you see a dead body.

It was cold but dry, January just heading into February. There'd been a heavy snowfall just after New Year's, but since then the weather had been crisp and freezing, frost-speckled landscapes the perfect canvas for my regular morning walks with Jazz. I loved the sound of frozen leaves crinkling underfoot and the sight of Jazz rooting through the undergrowth, sniffing out scents I would never know. She lived in a whole different world from me—one of exotic senses and tastes, different colours, and drives I can only pretend to understand—but that's why our friendship had always meant so much. She relied on me, I relied on her. I wouldn't have it any other way.

I held the mug tight in both hands, comforted by the warmth and staring through the steam. My back garden had the sparse, bleached appearance of winter, colours muted and growth paused between seasons. It felt like the whole world was holding its breath today.

I breathed out, and the steam spiralled and dispersed in the cool, clear air.

"A body has been found."

She has been expecting it. She'd convinced herself it was the only likely outcome, given the circumstances. But it is still a shock when the words come out of the policewoman's mouth. Taking form and meaning, given the weight of reality compressing air he had once breathed, the words' finality is like a punch to the chest. Her heart stutters and she blinks, eyelids fluttering as the echo of the statement weaves its way through the house and rebounds inside her skull.

"I'm very sorry, Mrs Jones. This is not a formal identification, but the clothing matches your description."

She can't look at the policewoman. She's been very kind, has sat with her for many hours over the past few days, but she is an invader in Jenny's home. Yesterday, Jenny went into the kitchen and found that John's cup had been washed and wiped and placed on the wrong hook, and the wrong way around. He wouldn't have liked that. They had their routine, their organisation, and John would have tutted and rolled his eyes. The policewoman didn't belong here. John did, sharing Jenny's space as he had done for the past four decades.

Jenny takes in a deep, shuddering breath and goes to stand, one hand flat on the table-top, the other pressed against her bad hip. She senses the policewoman moving close and concentrates harder, not wanting her help, not needing it.

"Maybe you should stay sitting down," the woman says, and

Jenny hears the pity in her voice. The caring, the humanity. It's been there all along.

"Yes," she says, easing herself back into the chair. "Maybe I should."

"I'm very sorry, Mrs Jones."

"Yes," Jenny says, and as she sits again she looks across the table at John's seat. He's there, newspaper folded on the table before him, toast and marmalade half-eaten on the plate, cup of tea half-empty, and he's frowning at the crossword as he has every morning for as long as she can remember. Soon he'll sigh and sit back, sliding the paper back across to her so that she can have another look. *Seven down's a bugger*, he'll say, and she'll hear him crunching the rest of his toast as she looks at the offending clue, half-hoping she'll get it instantly, half-hoping she won't. They both love their morning ritual. It is the foundation upon which the rest of their day is built, whatever that day is destined to bring.

John is not there. This day has no foundation. The previous few days have been the same, but now she knows that solid base will never be built again. She is floating free in her own home, her own chair. It makes her feel sick.

"We like to do the crossword," she says, and she senses the policewoman's discomfort. She hears movement behind her, a shuffling of feet, and Jenny silently berates herself for saying something so foolish. The woman will think she's just a confused old lady. She's not confused at all.

She's angry.

"He's left me," she says, looking up at the policewoman for the first time since hearing those dreaded words.

"I'm sure he didn't mean to," the woman says. She has a very caring face.

"I told him he was being stupid," Jenny says. She's already told the police about his failing health. They wrote down what she said with a blank expression.

"He sounded like a very proud man," the woman says, and the

past tense makes Jenny blink. John will never be in the past for her.

"Where?" she asks.

The policewoman scoots a chair over and sits down next to her, taking Jenny's hand in her own. It's a sudden, surprising gesture, the first time the woman has made physical contact, and it makes everything more real. *The foundation of my new future*, Jenny thinks. *A stranger holding my hand.*

"Up by the canal," the policewoman says. "I don't know where, exactly."

"Five days," Jenny says. "He's been lying there on his own for five days."

No answer. Only a squeezed hand.

"Who found him?"

"A man walking his dog."

Jenny laughs. She surprises herself so much that she pauses, then laughs again. The policewoman frowns, uncertain.

"Isn't that always the way," Jenny says. "Poor man. Poor, poor man. Just out for a walk with his dog and he finds . . . " *He finds my dead husband.*

"I suppose it is something you hear a lot."

"I'd like to meet him," Jenny says. "The man. His dog. I'd like to meet them to say sorry."

"I'm not sure if . . . "

"Not straight away. After all this is . . . " Sorted. Put away. After everyone but me has moved on.

"I'm sure it can be arranged," the woman says. Her radio makes a funny noise and she lets go of Jenny's hand, standing and moving to the doorway into the dining room to speak. She must be grateful for the distraction.

Jenny looks across the table at her husband's empty chair. *Seven down's a bugger*, he says.

"I'll get it for you," she whispers.

The policewoman glances at her and frowns. Just another confused old lady whose husband wandered away to die.

Jazz went off on her own again. I didn't mind, because she was a good dog and I knew she wouldn't get lost or run away. Jazz always came back.

But now, something was different. She was barking. She didn't bark very often, and it sounded agitated and afraid. I followed, slipping down the steep slope from the canal towpath and into the woods. A stream flowed down there. I'd heard it countless times, but I'd never been tempted from the path to go exploring. There was a barbed wire fence, fallen trees, holes from old forestry work, and I had no wish to injure myself and lie there in pain waiting for someone to come and help. I glanced back up towards the canal. It was interesting seeing it from this perspective. From down here, you could make out some of the heavy stone retaining walls that had been built over a century before, when the canal was being constructed. Such a familiar place, and now I was seeing it afresh.

"Good girl, Jazz," I said. She had shown me something new once more. She was always good company, and she enriched my life.

I heard another bark. I paused, head tilted, and the barking came again. I fought my way down the slope, climbing over fallen trees, avoiding the snares of tangled undergrowth.

The barking continued, guiding me, and by the time I saw her I knew that something was wrong. A darkness had fallen over the day. The sun was still out, but the fir tree canopy shielded me from the cool sky, and frost clung to the shadowy forest floor.

As soon as I saw the shape ten feet from Jazz I knew what it was. I froze, heart hammering, and for the longest few seconds of my life I waited for movement. *He's a drunk, a vagrant, a bird watcher, an explorer.* But all of those were wrong, and my first reaction was right. This was a dead man. From the state of his body, the colour of his skin, I believed he had been dead for some time.

I reached down to stroke and calm Jazz.

Which was when the man's head turned with a crunching sound and he said, "She's a good dog."

I snapped awake, gasping for breath. It was the third time I had dreamt about the dead man, the dreams waking me each morning since finding him. They unsettled me, because a dead man shouldn't talk. They were mostly the same—me and Jazz walking, her disappearing down into the woods, me looking for her. Then the barking, her calling me onwards with an obvious alarm. Drawing me closer to the body. The only real changes were the memories of how the weather had been that day. In one dream there was snow, a couple of inches coating the landscape and settling on the canal's frozen surface. In another, it was raining a constant, soaking drizzle. In this final dream, it was cold and sharp, and my exhalation of shock upon finding the body hung in the air before me. I didn't like waking to these dreams. It was as if the poor man's death drew me onwards, day by day, towards my own inevitable future.

Perhaps the events of today would help me move on.

I glanced at my bedside clock and sat up. Standing and opening the curtains, I was struck by the strange beauty of this normal, new day. It was cool and frosty once again. For the third morning in a row, I dwelled upon how the dead man would see no more mornings.

His wife would be here soon. A police officer would be accompanying her. After an initial deep sense of anxiety at the prospect, I had at last accepted to meet her. She was the one who mattered in this. The police had filled me in a little about her background, and the more I heard, the more I understood why this day must be so important to her. I might have been having strange dreams, but her waking hours had become a nightmare. If I hadn't found her husband's body, it might have been many days before his fate was discovered. Even weeks. Perhaps he might never have been found at all, hidden from the towpath as he was by a large holly bush and a couple of fallen trees. I was the person who had changed her life.

Jazz and I had changed everything.

I dressed and ate breakfast, then went about cleaning the house. I kept it in good condition anyway, but having a stranger visit gave me the impetus to vacuum and dust once more. Dog hair gets everywhere. But as I cleaned, I realised that I would not be letting the widow inside. Not after what had happened. Not after the dog had snuffled at her husband's corpse.

There was no way that she could meet Jazz.

"Why didn't you tell me this before?" Jenny asks. She's sitting in the back of the police car, and the policewoman is turned around in the passenger seat, eyes wide.

"I only found out myself this morning," she says. "And, really . . . " She shrugs. *Does it matter?*

Jenny frowns and looks at the hedgerows and fields flitting by. *Did* it matter? She wasn't sure how it could, yet it did. If this were a TV series or a book, not real life, it would hint at a malevolent pattern, a twisted thread leading to more murder and mourning. In truth, it's nothing but a sad coincidence. It is always a woman out for a jog or a man walking his dog, isn't it? They are the people out early in the morning. They are the ones who find what the night leaves behind.

"How long ago?" Jenny asks without looking at the policewoman.

"Fourteen years."

"Not the same dog, then."

"Huh?"

It doesn't matter. They swing from the main road onto a lane leading along the hillside, and across a couple of fields she can see the line of trees that marks the route of the canal, and the hump of an old stone bridge. They're still three or four miles from where John was found, but the towpath that leads there is now very close by. From here, all routes lead to his lonely, sad death.

A tear rolls down her cheek. She leaves it to drip from her jaw. She has wiped away too many tears.

"I hope he won't want to talk about it," Jenny says. "The other body he found all those years ago, I mean."

The policewoman doesn't reply. Jenny suspects that he's already had to talk about it enough with the police. She feels sorry for the man and hopes he's not nervous.

They finish the journey in silence, parking across the road from a neat little cottage. It's small but well kept, render painted a pale yellow, its garden large and ordered. There's a Ford in the driveway, and a curl of smoke rising from the chimney. Jenny realises that she doesn't know a single thing about this man, other than what he found three days before. She hasn't asked his name, whether he's married or alone, how old he is, what he does. She's suddenly embarrassed by that. He's been through a trauma too.

She wonders what he thinks about her wishing to meet him.

"Are you ready, Jenny?" the policewoman asks.

She nods. "Yes."

The policewoman leaves the car and opens Jenny's door for her, and as she does so the cottage's front door opens and a man emerges. He's tall and perhaps a decade older than her John, well dressed against the cold, and as he closes the door behind him and smiles, Jenny wonders, *So, where's the dog?* He crosses the country lane and stands close to the back of the police car.

"I thought we might go for a walk," he says.

He took the woman—the widow—and the policewoman along a track by his house and into a small woodland. They walked away from the canal, not towards it. The silence was awkward and heavy, punctuated only by the sound of their footsteps on the frozen ground, the crinkle of leaves beneath their shoes, the birdsong from the bare trees and bushes. He walked side by side with the woman, and if he glanced to the left and away from her he might have been alone.

He often came to these woods with Jazz. He knew the area well, and he led them to a place in the centre where several fallen trees provided somewhere to lean or sit.

"I'm so very sorry," he said at last.

"Yes," the woman said. She pressed her lips tight and a tear flowed down her cheek. It dripped to the forest floor, and he thought, *I wonder if it will freeze there?*

"I thought walking might be better, you know, fresh air and . . . "

"And you didn't want me to meet your dog."

He blinked, not sure what to say.

"I understand," the woman said. "That's very thoughtful of you." She looked around. "It's very lovely here."

"Yes, it is," he said. "You should see it in springtime. We walk here often, Jazz and I, most days in fact. Here and the . . . the canal."

"Good companionship, I imagine. Maybe I should get a dog."

"I couldn't do without her," he said.

"John and I used to walk," she said. "He liked getting up into the hills, but lately my hip's been getting worse and we've ended up finding flatter places to walk. Along the river, sometimes, you know? We always end up at a coffee shop somewhere. You feel like you've earned your cake after walking for several miles. John likes Victoria sponge, the bigger the better. He usually has two coffees." She paused, looking over his shoulder. "*Had* two coffees. *Liked* Victoria sponge." She was having trouble balancing the present and past, and he was not surprised. It was early days.

"Do you have a wife?" the woman asked. The question surprised him, and he took a few seconds to gather himself, moments in which memories danced and sang, and emotions made him their plaything.

"Not for a long time," he said at last. The woman smiled in sympathy. He smiled back. And like that the ice was melted, the awkwardness between them broken, and they were just two lonely people in their autumn years taking a stroll in winter sunlight.

Later, he went for his usual afternoon walk with Jazz. He left the cottage and headed up the gentle slope to the canal, crossing the small bridge and descending three steps onto the towpath. It would be getting dark within half an hour, but that was still long enough to stretch his legs and let Jazz have a good sniff around to do her business. And after today, he needed a walk.

For the first couple of minutes, he was on his own. He whistled softly and uttered her name under his breath. "Jazz. Jazz." He felt a faint tugging on the lead he was carrying. "Good girl," he said. He looked down and saw a shimmer around the end of the lead. "You always come when I call you."

It took his old dog a few more minutes to fully appear. And then he let her go and she was gone, darting along the canal to pick up the ghostly scents of other dogs, sniffing at forgotten dead things in the undergrowth, being with him as he had always been with her, and always would.

EMBERS

S tanding at the edge of a new housing estate, looking past a timber fence too high to climb into a woodland scarred with tarmac paths, he remembered the beautiful simplicity of childhood.

They knew the pillbox was in the woods, but for some reason they'd never got around to visiting it. Andy thought maybe it was because the older kids went there sometimes, smoking cigarettes and drinking cider and, so rumour had it, getting blowjobs from Mandy Sullivan. He wasn't entirely sure what a blowjob was—though his older brother Nick seemed to think it was something to do with sticking your tongue into your cheek—but those ideas were enough to keep the pillbox out of bounds.

Usually.

"We should go there," Joe said. "The old kids won't be hanging around this time of day. Just to see."

"To see what?" Andy asked, trying to sound cool but feeling scared.

"See what it's all about," Kai said.

"Yeah, that," Joe agreed. "Come on. Race you to the stream."

Joe went off quickly, Kai followed, and Andy pelted after them, sprinting through the blazing summer sunlight, legs thrashing through long grasses and raising clouds of tiny flies, dandelion seeds, and dust. It was the middle of a long hot summer, and school had finished a week before. Days of potential lay before them, and evenings of barbeques and bike rides around the village. His mum and dad had already told him that they'd give him a bit more freedom this summer.

The day rested heavily across the fields between village and woodland. The air was still, as if exhausted from the heat, and everything to Andy seemed large, wide, almost endless—the sun, the humidity, the fields and woodlands that were his playground, and the school holiday that was to last *all summer*. He whooped and hollered as he ran, overtaking Kai and closing on Joe. Just as they reached the stream he and Joe were neck and neck, and they leapt the old wooden fence together.

The timber rail beneath Joe collapsed, sending him sprawling into a thicket of stinging nettles. He yelped and rolled out, scratching all over, grinning from ear to ear.

"I am victorious!" Andy yelled, leaping into the stream and almost slipping on the slick rocks beneath the surface. Cold water hushed over his shoes and past his ankles, and he was tempted to throw himself in head-first.

"Only because I had an accident."

"Sore loser."

"No, I'm just saying, I fell into the nettles, my race-scars are better than yours." Joe reckoned that scars made girls like you more. He was scratching like crazy, his face tensed with the unpleasant tingling that would last for hours.

"Rematch?" Andy smirked.

"Screw you."

Kai arrived at the fence, panting. He leaned on the section just along from the collapsed rail and it broke too, spilling him to the ground.

"Fat bastard!" Joe shouted. Andy smiled but didn't join in. Kai *was* fat, and it didn't feel right taking the piss. Joe didn't care. He rarely did, and though there wasn't anything really mean about him, sometimes he was too brash for his own good. He was Andy's best mate. Kai had just begun hanging around with them, and Andy was growing to like the shy, overweight kid. It was only now that his parents were letting him out to play.

Andy loved the woods. There were streams to jump and dam, fallen trees to break apart and use to build dens, waist-high wood-ants' nests to prod and throw caterpillars in, places to hide, trees to climb, and animals to watch. It was a well-trodden woodland, but the paths were worn in by use, not formed artificially. There were still places in there that felt wild.

Andy, Joe and Kai played war all the way in, hiding behind trees and performing forward rolls to dodge each other's bullets. Kai was shot first, then Andy, and Joe declared himself the winner of the battle. That's just the way it was, invisible bullets obeying an unconscious social ranking. Andy's dad often commented that Joe would probably be in the SAS when he was older, and Andy wasn't quite sure whether he meant that in a good or bad way.

They played on the concrete bridge over the stream for a while, daring each other to crawl through the wide, twenty-feet-long pipes that carried water underneath, and as always failing to do so. There were stories of a kid getting trapped in there thirty years before and drowning when a heavy storm brought a flash-flood down from the local hills. It was the sort of tale Andy never asked his parents about, because a deep part of him wanted it to remain true. Such stories peopled the landscape with ghosts. And ghosts were cool.

Time passed, with the same oppressive heat resting over the woodland. Adventures were had. Eventually they found themselves close to the pillbox at the wood's far edge.

One of many built in the area during World War 2, it was part of a defensive line stretching past the village, intended to interrupt any German advance should an invasion have occurred. Andy knew of a couple of others in the area—one on Mr Eddles' farm, roofless and used for storing bags of fertiliser; another close to the local football club, its entrance and gun slots bricked up—but this one in the woods was the most complete. It was built of bricks laid around a shell of concrete, raised rapidly and made thick and heavy to withstand anything but a direct hit from a tank. It was square, with two gun slots in each face, and overgrown with ferns and brambles like waves of green fire.

"There's no way we'll get in there!" Kai whined.

"Yeah, we will," Joe said. "The older kids do."

"How?" Andy asked. He meant it. He couldn't see any sign of an easy approach to the squat building. Brambles grew higher than him in places. Their thorns promised pain.

"I don't like it, anyway," Kai said. "I'm going home."

"On your own? Through the woods?" Joe knew how to pick at his fears.

"Let's do a circuit," Andy said. He was excited, nervousness prickling his skin with a thousand pins. He wasn't even sure why. He paced left and Joe right, leaving Kai standing and staring after both of them.

"No!" Joe shouted. "Nothing!"

"Nor here!" Andy called back.

"No!"

"Nope!"

"Oh my God!" Joe screamed.

"What is it?" Kai yelled, but Andy already knew the tone of his friend's voice. Hidden around the other side of the building and undergrowth, Joe started laughing and Kai cursed softly.

That was when Andy saw the path. Beaten into the brambles, the route quickly jigged right, almost hidden from view. He was about to tell the other boys, but then had a better idea.

He followed the path. Turned right, then left again, circling around a tree trunk, then it stopped at the pillbox entrance. He'd already been stung on his bare legs by nettles, and pricked up and down his arms by thorns. But it would be worth it.

"No!" Joe called. "Still nothing."

Andy chuckled and wormed inside the building. It was cool in there and stank of piss. It was also filled with rubbish—cans, bottles, sweet wrappers, takeaway packaging—and a couple of old seat cushions propped against the wall.

"Andy?" Joe's voice sounded distant, swallowed by the walls. Only those gun slots and the rough doorway let in a hazy green light, and inside was almost completely silent.

"Woah," Andy breathed. There was plenty of evidence of older kids using this place to drink and do Bad Things, but he could only see Home Guard soldiers hunkered down with their rifles, firing through the gun slots as Germans advanced along the edge of the woodland towards the village. The sounds of bullets hitting the walls would be deafening. And one lucky shot would cause ricocheting carnage.

"I'm inside," he said.

"Andy?" Joe called again.

He moved to one of the slots and fired his voice outside. "I'm in here! Come around, there's a path hidden away. And it's *so cool!*"

Soon the other two were in there with him. Kai stood near the door wide-eyed, looking around and knowing they shouldn't be there. Joe kicked stuff around. Cans rattled, and a glass bottle smashed against one wall.

"Watch it!" Andy said.

"Why?"

"Well . . . " He wasn't really sure why. Equally, now that they were inside the pillbox he couldn't really remember why they'd wanted to come here at all. It was dirty and smelly, and now scattered with dangerous smashed glass. There was much more fun out there in the woods. He still had a couple of hours until he had to be home for tea—

"Wow, look!" Joe said. He bent down and picked something up, approaching one of the gun slots to see the object more clearly. A thin metal can, its end was topped with a narrow plastic spout.

"What's that?" Kai asked.

Joe started squirting something over one of the walls from the can.

"Joe, that stinks," Andy said.

"Pussy."

"No, I mean it's, like, petrol isn't it?"

"Lighter fuel," he muttered. "Look around for some matches."

"What? No way! I'm not setting fires, that's stupid."

"Why?" Joe asked. He continued squirting. Andy felt a splash of fluid across his hand and he shook it, backing away into Kai. Kai yelped and squeezed outside, yelping again when he lumbered into a bank of stingies.

"Joe, seriously, don't be stupid," Andy said.

Joe threw the can down and started kicking at the floor, sighing. Andy closed his eyes in relief. Maybe his mate would sulk for a bit, but he didn't care about that, he just didn't want—

"Yes!" Joe said.

In the shadows, Andy couldn't quite make out the object his mate bent to pick up. But after the scratch and spark it was no longer dark, and then he could see nothing at all.

Andy sighed and turned at the sound of kids playing in the street behind him. There were six of them, ranging from maybe seven to ten years old, scooting around the estate on a homemade go-kart and laughing as if the summer would never end. *I remember when all this was fields*, Andy thought, feeling so very old. He was only middle-aged. Forty-six . . . or was it forty-seven? Sometimes he had to pause to think about it, and he wasn't certain whether that was cheery or depressing.

His memory of those childhood times was still clear and fresh, even though so much had changed. Two of the three fields between the village and woods had been developed, with boxy brick houses struggling to find character and barely succeeding. The access roads curved gracefully, plots were set in artful disarray, yet the whole place still stank of new. The high fence between estate and the final field was attractive yet functional, the single gate prominently marked with "Public Footpath" signs and intended to guide walkers directly across the hardpacked path into the woods. Even from here Andy could see the beginnings of the paths that had been cast between the trees. They were breaks in the beauty, designed to provide easy access but taking away something of the wild, any sense of discovery. Part of him wanted to pass through the gate and walk on, but he knew it would feel too safe.

It was no longer the same place. Maybe tomorrow.

Sighing again, he turned his back on that last remaining field and the woodland it bordered and walked back through the estate. He shrugged the rucksack higher on his back and looked around, wondering if he'd see anyone he recognised but knowing that was so unlikely. He hadn't lived here for decades.

Climbing the gentle hill towards the heart of the old village, it was a relief when he left the last of the new houses behind and passed between the old. Whitewashed stone walls, deformed glazing, lush gardens filled with wild birds, and oaken doors, some of the houses were picture-postcard old. There were even a couple around the village square that were thatched. Andy remembered Joe telling him about how they'd used to build in a cat to the thatch to keep mice at bay, and he'd spent long nights afterwards imagining a still-living feline scratching its way through village roofs in search of prey.

He passed the church. He paid more attention to passers-by, thinking that if there were people he knew he'd see them here. But though he passed some old faces, and swapped a few smiles, none of them lit his memory.

He stopped in the village square and bought a coffee. The coffee shop was new, occupying the space that had once been the village bakery, but their coffee was good and the barista attractive and smiling, so he could barely complain. He sat outside and felt himself starting to relax. He'd arrived early and parked, deciding to walk around his old village before checking in to the little guest house. His meeting tomorrow in the nearby town would be boring and hopefully over quickly, but he'd leapt at the opportunity to come. Gone for over thirty years, in a strange way it felt just like coming home.

"Old face," a voice said.

Andy glanced to the left. An old chap was sitting at another pavement table, a pot of tea before him. He had wispy grey hair yellowed by cigarette smoke, a long thin face, and wore a shirt and tie and tweed jacket, even in the heat. It was nice to see an old man dressed like one, and Andy smiled.

"How do you mean?"

"Yours," the man said. "Old face from the village."

Andy squinted against the sun, struggling to strip thirty years from the old guy. *Huh, old,* he thought, laughing silently. *Thirty years ago he would have been around my age.* A sparkle of recognition teased him, dancing like a name on the end of his tongue.

"Yeah, I left when I was a nipper," Andy said.

"You that Joe Blake?"

"No," he said, frowning. "He was my mate. I'm Andy Randall."

The old guy frowned and stared across the square at the old church. It was twelfth century, apparently, founded by the Normans. Andy remembered going in there one evening with Joe and Kai and finding a grave dug for a funeral the next day. Joe jumped in first, Andy climbed in after some persuading, Kai ran home. Hierarchy maintained.

"Andy Randall," the old man said, almost to himself.

"From Oak Lane?"

"Huh." He looked at Andy again, smiling. Tapped his head. "Memory's gone to shit, sorry, son."

Andy smiled at being called son. "Aren't you Alf?"

"That's me," the man said. "Oh dear, now I'm wondering why the hell you remember me."

Cutting his lawns and pruning rose bushes; Andy always remembered that, because his mother had loved roses so much. Cycling to and from the village centre. Shouting at kids when their football bounced from the rec into his garden. Shouting at kids even when their footballs didn't. Shaking his fist if you rode by his place talking too loudly, laughing too much. *Miserable old bastard*, Joe had said once, shocking Andy with his use of the "B" word.

"Still living out by the rec?"

"Yep, and still using that." He pointed at a telegraph pole across the road, a bike leaning against it.

"No way," Andy said.

"Same bike."

Andy laughed. So did Alf. They talked some more, had another drink each and some cake, and chatting about village life from thirty years before was almost like being there. Andy's memories were sharp and vivid, and the older man's contributions carried less nostalgia and more simple recollection. Maybe because he still lived there, or perhaps because as you got older there were more memories than hopes for the future.

Andy enjoyed it, but all the way through there was something not quite right. A note of confusion in Alf's voice, a flicker of doubt in his eyes. *He can't remember me*, Andy thought, and that shouldn't have surprised him. Joe was the one his age that people would remember—lively, daring, cheeky, sometimes outright naughty. Alf had even thought he was Joe. Maybe they'd started to look more like each other as they'd grown older. He didn't know; he hadn't seen Joe for almost thirty years.

But when Alf stood, holding his knees and groaning but actually looking fit and lithe, he frowned at Andy, shielding his eyes from the blazing sun. For a while he just stared at him, looking him over as if trying to match him with a mental photofit.

"Andy," Alf said, nodding slowly. "Nice to see you."

"You too, Alf. I'm here 'til late tomorrow, maybe we'll chat again."

"Maybe," Alf said, and he crossed the road, mounted his bike and pedalled away without once looking back.

Left alone, Andy leaned back in his seat and looked around the village square, but it suddenly seemed like a strange place. He saw more of the new than the old, and he was sad at the changes rather than nostalgic for the places and features he knew. He finished his second coffee and stood, ready to walk across the village to the guest house on the outskirts. It was the old station house. Trains no longer stopped in Tall Stennington.

As he walked he started to sweat. The afternoon sun skimmed over the rooftops and probed beneath the trees overhanging the road. Houses became more occasional, and he waved at a couple of people working in their gardens. One waved back.

The skin of his face and balding scalp was tight, sore to the touch, and hot. He'd never learn. Should have used sun cream. He always seemed to burn more easily since that time in the pillbox.

Walking home through the woods, he'd been more afraid of being told off than he was worried about the damage to himself. Joe had held his arm and guided him along the paths, and Kai had kept his distance, staring at the boys wide-eyed. *It's the shock*, Joe had said, trying to explain why the two of them weren't screaming. *And it's not that bad. Like sunburn.*

Close to the edge of the village, about to turn right into Station Road, he saw someone further along the road, a man seeming to intentionally match his pace. When Andy stopped, so did he.

A flush of recognition filled him, and he felt inexplicably nervous.

"Joe," he said. "Joe?" Louder.

The man turned around. From this distance it was impossible to tell whether or not it was Joe, because age might have changed him so much. But the brash burn scar across the side of his face and head was obvious.

His image shimmered in heat haze, almost there, almost not.

Andy opened his mouth again but could not speak. The man stepped into a pathway between bushes and disappeared. "Joe," Andy breathed, but he doubted it had been him at all. He blinked, feeling suddenly dizzied from the sun. Blood roared in his ears like flames. He would get to his guest house, take a drink, and indulge in a long cool shower.

Andy must have been sitting outside the coffee shop for longer than he'd remembered. The sunburn across his scalp and face was uneven, brighter on the right cheek and side of his nose, his right ear blazing red. He was angry at himself. After all this time he should know better.

Standing naked in front of the big bathroom mirror, his burned bits looked blood-red in the late afternoon light, the rest of his body so pale it was almost translucent. He looked after himself, and considering his age he'd held up well. Had a bit of a pot, and small love-handles, but he was wide across the shoulders and his chest was firm and muscled. Women should love him. He could hardly remember the last time he'd been with one.

He dressed in fresh tee-shirt and jeans and slipped on his walking boots. It was early evening now, and he had a meal booked at the Farmer's Arms at eight o'clock. Still over an hour to kill, and he was bored of sitting in the room on his own.

Really, he knew where he was going even as his feet took him there. He walked back through the village, past the square and church and towards the new estate on the other side. The air was heavy and still with summer heat, and sound didn't seem to carry far. A few cars and vans passed along the road, pedestrians plodded lethargically around the village, but Andy felt very much alone.

Memories leapt out like teasing friends trying to startle him.

Joe and him playing with magnets outside the small industrial estate, rolling up iron filings and making patterns with them across the metal-clad gates.

Throwing knives at the big oak at the edge of the cricket field, trying to get them to stick. Joe had cut his thumb open with one throw, but his knife had quivered in the trunk, and he'd talked about how his blood would always be in the middle of the tree.

Mrs Chambers leaning from her front window and shouting at them when they'd fired their water pistols at the cat bathing in her front garden. Andy had fired a daring shot across the garden at her, to Joe's gasp of delight, but lucky for him it hadn't found its target.

Falling off his bike on the tight bend outside the village shop, skinning his knees, going home crying and watching his mum picking out grit with tweezers.

Letting off a smoke bomb by the bridge over the small stream.

Mandy Bucknall smiling at him as she rode by on her pony. She had been his first crush, their two-year age gap an eternity.

By the time he reached the new estate he was awash in childhood memories, and he jogged through to the field and woodland beyond so that he did not lose them.

Approaching the woods, he saw movement ahead of him, beneath the trees and away from the new path that had been formed. A shadow shifted. He shielded his eyes against the sun burning low above the tree line, squinted, and saw the figure again. It was moving further away from the path and deeper into the woodland, and just as it passed out of sight it turned to look back at him.

"Joe!" Andy called. "Wait! It's me, Andy!"

Joe or not, he did not wait. Moments later the movement ceased, and even though Andy ran the last hundred metres and stood at the new wooden fence between field and woods, there was no sign of anyone beyond.

"Damn it," he muttered. It troubled him that Joe didn't want to speak. Or maybe it wasn't Joe at all. *But the burns*, he thought, remembering the pink burn scar he'd seen across that guy's face earlier. It *must* have been Joe. Mustn't it?

He entered the woods through the new gate and walked along the path, and soon he was keen to get off the beaten track. He didn't recognise anything about the place now that it had been tamed, and he wanted to get in among the trees, where the bluebells were just fading away and his shoes would get covered in dust. Most of all, he didn't want to meet anyone coming the other way. This was his time, his memory, and he wanted to live it mostly alone.

Mostly. Because he also wanted to look for Joe. His old friend must have seen him earlier, and again just now, and if that were the case then perhaps he was following him. Could someone walking ahead be following? Andy didn't know, but the coincidence was too great.

He pushed through a bank of ferns and emerged into a shaded part of the woods that he remembered well. A dried pool was soft with a carpet of lush green moss, and he walked slowly in case there was still any water or deep mud there. It was only during the summer that this pool dried up completely, and it had been a hot one.

Really hot. Sweat dribbled down his sides and back. His sunburn hurt, even in the shade beneath the trees, and he wondered whether he should have used some moisturiser.

"Joe," he said, pausing, surprising himself with the utterance. Even hearing the name spoken aloud provoked memories that brought tears to his eyes. He walked onwards, avoiding places where he could see new pathways cut through the woodland like pale scars on a rugged face. Some places were so familiar that he had to stop and stare. Time had worked on the woods in the three decades since he had last been here—many trees had fallen, and new ones grown in their place—but he still knew the place so well. The woods were timeless, and thirty years were barely the flutter of the last leaf to fall before winter.

Eventually he found the pillbox. It was buried even deeper beneath undergrowth. Someone must have planted rose bushes around it some time ago, and they had gone wild, twisting and merging with the forest's natural plant life to form a thorny tangle. Though he circled it several times he saw no easy way through. He had mixed feelings about that. It was good because it meant that local kids didn't use it anymore. But that also saddened him, because coming in here and having adventures, exploring places like this, was what kids *should* be doing. Now it was all computer games and TV.

He was also disappointed because he thought that perhaps he'd have liked to have gone inside.

Joe was watching him through the trees. Andy caught sight of him and held his breath. He was like a tree himself, motionless and expressionless, staring across at Andy as if he had no real thoughts in his mind, no words on the tip of his tongue.

"Joe!" Andy called. His old friend was a hundred metres away, visible between trunks because he wanted to make himself so. His image shimmered in the afternoon heat. "Wait there, I'll come and . . . " Andy hurried away from the pillbox, but as he left he felt a vicious burning sensation across his arms and neck, his face, his scalp, like the memory of flame. It scorched. He gasped, and when he wiped his hands across his face and head, his skin was tight and hot.

He smeared sweat, surprised at how much he was perspiring.

Looking back he saw that he'd shoved past a bulge of nettles growing beside the pillbox. He smiled through the tingling, burning pain, remembering when Joe had fallen into the stingies that day. The last day they had been together.

Joe was gone. Where he'd been standing Andy now saw only the pale trunk of a silver birch. Maybe he'd never been there at all.

Wincing against the pain from the nettles and the pulsing ache of sunburn, he started to make his way back out of the woods. He was hungry. It would be dark soon. And suddenly, he no longer wanted to be there when shadows began to grow.

Just ahead of him, visible several times through the tree, the shape that might be Joe. Why his old friend was doing this, Andy couldn't figure out. Didn't he want to speak to him? Or perhaps he was as much a joker now as he had been back then, and he was just attempting to spook him.

The pain of the stings and sunburn continued to trouble him, and now and then it made him feel sick. He moaned against it, as if noise might drive it away. Blood pulsed in his ears, and then roared, blurring his vision with dancing shapes that twisted trees and bushes, catching the sun and concentrating it in flaming arcs that seemed to hang like giant spiderwebs all around. He reached out to lean against a tree but drew his arm back, afraid that he might set it on fire.

"Joe!" he shouted. "Joe, help me! It hurts!" He'd screamed the same all those years ago when the lighter fuel ignited, or thought he had.

Andy tripped and hoped he was falling into a stream. But it

was the green flow of more brambles and nettles that caught him, piercing skin, speckling mild poison that added to the fire. He dragged himself upright. What was happening to him?

"What's happening to me?" he screamed. Through his swimming, burning vision he saw that shape again, closer than it had ever been and gesturing him forward. He followed because he could think of nothing else to do. Why weren't his clothes burning beneath such intense heat?

It's just the sunburn and the stings, he thought, *an allergic reaction.* But he didn't want to collapse out here, not alone, and not when he'd done his best to avoid the paths that people would undoubtedly stick to.

He staggered through the undergrowth and kicked against a wood-ants' nest, backing away quickly even as he felt the first few acid stings on his lower legs. The shape—

"Joe? Joe? Joe?"

—waved its arm furiously and moved ahead of him. Andy followed, gasping against the fire that seemed to be deep within him now, singeing his organs, set deep in his bones where it might burn forever. And when he saw where the shape was taking him, the first glimmer of calm touched his skin.

The pillbox was no longer overgrown and inaccessible. Even with his senses reeling he was able to find that path beaten into the brambles, turned left and right to hide it from the casual observer. He wasn't sure whether or not that shape had gone ahead of him, but just as the entrance came into view, he saw a shimmer of movement as something passed inside.

As Andy stepped over the threshold and entered the pillbox, the blinding pain of fire seemed to lift from his body and seed itself inside.

Small flames flickered over the floor, walls and ceiling, following the swirled lines where Joe had squirted lighter fluid. Andy could smell the tang of burning material and hear the gentle *pop-pop* of discarded litter shrivelling beneath the heat.

"Joe?" he said. But though there was a vague shape in the opposite corner, turned to face the junction of two walls as if ashamed at what it had done, Andy no longer wished to see its face.

As the heat inside him dissipated to nothing and the fires began to grow, he wondered whether he had ever left that pillbox, or if he had spent his life nightmaring about it.

If he kept the flames at bay, he would never have to find out.

FLOTSAM

Since her husband had died, Debbie always tried to sleep on the beach. The feel of sand slowly giving out the day's heat mimicked his warm touch. The smell of drying seaweed and decaying crabs and fish reminded her that he was dead. The constant hush of waves onto the shore might have been him sighing in her ear. An unseen creature's delicate legs trailing across her stomach were his fingers soothing her skin, and the stark sea breeze preceding dawn was his last gasp of air before he went under that final time. Everything was Marc. All that she had known, and all that she would ever know of him again.

She could never abandon that.

But three years is a long time. Plenty long enough to get over things, her friends had tried to tell her, before they ceased being her friends. And more than long enough for others to start seeing her in a different light. Mad old sea woman. The lonely mermaid. Beach bitch.

She'd heard it all, and cared for none of it. The sea entranced and intimidated her, and sometimes she went a whole day without even remembering Marc at all. Beaches became home. Sand became habit. Life wasn't always about mourning and loss. Sometimes, life was driven by the tides.

By day she would sell homemade jewellery to tourists from the small home they'd once shared. It backed onto the beach and was becoming ever-more rundown, its wooden boarding scoured by the salt breeze. The sea eroded her home just as it had eroded her life.

She never told the tourists her story.

Some nights when Debbie slept on the beach, she spoke to him. But the times she spoke out loud were becoming less frequent. Memories were a form of communication, more personal and internalised. Sometimes it felt like they were impressing themselves upon her rather than forming from the shadowy depths of her own experience. On occasion, though, it simply felt good to talk.

"See the stars?" she would ask, lying back in her sleeping bag and tracing one hand across the clear sky. In moments she swept whole galaxies aside. Marc had loved looking at the stars. Sometimes she'd find him lying on the decking at the bottom of their garden, mildly drunk and grinning in delight as he stared, and stared. She'd join him for a while, but the cold always got to her, or the thought of unseen insects and other crawling things exploring her loose night clothing. A few times it had been his hands doing the exploring, and she had stayed with him a while longer. He had always insisted that she sat astride him, so that he could see her against the universe as they made love.

Other times she would say, "It's so cold tonight," wrapping herself tighter, curling up in the sleeping bag so that she looked like a giant shell among the dunes.

"Maybe I should go home." She said that less frequently. It was a strange concept, when home was rarely more than a mile or two along the coast. But sleeping out here, beside the sea, beneath the stars, felt like a way of honouring her husband's memory. Returning home to sleep would be moving on. She was not certain she was ready to move on so far.

So she bought thicker sleeping bags for the winter, and invested in heavy duty tents, and weathered the storms of water and wind and people's scorn. And even after three years, on occasion she still spoke to Marc.

Debbie had never expected a reply.

The bottle was wedged between two rocks at the edge of a rock pool. It was almost buried in sand, and she wouldn't have seen it if she hadn't slipped on a slick stone. She did not quite fall, but her foot splashed into the pool, water entering her boot. When she looked down she saw the opaque curve of glass. There was often glass on the beach, cruel edges smoothed by time spent washed back and forth across the sea bed. But this bottle was whole. Even more intriguing, it was sealed with a cork and wax sealant.

She tugged its neck. It came out of the sand with a slow pop, as if the beach did not wish to relinquish its grasp.

She held it up to the sunlight, trying to peer inside. The glass was cloudy, completely smooth, and speckled here and there with tough green algae. The seal appeared whole.

Tucking the bottle into her backpack, Debbie walked up the beach until she reached the first of the dunes. They were large here, frequented by dog walkers, runners, and lovers, and she sat atop one of the highest so that she could see all around. She loved the views over the water, the world at her back. Though familiar, they never grew boring.

Carefully, she worked at the wax seal around the bottle's neck. When she could grasp the cork's top she twisted, bottle one way, cork the other. It came out with a pop that reminded her of the beach giving up the bottle, though this was more musical. It sounded like a gasp of delight.

Inside the bottle, a single sheet of paper was rolled and tied with a grass-like twine. Excitement building, she tipped the bottle and caught the paper as it slipped out. The twine was old and crumbled beneath her fingernails. The paper was dry but brittle, and she unrolled it slowly to prevent damage.

There were three words written in a simple, neat hand.

I'm not gone.

She recognised Marc's writing.

There was no profound shock. No cry of surprise or fear, no disbelief, no throwing of bottle or paper, as if to discard the possibility of what she had just read. No histrionics at all. She simply read the words again, three times, just to make sure. Then she rolled the paper, slipped it back into the bottle along with the cork, deposited it in the backpack now resting beside her, and took in the view once more.

The sea was rough today. White horses broke across the beach, never quite making land. She wondered what would happen if they did.

Marc was dead. Even from the beginning there had been no hope, and she'd told those who questioned her reasons for living on the beach that they did not understand. In truth, she wasn't quite sure that she did. But she allowed those words, in that handwriting, to sink in.

That evening as she built a fire and ate supper she had brought from the house, she opened her rucksack to hold the bottle again, and to touch what was inside. But the bottle was gone.

Marc had insisted on calling their sailing boat *Doot*. It was what he had used to call boats when he was barely old enough to talk, or so he said. His parents had been dead for years, so she wasn't sure how he could even know. But owning a boat had always been his dream, not hers. She didn't really care what he called it.

The day the *Doot* went down, they sailed along the coast and pulled into Polperro for lunch. It was thronged with tourists as usual, but Marc quite liked the hustle and bustle. He said it made the solitude they both enjoyed so much more precious.

They walked through the streets, watching families herding their children, ice cream around the kids' mouths, parents sporting sunburn lines that would blister and peel. They'd talked about having a family of their own one day, but neither of them was in a rush. They were enjoying life as it was. They were still young.

They ate fresh crab and winkles on the sea front, followed by a pint of local cider. They laughed. They held hands walking back to the boat, then jumped on and hurried, conscious that the tide was going out. Marc used the motor to cruise them back past the long stone pier, and she sat beside him, waving to a group of children fishing with crabbing lines.

It was a sunny day, with a slight westerly breeze. It was only a few miles home, and there was no sign or forecast of any bad weather closing in. The *Doot* was newly serviced, with plenty of fuel and all the emergency gear required. Marc had logged their journey with an online port master. Nothing should have gone wrong.

Debbie was dozing when it happened. Lying on the upholstered bench at the boat's stern, Marc standing at the wheel, she was conscious of the sea's constant movement and sound, Marc's soft singing voice, the sun on her face, and the subtle movements of her body as the boat dipped and rose. It was one of those moments when everything was perfect, and a rush of sheer ecstasy at life washed over her. She kept her eyes closed and smiled, trying to hold onto the sensation. Living in the moment.

Marc's song ceased.

"Oh my—" he shouted, and then came the impact. It was huge, shattering, and it tore their world apart. She didn't know whether they had struck something, or something had struck them, but she was thrown aside, smashing into the boat's small cabin. Water poured down on her, filling her mouth and eyes and drowning her senses. The world turned. The sounds of breaking things smothered everything else. She was being thrown around, battered from all sides, dipped in the sea and pulled out again, and whenever she tried to open her eyes she was blinded by salt water, crashing into her face as if wave after wave was attempting to drive her down.

She tried screaming for Marc, but she gagged, swallowed, vomited it back up. Something struck her hard across the back. Something else punched her face, and it was only later that she'd find out she had four parallel gashes across her cheek from ear to jawline.

Struggling to swim, to breathe, to live, it seemed like forever before Debbie was flung from the chaos into calmer, flatter seas. She had always been a strong swimmer, but she flailed. Almost drowned.

Behind her, the boat was in pieces, the sea still whipped into violence by whatever had taken it. As the hull reared up one last time, she saw a swathe of blood splashed across the ruptured deck. Between blinks, the sea came in and washed most of it away. A few blinks later and she was floating on her own. Waiting for rescue.

By the time it came she was almost dead.

The life she was brought back to was nothing she really recognised.

Debbie found the second bottle three days later.

She had been looking for it, never quite sure whether it would be there or not. But she desperately hoped that there was more than one. The first bottle had come and gone, leaving doubt that it had ever been there at all.

The second convinced her.

Tangled in a mess of seaweed and driftwood halfway up the beach, it must have been brought in with the recent tide. It was smooth and clear, newer than the first, the glass chipped here and there from impacts with rocks as it was washed ashore, the chips' edges still sharp.

She picked it up nervously, wondering whether it was just a random piece of rubbish. Knowing at the same time that it was not. The rolled message inside was visible, the sealed cork top untouched by algae.

Looking around, Debbie wondered who might be playing a trick on her, and who would ever want to. It was a cool day on the beach, summer giving way to autumn and a different type of beach dweller. There were fewer sunbathers and more walkers, not so many children and more lone adults. Along the beach, an old woman and her three dogs faded into uniform grey specks. A jogger splashed through the surf. A man and boy flew a kite.

No one was paying her any attention. The beach was a wide-open space where she could be alone, and everyone had their own reasons for being there. Hers were at last becoming more clear.

Debbie plucked at the wax seal, popped the cork and opened the bottle. She tipped the message out. Unfurling the paper, she looked around once again to see if anyone was watching. Almost wanting them to. If someone else bore witness, she would not have to doubt herself.

Marc's words saw away her doubt

Go to our Cove and you'll understand.

The Cove was a secluded beach two miles along the coast from their home, accessible only via a precarious cliff descent. The beach was only exposed at low tide. It was small, pebbly, dangerous, with several small caves and one larger cavern. They had been to the Cove three times, and on their final visit they had made love in the largest cave, the echoes of their passion merging with the sea's constant murmur.

It was late afternoon, too late to walk to the Cove. And perhaps she was scared.

Heart thumping, she slipped the message back into the bottle and held it in her hand. She felt its reality, and replayed the words over and over as she walked back up the beach.

The Poop Deck was still open. A quirky beachfront café, its owners had done their best to turn it into a pirate-themed restaurant, hoping to attract families. It was tired now and in need of a paint job, but that added to its rugged charm, and Mags and Chris still served good coffee and great fish and chips. She knew them well. They were always welcoming and kind.

They had known Marc.

She sat in a window seat, the only patron, and placed the bottle on the table before her. She was afraid that if she glanced away, it would disappear just like the first. But this one felt more real, more solid, and its message could only be for her.

"Debbie," Chris said. For such a big man, she was surprised that she never heard his approach. "Usual?"

"Just a coffee today, thanks."

"Not hungry?"

She considered a moment, glancing up at him only briefly before staring at the bottle again. She didn't feel like she could eat a thing.

"Slice of Mags's carrot cake?"

"Sure. You okay?"

"I'm fine."

"Find some beach treasure, eh?" he asked, leaning in to look at the bottle.

"You see it?" she asked. Chris gave her the look. She was used to such a look from many people, but Chris and Mags seemed to understand her more than most. Or maybe they only pretended to.

Eyebrow raised, a cautious smile, the *Maybe she's mad* sort of look.

"Sure you're okay?" he asked, and the look dropped away to reveal the Chris she knew. He was a grizzled old sod, face craggy and leathered by decades of exposure to the sea. Difficult to age, he claimed to have served on a merchant ship during the war, but he varied which conflict with each telling of the tale. His beard could have abraded metal. He even smoked a pipe, though only once each day just after closing time.

Debbie shrugged.

"Marc's birthday coming up, huh?" Chris asked, and it hit her like a shot, because she had not remembered.

"Yes. Birthday."

"And he's still gone." Chris rested his foot on the chair opposite her, elbow on knee. All he needed was a parrot on his shoulder.

Debbie smiled. She knew that Chris was about to indulge in one of his ocean monologues. She touched the bottle with her fingertips, tracing its rough exterior. It was still warm, as if she had only just been holding it.

"Thing is with the sea, it's all hidden," he said. "We see the surface and it's vast, but we only see it in two dimensions. Even that scares us, but its real scope is beneath. Depths we can't imagine. Whole worlds down there, and we hardly know any of it. The oceans have more secrets than we'll ever know, and Marc's one of many lost to that world. Maybe there's a hundred thousand lost souls being swilled around in its currents, buried in deep sea beds, tangled in ocean forests, washing up and down the sides of deep sea mountains. Fishermen and soldiers. Lovers and monsters. Maybe there's a million of them, and they're souls that'll never be seen again."

"You really should write some of this down, Chris," Debbie said.

"Who'd read it?" He was staring at her. His eyes were sharp, blue as the sky and deep as the ocean. "If his time was up, I think Marc would have liked it that way, don't you?"

"I'm not so sure," Debbie said, frowning. She'd tried putting herself in Marc's head for his final moments, and sometimes she thought she was almost there. But now with these bottles and their messages, she was confused and messed up once more.

"Hope that's not dirty," Chris said. He gestured at the bottle as he walked away to get her coffee and cake.

"I don't know what it is," she whispered. She held the bottle again, comforted by its solidity.

Later, after she spent some time watching the sun sink over the headland and set fire to the sea, she reached out to finish her coffee. The bottle had vanished.

She held the coffee mug against her mouth, searching across its rim. Scanning the table. Looking at other tables, down at the floor, in her lap. Even lifting her left hand to make sure she wasn't still clasping it.

Chris and Mags were sitting in the far corner cubicle. He was filling his pipe, a signal that they would be closing soon. They were waiting for her, she realised, and Debbie felt a pang of affection for them. Sometimes they hardly spoke to her at all, but she could feel their concern. Good friends didn't always need to talk.

She thought of asking them about the bottle. Maybe Mags had cleared it away while she'd been hypnotised by the sunset. But for some reason, she kept it to herself. A mystery was forming around her, its shape taking on Marc's dimensions. She had no wish to break it.

On the beach that night she heard sounds from the sea. She was familiar with night sounds of the ocean. The swell was a constant hush, waves washing onto the beach an accompanying whispered concerto. Sometimes she heard stranger noises from further out, attributing them to birds or perhaps seals floating on their backs and wondering at the stars. But this sound was different. It sounded like an incredibly distant shout, carried across waves from far away and merged with spray, changing the voice's language and pitch. There was no way of discerning what it said. And perhaps she was simply listening too intently, hearing things that were not there.

She fell asleep sitting up, sleeping bag unzipped and hugged around her shoulders.

When she awoke, the sea had receded down the beach, distant and silent once more.

Debbie was already on her way to the Cove when she found the third bottle. She saw it from a distance, propped against the rotting timber upright of an old coastal erosion defence. Most of the structure had long-since been washed away, but the post was still there, spotted with crustaceans, its surface slick and wet. Sand was piled around its base from the recent tide. Sat on top of that sand, as if placed there intentionally, was the bottle.

It was a milk bottle the likes of which Debbie hadn't seen for some time. It was clean, undamaged by the sea, and its neck was sealed with a knot of wood and melted wax. She could see the message rolled up inside.

And she did not want to read it. She approached the bottle and paused a few steps away, sitting in the sand and looking around. There was no one close. She was nearing the end of the beach, and looking up at the low cliffs she could see no one watching, no walkers looking down, no one waiting to see her find the bottle.

I'm already on my way, she thought. *Why send me another message?*

She took a couple of steps closer. The bottle was solid. There was little doubt about that, and when she reached out and touched it, it was as real as the sand, the wood, the sea and sky.

As real as me.

"I'm already coming, Marc," she whispered. She usually only spoke to him at night, and the sea muttered in reply.

She stood and walked past the bottle. But its pull was strong, and she could never leave it like that. Every step she took, she'd be wondering what she was leaving behind.

The plug popped out easily enough. The scrap of paper was the same at the others, brittle and tied with some sort of dried grass. She paused before unrolling it.

If his time was up, I think Marc would have liked it that way, don't you?

Instead of reading it, she tucked the paper back into the bottle and plugged it again, holding it in her right hand as she walked towards the end of the beach. She faced a climb up a rough stair-case, a mile walk along the coastal path, and then a difficult descent to the Cove. If she decided to read this latest message between now and then, she had to ensure the bottle remained real.

Of course it will, she thought. *Until you read it. Because it's only meant for you.*

Debbie didn't know what any of this meant. Her memories of Marc and that night were confused. She was not quite as mad and lost as some people liked to believe, and she knew that these mes-sages could not be from Marc. But she had to find out just what they were. Someone fooling with her? Or someone else trying to get her attention? Messages in bottles . . . intimations that there were answers at the Cove . . . shouting, far out to sea.

Fit from her constant beach and cliff-walking, she reached the path above the Cove before lunchtime. The tide had turned and was coming in, but it was still far enough out for her to be able to climb down.

She edged forward, watching her footing amongst the brambles and ferns, and tried to look over the cliff's edge. But she couldn't make out much down below. Only the white lines of breaking waves and a few feet of pebbly beach.

As she took the path less trodden that headed towards the hazardous climb down, she slipped, dropping the bottle as she reached to break her fall. She landed with a heavy thump, winded. The bottle rolled. She dived for it, but her questing hand merely gave it a shove towards a sheer drop.

It disappeared from view, and a few seconds later she heard it smash onto the stones below.

"Shit!" She lay there panting, heart hammering from her near miss. A foot to the left and she'd have gone over, too. She might have been down there for days or weeks before anyone found her, washed into one of the caves, rotting, crabs taking their fill. Or if the tide dragged her out into the sea, she might have never been found at all.

Debbie climbed down. Each footfall, every hand grip on the cliff's face, reminded her of coming here with Marc. It was a scramble more than a climb, but still treacherous enough to kill herself if she missed a handhold or her feet slipped on loose soil. So she took her time, despite how keen she was to reach the beach. She made sure she got there in one piece. More and more, she was starting to believe she would learn something down there, and that her life might begin again.

When her feet met pebbles at last, she breathed a deep sigh of relief.

The smashed milk bottle was still there. But the rolled message inside was gone, nowhere to be seen. She suddenly felt a pressing need to read it, berating herself for being so hesitant before. She dashed back and forth searching for it, testing which way the breeze was blowing to see where it might have been carried. But there was no telling. The Cove was small, cliffs surrounding it on three sides, sea on the fourth.

The paper could have been anywhere.

She eyed the caves. The smaller ones were piled with seaweed and sea-smoothed timber. The larger yawned further up the small beach, sunlight revealing wet walls and a dripping ceiling, and making the shadows further in deeper, almost solid.

We loved there, she thought, and the memories were rich and precious.

"I'm here!" she called. Her voice was dull, the cliffs offering no echoes. Perhaps her shout travelled further into the cave. Perhaps somewhere in there, deeper down, their cries of passion still pulsed.

Debbie walked back and forth across the beach, looking for the scrap of paper from inside the smashed bottle. The shattered glass remained, the vessel's message still unread. She lost track of time. The sea's sounds were amplified here by the Cove, hush and roar, hush and roar, and her feet passing over pebbles added to the ocean's song.

She sat on the stones and stared out, realising that the tide was coming in quickly now. But she didn't mind. She could reach the cliff in a few seconds and be climbing, back on the path high above in five or ten minutes. And she could not simply leave. Not after being drawn here, and not before reading that last message.

"Oh please, Marc," she said, hopeless, lost. No one, nothing replied.

Hush . . . roar. Hush . . . roar.

The tinkle of glass on glass. Bottles, dozens of them, were floating in the surf, clinking into each other with every watery shrug.

Debbie stood and waded out, reaching for a bottle. It bobbed just out of reach.

Another came close, and she went deeper. Up to her thighs now, her shorts wet, she leaned forward and clutched at the bottle as it floated nearer.

It sank out of sight.

She frowned. *Being teased.* She took one step back.

The wave came from nowhere, forming out of the surf and powering towards her, knocking her over, crushing her down against the beach, the rocks. Breathless, she tried to gasp in air but sucked in water instead. The salty tang burned her throat. She gagged, vomited, thrashing as the wave dragged her back out.

Managing to find one breath, she screamed long and loud, her voice instantly smothered by the next huge wave. She was bashed down against the beach, winded. She rolled, grasping for something solid but finding only water. Around her in the tumult, bottles clashed and broke, spilling their secrets to the ocean forever.

She wondered what had been written on that final note. Perhaps it had been a warning.

The more Debbie struggled, the further out she was being pulled, violent seas spinning and swirling. She sucked in another chestful of water, and for an instant she thought it might take her closer to Marc.

But there was nothing of Marc here. There never had been. No voices in the waves, no warm touch, only false messages of hope. He was one of the ocean's lost souls.

Debbie joined him.

INTO THE DEATH ZONE

I'd been one of the first to volunteer, so as I dragged the corpse down from the death zone towards Everest Base Camp, I could hardly complain. This was an adventure. This was something I'd be able to tell my kids and grandkids about. This would be written about in the press, a film crew was interviewing everyone, and a special team were examining each body we managed to retrieve, gathering personal effects and doing their best to contact any next of kin.

This was important, and I should have been *enjoying* it.

But the dead were talking to me.

At first, it might have been the wind playing around my frozen ears, or ice crackling in my hair. Or maybe it was my breath freezing and dropping into the snow, crystals of unuttered fears. But then I heard my name.

Richard.

I didn't tell anyone. In such conditions, you can hardly admit to something like that. But looking around the camp that evening, I could see at least three others who seemed quiet and withdrawn, their eyes distant. I wanted to talk to one of them. But evening came, and with it exhaustion.

We all retired early to our tents. The last thing I saw outside was the glaring red bulk of the tent where they kept the corpses.

There were varying accounts of how many people had died on Everest and been left frozen to the mountain's skin, fixed there like dead parasites. Before I volunteered to help retrieve some of them, I'd always wondered at the teams who could leave their dead behind. *It can't be that hard*, I'd thought. But then the mountain had clasped me in its teeth, and I'd come to understand.

There is no normality in places like this. I was in the wild, at the very edge of survivability. This was a place of extremes, where a sprained ankle or a stomach bug could mean a slow, cold, lonely death. I'd heard many stories of climbers leaving wounded companions behind, vowing to return but sometimes unable to save even their own lives. And I imagined that their empty promises of sending help were lost amidst Everest's storms, forever echoing around the mountain. It gave the wind a haunting lilt.

Perhaps it was one of those whispers I had heard.

The last day we went up, I travelled with sixteen other climbers. We'd come to know each other quite well during the seven days we had been working, and it would be a sad final journey off the mountain and away to our separate corners of the globe. It was a strange endurance challenge—most people ran marathons across the Sahara, or cycled across Australia—but we'd all wanted to feel that we were making a difference.

Nineteen frozen corpses in the red tent paid testament to that. I'd already vowed that I would visit them one more time before leaving, though such snooping was strictly forbidden.

We found the body of a German woman that afternoon, frozen into a small cave in the rock face just where several expeditions had marked on their climbing maps. The researchers at Base Camp thought she had been there for at least thirty years, so contacting her relatives would likely be a time-consuming effort. Something for them to do after I was back at home, running the hills of South Wales and remembering my great adventure. Perhaps one day I would even—

Richard.

I looked around at the other climbers. The body was close behind me, bound in canvas now and being towed by two American men. They were quiet and respectful, and one of them returned my haunted gaze.

I went to ask if he'd heard anything, but a gust of wind stole my words before I even spoke, and a haze of snowflakes blurred my surroundings.

The storm came in quickly, and because we'd not anticipated it, getting down safely became a real challenge. I concentrated hard, sweat warming and then cooling my skin inside my layers, my backpack frozen to my coat, ice pick swinging and spiked boots stamping at the ice.

Richard.

I looked left and right, but there was only the wind. It spoke again. I could not decipher what it said. All the way down to Base Camp through that long afternoon, through all the effort and the slips and stumbles that could have led to injury and death, the wind whispered to me.

There was no way to ask anyone else what they were hearing. And by the time we reached camp and collapsed into our tents, I no longer wished to know.

Sleep came and took me away, and the frozen German woman haunted my dreams with her half-open eyes.

Next morning when I woke, my kit had been packed and stacked outside my tent. The realisation that I was leaving caused a brief panic in me, and I had crazy ideas about fleeing the camp and climbing on my own, going as high as I could until the freezing wind and snow ensured that I would remain forever.

But I quickly gathered myself. My companions were sitting around the fire pit, hands wrapped around mugs, staring into the flames. Some of them spoke softly, others seemed silent. Everyone was feeling the pull of the mountain much more now that we had to leave.

I took a step towards them, then quickly changed direction. Head down, as if not seeing them meant that they would not see me, I marched across to the closed red tent and ducked inside.

The first thing that struck me was the smell. This was not decay, or age, but the muggy, warm odour of climbing clothes and sweat-soaked gear that I'd become used to since hiking into the Himalayas. Not unpleasant, I found it a compellingly personal smell. It was honest and human—the bare scent of extreme effort and the will to survive.

I smiled and went to speak to whoever else had come into the corpse tent. Then I realised that no one had.

The first man who turned his head was a sherpa who had been lost on the higher slopes eighteen years before. I could hear the crick of his neck, and his skin had turned leathery and smooth, like a china doll's. His eyes were withered, too small for their sockets. He smiled, and I could not understand what he said.

Others turned to look at me. One retained very little skin on his or her skull, and I was not sure whether they were smiling. Another was swollen within her bright red coat, the exposed skin of her face black and brittle. They looked at me and welcomed me in. A man raised one hand offering me something.

I stepped forward to find out what. I was not afraid.

His had been a more recent tragedy. Part of an Indian expedition, he had died less than twenty years ago, and his eyes seemed to retain some of their shine. I smiled, and he lifted my hand, turning it over so that I could see the waxy effect of my flesh, and the blackened stumps of frostbitten fingers.

From outside I heard the faint sound of crying. But outside the tent was now somewhere else.

The dead spoke, and though I could still not understand, I knew that they sounded lost. Perhaps that was the true language of the dead.

I sat with them, and the mountain breathed my name one last time.

EMERGENCE

Sometimes it's turning left or right that changes your life. Sometimes it's staring straight ahead, not paying attention to what's around you in case it's dangerous, or unpleasant, or something you wouldn't want to go to sleep that night remembering. On occasion closing your eyes and just standing still will alter everything, because as the world parts and flows around you, you cannot help but feel its tides.

Sometimes, it's recognising that a place you once thought of as normal really, really isn't.

That was why I went closer to the tunnel. I'm naturally curious, and hidden places fascinate me as much as paths that lead away from the beaten track. I like to explore. I don't know why it was that particular day and hour, but something about it drew me when I passed. It could be that I glimpsed the skull from the corner of my eye. Maybe it was the smell.

I'd climbed this steep path and run back down it thirty or forty times. It was a favourite run of mine, starting with a solid, unrelenting thousand-foot climb from the small car park to the top of the mountain, then a good trail run around the summit until I descended back down to the car. I'd cover seven or eight miles and spend two hours on my own, just me and the wild and the breeze, the views and the sheep, the sense that I was alone in a wilderness only barely touched by humankind. It was glorious.

Halfway down the heavily wooded lower portion of the slope, I skidded to a stop and stood staring at the tunnel mouth. I was panting, sweating, and I couldn't quite explain the draw it had over me. I'd glanced at it a dozen times before but never gone closer than this. It was little more than an arch of rough brickwork, partly broken away by years of plant growth and frost damage, half-buried by leaf falls and tumbled tree branches, and enclosing a half-moon of deep darkness that seemed to lead nowhere. I'd often wondered why it was there and who had built it. I assumed it was the remains of an old drainage culvert constructed by some farmer or land owner long ago. The hillsides were scattered with such remnants, evidence of past labours that seemed to serve little or no purpose. It was something else that attracted me to places like this.

I climbed the small bank and moved closer. The darkness inside didn't feel intimidating, I wasn't afraid, but it was deep and heavy, like a weight luring me down. In the shadow of the brick overhang was a skull, picked clean by birds and insects. It sat on a carpet of old leaves and twigs. Scattered around were smaller bones, the shattered remains of whatever creature had come there to die. A sheep, probably. I'd seen them before, corpses taken apart amongst the heathers and ferns of the wild hillsides. The skull was smallish, and there were scraps of wool snagged on brambles and rolled into dirty clumps. A lamb, then. I wondered what had killed the poor creature.

I edged closer and saw more of the tunnel mouth. It was strange seeing such skilled brickwork in this wild place, and I tried to imagine the people who had worked there. It must have been an effort lugging bricks and mortar up the steep slope, and the purposes of the tunnel still eluded me. It was set deep into a steep bank, trees growing above it. I could see heavy roots dangling down inside, and dislodged bricks littered the ground.

The entrance was half-buried by years of leaf falls, much of it turned to mulch and providing home to ferns and a bramble bush on one side.

I dug into the hip pocket of my rucksack and pulled out my head torch. The batteries were new, but I paused just for a second before turning it on, wondering how long it had been since the tunnel's interior had been touched by light.

I looked down at the skull close to my left knee. "So what were you doing here?" I asked. For a second afterwards, the silence was loaded. I laughed and turned on the torch.

It revealed no surprises inside. The curved ceiling sloped down, as did the floor, the tunnel burrowing gently beneath the bank. There were fallen bricks, plants, dead leaves, a few pieces of lonely litter either dropped there by snacking hikers or blown by the wind. I played the light around, crouching in an effort to see further. I already knew I was going to venture inside.

When I was a kid, myself and some friends found the remains of an old air raid shelter close to some allotments, left over from when a row of houses had been demolished. We'd all got cuts and bruises from going down there, and Gavin had ended up in hospital having a gashed thigh sewn up. But we'd all come out with something, too. I still had the old gas mask I'd found in its cloth bag, tucked away in the attic at home where plenty of old memories withered and faded away.

Faded until something like this brought them crashing back again.

I remembered Jimmy's taunting when the three of us were egging each other on, all afraid, all trying to be brave enough to go first. Gavin had been the brash one, but his fear of the dark had made itself apparent. We'd gone exploring down there three times before Gavin slashed his leg open on a ragged shard of metal protruding from the old brick wall. They were good times. I hadn't seen either of them in over fifteen years.

"Not worth it," I said, glancing down at the sheep's skull one more time. It grinned up at me. Maybe I'd seen this creature alive on an earlier run that year. A memory of me might once have resided within its now-empty cranium.

I slipped the head torch around my head to free up both hands, then slipped feet-first into the low tunnel.

Enveloped by the tunnel's darkness, everything felt very different. The smells of the hillside changed, becoming wet and dank, the scent of old things and decay. As I slid down the gentle slope, my boots dislodged clumps of mud and rocks, and the rich fug of darkness was released to rise around me. The cool, wet ground soaked through my long-sleeved tee shirt, and my shorts were soon heavy with mud.

I shone the torch all around, moving slowly, checking the tunnel structure above and around me, and the floor ahead. I probed with my boot, digging at the ground in case any holes had been covered over with detritus. Fall in, break a bone, shatter my torch, and over time my bones would join those of the dead sheep guarding the entrance.

Soon the tunnel levelled and the ceiling grew a little higher. The floor was comprised of damp, hard silt rather than leaves and loose soil, and I guessed I was far enough in so that leaves were not blown this deep.

I crawled on. It would have been easy to lose track of time down there. I checked my watch and realised it was still ticking along recording my run, although it had lost satellite reception so the GPS would no longer be working. I paused it and switched it back to showing the time. 11:18. I'd been in the tunnel for maybe five minutes.

It felt longer.

I should turn around and go back, I thought. *There's nothing down here. It's just an old drainage tunnel, or something. Goes nowhere. I should go back.*

But I didn't, because that old curiosity drew me on. Though there was still a vague light behind me from the entrance, my main source of illumination was now the head torch, and I played it around as I continued to crawl. The walls were wet and slick with moss, the ceiling broken here and there where tree roots had grown through. They hung like pale, fleshy decorations. I had to push some of them aside and they trailed cool fingers across my skin.

The tunnel seemed to be growing wider and deeper. I crawled on hands and knees, careful where I placed my hands, watching every move. Glancing left and right, I saw hollows in the vaulted walls that might once have led elsewhere, but each one was blocked from a cave-in, bricks and soil forming solid barriers.

This tunnel will cave in one day, I thought. I was moving deeper on trust, hoping that my being there didn't cause a fault, a tumble, a roar of old frost-shattered bricks, soil and rock thumping down from above to trap me there forever. Jayne knew where I'd gone, but there was no phone or GPS reception this deep. If a search party did come looking and eventually found me, it would likely be way too late.

The danger was something of a thrill.

Next time I glanced at my watch, twenty minutes had passed. I paused at that, blinking, staring at the illuminated digital time blinking back at me. It hadn't felt like that long at all, but I couldn't doubt what I saw. I'd reached a place in the tunnel where the walls were slick and wet, the floor increasingly boggy, and the roots protruding through the joints between bricks in the ceiling were pale and fine, hanging still like an upside-down forest. Some of them snapped as I brushed by, as if dead and petrified. Others caressed the back of my head and neck.

"Time to turn around," I whispered. My words carried, and as I glanced ahead—imagining my voice winging its way deeper, into a darkness that might not have heard a human voice since this place was built—I saw the faint glow of daylight.

Excitement took me once again. The idea of seeing where this tunnel ended gripped me, and I felt like a true explorer. Maybe I'd emerge wet and muddied, and surprise someone looking into the far entrance and wondering where it went.

I scrambled onwards, and this lowest part of the tunnel was also the wettest. I slopped through mud, shaking my hands and spattering it up the walls. It was thick, black, and it smelled of for-gotten places and age. I hurried on towards the glow, and soon the ground sloped up enough for me to see daylight.

Minutes later I approached the opposite end of the tunnel. I could see that it was somewhere still within the woods, and for a moment I was disappointed. I'd imagined emerging into an old tumbled building, or perhaps onto part of the barren hillside where I had never been. In truth, it was probably only a hundred feet from where I'd gone underground.

As the daylight grew stronger, so I anticipated its touch even more. I had no wish to go back into that gloom. There was nothing down there to concern me, but something about the darkness I was leaving behind started to repulse me, urging me onwards into the light.

Close to the entrance I saw the pale gleam of a skull.

I frowned. I was convinced that I'd crawled into the tunnel at one end and out of the other. I moved closer, and as the sun touched my skin I realised that it was the same lamb's skull.

Weird.

The sun felt good, dappling down through the tree canopy to speckle my arms and face. I stood and stretched, shaking mud from my hands, brushing it from my knees and bare legs, hearing the slosh of water in my backpack's water bladder. I hadn't taken a single drink while I'd been underground, and now thirst burnt in with a vengeance across my throat and tongue.

I sucked at the nozzle. The water was warm but welcome. I blinked and sighed, then looked up.

The sky past the trees was a blazing blue, scorched by sunlight. Wispy clouds streaked the heavens high above. Closer, the trees swayed in a gentle breeze, leaning back and forth as if whispering to one another about me. I looked up as they looked down.

I shivered. It was an unsettling thought.

Dropping back onto the path leading down through the woods to the road, I pushed through a spread of nettles. They kissed against my bare legs and fire tingled there, spiky, almost pleasant in its low burn. I didn't recall the nettles being there a couple of hours before when I'd climbed up towards the summit. Their leaves were speckled with some sort of fungus, making them hang heavy and low. I crouched down to look. Maybe being underground in the dark had made me so much more receptive to detail.

The fungus was pale grey in colour, each growth the thickness of a matchstick and just a few millimetres long, topped with a darker, globular speck. There were perhaps a hundred stems on each leaf, all of them curved and pointed in the same direction like miniature soldiers stood to attention. Although the nettles were still a rich, healthy green, I couldn't help thinking that the fungal growths were parasitic.

Energised by my unexpected mini-adventure, I scanned the ground ahead as I started running downhill, dodging rocks, leaping down some of the steps that had been built into the path by local scouts a few years before. I always enjoyed running downhill, even though I was heading towards fifty and becoming more concerned about my knees. I needed to look after my joints if I was going to continue doing what I loved into my old age. But every time I thought that, I countered with, *But this* is *looking after myself.*

Something about my visit down into the tunnel niggled at me, like a whisper behind a door I couldn't quite make out. It worried and scratched, and as I glanced around I felt unsettled in this, one of my favourite places, for the very first time.

The path followed a wide gulley carved into the mountainside over millennia by a stream. There were a few small waterfalls along its course, and now I noticed that the pool at the base of one was dammed with several fallen trees and debris accumulated against their trunks and branches. It formed an expanded lake where water gathered before slinking its way past or through the blockage. I briefly considered stripping off and taking a dip. The water looked cool and inviting.

It also looked dangerous.

I paused and frowned, catching my breath and trying to open the door on those niggles and whispers. Being belowground had unsettled me more than I'd believed, and I'd brought that feeling up with me, carrying it down towards the road, car park, and the car where a fresh change of clothes and a flask of coffee awaited.

I haven't seen this pool before, I thought. I had no recollection of the falls being dammed like this, but then I always climbed the hill with my head down, checking the uneven path for trip hazards, pushing down on my knees so that I could achieve the best climb possible. My record so far was a little under half an hour. Maybe today I'd have broken it.

I glanced at my watch. It was still searching for a satellite signal.

Passing the pool I carried on, and it was only as I approached the bottom of the winding path that I acknowledged what was worrying at me. The door opened and the truth roared in.

Everything was different. Only slightly, but there was a rough edge to things, like a sheen of wilderness smothering my surroundings.

The trees above me were heavier with leaves. A few had fallen, with several lying across the path and forcing me to squeeze underneath or climb over them. They had not been there before my ascent, and I could tell from one of their exposed root balls—the hole filled with a swathe of nettles, no bare soil showing, and the cracked timber pale from weathering—that it had not happened recently.

The path emerged onto a gravelled area beside the canal, the wide driveway and parking area attached to a low wooden house. There was a narrow tunnel leading beneath the canal and down to the car park beyond, but this side was a private residence, the public footpath running across the gravel to the tunnel. I'd seen the elderly owners of the house several times, and they always spared a wave or nod for those passing across their land to or from the steep path up the mountain.

The gravel was churned, and in places it was overgrown with weeds. The house looked abandoned, with smashed windows and paint flaking from its previously pristine woodwork. A Range Rover rested on flat tyres beside the house, its windows misted with a hazing layer of moss on the insides.

"What the hell?"

I stopped and looked around. Birds flitted from branch to branch, a few of them landing in the long grass of the canal's towpath on the opposite bank. The towpath was overgrown. I could just make out a bike leaning against a wall. Plant tendrils had curled around its spokes and uprights.

"Hello?" I called. Some birds took flight at my shout, but they quickly landed again and started singing as if I wasn't there. I frowned and shook my head. Maybe I was dehydrated. I took a drink and suddenly the taste of my water had changed, from warm but clean to stale and dirty, as if I was sucking up water from the canal.

This was all wrong. There was so much I hadn't noticed on the way up the mountain, so much that I'd been certain of but which now was being proved less certain. When had the old couple moved out of their home and left it to decay? Why leave their vehicle behind?

I took a few steps towards the tunnel beneath the canal, and paused.

It had caved in. The steps down to it were piled with tumbled stones, and the tunnel itself was filled with dried mud and rocks, blocking it completely. If I hadn't known it was there, it would not have been at all obvious.

"That's just not right," I said. "I came up through there two hours ago. Just a couple of hours." I checked my watch. It was still searching for a satellite signal. *Not right.* "Hello?" I shouted louder, the sound of my voice the only thing pinning me to the world. Birds took flight again, but I didn't seem to trouble them unduly. If I remained silent, if I did not interact with the world, I might as well not be there at all.

The canal bridge was fenced off, meant for exclusive use by the owners of the dilapidated house and enclosed within their garden and land. The tunnel was the public access, but now that it was blocked there was no other way across the canal. I skirted around the garden, pushing through waist-high undergrowth until I passed the garden area and stood close to the canal.

The water level was vastly reduced. *That's what's happened*, I thought. *Maybe there's been a breach and everything has changed.* But a breach in the canal wouldn't have changed so much in such a short time.

And this damage had been wrought a long, long time ago. There were still pools of water across the canal's bed, but most of it had gone, perhaps flowing downhill from the fracture that had filled the tunnel. The pools remaining looked surprisingly clear, reflecting the blue sky and fluffy clouds as if presenting a memory of better times. Weeds grew across the rest of the canal's uneven, dried-silt bed.

I climbed down, walked across, and scrambled out onto the towpath. It was deep with knee-high weeds.

It was impossible, yet the evidence was there before my eyes. *Everything has changed.*

I made my way to the steps that led down to where the tunnel emerged on the other side, at the top of the gentle slope that led down to the car park where I'd left my car. I needed to be there. I had to reach the comfortable Mazda, to see whether it was new and clean from the polish I'd given it last weekend, or old and rusting, wheels flat, windows grimy, metalwork fading from so long sitting unused and exposed to the harsh sunlight.

While I'd been down in the tunnel the world, and time, had moved on. All I could hear was the chatter of birds and the conspiratorial whispering of the trees as they observed my growing panic, laughing amongst themselves.

I climbed down the steps and saw that much of the landscape on this side of the canal had changed. The breach must have caused the cave-in, and tens of thousands of gallons of water had cascaded down the slope, carrying silt and rocks with it and washing away the gravelled road, hedges, and many tonnes of soil. The resulting slick had spread wide, and in the time since the breach had provided fertile ground for new plant growth. I ran through the low shrubs and long grasses, hearing creatures scurrying from my path, kicking my way from the canal and down what was left of the path to the car park. I heard no traffic. I smelled no fumes, and I realised just how clear and clean the air seemed, untainted by humankind.

I'm still underground, I thought. *I fell and banged my head. I'm semi-conscious in that tunnel, and unless I wake and move I'll be there until dusk, and then I might never find my way out.*

The grasses felt cool and sharp against my bare legs. Seeds carried on the air tickled my face. Sweat ran down my back. Everything looked lush and rich, as if the plants were relishing this new-found freedom. And yet many plants were also home to that strange fungus I'd seen on the nettles back up the slope. It provided a haze across everything that seemed to knock my vision out of focus.

If I was still beneath the ground, my imagination was running riot.

I reached the road and ran straight across. The buildings to my right were familiar, but I barely glanced at them. I knew what I would see.

I knew because I could see my car. It might have been there forever.

I ran the three miles home. It was the strangest journey of my life, but running gave me the rhythm, pace and room to try and rationalise what was happening. It didn't work, but just as concentrating on my breathing and footfalls helped occupy my mind, the attempt to make sense of what I was seeing, hearing and smelling diluted some of the terror that was settling over me.

I'd tried starting the car, of course, but the battery was flat. It was strange sticking the clean, shiny key into a vehicle so obviously degraded by time.

I was worried about Jayne. If everyone and everything had gone, then what about her? Where was she? *On the other side of the tunnel,* I thought, but I tried to silence that idea.

I lived three miles from the bottom of the hill. Usually I would have run that distance in a little under half an hour, but today I was faster. Everything I saw gave me energy, fear driving my legs and muscles.

The town was empty of people, but far from dead. By the Indian restaurant where we had celebrated our tenth anniversary I saw a small herd of deer, milling in the overgrown car park, wary as they watched me pass. A pack of half a dozen feral dogs stalked from an alley a few minutes later, and the hairs on the back of my neck bristled as they growled. I threw stones at them and they stalked away. Squirrels sat on rooftops and window ledges, rabbits frolicked across roads where weeds grew through cracked tarmac, and what might have been a big cat flowed through the shadows beneath a bridge. Nature had made this place of people its own now that the people were gone.

If I wasn't so terrified, so confused and frightened, it might have been beautiful.

Just past an old car showroom, now displaying a score of vehicles resting on flat tyres and with rust eating at bodywork, I drew level with the local park. It had once contained a playing field, a band-stand, and a play area for children, but now all that was gone. Close to the park gates and fence were three JCBs, motionless and dead. Beyond them, the park had been excavated in several long, wide strips. Some of these massive trenches were partly filled in, but most remained open to view. One was filled with rough timber coffins, piled in without any real care, like a tumble of giant Jenga blocks. The next trench along was filled with skeletons. They had run out of time to box up the dead.

I stopped and leaned against the cast iron fence at the park's boundary. I felt a deep, cool shock settling in me, a sickness of the soul as similar images from history sprung to mind. But these were no murder pits. Piled beside one trench were hundreds of simple wooden crosses, unplanted. I wondered if each of them bore a name, and my eyes were drawn back to the countless skeletons settled in the open excavation, staring at the sky with hollow eyes as they waited forever to be hidden away from this cruel, dead world.

I tore myself away from the dreadful sight and moved on. I saw no other mass burials, but the memory remained with me, an awful visual echo to everything else I witnessed.

When I reached my house there were no surprises to be found. It was the same as everywhere else. My home, the place where I lived and loved and felt safe, had fallen into ruin.

Seeing a place I knew so well in such a state was shattering, hitting home much harder than anything else I had seen. The house name Jayne and I had screwed to the front wall together was broken in two, half of it fallen away. She'd cut her thumb while we were fixing the plaque to the brickwork, and I'd put it in my mouth to ease her pain. The garish red paintwork she had chosen for the front door was faded, much of it peeled away to the bare wood beneath. The hawthorn tree we had planted in the front garden, and which had become so much work to keep under control, had grown wild, its spiked branches reaching forward for the street and back towards the house as if to embrace the place for itself. I remembered clipping those branches one by one, while Jayne snipped them small enough to feed carefully into the garden waste bags. We'd both suffered pricks and wounds that day. She'd laughed at my pin-cushion hand that evening, and I'd rolled her onto the sofa and silenced her with a kiss.

I sobbed, standing in the street and staring at the place I had once called home.

I'd only left three hours earlier.

"Somebody!" I shouted. "Jayne! Anybody!" My cries echoed from buildings close by, but were soon swallowed by the wild trees and shrubs along our street. I reckoned that within another ten years much of this place would resemble an infant forest. Twenty years after that, new trees would be higher than the house roofs. And a century later, the houses would be little more than piles of rubble subsumed by undergrowth, hugged to the land's embrace by brambly limbs.

I shouted again, the only reply my despairing and muffled cry echoing back at me. I took a step towards the house. It was desolate, silent and dead, and I dreaded what I might find inside. Nothing would be bad. The bones of my wife would be so much worse.

And then, as I pushed past the rotten front fence and the clasping plants that held it upright, movement. A shadow shifted in one of my home's upper windows. Sunlight glinted from fractured glass. A pale face appeared at the window, still too far inside to make out properly, but definitely there.

Jayne, I thought, and I took a step forward.

But this was not Jayne.

The face that appeared at the window was wild, heavy with beard and framed with long, straggly hair, thin and sunburned, eyes staring and mad. I felt a moment of rage at the man who had made my house his own.

Then I realised that this was the only person I had seen since leaving the tunnel, and my rage became confused. Tears came to my eyes, and I felt a pang of deep loneliness. I wanted to rush in and hug this man, speak to him, and hopefully understand that this strange situation was not merely my own personal madness. I wished it was.

"Hello!" I called. I took another step forward into the front garden, edging around the clasping thorns of the hawthorn. "What happened here? I went for a run and when I came back—"

He lifted an object and pointed it at me. I heard a low *twang*, and something sliced across my right bicep.

Shock rooted me to the spot as the man flustered with the object and raised it again. I fell to the left just as another arrow whispered by, bouncing off the road behind me. Then I stood and ran.

Another arrow struck my bare left thigh, and I felt the piercing cool kiss of the tip slicing into my skin. I yelped and reached back, but the arrow had fallen away. Its head had merely cut my flesh, and when I brought my hand up it was smeared with blood. The pain was keen and sharp, the wound superficial. It didn't seem to have affected my ability to move.

I did not stop running. I could not. I had to run as fast as I could, back across that strange town I had once known and over the drained canal, up the hillside, into the tunnel where everything had changed. There was no discernible thought process leading to this action, no consideration. It was the only thing to do, and it felt like the only way I might find my way back to normality.

From the house I had once lived in came a dreadful, guttural roar, a scream of such hopelessness that my blood ran cold and every hair on my body stood on end. I sprinted back the way I had come, fearing another arrow. The buildings around me now loomed, and every dark window or open doorway might have been the source of another deadly shot. But no more came, and it seemed that the person in my old house might have been the only one. I glanced back when I felt it safe, and for a second—just as I checked the ground ahead before twisting around to look behind me—I knew that he would be there with me, a ragged, wild shape so close behind that I could smell his breath, feel his body heat as he ran after me in complete, monstrous silence.

I was alone. I reached the bottom of the hill and retraced my steps, crossing the drained canal, climbing, arriving at last at the tunnel mouth beneath the steep bank. Panting hard, sweating, I hesitated only for a second before ducking inside. I glanced at the skull as I did so, suddenly certain that it would not be a sheep's skull at all, but a human's. Buried there at the tunnel entrance, it was one of the few things about my world that had not changed.

I moved much faster than I had the first time. The tunnel seemed smaller, the floor higher. My headtorch lit the way and I ducked my head to avoid banging it on the low ceiling.

He's behind me, I thought, *crawling, hands clawed, so quiet that my own gasps and scramblings covered his sound.* I looked back but I was alone.

Every shadow was danger. Only the small splash of light ahead offered any hope of freedom and salvation, but the sinking conviction came that I would emerge into that desolate landscape once again.

The first time I'd come in here I had somehow turned around, exiting the way I had entered even though I had continued through the tunnel towards daylight at the other end. I had no wish to do that again. Reaching into my backpack's hip pocket I pulled out the small penknife I always carried with me. Jayne had given it to me for my eighteenth birthday, our first year together.

I opened the blade and crawled to the tunnel wall, ready to carve in a simple arrow to show me the direction I was taking. When I aimed my headtorch at the old brickwork, at first I thought it was laced with a network of thin white strands, roots from one of the trees growing above. Then I saw the arrows.

There must have been fifty of them, maybe more, carved into the brickwork and all pointing in the same direction. A few of them were recent, their edges sharp and clear. Others appeared older, with moss dulling their clarity. Some were faded almost to nothing.

I stopped, gasping as I tried to catch my breath. *Not my arrows*, I thought, because they could not have been, I'd only been inside this tunnel once before and I hadn't taken out my penknife.

I carved in a new arrow nonetheless, finding a bare spread of pitted brick and leaving my mark. I tried not to touch any of the others as I worked. Touching might link me to them, draw me in and make me part of the experience that had etched them there. All I wanted now was to find my way home.

It was like waking from a bad dream.

When I emerged from the tunnel at the same location where I'd entered—even though I *knew* I had not turned around down there—I could sense that everything had changed once again. Birds were singing a more familiar song. The light was softer and less threatening. Trees no longer whispered in the breeze. The skull close to the tunnel entrance was more exposed, and when I ran downhill and approached the canal, the old man who lived in the house there gave me a gruff nod.

I drove home faster than I should have, to find a jug of coffee on the warmer and Jayne in the shower. I stripped and got into the shower with her, and she reached for me as I started to cry, shivering uncontrollably even though she turned up the heat and hugged me to her, confused at my reaction and almost crying herself. I welcomed her touch and smell. I never wanted to let go.

By the time we went to one of our favourite riverside pubs for lunch, the things I had seen and experienced were starting to feel like a dream. The memories were woolly, although they did not fade. I drove so that Jayne could drink, but the real reason was that I did not want to muddy my thoughts and allow back in the fears and confusion.

Later, with Jayne snoring softly in bed beside me, moonlight passed through the curtains and cast uneasy patterns across the ceiling, shapes in which I perceived uncertain truths. But they were only shapes in my imagination, it was only moonlight, and I eased into a comfortable sleep listening to my wife's breathing and feeling the weight of night as a comfort rather than a threat.

Upon waking, the previous day's events had faded even more into that place where bad dreams inevitably dissolve.

Two days later I started climbing the hill to fill in the tunnel. Jayne knew that something had changed within me on that early morning run, and she did her best to draw it out and help me move on. But she also acknowledged my need to return on my own. The first time, I sat twenty feet from the tunnel and just stared, tempting the darkness to reveal to me what had happened. *Something in there*, I thought, and I imagined old discarded cannisters of degraded gas, natural fumes from an unknown cavern system, tainted water dripping from the tunnel ceiling and entering my mouth. Something had taken me and edged me towards a terrifying madness, holding me over the edge of a terrible, deep ravine. Only my determination had prevented me from falling.

That first day I kicked the sheep's skull into the tunnel and piled a few rocks into the entrance, sweating and panting with the effort. When a family climbing up for a walk on the mountain gave me a strange look, I paused in my efforts and smiled back. I offered no explanation. There was none that made any sense.

From then on I returned in the early mornings, telling Jayne that I was going for a run up and around my familiar route. I halted every time at the tunnel, and after five days I'd piled in enough scattered rocks and fallen bricks to clog the entrance. On day six I used a heavy block to loosen more bricks, encouraging heavy falls of damp dirt from the banking above the tunnel, pushing it into hollows to bind and seal, testing the new barrier by standing and jumping on it.

It still was not enough. At night the bad dreams lurked, and sometimes they came fully-fledged, pursuing me like that mad, raving shape from my own ruined house as I thrashed and groaned myself awake and submitted to Jayne's concerned hugs. She suggested I see someone. I agreed. I never kept the appointments, instead climbing the slope with bags of sand and cement in my rucksack. I buried them close to the tunnel entrance, and when there were enough I dug them up again, mixed the concrete, and probed it deep between rocks and bricks, filling hollows and smearing it across the filled-in tunnel entrance until I could see no holes at all leading inside.

Once dried, I covered the rough structure with mud and leaves and fallen branches. I planted several fast-growing shrubs around the area. By the time winter came, all evidence of the tunnel entrance was gone. Some people might have remembered it being there, but soon they would forget.

Sometimes I had nightmares about being buried alive, following a thousand arrows to an entrance that no longer existed. Often I believed that my waking life was the dream, and the tunnel was my dark, damp reality.

Jayne became tired of my nightmares. She found out that I had never gone to any appointments with doctor or therapist. She left, accusing me of not doing anything to help myself.

In truth, I'd done everything I possibly could.

I've become one of *those* people. You know the type. People talk about me behind my back, sometimes in pity, more often with humour. Teenagers giggle and whisper when they see me in the street, or sometimes shout and mock. Part of me wishes it was all back to as it was before, but another part of me knows that I'm doing the right thing. This isn't madness. I left madness down there in the tunnel, scratched on the wall and shut away with tons of stones and bricks, soil and cement. This is the exact opposite of madness. This is clarity. This is being prepared.

People have started to die. I'd been expecting it, and I've always been certain of who would go first—the closest person to me, though that closeness has changed. At least Jayne welcomed me to her bedside as she was ailing, and when I told her I loved her she smiled and said she loved me too. That means an awful lot and such knowledge will, I hope, give me courage in the times to come.

Times of plague and death, confusion and chaos. Times of silence. Times of decay.

I still go running every day, sometimes covering upwards of twenty miles. I pass by the hidden tunnel mouth occasionally, but I have no worries about anyone emerging from there. It's solidly plugged. Besides, there are countless other places. Manholes and culverts, drains and caverns, riverbank hollows and old, forgotten tunnels under churches and castles, car parks and hotels.

I'm collecting as many weapons as I can find. I target houses where people have died, and it's easy because the authorities have started painting these places with red circles. So far I have seven bows, three crossbows, and two shotguns. Hardly a stockpile, but it will only be one man, and it will only take one shot.

I brought something back with me through that tunnel. A disease that is making this world its own, and which does not touch me. Thinking about why that is will send me mad, because I've heard no evidence of anyone else being immune. I'm cursed with a terrible purpose. I saw evidence of the contagion on the plants over there, the strange fungal-like growths, and perhaps I should have thought more of it when I found the empty town, the dilapidation, the mass graves. But I'm not in the business of regret.

Today, the traumatised authorities started digging a huge trench in the local park.

One day soon, when the world is dead and I'm one of the last left alive—perhaps the only one left—he will emerge from somewhere else and come to pay me a visit. He'll know where to come because home is an important place. It's somewhere you're meant to feel safe. Once here, there's no way I can let him return and take the infection back through to where he came from. It's a heavy responsibility, but one which I know I was destined to shoulder.

I have no idea what shooting myself will feel like.

This time I will not miss.

LAND OF MANY SEASONS

He wasn't there when I began. I wouldn't have stayed if he was. The whole point of what I do is the loneliness and solitude, the escape from my troubled existence. I hike out to these places to be alone, and sketch and paint them so that I can take them home with me. They are my escape. From the first pencil line or brush stroke, the canvas becomes a reality where I can live alone for a few hours or days, free from the real world.

The real world isn't very nice.

"Kes! Here!" My little collie scampers across the heathers and weaves through a stand of ferns, back to where I have set myself up for the day. He's a good dog. Dogs are undemanding and kind, their love a simple thing. That's why I like to bring him out here with me, because his simpleness, his dogness, doesn't taint this place.

The figure in my painting does.

Kes nuzzles against my hand. I tickle him behind the ear, and he grumbles and tilts his head in satisfaction. There's a warm breeze flowing across the hillside today, carrying scents of heather and wet mud, and the fresh, wild smells of the mysterious mountains. If it shifts ninety degrees and breathes at me across the town, I'll pick up aromas from the bakery close to the river, or the building site where they're constructing another two hundred homes. I hope that doesn't happen. This is my fourth day coming to the same spot, and I've been lucky so far—the weather has been consistent, the sky cloudy but witholding its rain, the breeze wafting in from the same direction.

The painting is progressing well. Apart from him. But right now, I'm avoiding thinking about him.

Kes growls and lopes off again, and this time I let him. I watch as he springs through the high ferns like a lamb, leaping to find his bearings, running again, leaping again. He reminds me of myself, ploughing blindly through life and coming up here, or places like this, to raise my head above water.

"Go get 'em, boy," I say under my breath. Kes barks as if he's heard me, and several startled birds take wing.

I look at my painting and consider adding the birds in, specks in the sky that might remind me of this place and time, but my attention is drawn to the figure once again.

He's little more than a few brush strokes right now. He appeared on my version of the hillside just an hour ago, and I surprised myself by painting him in. However much I stare at him, and then sit back and look across the hill, he's only there in my painting.

Maybe I saw a shape in the air? A shimmer in heat haze, or a waft of mist from the damp grass? The shadow of a red kite circling high above?

I can't fool myself. I saw nothing, yet still I felt the need to paint him into my picture.

It should not matter, and yet it does. My paintings are rarely literal representations of the world. The general lie of the land is as I view it, but the skies are inevitably more stormy and violent in shades of red shadow, the hillsides more desolate and windswept. I paint my mood and my soul onto the canvases, and sometimes I frighten myself with how I see the world.

It should not matter. But it does.

In my painting he is a long way away, but he is walking straight towards me.

Later that afternoon I come down off the mountain. The Blorenge is my favourite of the three hills surrounding Abergavenny. Although it is perhaps not the most dramatic to draw or paint—that might be the Sugarloaf, with its distinctive volcano-shaped peak, or the harsh knife-edge of the Skirrid—it is the quietest of the three. I can sometimes follow a familiar seven-mile walk across and around the mountain without encountering another soul, and sometimes when I'm up there I imagine that I am the last person on Earth, wandering with my rucksack full of art stuff and my dog, and recording the end of time for the no one who will come after me. For someone so lonely, the fantasy is strangely calming.

Kes runs ahead of me down the steep slope through the woods. There are old stone railway sleepers here, the track long since gone, the chains that hauled carts up and down the mountainside now rusted away to nothing. Perhaps their remains are close, fragile remnants buried deep.

I pass the old tunnel mouth. It's a strange structure, an arch of brickwork protruding from a steep bank with only darkness beneath its mouldy embrace. I've stopped a few times and looked inside, but Kes has always been uncertain, sometimes standing with hackles up as if sensing something in there, perhaps sensing nothing. Maybe it leads to other worlds. Maybe it leads to different versions of this one. I wish I was brave enough to venture in.

Further down the hill I start to hear distant traffic, and experience the familiar sadness that my time alone is over. I consider turning around and going back up. It's summer, warm and bright, and I know I could probably sleep on the mountainside. But it's late afternoon now, and I have no food or water left.

Kes whines softly. He's hungry, and probably eager to get home. He's not as young as he used to be.

"Okay, boy," I say, and then another voice pipes up and surprises me.

"Nice dog."

I jump.

"Sorry. Sorry." The old man is beneath the trees to my left. I've seen him before out in the hills, usually from a distance. I recognise his long grey hair and red bandana. I sometimes think he's as lonely as me, but who am I to judge? I have no right to project my problems or faults onto him. Just because he walks the same paths as me doesn't mean he's heading in the same direction.

"It's okay," I say. "I was miles away."

"Look like you've seen a ghost." He's looking at the kit I'm carrying. If I've seen him he must have seen me, but maybe he was too far away to make out what I was doing.

"Just tired," I say. "All this fresh air."

"Lovely up there," he says. "My favourite mountain."

"Mine too." Kes has trotted up to the man, confident and unconcerned, and that puts me more at ease. The dog's a good judge of character, and he can usually smell the crazy on people. The old man kneels and ruffles the back of his neck.

"You seen the Walker." Even in that simple remark I can hear the capital letter for Walker. He gives the word a peculiar weight.

"What do you mean?"

He doesn't answer at first. He looks down at the dog, and something about his manner makes me think he's sorry that he spoke.

"What Walker?"

"Oh, nothing. Silly old story. The hills are full of them."

I think about asking more, but don't. He seems like a nice old man, but I'm tired from the day's work, and I'm eager to get the painting home and set it up to dry. It's almost finished, and the more I carry it around, the longer I hold onto it, the more chance there is of causing damage.

"Nice to meet you," I say. "I think Kes has a new friend."

The old man nods and smiles, then waves as he heads past me up the hill.

"It'll be dark soon," I say.

"I like it up here in the dark," he says. "See you around, I'm sure."

I head down to the road, and cross to the small car park. Kes walks beside me, obedient as ever. I open my little car and place the painting carefully on the front seat, propped so that it will not slip or tumble on the short ride home. Kes jumps into the back and snuggles down on the seat. By the time I start the car the dog is already asleep.

I sit for a while, thinking about the old man walking up onto the mountain to meet the dusk. I wonder what else he might meet up there.

He seemed unafraid.

I do not talk to anyone else that day.

Back at home, Kes trots into the house and waits patiently in the kitchen for his tea. After feeding him I feed myself, some salad and cured meats from the fridge, followed by a whole packet of biscuits and a big mug of coffee. I stare at the painting as I eat. It's propped on a stand in the large kitchen. I've been working on it for four days and I'm starting to consider it complete, but the more I stare at it, the less it seems like a painting I would have done. The landscape is familiar, and the stormy sky giving voice and scope to my constant inner turmoil and loneliness. But there's something about the shape—cast onto canvas with a few brush strokes, shadowy and yet obvious—that speaks of familiarity.

I cover the painting before going to bed.

I wake up before the dawn, as always. Kes has crept upstairs during the night and made his home on the foot of my bed. I don't mind, and he knows that, stretching out as I stretch, crawling closer to me so I can pet him as I lie awake and watch shadows retreating across the ceiling.

Something plays at my mind as I use the bathroom and dress. A certainty that is left over from my dreams, a vaguely haunting idea that I sense plagued my sleep, but which I can no longer recall. Something to do with the Walker.

As I enter the kitchen, I know what I'm going to see. He'll be closer. He'll be a greater part of my picture, a larger part of my life.

The shape of the figure in my painting is as I left him the night before, and I breathe a sigh of relief. The idea of painting him out of the picture never even occurs to me until much later.

By the time I see the Walker again I have almost forgotten about him.

He remained with me and visible, of course. I hung the picture in the little studio I rent in town, but it never sold. No one ever commented on why they didn't like it, but I started to think perhaps they were put off by the strange smudge, the errant brush strokes that they saw as a fault or a mistake. Only I seemed to recognise him for who he was.

The next time I go up onto the Blorenge to paint, it has passed from summer into autumn. I'm wrapped up warm, and although the forecast is for a dry day, I have a rucksack containing waterproofs and wear walking boots. I've been caught out in bad weather on the hillsides before.

Kes lopes ahead of me. I decide to let him find a place for me to paint, and for an hour or so he leads the way up and across the mountain, smelling his way towards the old surface mine workings that make for such an interesting landscape. After a while I call a stop and Kes comes back to me. I give him a treat from my pocket, then look around and select somewhere to set up my kit.

The easel is steel, with spiked feet to hold it fast. The canvas I've brought today is smaller than usual. I paint standing, enjoying being able to pace back and forth to gather different angles and aspects.

I open my flask and pour a steaming coffee, then begin.

For me, painting slows things down. My life is not lived fast anyway, but I always feel that it is out of my control. Both of my parents died when I was a teen, I grew into my twenties living with an aunt, and then when I started living on my own the tides of life washed over me, always threatening to drown. I'm not self-pitying. That's just the way I am, and I sometimes welcome my loneliness rather than regret it. Without being alone, I would not be able to create the art I do, and it's the art that defines me. It pins me to the world, and when I slow the world down I start to believe I might be able to grab on and go alone for the ride.

The morning passes. I drink more coffee. The painting grows. I fill out the lie of the land, impatient to move onto the part of any painting that always excites me most—the sky.

As I start to address the sky above the slope of the land, it is marred by a silhouette I have not seen.

I pause and take a step back. I hold my breath. A bird calls somewhere, a buzzard circling high above. A rabbit rustles through undergrowth nearby, Kes chasing it, flushing it out, and I wonder if the buzzard will swoop and clasp it in its claws. I think what the world would be like if birds of prey were ten times larger, and we were their prey.

Perhaps we are all prey to something, I think, and the shape on the painting manifests as the walking man once again. He's more defined than he was before, on the painting that still hangs in my studio. There he was merely a hint, a few brush strokes. Here he is more angular, more solid. More formed.

I gasp and look past the painting towards the spread of mountainside where I have painted him, and of course there is nothing there. If there was I would no longer be alone.

"Kes!" I say. The dog perks up, head raised. "Who's that?" He looks around, darting here and there, sniffing and whining softly. Kes always likes meeting people—perhaps because he knows I'm not so keen, and he wants to guide me away from being so alone—but he sees and senses no one.

I'm not sure I do either.

I return to the painting and hover my brush over the shape in the distance. A few strokes of green and blue and the Walker will become hillside and sky once again, swept from memory with a few casual drifts of my hand, like a conductor orchestrating a sudden silence. I am a god with the power of being in my hands. It's not a feeling I like.

I leave the shape alone, but my painting is done for the day. Finding the man on my canvas has made me feel more alone than ever before. I crave the company of people, and that's a feeling I am not used to.

I pack and rush down the mountain, not afraid, but needy. Kes comes with me, and an hour later we're at the coffee shop in town. We sit outside, even though autumn's breath keeps most people behind door and glass, and after an hour watching people passing by, I see the old man walking towards us. He has his head down but is dressed as he was the last time I saw him, the bandana no longer looking out of place in the cool, breezy day. It seems that he hasn't noticed us, and I wait until he's passed us by and is walking away until I say something.

"Tell me about the Walker."

The old man pauses, and for a moment I wonder if *he* is the Walker, and if in some strange way he's down here with me, as well as up there on the mountainside. But he's shorter and squatter than the figure in my painting, more present. When he turns around I see a strange look in his eyes. Maybe it's confusion. Perhaps I've stirred him from a deep reverie, and I'm instantly sorry for calling out to him. I know what it's like not wishing to be disturbed.

"Oh, it's you," he says, and he sits across the picnic table from me as if we've sat and spoken many times before, not just bumped into each other for a brief time on a hillside months ago. He pulls his coat around him and takes some time to get comfortable, finally looking up at the sky, and at the clouds drifting by. "Coffee'd be nice," he says.

I half-stand, then pause, thinking of Kes.

"I'll look after your dog," he says. He clicks his fingers and Kes trots around to him, and the old man strokes and pets him. Kes is instantly at ease, and that puts me at ease as well.

I go inside and buy two coffees and a couple of cakes. Returning outside, I'm not surprised to see Kes lying on the bench with his head on the man's leg.

"You've seen him again," the old man says.

"Yes. Today. Or rather, no, I didn't see him. Not with my eyes."

He glances at me, one eyebrow raised. "And they call me mad."

I laugh, placing the coffees and plate on the table. He grunts his thanks.

"I painted him," I say. "Don't remember seeing him, but he's in the landscape I'm working on. It's strange. I'll show you, if you like." I reach for the folder I use to carry my canvas, and the man shakes his head and holds out one hand.

"No need," he says, a little too quickly. I get the feeling he really doesn't want to see my painting. He softens, though, and smiles. "I know what he looks like well enough. I see him too."

"You do?"

The old man nods, drinks coffee, eats cake. Kes looks up and he drops a corner of Welsh cake into the dog's mouth. "He's always up there, if you know where to look."

"Do you go looking for him?"

"God, no. I just see him now and then."

"You're talking like he's a ghost," I say, thinking, *What the hell else could he be?*

"Not sure what he is," the old man says. "I only know the story. Four decades ago, he appeared in town. Came from somewhere else, and it's said he carried trouble with him like a stain. Rumours are he was a murderer, or something worse. Sometimes a stranger attracts such stories, I suppose. Anyway, he started going up the mountain on his own. He went there more and more, loved the place, spent longer and longer walking up there. Couple of people in town still remember him, and if you buy them a drink they'll even talk to you about him. They say he wasn't happy with the way the world was going, but he was happy with things up there. That's the only place he felt alive."

I look down at my cappuccino. It's difficult meeting the old man's eye when what he says sounds so much like me.

"Anyway, one day he went up there for a walk and never came back."

"He vanished?"

"As good as. Left his clothes and belongings in the room he was renting in town. Never seen again. By most people, at least."

"So you think he died up there? You think I'm seeing his ghost?"

"Like I said, I don't know what he is. Could be that he died and he's a ghost. Or maybe he's still walking around up there."

"How could that be possible?"

The old man shrugs and smiles, as if what he's about to say is preposterous and embarrassing. He sips the rest of his coffee. "Maybe he lives somewhere up there now," he says. "There are . . . places. Old mine workings. Brick tunnels that don't seem to lead anywhere. Drainage culverts. If you get to know the mountain well enough, you soon realise you don't know it at all."

"You think he's living in a hole in the ground."

"I don't think at all. Best not to. None of my business, and he's never done me any harm. Live and let live, that's what I say."

"I say that too," I mutter, and the old man stands ready to leave. Kes lets out a little whine.

"He's just part of the mountain," he says. "Sounds to me like that's what he always wanted."

As the old man walks away I think, *Maybe that's what I want too.*

It is a mountain of many seasons, and I have painted them all but winter.

Kes likes the snow. By the time we reach the trig point on top of the mountain there is four inches, and the forecast says we might have more tomorrow. But for this afternoon the skies are clear, the sun shines, and the world is a shimmering blanket of glorious white.

This mountain has become a familiar place to me. I am known in the town for painting it, and I've sold more than twenty canvases of various sizes over the past nine months. Three still hang in my studio, unsold. Each of them has a shape, a figure, and to me the Walker is very clear. I'm starting to believe that to other people the Walker is simply a smudge on the paintings, and that most believe it to be an error on my part but are too polite to say.

I am certain he is not an error. My autumn conversation with the old man convinced me of that. I've seen the old man several times since our chat, but always at a distance across the rolling terrain of the mountainside. Once, Kes saw him and ran all the way over to him, further away from me than he has ever gone before. Another time he raised his hand and waved, and I waved back. There is something profoundly comforting about our familiarity, as if we share a wonderful secret that no one else knows.

I settle down to paint, and set against the virgin snow my skies are darker and more tumultuous than ever before. Whenever I paint angry skies, I feel myself becoming more at ease with who I am. I'm still young, still finding my hand with painting and my way in life.

It's cold, and although the sun is out the breeze drifting across the mountainside makes it feel colder. My paints are thick and sticky, and I hold the brush over my mug of coffee to soften the bristles. I don't mind my work being a tough process. I think it benefits the final product, and if anyone asks—which they often do when browsing in my studio and commenting on the wildness of my locations—I can give them a wide, deep history of how art often grows out of discomfort and difficulty.

By mid-afternoon I have the shape of the painting set, and I'm spending some time examining the skyline, seeing boiling clouds in my mind's eye, when I see the shadow on the left side of the canvas.

I gasp, almost winded with surprise. I didn't see anything, didn't do anything, and the shape has come from nowhere. It's like a shade against the snow and sky, and I step left and right to ensure I am not throwing a silhouette.

It's not me.

"It's him," I say, and my voice is captured by the breeze and taken across the mountainside. Kes's ears prick up and he turns to look up at me. "It's him," I say again, and this time I look at Kes. He trots off ahead of me, past the canvas, and he strays into the spread of mountainside where the shape has found itself. He sees and senses nothing.

This feels like an intrusion. The Walker is too close. Before, in the distance, he was like the old man, a presence I do not mind and which I actually enjoy. But this is personal space.

I pass my brush across a smear of white paint and spread it on the canvas. It's a crass, damaging application, and I can see that it has lessened the painting even though it is only just begun. The shape vanishes. What once was the outline of a human figure is now less than a shade.

My heart beats, my stomach sinks, as if I have done something bad. A flush of loss surges through me, a feeling deeper and more profound than the loneliness I grow used to. I have been painting the Walker all year, allowing him to inhabit my paintings as he comes closer, closer, and now I have shunned him.

But what if he really came that close? What if—?

Across the hillside, Kes turns back towards me and growls.

I feel a heavy presence behind me.

Brush poised, breath held, I wonder whether I should paint this moment away.

THE LONELY WOOD

"But the sensitive are always with us, and sometimes a curious streak of fancy invades an obscure corner of the very hardest head; so that no amount of rationalisation, reform, or Freudian analysis can quite annul the thrill of the chimney-corner whisper or the lonely wood."
—H. P. Lovecraft

The timing was perfect. Some might have called it divine. But as far as Guy was concerned, he was just in time for a song.

On his own in London with a couple of hours to kill between meetings, he'd headed to St Paul's Cathedral. Marie had always wanted to go, but for some reason they never had.

He hadn't been there since a primary school trip when he was ten years old, and thirty-five years later he wondered how much it had changed. In truth, not much at all. Buildings as old and grand as this wore their age as a disguise from which time slipped away, years passing in a blink, centuries in the space between breaths. It bore scars from the war, its walls were stained with decades of smog and exhaust fumes, yet it stood almost aloof amongst those far more modern structures surrounding it. It had existed before them, and it would likely persist long after they had fallen or been demolished. The cathedral was timeless.

Guy found that funny. Not humorous, but in an ironic, isn't-it-typical kind of way. He saw the building as a vast folly erected to

223

superstition and vanity. That it would outlast them all only gave its uselessness a deeper melancholy.

Yet it fascinated him, and he found the building truly beautiful. It was the same with any old building—castles, churches, old houses or hotels. They dripped with character and history, and he'd come to realise that it was the hidden things that fascinated him. St Paul's revelled in its beauty and majesty, but he knew that it had more secret places than most.

He'd toured the crypt, pausing beside Nelson's tomb, hurrying past Wellington's tomb when he'd found it surrounded by a gaggle of school children, resisting the lure of cake in the café, and upon returning to the nave he'd seen a girls' choir preparing for song. Tourists milled around, many of them listening to recorded information and looking at hand-held gadgets that told them the history of this place as they walked. Guy thought that perhaps they might enjoy it more if they experienced it for real, but he wasn't the one to tell them. Others stood staring at the incredible architecture, graceful statuary, and vivid mosaics. But he decided to join those others who had taken the time to sit and rest.

That was another strange reaction that he was comfortable with, and had never felt the need to analyse. Even as a non-believer he found such places of worship incredibly peaceful and contemplative.

A moment after he sat down, the organ breathed, and the singing began. The whisper of a dozen headsets, the mumble of feet, the swish of coats, all were swept away. Guy sat quite a distance from the choir, but he could see the conductor clearly enough, and the first few girls in line with their red gowns, flexible lamps and song sheets. His vision became focussed and narrowed upon the choir as the first sounds soared, and a thrill went through him.

The organ notes and the caress of voices filled the cathedral. Guy shivered, a tingle that rose to his scalp and down his back. Calmness descended, a type of tranquility that he was not at all used to in his busy, full life. Not since his teens had he listened to music for music's sake—it was always background to something else, whether he was writing a report, cooking, or working out. Now he could not imagine doing anything other than listen. It was beautiful. It was art splashed across the air, perfection given voice and then allowed to fade away. He mourned every note that vanished, but then revelled in the new ones that sang in afterwards.

I want to hold onto this forever, he thought. He leaned back in the chair, tilted his head back, and closed his eyes. He could not make out any words. The hymn was probably in Latin, but meaning was unimportant.

Wonderful. Beautiful.

He opened his eyes. Above him was St Paul's huge dome, the Whispering Gallery encircling it at a lower level. There were several people up there now leaning on the handrail, looking down, swallowing up the transcendent song rising to them. On the walls lower down were immense paintings or mosaics of the four disciples that had supposedly written the Gospels.

"Come on, then," Guy muttered, surprising himself. He had no wish to disturb the music, but something was settling around him. At first it was a playful notion, an idea that if he was ever to receive the touch of Christ, or to find his heart opened to the God he had never believed in, now would be the time. He'd never thought himself an on-the-fence doubter, was comfortable in his convinced unbelief. Yet he'd often had that discussion with Marie—*If God exists, why doesn't he just tap me on the shoulder and show me the smallest sign?*

"Come on, here I am," he whispered. "Do your worst. Do your best. Just do anything."

Proof denies Faith, was always her reply.

Why?

"I'm waiting."

Nothing happened. Guy chuckled. Of course not. He stared up at the amazing ceilings above him, the incredible artwork, and marvelled at the dedication and commitment of those who had created it hundreds of years before. To build this place now would be almost impossible. The cost would be into the hundreds of millions, the skills all but vanished in a time of steel-and-glass altars to commerce and excess.

And suddenly, in that place of wonder and grandiosity, he felt a flush of disgust. How many lives had been lost building this place? He doubted they were even recorded. How much money spent while the rest of London had lived in conditions of poverty, filth, and plague? The true cost of places such as this was never known. The music and singing soared, and it felt like the only pure thing. He appreciated the beauty of the architecture, but he could no longer admire it.

Guy stood, chair legs sliding against the floor. One of the choir girls glanced at him—it must have been the sudden movement, she couldn't have heard his chair move from that far away—and he tried to smile. But she had already turned back to her music sheets.

The conductor waved, body jerking like a marionette.

The organ groaned and moaned, exhalations of distress given wonder.

Guy turned his back on the choir and walked away. He headed for the front of the cathedral and the impossibly high doors which were only used when *important* people came. Not people like him. But somehow he drifted to the left, and then he found himself at the entrance to the staircase that wound its way up into St Paul's massive dome, and the famous Whispering Gallery it contained.

He started up the wide spiral stairs. The risers were low, the stairs wide, so it almost felt like he was walking on the level. Each stair was identical to the ones just gone and those ahead—smooth concrete, narrow to the left and wide to the right, a dark line drawn along the stair's edge. His blood started pumping, heart beating. But Guy was a fit man, and his level of exertion was low.

The movement seemed smooth and almost distant from him, as if it was someone else walking. The steps passed beneath him as the tower turned and he remained in the same place, pushing the stairs behind and below him with his feet, turning, moving the tower while he himself remained immovable.

Nothing can move me from here, he thought, and a man ran past him down the stairs. He wore jeans and a leather jacket and was gone in an instant, but Guy caught a glimpse of his wide eyes and slack-jawed mouth, and smelled the rank odour of sweat.

"Everything all right?" he called after the man, but the figure was already out of sight. The muttered words in French that echoed from stone walls seemed disassociated from anything, mere phantom pleas.

Guy carried on climbing, soon entering that hypnotic rhythm once more. And he heard the music again. Each pulse of its rhythmic heart seemed to match a footfall, and he found himself humming along, an inaudible vibration that seated itself in his chest and travelled out through bones and sinews, veins and ligaments, kissing his extremities. *How can I hum to music I don't know?* he wondered, but then realised that he might know it after all.

All her life, his wife had wanted to hear him sing her own song. It had never been a big thing between them—no pressure, no major disagreements—but her devout faith and his lack of it had sometimes felt like a repulsion pushing them apart. He believed that she'd felt it much more than him. Sometimes waking up in bed he'd wrapped his arm and leg around her, drawing her close, holding her there.

Thinking of Marie now almost caused him to trip. But the steps kept moving, and he felt himself rising.

Firmly though he did not believe, he couldn't help thinking of Marie still watching him from somewhere. Looking down. Being his guardian angel.

He chuckled, and even that seemed to match the music and singing he heard. *How foolish*, he thought. *She's dead, and the only person that matters now is me. She's gone, and I'm the one hanging on.* But he couldn't shake that fanciful idea. Sometimes in the dark, alone and cold in bed, tears drying on his face, he spoke to her. He supposed it was very much like praying.

Footsteps approached from above, and they were breaking the rhythm. Sometimes they hurried, sometimes they dragged, and just before he saw who made them he heard a soft impact. He continued walking, rising, and a woman appeared on the steps before him. She was holding her hands against her stomach and repeating something over and over.

Guy paused and lifted the hair hanging down over her face. She looked up at him, still speaking, her words lost in a language he could not place. She looked terrified.

"What is it?" he asked. "What's happening?"

Because something was. Something had been happening since he'd sat down and started listening to the choir. He thought of the girl who'd looked at him then looked away again as he waved, and wondered whether she'd even been there at all.

"It's . . . all . . . real," the woman said, struggling to form the unfamiliar words before muttering again in her own language. She lowered her head and kept her hands clenched to her stomach. Maybe she was hurt, but Guy could not tell. He didn't want to touch her again. Something about her terrified him.

He moved on, and soon he came to a sideways branch in the stairwell that opened out into the Whispering Gallery. There were others there, at various points around the walkway. Some sat on the stone steps, heads back and eyes closed. Others hung over the cast iron railing and looked down.

Guy reached for the railing and followed their gaze.

It was pandemonium. People, tiny people, ran back and forth across the mosaic floor of the cathedral. Some collided and fell, either getting up to continue their run, or remaining on the floor, curling up and hugging themselves into a ball. A small group of people knelt in front of the chairs and seemed to be praying. One man was splayed out with blood pooling around his head. Maybe he'd jumped.

The music and singing continued to soar.

"What's happening?" Guy whispered to himself, and a disembodied voice answered.

"This is it," the voice soothed. "This is the end. Now we all know the truth, and we can't be allowed to live." The speaker laughed. "What a load of shit!"

Guy looked directly across the wide dome at the man standing opposite, his head back as he guffawed.

"You believe a word of this?" the man asked. Guy could barely see his mouth moving from this distance, but the words were crystal clear. Even over the shouting. Even above the singing, and the laboured breaths of the organ.

"I don't know," Guy said, surprised at his doubt. "I don't even know what's happening."

"Go up," the man said. "See. See if you believe. I still . . . I . . . " Then he started walking around the gallery and his words faded away.

Guy moved to the left, heading for the route up to the next level on the dome. He ran, passing people sitting silent and still, and others who were speaking softly. Maybe they were praying, but Guy didn't stop to listen. It had always been a private act for Marie and he had respected it in others ever since.

The stairs to the next level were much narrower, stone treads worn down by a million footsteps over hundreds of years. Time weighed heavy. He hurried now, feeling a pressing need to discover what might be happening, even though he was quite certain he wouldn't want to know.

The choir's song and the organ's lament accompanied him on his climb. *Where is everyone else?* he thought. *Why isn't everyone climbing these stairs?* He paused to listen but heard only those haunting hymns, exultant one moment, screeches of terror and torment the next. That had always been Guy's problem with religion—the ecstasy and the horror.

He walked on, enjoying the feeling of exertion. He was sweating and panting. This felt good and right, and he only wished that he and Marie *had* come here together.

He reached the top of the staircase and emerged onto the external balcony surrounding the dome. To his left was the tall railing, heavy bars offering a partitioned view out across London like an old zoe-trope. To his right, the dome, still exuding warmth from the day's sun.

And everything, and everyone, had changed.

"You're so bloody stubborn!" Marie said. There was a lightness to her voice, but he had known and loved her long enough to know that she was also frustrated.

Welcome to my world, he thought, and he said, "I'm not! Just because I don't suffer from blind blinkered faith you say that—"

"Blind *and* blinkered?" she asked.

"You know what I mean."

"Well, no, not really, 'cos like if you're blind why bother being blinkered, 'cos if you—"

He leaped across the picnic blanket, rolled her over an open foil packet of uneaten sandwiches, and shut her up with a kiss. She fought him off but he pressed his mouth to hers. She was tough and strong, but he could also feel her starting to giggle.

Birds sang around them. A gentle breeze whispered secrets through the tree canopy. This was their place, or when Marie spoke about it, it sounded like Their Place. They'd come here on three occasions to spend time in the woods, and they did their best to ignore the scraps of litter and broken vegetation around the clearing, shoving aside the fact that other people probably also knew this spot as their own.

Their Place.

She pushed him off at last and peeled a flattened sandwich from her butt. She held it up and it flopped down limp. She raised an eyebrow, and Guy burst out laughing.

"I believe in the god of limp sandwiches," he said. "I'll worship him forever, and sacrifice every third sandwich to his most glorious and—"

"Oh, fuck off!" she said, lobbing the bread and catching him perfectly across the nose.

They stopped talking and started kissing, and that suited them both just fine. In Their Place they found proof of love.

London danced and sang. From all across that great city voices rose, crying and chanting and singing, rippling over the built-up landscape like an ocean's tides. They sang of joy and wonder, delight and ecstasy. Down below he could see people in the streets around St Paul's, dancing and relishing this momentous, amazing moment. Most vehicles—cars, taxis, buses and motorcycles—were motionless. London was still but for the people, and the birds that swooped and swerved along streets and around tall buildings. He knew London so well, and the feelings he usually experienced when looking out over the city from a high vantage point had changed. Usually he thought of the millions of people hidden away in the sea of grey buildings, working and striving to earn their keep, stressed and traumatised by whatever lives they had chosen or fallen into. A smog of desolation constantly smudged the city in his eyes, however clear the weather. He never *liked* that feeling, but struggled to work his way out from beneath it.

Now he thought of every beautiful, complex mind, every cheerful thought, each wonderful story of every single person he could spy down in the streets and the many more inside the buildings. They were no longer grey lives. It was no longer an anthill of workers edging towards extinction, but a sea of hope and potential.

In Guy's mind it was a moment of pure revelation.

But also a time of pain.

Here and there across the great city he saw the flickering signs of small conflagrations. A couple of miles to the south, great flames reached skyward, much taller than should be possible, flexing and stretching in majestic slow motion like the fingers of a fire-giant being born from the earth. Smoke rose around them, deep black and almost oily against the sky, as if extensive piles of fat sizzled and burned beneath them. What he had taken to be musical accompaniment to the joyous ululations were the coughs of thousands of windows bursting out beneath terrible heat.

The Thames flowed red.

Guy grasped the railings and pressed his face to a gap. The feel of cool metal framed his face and pinned him to reality, and he tried to blink the sights away. They would not go. Neither would the sounds of ecstatic song and breaking glass, nor the smells of jasmine, rose petals, and burning flesh. He was a man who trusted his own senses, and he did so now more than ever before.

Do your worst. Do your best. Just do anything, he'd said, glibly challenging the beastly god he had never believed in. And whatever Marie had believed, he had always attempted to keep an open mind.

"Marie!" Guy shouted. He talked to her often in his mind, but this was the first time since she died that he had cried her actual name aloud. "Marie!" It felt good. It felt right, and he started to run around the circular walkway looking for her.

Surely if this was some divine demonstration, a sliver of proof for a world slipping into doubt, then Marie would be with him once more?

That was what he required to believe and care. That would be his proof.

So he ran, calling her name, circling the balcony that skirted around the dome. There were others up here too. They were doing their own thing, and he ignored them as they ignored him. This was a personal time—whatever they saw, smelled, tasted was all their own. He saw one man praying and one woman hiding her eyes, and he wondered what he might be doing when this day was done.

"Marie! Where are you?" He ran on, and a transformed London lay all around. Eventually he came back to where he had begun, his route blocked by the entry lobby out onto the balcony. So he turned around and ran back again, calling his dead wife's name. Senses could be fooled. A mind could be tampered with, cajoled, distorted. But he would know Marie.

He circled around to the lobby, pressed his face to the railings once more, and London blurred in his tears.

"What is this?" he screamed. Voices sang in answer but he could not understand their words. *You never did*, Marie might have said, but that was only in his mind, a precious memory of her face and voice, her sweet smile and gentle touch.

The singing continued, a million voices rising in celebration, setting the cathedral behind him shimmering and crackling with an amazing energy. The flames rose in unison, dancing to their tune. It might have been proof undeniable, belief unstoppable. But in any world where Marie remained dead—in the face of any bastard god who could push her into the path of a foolish, drunken driver—Guy remained immovable.

He turned his back on everything, entered the dome, and started back down the winding staircase.

On that journey down the first staircase to the Whispering Gallery level, he met no one coming up. He was on his own. He moved quickly around the outer edge of the stairwell, using the wider part of the stairs so that he didn't trip and fall. He watched his feet, saw the steps passing below him and the core turning as he descended, and for some reason he came to believe that the drop below him was far, far deeper than it really was, and that if he fell he might tumble forever. It was dizzying and hypnotising, and he trailed his fingers along the outer wall where a million people had touched before. He brushed fingertips with every one of them.

He reached the Whispering Gallery level and moved out onto the inner balcony. All was silent. There was no one there, and looking down he could see no people on the cathedral floor below. The singing had ceased, the organ had breathed to a halt.

He felt completely alone.

"Hello?" he asked. He closed his eyes, and for a loaded moment that seemed to stretch forever, he firmly believed that he would be answered. But his voice whispered away to nothing.

He circled the balcony and started down the wide staircase that led to the cathedral floor. Every thirty steps or so he paused to listen.

For voices, footsteps, singing, screaming, *anything*. Only his heavy, fast breathing broke the silence.

Moving faster, the steps speeding up beneath his feet rather than feet accelerating down the stairs, he finally tripped. A blade of fear sliced into his core, and in panic he held out his hands to break his fall.

He hit the steps and rolled.

Down . . . down . . . forever.

When Guy was in his late twenties, a year after falling in love with Marie, he'd gone on a business trip to Scotland. He'd just started his own web consultancy business, and he was investigating the possibility of a partnership with another young, forward-thinking entrepreneur. He and the man had gone out on the town in Edinburgh, and Guy had learned his most important lesson of the day—never drink whiskey with a Scotsman.

Several pubs and a dozen single malts later, he was paralytic. He'd made his excuses and stumbled back to his hotel room already fearing the next day's hangover. His head had felt like the only fixed point in the universe, with everything else in a state of turmoil. He fell twice on the stars up to his room. Once in his room he took a piss, drank a pint of water, then fell on the bed and went to sleep fully dressed.

He woke in the early hours. The headache throbbed in first, consuming his entire body, and then he heard someone groaning. He stirred quickly, fumbling for the bedside light, missing, rolling from the bed. Hurt his shoulder on the floor. Then he realised that the groan was his own, and he climbed slowly back onto the bed and turned on the light.

It melted his eyeballs to the back of his skull.

Squinting, slowly stripping off his shirt, he hobbled to the bathroom. Here he stripped naked and propped the door open so that he didn't have to turn on the harsh light. His head throbbed. His stomach churned. He burped and smelled whiskey, and groaned all over again.

As he took a piss he stared at his darkened reflection in the mirror, and then he saw Geraldine. She was Marie's mother—funny, intelligent, a widow far too young, Guy got on with her amazingly well. He was already starting to think she might one day be his mother-in-law.

But now she was in pain. Her reflection was much hazier than his, as if in a much darker room, but he saw her features twisted in agony, her body shivering, and he pissed all over the floor.

Rushing back to into the bedroom, his hangover seemed to have vanished instantaneously. Without stopping to think—how stupid this was, how unlikely, how bloody annoyed Marie would be when he phoned her in the middle of the night because of some weird just-surfacing-from-a-drunken-sleep dream—he dialled her mobile. He told her that there was something wrong with her mother, and when Marie asked how he knew he said he didn't know. Yes, he was still in Edinburgh. Yes, he'd been drinking, but no, he was sober now. No, he didn't know how, but could she just . . . ?

Half an hour later Marie rang from her mother's flat. She'd fallen down the stairs and broken both legs, and was suffering from concussion and shock.

Next morning Guy's hangover landed with a vengeance, and he spent the whole morning in his room puking, sleeping, and vowing that he'd never drink again.

Marie called it a miracle. Guy, who had time to think about it on the long train journey home, and who could not really remember if he'd actually seen Geraldine, or whether he'd been anything other than drunk when he called Marie, shrugged his shoulders.

"Just one of those things," he said.

He was lying on the cold stone floor, head lower than his feet, arms splayed out. He was still on the shallow staircase, but ahead and several steps down he could see the arch of the doorway leading back into the cathedral's cavernous interior. Light flickered in there, a thousand dancing candles. But it shifted slowly, almost sensuously, as if the air was almost still.

Groaning, Guy rolled onto his front and pushed down, lifting his upper body from the step beneath him. The stone was speckled with a few droplets of blood. He swung his legs around and sat on a step, then put a hand up to his face. His cheek was sore and bruised, nose a little bloodied. He looked at his watch—almost six p.m. He couldn't have been out for long.

Breathing softly, Guy stood, hand against the wall in case he was woozy. A dull headache thudded against the inside of his skull, each pulse matching the beat of his heart, but he did not feel unsteady.

Something had happened.

He started to shake, but it was nothing to do with the fall. This was uncertainty and fear. It was worry and confusion. The silence was wrong, the stillness was something that should not be. He walked down the final few steps and then stood in the arched doorway.

The cathedral was deserted. High windows let through a rainbow of light, subdued now that evening was falling. Dust motes drifted in the light, and tides of colour shadowed across the cathedral's interior. Around the central area, directly below the huge dome, giant candles burned in tall braziers, their flames almost motionless.

It looked like a place that had not been disturbed by human presence for years.

Guy took a tentative step out from the staircase enclosure and looked around. It was truly deserted. The choir stalls were empty. No songbooks were present, and the angle-poise lamps were all off and aimed down. The curve of seats where visitors could sit— where *he* had sat, head back, staring up at the mosaics of the four disciples and inviting something in—were empty, cushions hanging from small hooks on the seat backs. He turned and looked along the cathedral to the giant doors, only used now on occasions of high ceremony. Down there, close to the entry and exit, a rack of candles lit by visitors burned gently. Some of them had already sputtered out, and as he watched one more died a smoky death.

"Hello?" Guy whispered. His voice was quickly lost to the massive, motionless space. He thought of calling louder, but he was suddenly terrified of what might answer.

This was not a space meant to be so empty.

He started walking towards the exit, a hundred metres away. He looked around constantly as he went, not sure what he expected to see, not wishing to see anything. He passed the tombs of forgotten priests and looked away, catching stony movement from the corner of his eye. He walked across a solid brass grating that looked down into the crypt, but it was fully dark down there now, and anything might be staring back. He felt the air moving around him as he walked, but when he looked behind him he could see no sign of the disturbance he had made. It was as if he wasn't really there at all.

Guy paused and listened, head cocked on one side. Maybe everyone had abandoned this place when they saw what was happening outside. Maybe they'd vacated the cathedral to leave room for what might come next, or perhaps they had fled in terror.

He could hear nothing. In a space like this there should have been echoes, whispers, the groan of memory or the reverberation of the building's great weight settling for another long night. But other than the frantic beating of his heart, there was utter silence.

He lit a candle. He should have felt ridiculous doing so, but it was all for Marie. He held the wick against another candle until it caught, then placed it gently in the small holder. Its flame shifted for a moment, as if excited at being given life, and then it settled into a steady burn, mimicking all the others. If he turned around and then turned back, he might even forget which flame was his.

The exit was close. He took slow, gentle steps, listening for any sign that the cathedral knew he was there.

"Oh, I thought I was the last one," the voice said, and Guy screamed.

The old man stood from behind the reception desk, hands held out, an apologetic smile on his lips. He looked so human.

"Sorry mate, hey, didn't mean to startle you." He came out from behind the desk, hobbling with arthritic pain. "Where'd you come from, then? I thought everywhere had been checked."

Guy stared at the old man for a few seconds, certain that he'd see something horrible or terrifying. But the man's smile only faded into a troubled frown, and that made all of Guy's stress drain away. His shoulders slumped and he chuckled, shaking his head.

"Sorry. I fell and banged my head, and . . . " He held a hand to his face and felt the bruise starting to form. The blood was already drying in his nose. "I'm sorry."

"No need to apologise to me," the old man said. "You're lucky! I'm just about to lock up, you could have been in here all night." He looked around and actually shivered. "Not something I'd like to go through."

"Something's happened!" Guy said. "Outside, something . . . have you been out? Have you seen?"

The man smiled and shook his head. "This is my place. I sit here from three 'til six, then lock up a little while after we close to the public. Nope. Not been outside. Though I hear it's getting cold."

"Have you seen Marie?" Guy asked. There was something about the security guard. Or perhaps it was merely Guy's own mystery reflected in the old man's eyes.

"No, no Marie," the man said. He turned and started walking, and Guy found himself compelled to follow. They reached a small side door set beside the circular entrance door, now motionless.

"But something happened."

The man turned and smiled.

"What are you smiling at?" Guy asked.

"You. Your face. Lots of people have stuff happen to them here, good and . . . not so good." He mused, looking over Guy's shoulder into the deep spaces beyond. "First time one of them's talked to me about it, though."

Guy frowned, trying to recall what he'd seen. Maybe the bang on the head was mixing things up.

"But there *was* something . . . " he said.

The man shrugged and opened the door, inviting Guy to step through. "Just one of those things," he said.

Outside, London roared.

The streets around St Paul's were buzzing with taxis, cars, motor-cycles, buses, and cyclists braving the darkness with little more than flashing lights for protection. Horns blared. Tyres squealed and someone shouted. Pedestrians weaved around each other on the pavements, some chatting and laughing, others focussed on getting home from work as quickly as possible. Shops around the cathedral were closed or closing, security grilles splitting the subdued lighting from inside. Restaurants and pubs spilled laughter and music across the streets. Streetlights glared, several flickering in their death-throes. The smell of London was heavy and rich—cooking food, exhaust fumes, and an occasional waft of sewage beneath it all.

There was no singing, other than a drunk man leaning against a wall with his hat upturned on the floor. There was no dancing. There were no raised hands and joyful chants, no fires melting the city's distant shadows, and no impossibly tall flames licking at the underside of clouds. London was the place he had always known, loved, and hated.

But perhaps it was a very different world.

Guy had yet to decide.

IN THE DUST

We should have known that one day they'd refuse to let us leave.

I'd already seen the fresh smoke rising from the cremation pits, and a sensation of cold dread had settled in my stomach. But I chose not to mention it to the others. Jamie's bluff and bluster would only piss me off, and I feared it would send Bindy over the edge. If in the end events drove her to madness or suicide, I didn't want to be the catalyst.

So it wasn't until we reached the old stone river bridge that the truth began to dawn.

"What the fuck?" Jamie said.

"Tobe . . . " Bindy let go of the cart and grabbed my hand. Before the plague we'd only known each other in passing, and there was nothing sexual here, but contact helped her cope. As for me . . . it only made me think of the past.

"They've blocked the bridge," I said.

"And they're burning something in the pits." Jamie jogged off ahead of us, approaching the barrier of roughly-laid concrete block and barbed wire they'd built while we'd been searching.

"Tobe . . . ?" Bindy said again, her hand squeezing hard.

"It's okay," I said, squeezing back. Though I knew it was not.

I looked down at the cart we'd been pushing. The body of a small child stared back at me. She had died during the initial outbreak, and been motionless since the Purge three weeks earlier, but her eyes still held a glimmer of something resembling life. That was always the worst thing for me—not that they'd moved when they were dead, and were mindless, and craved the gristly hearts of the living, but that in their eyes they looked so alive.

The girl stared back at me, unseeing. I looked away.

"Hey!" Jamie shouted. "Come and see!"

"Tobe, I don't want to go up there," Bindy said.

"Then stay with her," I said, letting go and walking after Jamie. I heard Bindy's sharp intake of breath, and knew that I could be cruel. But she was weak, and sometimes I lost patience with her.

I reached the block wall and climbed, joining Jamie where he looked through the swirls of razor-wire topping it. I could still smell the rich, warm odour of wet cement.

"Something's happened," he said. For once, his understatement was surprising.

There had been an army camp on the other side of the bridge. For three weeks, the three of us had been bringing bodies out of Usk, back over the bridge and delivering them into the hands of the scientists. We each had different reasons for doing so, and all of them involved dead people. Jamie's sister we had found on day one, torn apart in a pond in their garden, her chest opened and heart ripped out. There had been a squirrel feeding on her eyes, and I'd been shocked, because I never knew a squirrel would eat meat. Bindy's parents were two of the infected killed during the Purge, and we'd brought them both out during the second week. Her mother had been covered with dried blood, and in her father's hand was the remains of something meaty. They'd had those same staring, glittering eyes, wet and knowing even in true death.

My own dear Fiona eluded me still.

Now, the camp was abandoned. There were still a few of the prefab huts they'd used, and a tent flapped in the lonely breeze. The field was churned up, and the old cottage they'd requisitioned as a command post was empty. Its windows and door had been left open, and that just seemed so careless. *The rain will get in*, I thought. I laughed softly.

"What is it?" Jamie asked.

"Nothing."

"So where the fuck have they gone?"

I shrugged, but my eyes were drawn to the smoke still rising from the pyres, the fires and pits hidden beyond a thick copse of trees. After we brought the bodies out and they'd done their tests, that was where they disposed of them. Someone was burning now. The smoke was black and greasy, the smell sickly and mouth-watering.

"Moved back," I said. "Pulled the perimeter out away from the village."

"Why?" he asked, but I could see him looking at the smoke as well. "Fuckers," he said softly.

I turned and looked back down the curve of the bridge at Bindy. She'd stepped in front of the trailer so she did not have to look at the little dead girl, and she was staring up at us, eyes wide and hands clasped between her breasts. When she saw my expression she looked at the road surface.

"They should tell us what they found, shouldn't they?" Jamie asked.

"So ask them."

"What do you mean?"

I nodded across at the torn-up field. Birds were flocking across it, exploring for worms where the soil had been recently turned. "You don't think they'd leave us alone, do you? We could climb the wall, swim the river. Walk out of Usk." I was scanning the landscape as I spoke, searching for movement, or the tell-tale glint of sunlight on binoculars or rifle scopes. I could see nothing, but that didn't mean they were not there. "They'll be there to make sure we don't."

"Well I'm going to try," Jamie said.

"Don't be a fool."

"Fool?" He turned to me, eyes wide and glaring, and the fear beneath his constant outrage was patent. "You've been treating me like a kid ever since we started this, and I'm a lot younger than you so I can take that. But I'm not a fucking fool."

"Fair enough."

He turned back to the view, scanning the hedgerows and hillside beyond as I had.

"They'll let us out, Tobe, won't they?" Bindy said behind us.

"No," I said. It was so quiet that she didn't hear, but Jamie did. He glanced at me again as he jumped down from the wall.

"Later," he said. "I'm going to swim the river and get out of this shit-hole later."

I followed him back down to the street.

"What do we do with that?" he said, pointing at the girl's body.

For a second, I was at a loss. By discovering the corpse splayed on a tomb slab in the churchyard, we had effectively taken owner-ship of it, and the thought of simply dumping her somewhere felt terrible. She was somebody's daughter, someone's little girl, and she deserved more than that.

"Well, chuck her down a drain somewhere for all I care," Jamie said when neither of us answered. He walked off along the street. "I'm going to the Queen's. I'll be in the bar."

Bindy turned to me.

"Let's put her back where we found her," I said, and she seemed to find that acceptable. She almost smiled.

Jamie was on the way to drunk by the time Bindy and I arrived at the Queen's Hotel. He was sitting at a table in the bar, and we arrived in time to see him stagger across, lift the bar flap, pour him-self a single whiskey, and then sway back to his seat. By the time he sat down again he'd almost finished his drink, but perhaps there was something comforting in the process.

"Whaddya do with her?" he asked.

"Back in the churchyard," Bindy said.

Jamie snorted, but I wasn't sure what that meant.

"I'll get food," I said. "Then we should talk about what to do."

"Talk?" Jamie shouted. He looked ready to rage, and I tensed. Then the glass slipped from his hand and dropped to the table, landing upright without spilling a drop, and he put one hand to his forehead. He sobbed, once, then looked up at us again, putting on his hard face.

"Jamie—" Bindy began.

"Fuck it!" he said. "There's nothing to do but get out. I've done nothing . . . nothing wrong. Nor you." He pointed at us, and I wondered how many people he saw. "It's wrong, them keepin' us in, and . . . I'll get out."

"I'm getting food," I said. I sensed Jamie about to break—it had been coming for days—and I had no wish to see that. I went through behind the bar and into the big kitchen, glancing at the huge walk-in freezer door we hadn't dared open since the power had gone off. There was still enough food in the larder: tinned stuff, packets, dehydrated fruit and vegetables. At lunchtimes over the past few days we'd almost laughed about how disgusting it was, but knowing we were now trapped here with no chance of escape, laughter was distant.

I knocked together something quick to eat, because there were more important things to do. I carried it back through to the bar, and was amazed to see that Jamie had calmed down. He was still drinking steadily, and Bindy sat at the table opposite him with an open bottle of wine and two glasses in front of her. As I sat down she poured me a glass. Jamie stayed on the whiskey.

"That fire," she said. "We haven't taken a body out for two days. Could it be that one?"

I remembered the body she meant—a huge, fat woman, naked, her breasts pawed and scratched and teeth clotted with rotting meat. And those eyes, so falsely alive.

"They burnt that one the day we took her out," I said.

"Right," Jamie agreed.

"So there's been another outbreak," Bindy said. She was staring into the deep violet depths of her glass. The drink had already stained her lips, an effect that I had always found unbearably sexy in women drinking red wine. Not in Bindy, though.

"Not necessarily," I said. "If there had, why trap us in here?"

"It's in the dust," Jamie said. "I've told you, haven't I? I've been saying it all along." He ran one finger around the inside of his glass, smearing whiskey and touching his finger to his tongue. From day one, Jamie had been suggesting that the plague—virus, bacteria, nobody yet seemed to know exactly what caused it—could be alive in the dust of the deserted town. He'd seen dust settled on the eyes of the bodies we'd found, filtering the light that entered their dead eyes, and I think perhaps it had driven him slightly mad. We were all allowed our own madness.

We drank some more, but didn't really come up with anything like a plan. Jamie was drunk and bitter and scared, Bindy was too distant, and I really had no need of a plan at all. My aim had always been to find Fiona's corpse, wherever it might be, and only one thing really kept me going: the hope that she had been killed and eaten by what people had started to call zombies.

The alternative was that she had become one herself, and the thought of looking into her dead eyes knowing that was just too terrible to bear.

We took three en-suite rooms next to each other. Bindy and I carried Jamie to bed, trying to ignore his rantings and tears, and then back in the corridor I bid her goodnight.

"Tobe," she said, and her voice sounded different. "I know what you think of me, but I'm trying. I'm really trying." She slurred slightly, but she was more in control than I had ever seen her. She'd once served me breakfast at a café in town—maybe four years ago—and I'd flirted with her. "I keep thinking tomorrow will be another day, but it won't. It'll always be today." She turned to go to bed, and I reached out and held her arm. She touched my hand and smiled sadly.

"Maybe they've just upped and left." It was fucking stupid, and I knew that, but I couldn't think of anything else to say.

"They built a wall," she said. "And Jamie's right—none of us has done anything wrong." She went to bed then, and so did I.

I lay there for some time trying to sleep. The town lay around me, its geography altered completely by what had happened. The town square, its attractive clock tower bedecked with flower troughs, cobble paving slippery in light summer rain, was now the place where I had found six dead zombies with the remains of several small children they had been fighting over when the Purge came. Where the old castle once stood, I could now only recall seeing the family that had fled there to die—father, mother, and two children, surrounded by their mingled blood vented by the knife in the man's hand. Streets where I had walked with Fiona, pubs we had drunk in, restaurants where we had eaten and laughed and talked quietly of the possibility of children, all now tainted in some way by what had happened. Some taints were simply the silence; others, blood and rot and death.

I was trapped in my home town, but I had never been in a place so strange.

As I drifted to sleep I wondered yet again what had happened to the rest of Usk's residents. Most of them had fled after the first few attacks, but they were soon rounded up and kept in confinement in the old military base in Glascoed. The majority of those who stayed behind were killed or infected, and then came the Purge, where the whole town was sprayed hourly for three days with what the military had called an "antidote". When Bindy, Jamie and I walked out of town across the stone river bridge, the only reason we weren't shot is that their solution hadn't killed us.

They'd let us stay, suggesting that we help appropriate zombie corpses for the scientists to study. Every day they let us out to sleep in comfortable quarantine, and each morning, I expected it to be the day they no longer let us out. I didn't care, because Fiona had remained behind and had not yet been found.

Faces of old friends and people I knew from the town appeared to me as I dropped into an uneasy slumber. Some of them smiled, some were slack in death.

Some of them raged.

The sound of helicopters woke me up. I went to the window and saw a military chopper buzzing the town. At first I thought they were spraying again, but then I noticed the cameras mounted under its nose.

"Please come out into the street where we can see you," an electronic voice said. "Stand at the road junction, and make yourselves known."

Make yourselves known! I thought. We'd been dragging corpses from the dead town for three weeks for these bastards, and they couldn't even use our names.

I met Bindy out in the corridor, and we knocked on Jamie's door. *He's dead*, I thought, *veins slashed, heart given up, brain popped with the pressure.* But then he opened the door, squinting in the dawn light. He had a hangover. I chuckled.

"Fuck's wrong with you?" he growled.

"Nothing. Come on, let's find out what's going on."

Bindy and I waited at the road junction outside the hotel for several minutes before Jamie joined us. In that time the chopper swept past three times, the cameras seeming to turn slightly as it went. It was warm already this morning, but the rotors caused a storm in the street that blew waves of dust against smashed shop windows.

Jamie coughed and spluttered, washing dust from his mouth with a swig from the whiskey bottle he carried.

"You're kidding me," I said.

"Hey, it's a free country!" He giggled maniacally and took another drink.

The chopper came in again and hovered a hundred feet along the street. We could barely see against the dust and grit, and the sound was tremendous. The speakers were even louder.

"For your own safety, you will remain in quarantine within the town limits for the next forty-eight hours."

This is unfair, I thought. *We can't ask them anything.*

"During that time, certain work will be undertaken. You must not attempt to impede or interfere in any way. You must not attempt to escape."

"Try and fuckin' stop me, you bastards!" Jamie shouted. I realised that he was still drunk.

"Any escape attempt will result in the use of deadly force."

The sound seemed to decrease, and the three of us were trapped in a surreal bubble of shock. *They'll shoot us*, I thought, and their military-speak suddenly annoyed the hell out of me. Why couldn't they just say what they meant?

I glanced past Bindy at Jamie. He caught my eye, smiled and shrugged. Bravado.

"Toby Parsons, please proceed alone to the road crossing outside the primary school. There you'll be given more instructions, and any questions will be answered."

I hated the sound of that voice, distorted by technology. The speaker could have been laughing or crying, and we'd never know.

The chopper lifted away quickly and disappeared over the roof-tops, and Jamie gave it the finger.

"What does all that mean?" Bindy said. "What work are they going to do?"

"Hopefully I'll find out," I said.

"Why just you?" Jamie said. "Why the hell is it you who—"

"Jamie," I said softly, quietly, and he listened. Maybe I'd never spoken to him in this tone of voice before, but it was about fucking time. "Stay here. Drink coffee. Have a wash. I'll go and find out what's happening."

I glanced at Bindy, and though she was frowning I could see that she seemed comforted somehow with me taking charge. Not that I wanted to. Last thing I wanted was these two hanging on my back.

The only thing I wanted . . .

But we'd been looking for three weeks, and if Fiona had been a victim rather than a zombie, I was sure I'd have found her by then. I knew all the places she knew. I'd checked all the places we'd been together. And if I really thought about it, I didn't really want to keep looking at all.

I started along the street. It took me five minutes to reach the school, and all the while I could hear that chopper somewhere in the distance. It was the first time I'd been alone out on the streets since the Purge—every other time one or both of the others had been with me. I thought I'd be scared, or at least nervous, but I found it quite settling. Most things had changed, but liking my own company was not one of them.

As I reached the zebra crossing by the school, I looked along the curving road at the roadblock. It had been there since the first plague outbreak in the town, and I'd seen it a couple of times in the past few days when we went looking for bodies in the school. But now it looked different—larger, for a start, and it had also been added to. Whereas before it had been constructed of a couple of cars turned on their sides and piles of sandbags, now there were several heavy, dark metallic structures behind that. Tall fences stretched away on either side, the one on the left disappearing behind a house and heading uphill, the one leading right forming a straight line right across the school's playing field, merging with the woodland beyond.

Either side of the road stood tall posts topped with cameras. They both turned slightly, and I imagined them as eyes observing my approach. Fifty feet away, an amplified voice said, "Remain where you are."

I stopped, sighed. Everyone was shouting at me today.

A man appeared atop the roadblock, obviously standing on a raised section on the other side. He looked across the town behind me before focussing on my face. He appeared nervous.

"Toby Parsons?"

"That's me."

"I'm Peter O'Driscoll. I'm a doctor assigned to the research team looking into—"

"You're one of the scientists been cutting up the bodies I've been hauling out of here."

"Yes, if you like." He did not seem at all perturbed by my comment.

"So what have you found out?"

He paused, but only for a second. "I'm afraid that's classified."

I laughed. It was the first real laughter I'd uttered since the plague, and since losing touch with Fiona. We'd been half a mile apart when the first attacks came, by my reckoning. Close enough to hear each other screaming.

"You're joking!" I said. "What movie are you trying to be?" I laughed some more.

"Your help has been appreciated," O'Driscoll said.

"Got a medal for me?"

"No, no medal."

"So what do you want? Is there another infection? Has it spread?"

"It's still contained," O'Driscoll said. "But there's been a recurrence, yes."

A recurrence. My blood ran cold. The Purge was supposed to have been the end solution, the final cleansing of what had happened in Usk. Blame went everywhere from the moment it struck, the media filling the channels with political and religious pundits, ex-military personnel and any c-list celebrity who had a fucking opinion. When the military had issued assurances that the Purge would end the slaughter, such assurances were taken as an admission of guilt. How could they know how to stop it if they claimed not to know how it began?

"Where?" I asked. And then a greater chill ran through me, and I couldn't prevent myself from spinning around. The chopper, the cameras . . . "In the town?"

"No, Mr Parsons. Usk is clear . . . or so we believe. The recurrence was in one of the corpses you brought out."

"So the infection is still here."

"We hope not. We hope it was an isolated case, and we're looking into it. But . . . " He glanced down at something in his hand.

"Okay," I said. "So you're watching us, just in case."

O'Driscoll nodded, lips pursed. "Just in case."

"And if we're still fine a week from now? Two weeks?"

He went to leave.

"Hey!" I called. "You can't just go!"

He paused, squatting down ready to jump away from the road-block. He seemed to have nothing else to say.

"You can't just leave us in here like this. We haven't done any-thing wrong!"

"But you might," he said, and dropped back into his world.

I was left staring at the roadblock while the cameras stared back. I gave them the finger; it felt childish, but made me feel better.

Turning to walk back into town, I felt watched every step of the way. As I passed the school I looked at the low brick building, infant class windows splashed with colourful drawings. Self-por-traits, with big round pink faces, bright blue eyes and smears of yellow or brown hair. If I went closer I'd probably see the names, but I had no wish to do that. I might end up seeing the cartoon-face of the little girl we'd left back in the churchyard.

The chopper drifted in again, skimming low over the trees beyond the school and disappearing from view. I jogged along the street, eager to see what they were doing, and as I passed the burned-out fire station I saw through a gap between buildings. The chopper was hovering above the four-storey block of flats—one of the tallest buildings in Usk—and two men were abseiling down a rope to the rooftop.

"What the hell . . . " I muttered.

Maybe they wanted us. They'd confine us somewhere, send in their teams of doctors and scientists like O'Driscoll with their syringes and knives, slice us open one by one to see if they could find out what was happening. Because even if they'd known at the beginning, I had the feeling that they were lost now. The plague had progressed—evolved, perhaps—and with a recurrence somewhere beyond the town's perimeter, their understanding of whatever caused the plague had lessened considerably. Desperate times called for desperate measures, I knew that. But suddenly I was very, very afraid.

We're expendable, I thought. *At least we know the town, the streets, know the places to hide . . .* But that was just foolish. If they sent in forces to find us, we would be found.

But the two men on the roof did not look like they were here for long. They were setting up a large tripod topped with a box, weighing down the feet, clipping some sort of cover over the box. The chopper had drifted away, but it was merely performing a circuit of the town.

More cameras.

Even as I realised that, the helicopter came in low and lowered a rope ladder, and the two men climbed back up.

I could just see the smooth movement as the camera turned this way and that. Someone back at control was testing it. I waved.

Walking back to the Queen's Hotel, I heard and saw several more choppers coming in. They chose the tallest buildings.

"What are they doing?" Bindy asked as I arrived back. She was sitting on one of the hotel's wide stone window sills, waiting for me. For a moment I was irritated at her question, but then I sighed softly and sat beside her.

"Setting up cameras to try and keep track of us," I said.

"Why?"

"There's been a recurrence in one of the bodies we took out. I guess they want to watch in case we're infected too."

Bindy nodded grimly. "So that's it then," she said, and I couldn't bring myself to answer. I didn't want to admit the end of anything.

"Where's Jamie?"

"Went inside. I expect he's in the bar."

"Right. I need to tell him what's going on."

Bindy stayed where she was, which surprised me a little. I thought she'd latch onto me again like a lost puppy, her eyes wide and expectant. Maybe somewhere she'd found her own strength.

"Bindy," I said from the main doorway. She glanced at me. "We'll get out. When they've sorted it all, when they know exactly what's happening."

"Thanks, Tobe," she said. Then she looked away again.

I went inside to find Jamie.

The first plague victim I had seen was an old man who used to run an opticians' on the main street. He was in the early, raging phase, and he stalked the street smashing shop windows with his own hands and head, picking up big shards of glass and slashing at passers-by. This was still early on, and though most people knew that *something* was wrong with Usk, few knew exactly what. People screamed, the old man shouted and growled, and then he pinned a woman down and started cutting her up. He was completely insane

A teenager smashed him over the head with a golf club, five times. He fell on the bleeding woman and died in the street, and seconds later he hauled himself slowly upright again. The rage was gone now, and he started digging into the woman beneath him for her heart.

When I entered the bar, Jamie was raging.

My heart stuttered, my balls tingled with fear. I stood back against the wall, and watched.

He was overturning tables and chairs, smashing bottles, kicking out at the bar, spitting and shouting. *This is it*, I thought, *it's all over for us now*. And suddenly, facing that, I found my purpose again: I could not die here, because I had to find Fiona.

As I was backing away, Jamie saw me. He stopped and fell to his knees, crying.

"It's not fair," he said. "None of it's fair."

I let out a breath, sagging against the wall. *Just drunk. Christ.*

"You heard what I told Bindy."

"Through the window." He lay down amongst smashed glass on the whiskey-stained carpet, and I left him there. There was little I could do, and for a moment he'd scared the hell out of me. I wondered what they'd do if they saw him raging like that.

I went back outside but Bindy had gone. So I went to look for Fiona.

We'd lived in one of eight flats in an old renovated church in the town square, and the building had been gutted the day of the outbreak. Fiona was gone by then, and since the Purge I'd been back into the church three times looking for her body. So I went there again, climbing the warped metal staircase, and however hard I tried to avoid touching any surfaces, by the time I reached the first floor my hands were black with soot. It was as if the air itself was stained. If Fiona *had* died here, my breathing helped her mark me inside.

Our flat was at the rear of the church, and I had to pass two others to get there. They were both ruins, and empty of bodies or bones.

I reached the place we had shared and loved, and I was thankful that it looked nothing like home. That would have been hard to take. I felt no hint of nostalgia, because the place was black and burnt and there was little to recognise. The layout was familiar, but even that had changed where walls had burned through and ceilings had fallen. In what had been our bathroom the floor was gone, and I could see the shattered remains of our bathroom suite in the flat below. In the bedroom, the bed was a charred mound, and none of the wardrobes had survived.

I'd done it before, but I sifted again, moving ash and blackened wood around with my feet. Clouds of dust rose up, and soon I knew my vision would be blurred, so I worked quickly. Bedroom, living room, kitchen, there was nothing to suggest that Fiona had been here when the fire broke out.

I loved her, but right then I so wanted to find her bones.

Leaving the church, I realised that I would never go home again. There was no need, because it was no longer there. So I walked the town once more, looking in places where I had already searched, glancing into gardens which were already becoming overgrown, amazed at the silence of this place. That was something I could not grow used to. Never a particularly busy town, nevertheless there had always been atmosphere of bustle. The main street was where most of the shops were, and it was forever frequented by the town's retired contingent going for coffee or their morning papers, and at lunchtime office workers would visit the several restaurants and pubs. In the evenings, too, it was a lively place, though rarely any more than that. Now, even though the place was not completely silent, it was devoid of the chatter of people.

Birds seemed to have taken over. Perhaps their song had always been there, subsumed beneath the constant rattle of traffic, but now it was given free rein. They lined the rooftops and window sills, pecked around on the roads, and flitted overhead in manic celebration.

It wouldn't be long, I knew, before Usk began to take on a wild appearance. Always proud of their town, most of the residents had gone to great lengths to make sure their gardens were well planted. Those plants would no longer have to fear the shears or clippers of artifice.

"Toby!" The shout came from far away, direction confused by echoes.

"Bindy?"

"Toby, the river!"

I ran. Past the old law courts, across the car park, through an alleyway, and out onto the main street. I was gasping already, and cursing the middle-aged spread that I'd willingly let settle. *Something for me to hold onto*, Fiona had said once as we made love. As I pelted along the road, the river bridge came into view around a curve in the main street. Bindy was standing on it, not far from the block wall, leaning over the stone parapet and looking down.

"What is it?" I called as I ran.

She glanced up and pointed. "Jamie!"

I heard his voice then, more drunken shouting and rambling, and if he'd been close to me I'd have gleefully punched him. He was a tiresome idiot. *Am I really trapped here with him for however long?*

I ran up beside her and looked over the stone parapet. Jamie was down at the river's edge, and he had something slung over his shoulder. His things?

"Don't be an arsehole!" I shouted. "You get over, they'll shoot you before—"

"Fuck off," he said wearily.

"He won't listen," Bindy said. "And he's not going to swim."

I realised what he had over his shoulder then—the little dead girl from the churchyard.

I climbed onto the parapet and judged the drop. Maybe twelve feet. *And if I break my leg?* I thought. *I'm stuck in Usk with a waitress and a loser, and I'll end up dying in bed.*

"Jamie, what are you doing?" It was a stupid question, because I could already guess. As ever, he was trying to be defiant because that was the only way he could hide his fear.

"Helping her escape," he said, giggling. "See how far she'll get."

"They're trying to keep this thing contained," I said, and I blinked, confused. Did I *agree* with what they were doing? I hadn't really given myself time to consider that, not yet.

"You're a pompous shit, Toby. Y'know that? You should listen to yourself sometimes, look at yourself." Jamie stepped down the river bank onto some mud flats. The river rushed by several feet from him.

I almost jumped. If I had, perhaps I would have stopped him. But the real reason that kept me up on the bridge was the idea that the trees across the river could be home to snipers. I didn't want to be close to Jamie when they started shooting.

But there was no gunfire as he approached the river, and none as he shrugged the girl off his shoulder and into the mud. Her limbs were still loose, eyes clear. *There's been a recurrence.*

"Jamie, do you want other people to go through what you're going through?" Bindy asked.

"Yes," Jamie said. He pushed the child into the water. I winced, expecting gunfire, and as we watched her float away, I realised that I had failed. I was a coward. A jump, a punch, and I could have stopped him.

"Fuck," I said.

"Yes, 'cos if I have to go through it, why shouldn't other people?" There wasn't an ounce of regret in his voice. In fact, I thought I heard an element of glee as he giggled again, took a half-bottle of whiskey from a pocket in his cargo pants, and started drinking.

"You're a fucking idiot, Jamie," Bindy said, "and you'll get us all killed." She was watching the little girl carried out by the river.

The water flow was quite fast here after being channelled through the bridge's three arches, and the body started to turn as it moved downriver, spinning clockwise with arms and legs splayed, hair billowing out around it. *The dust will be washed from her eyes now*, I thought. A tree overhanging the river snagged her clothing for a beat, but then she moved on, and soon she was out of sight around a bend.

I realised that Jamie had already walked back up the bank and skirted around the old toll house at the bridge's end. He was heading back along the main street, bottle clasped loose in one hand, and he swayed slightly as he walked. Still drunk. Jamie would always be drunk, and I wondered how much worse he'd be sober.

"What do we do now?" Bindy asked. She had moved closer to me, and she reached out as she spoke. I took her hand.

"Just carry on," I said. "I'm still looking."

"But if you *do* find her—"

"I'm still looking." I let go of Bindy and started following Jamie.

"You're not, in case you were wondering," she said where she followed on behind.

"Not what?"

"A pompous shit."

I shrugged as if I didn't care.

Jamie was sitting on the kerb close to the post office, a stupid grin on his face. Waiting for us. Waiting to gloat.

"What?" Bindy said. I cursed her silently for encouraging him.

"Showed them," he said. He laughed, but I detected an uncertainty in him. The laughter was there to cover that, perhaps for himself.

"Yes, you really showed them Jamie," I said. "They're sure to buck up their ideas and let us leave now. Prick."

He went to stand, swayed, and I saw violence cloud his face. I didn't want to fight him, because I'd never been a fighter. But I realised it was something else that would come between him and his uncertainty, and he was set on the course now.

He threw his empty bottle away and took a step towards me, and then the chopper came.

"What do they want now?" Jamie said. He sounded scared.

"Stay where you are," that mechanical voice instructed.

"Lecture," I said. "We're their pets, and they're going to give us a good talking to."

I was right. But they didn't say another word. Instead, as the chopper hovered just above the buildings fifty yards along the street from us, a man leant out with something in his hand. *Camera and microphone*, I thought, and then Jamie flipped back onto the pavement, blood spewing from his throat just below his Adam's apple. His eyes were wide, hands waving like separate animals as they tried to find the wound, and before they could a second shot rang out. This one was right on target, and the top and back of his head splashed across the post office's front steps.

The helicopter left. Bindy had turned away, but I couldn't help but look. I'd seen a lot of death, but there was something worse about this one. For a few seconds, as blood dripped, his left foot twitched, and his eyes slowly turned up in his head, I couldn't work out what it was.

"And then there were two!" Bindy said, verging on hysteria.

And that was it. Because inside I knew we'd be in here for a very long time, and prick though he was, Jamie was company. And prick though I was, distant and aloof, I knew I could never hope to survive this on my own.

I went to Bindy and held her, and this time it was me taking comfort from the contact as well. She felt warm and alive, and I held onto that with everything I had.

That night, Bindy moved into my room at the hotel. I did not object, and she didn't ask. She simply dropped her small bag of belongings next to mine, stripped to her underwear and climbed into bed. I put my arm around her shoulders and she rested her head on my chest, and soon she was asleep. There was nothing sexual at all. I smelled her, felt her heat, felt her heavy breasts pressed against my side, but I didn't stir. This was pure survival instinct, and though we didn't need each other's bodily warmth, there was so much more to share.

The next day we went about burying Jamie. I tied a bag around his head so that we didn't have to look at where wildlife had been picking at him, and Bindy broke into a hardware and DIY store to find a shovel and pick. We carried him together across the main street and through a small alley that led to a pub garden. There were rose beds here, ground still quite soft even in the summer heat, and I saw no reason to carry him all the way to the church.

We took it in turns digging. While Bindy dug, I squatted and watched her. There had never been any attraction—and the thought of betraying Fiona's memory was terrible to me—but for the first time I realised what a striking young woman she was. Perhaps fear took this away from her, but now, digging in shorts and a vest top, sweating in the morning sun, mud streaked up her legs, she was quite beautiful. I enjoyed watching her, and that enjoyment ceased only when I saw movement from Jamie's body.

I gasped, stood upright, and saw the sparrows flitter away from his bloodied chest. *Only them*, I thought, *it was only them*. But when it was my turn to dig again, I used the pick and made sure we planted him deep.

It took a couple of hours, and halfway through Bindy went to the shop and came back with a couple of bottles of water. The shop stank now—so much stuff in there had rotted, its stink still rank and stale—but there were enough canned and bottled goods to see us through for a long time.

"Are we going to be here forever?" she asked as I shovelled dirt in on top of Jamie.

I paused, panting and sweating hard, and leaned on the shovel. *She doesn't seem so scared now*, I thought. And there *was* something changed about her. Maybe it was because Jamie had gone, or perhaps it was the simple fact that we'd slept comforting each other, holding the nightmares at bay.

"Maybe," I said. "Or at least until they know exactly what happened here." Past her head I could see one of the camera tripods on a building's rooftop. It wouldn't be long before they could watch us almost anywhere if we were outside.

Bindy nodded, then looked down at Jamie's grave. "We'll be okay," she said, and she sounded so certain that I wondered if she'd been stronger than me all along.

The helicopter overflew the town all day, turning a tight circle several times if it saw us in the street. It dropped those two men down a few times, letting them set up other cameras before lifting them away again. I supposed we could have gone to those buildings and smashed up the cameras, but maybe there would be a punishment for that. These people seemed keen to keep their own special lab rats in order.

Bindy helped me look for Fiona. I couldn't find it in me to say I wanted to do it on my own, then after we stopped for lunch I realised that I *wanted* her with me. She was good company, she seemed to have taken her fear under control, and I found myself stealing more glances at her as we walked. *I really am a pompous shit*, I thought, because I'd never given myself a chance to know this woman at all.

We started going into houses we hadn't had a chance to explore before, and we found the remains of eight people. None of them were zombies, that we could tell—rot had taken them all, and some of them were badly mauled and chewed, their bones and remains strewn around. None of them were Fiona. I went to great pains to sift through the remains, gagging, puking several times when the smell became too much, and I never found anything of her I recognised. No jewellery, no hair, no clothing. It was a continuation of the most terrible thing I had ever done—we'd been shifting and hauling bodies for three weeks—but I had to make sure.

Bindy came with me every time, but she always stayed outside those rooms. I could not blame her at all, though as time went on that day I found myself missing her company more and more as I moved splintered bones and stinking things aside.

By early evening we were exhausted, and we went back to the hotel. They'd been while we were away and installed cameras in the upper corners of the hallway, bar, kitchen, pantry, and the corridor upstairs outside our room. Greasy footprints marked their route up and down the stair carpet, and I was outraged at them for not removing their boots.

"They're really interested in what happens to us," she said, as if truly realising our predicament for the first time.

I nodded, not wanting to speak. *They're watching us right now. Maybe O'Driscoll is with them, drinking good coffee, eating a doughnut, and they'll be looking for signs of infection, or madness, or rage.* I had no wish to say anything to them, so I motioned for Bindy to come into our room.

I spent some time looking around for cameras and microphones. Would they really have any respect for our privacy? There were no bootprints on our light room carpet, but maybe that was just them being sly. I could find nothing—no cameras, whose presence would have been obvious, and no microphones either. I actually caught Bindy smiling as I looked inside the lamp shades and behind the mirror, and I smiled back, remembering what I'd said to O'Driscoll. *What movie are you trying to be?*

We ate downstairs in the bar, sharing a bottle of wine, and it was the most relaxed meal we'd had since being thrown together by this. Jamie's agitated presence had always been a pressure, but something about Bindy had changed. I thought that Jamie being gone perhaps allowed her to assess her panics and fears without his own stoking them.

We slept in the same bed again that night, sharing comfort, relishing contact. Though I was aware of the heat of her more than before, and the feel of her moulded to me, still there was no tension at all. I appreciated that, and I fell asleep dreaming of Fiona planting roses in our garden, laughing, and scooping dust out of her eyes with delicate thumbs.

The helicopter didn't come the next day. And it was as we continued our search through the deserted town, and the sun reached its zenith, that I saw the column of smoke rising far in the distance.

"Is that another cremation pit?" Bindy asked.

"I don't think so. Something about it's different."

"How do you mean?" She came closer and held my hand.

"It's a long way away."

She squeezed. The implications of that did not need stating. It was a wide column, and high, and if it was several miles distant, the fire must be huge.

When I said that I was going to the edge of town to see what I could see, she shook her head and backed away from me.

"I don't want to see," she said. "I don't want to know."

"Bindy, the chopper hasn't been around this morning."

She nodded, looking away from me.

"And you've noticed the cameras?"

"Yeah." They weren't turning to follow our progress. I'd been keeping a wary eye on them since I noticed that first thing in the morning, but I hadn't wanted to mention it to her.

"We have to know."

She was shaking her head, but there were no tears. She was far from the Bindy she'd been just a couple of days before. Now I saw calculation and consideration in her eyes, not blind panic.

"*I* have to know." I went to her and held her, and she was hot, her skin already tacky with sweat. It was the hottest day I could remember, and I felt a rush of affection for her then. I kissed the side of her head, she kissed my shoulder, and we both hugged tighter.

"I'm going to keep looking," she said, nodding along the street we'd been searching. They were big houses, and there were five left on this row.

"You're sure?"

She touched the claw hammer she carried in her belt. We'd both agreed that it would be handy for breaking the locks out of doors, but it didn't need saying that it was also a weapon.

"I won't be long," I said, but that turned out to be a lie. It would be evening before I saw Bindy again, and by then our whole world had changed once more.

I went back towards the roadblock by the school. I stood there shouting for a while, waving at the cameras, trying to get their attention. Stepping left and right across the road, the cameras did not follow my progress.

"I need to speak with O'Driscoll!" I shouted. Silence was my answer.

In the distance to the south, beyond a range of hills, the column of smoke still rose. It could have been Cwmbran several miles away, or maybe Newport, several miles farther. Whichever it was, I judged its fiery base to be miles wide.

Waving at the cameras was stupid. There was no one there to see.

So I climbed the roadblock and started walking along the road. To begin with I cursed myself with every step, knowing how foolish I was being, wincing at the expected sound of a high-powered rifle shot. *I'll be hit before I even hear the shot*, I thought, and that was no comfort at all. But there was no gunfire, no helicopters, and no loud mechanical voices exhorting me to, "Please don't attempt escape." Right then there was nothing I wanted to hear more.

The road ran for a mile before splitting and filtering down onto a dual carriageway heading north and south. It was deserted and quiet, save for the wildlife that was becoming braver day by day—I saw a fox watching me from a large house's garden, and a buzzard sat on the road eating something it had just caught, not even glancing up at me as I passed within fifteen feet of it. I tried to identify what it was eating, but I could not. There was no fur.

I saw them from far away. I knew what they were. And I gave thanks to gods I had never believed in that the military had seen fit to erect a second line of protection.

The fence spanned the road just before it split to curve down to the carriageway. It was high, heavy-duty, and I could track its route across fields and in front of a distant copse of trees, curving around the north end of the town. In the other direction it was soon lost to view, but I hoped it was just as long, and just as strong.

I sat down in the road and watched them pressing against it.

Most of them wore army uniforms, those who weren't in underwear or naked. Many bore terrible wounds, and the blood still flowed. Dead blood must have been different, though, because its stench did not attract their brethren. A zombie's heart, it seemed, did not taste so sweet.

There were maybe fifty of them. Most were clumped against the section of fence built across the road, but I saw a few down in the fields as well. One of those still seemed to be carrying a rifle across his back, though now I hoped he no longer remembered how to use it.

They were making very little noise. A few moans and groans, but none of the raging growls that had marked the first phase of infection. All these were past that now—they'd gone mad, and killed, and died, and now they were back again, and all they saw when they looked at me was my succulent still-beating heart.

There's been a recurrence, O'Driscoll had said. Smug prick. I looked for him, but didn't see him. I hoped he'd been killed and torn apart, found true death, because however much I hated him I'd had contact with him, and he was a human being like me. He was only doing what he'd thought was right, and this was no way to end up.

I tried to make out exactly what this meant. The Purge had worked in Usk, for a while at least, and now that there had been an outbreak beyond the town, surely the military would launch another Purge? But there was no sound of vehicles anywhere, neither ground nor air, and I could see no plane trails in the sky.

And there was that burning city.

I sat and watched them for a while, trying not to appreciate the stark truth of things: that this plague had gone further, and perhaps was still travelling.

Then I knew what I had to do before returning to Bindy, because I couldn't go back to her with half-truths and suppositions. I had to make sure that we were safe, and that our prison had become our refuge.

I walked north first of all, following the fence all around the town until it reached the river. I looked into the town at the stone bridge, and from here I could just see the clumsy block barrier that they'd built at its centre. The fence extended right across the river and continued on the other side, obviously encompassing what had been their encampment.

I followed the fence back around the town, crossing the road where most of them were still gathered. They pushed and shoved, but it was solid, and they had no real strength.

A mile to the south of town I saw O'Driscoll. He was naked, and his entire front was a mass of dried blood. I couldn't make out whether or not it was his own, and I gave him a wide berth. He leaned against the metal upright, banging his head rhythmically against it as he watched me pass.

The fence reached the river on that side too, and crossed over, and I knew I had to swim over to make sure. I half-swam, half-walked, and on the other side where their encampment had been, I found that the fence only enclosed a small part of it. Gates were built in at two points, both of them padlocked and chained. I'd found no breaches, and no areas where any of them could climb over. The military had been very thorough and determined to keep us in, and as I forded the river again and walked back into town I thanked them for that. It was a good job they'd realised how dangerous we could be.

Bindy was in the hotel bar, sipping nervously from a glass of wine. When I entered she jumped up and ran to me, cursing and crying and wrapping her arms around my neck.

"Where the fucking hell have you been?"

"I'm sorry," I said, "I'm sorry."

"You're all I've got, Tobe, you're all that's left. Don't you dare scare me like that again, *ever*!" She pulled back and held my face, staring into my eyes, and I realised something both striking and comforting then: in her own quiet way, Bindy was in charge.

"I won't," I said. She held me tight again, and I hugged her back. "You're all I've got too, Bindy."

She pulled away, stalked back to the bar, poured some drinks. She wouldn't catch my eye.

"It's spread outside," I said.

"I know. I guessed. I walked and saw the fence, and some of . . . them."

"That big fire's still burning."

"Yeah."

"Maybe they'll starve."

We sat down together and drank, shoulder to shoulder on a leather sofa, the contact so important. There was so much more that needed to be said, but I knew it could wait. We both realised the truth—that our entrapment had become the only freedom left.

Later, just before midnight, I asked her what she'd found as she continued searching the big houses on that street. Her hesitation was just too long for me to ignore, and she would not meet my eye. But when she said, *Nothing*, I nodded and let it stand. For then, at least.

That night in bed, we began our future together. It was beautiful and intense, and I think the passion came more from our continuing freedom than anything else. I should have felt guilt, but there was none, because the past was now so far away and obscure that it felt like someone else's memories. Maybe in the daylight things would be different, but then it felt so right.

Afterwards, lying in the dark listening to a silence that would become the norm, she told me.

"I found her," she said.

"I know."

"In the last house. I nailed the doors shut."

"Good."

"So . . . ?"

"Tomorrow, yes. We'll go and set a fire."

I did not sleep at all that night. The fear was there that we had left it too late, and I listened every second for sounds that did not come: the creaking of footsteps on the stairs; the low grumbling of my wife come to berate me and regain my heart.

Even though she said nothing, I knew that Bindy remained awake as well. She was looking after me.

Dawn brought the smell of burning from afar, and we went out together to finish cleansing our town.

MAY THE END BE GOOD

"Things went ever from bad to worse. When God wills, may the end be good."

—Unknown monk, Worcester, England, 1067

As dawn broke it started snowing again, and Winfrid saw a body hanging from a tree.

He paused downhill from the grisly display, catching his breath and shrugging his habit and sheepskin in tighter. Nothing could hold back the shivers. They were mostly from the cold, but over the last ten days he had seen things that set a terror deep in his bones. Fear of God he had, as did any monk; a complex, rich emotion that seemed to both nurture and starve. But this fear was something new. He had yet to define it fully.

Perhaps the body in the tree would feed him another clue.

As he crunched through the freshly falling snow, softly layered over the previous week's falls, several birds took flight from the corpse. A rook he expected, but some of the smaller creatures—finches, a robin, several sparrows—were a surprise. With fields of crops burned, villages put to the torch, and the dead more numerous than ever before, perhaps these previously cautious birds were taking whatever they could get.

"Even the animals are against us," he muttered as he moved

cautiously uphill. He didn't truly believe that, because the animals served only themselves. But if they *had* turned, it would have been the fault of the French. This brutality, this scourging of the land, was all their doing. William the Bastard and his mounted armies had not stopped when they defeated the English uprising in the north. They had carried on, shifting their attention from soldiers to farmers, peasants scraping a living from the land. The cattle fell beneath the sword first, then homes were put to the flame. Anyone who objected received the same—sword, flame, or sometimes both.

Winfrid had seen a child speared onto the side of a burning home. A man split from throat to crotch and seeded with the torched remnants of his stored harvest. Women tortured and raped, left as barren as the land. Whole villages torched, populations massacred or left to fend for themselves from a blasted landscape where nothing would grow, no livestock remained alive, and no building was left standing.

The north had paid a hundred times over for rebelling against he who called himself king, and that debt was still being gathered.

The body was relatively fresh. A man, stripped of clothing and hung from his neck that was stretched thin and torn, head blackened and tilted to one side. His swollen tongue protruded from his mouth like a final scream.

Winfrid muttered some prayers and tried to unsee the signs of scavenging. He had witnessed them on several bodies over the past few days, and rumours of cannibalism muttered in the darker parts of his mind. Prayers would not hide them away.

The man's legs were mostly stripped of flesh, bones plainly visible in several places, knife marks obvious. His cock and balls were gone, his stomach slack and drooping, and his stick-like fingers seemed unnaturally long.

Winfrid's prayers froze when he heard a sound. It might have been a song being sung in the distance, or a whisper from much closer. He stared up at the dead man's face and saw no movement there, but still he hurried on, pleased when the trees and snow finally hid the grotesque sight from view.

"Just the wind," he said. His voice was muffled in the landscape, the white silence of snow and woodland showing only scattered signs of life. Birds pecked ineffectually here and there. Rabbits scampered from shadow to shadow. He saw prints that might have belonged to a fox, but then found larger marks that were undoubtedly those of a wolf. Winfrid had heard that wolves had ventured north and east from the borderlands between England and Wales, but he was surprised that they had come this far. The slaughters in the north would have left little for them to eat.

He would have to be careful. Hungry wolves had been known to take down a grown man, and with the snows falling later this year, a pack might become desperate.

He heard the sound again, from ahead and above, drifting down the hillside and twisting between the trees. Perhaps it *was* the wind, but it had a haunting quality that stopped him in his path. It lured him in and scared him at the same time. *I believed I was away from the horror*, he thought, but perhaps he never could be. The body hanging from the tree was yet another sign of that, and he had no way of knowing just how far King William's fury might extend.

The wind, the voice, suddenly ceased, and the silent snowscape surrounded him once again. Frightening though the sound was, in a way the silence was worse. He moved on, listening for more sounds and keeping alert for movement.

It was difficult. He was cold and tired, and a man in his fifth decade was not meant to be wandering the landscape, especially one as harsh as this. He had spent his younger years spreading the Word, and now in his old age he should be comfortable in the monastery, waking early to pray, tending the gardens, brewing mead, and waiting for that approaching hour when God called him home. But instead the monastery had been sacked, riches plundered, and the monks turned out to fend for themselves. Never a material man, even so he had cried at the sight of French knights and their horses trampling the fields he had toiled in for so long.

Winfrid started a low, soft prayer, the whispered words calming and comforting. It reminded him of friends and peace, and right then he would have given anything for either.

"Did you hear her?"

The voice shocked him and he started upright, staggering into a young tree. The impact shook dead leaves and snow from a fork in its branches, and he saw the man through a haze of falling leaves and ice.

"You. Did you hear her?" The man seemed frantic, head jerking left and right like a chicken's. He had one hand cupped behind his ear.

"Did I hear who?" Winfrid asked.

"My Lina. My sweet girl Lina, singing so that we can find her, though we never can, we *never* can!"

"Who's there?" a woman's voice called. Winfrid saw them both more clearly now that the falling leaves had settled. The man was twenty steps away, the woman close behind him, and he had seen healthier-looking people dead by the trail. How they could still be alive he did not know.

"My name is Winfrid," the monk said. He offered them a prayer in Latin, aware that they would not understand yet eager to ensure they knew who he was. They looked hungry. And Winfrid could neither forget, nor unsee the cannibalism he had seen.

"So you *did* hear her," the woman said.

"No, I—"

"You're praying to bring her back to us. So keep praying. Tell God to give her back!"

"I can't tell God to do anything," Winfrid said.

The man and woman stared at him for a while, the snow floating between them doing little to soften their skeletal forms. Then the man began to cry. They were dry tears, but his shoulders shook, and his chest emitted a *click-click* like bone tapping against bone.

"Will you eat with us?" the woman asked. She held out her hand even though they were twenty steps apart.

Winfrid's stomach rumbled. He could not recall the last time he had eaten anything resembling good food, and as if bidden by her invitation, he caught the scent of cooking meat on the air. *They'll attract wolves*, he thought. *Or Frenchmen might still be close, looking for survivors to kill for fun.*

"Eat what?" he asked.

"Rabbit," the woman said past her husband's shuddering, shrivelling form.

It was through hunger that Winfrid let himself believe her.

They had a weak fire burning on a small, rocky plateau shielded by a steep hillside. Several sticks spanned the fire, with chunks of speared meat spitting fat into the flames. Snowflakes hissed into oblivion in the smoke. Burning logs jumped, settled, coughed ash.

Winfrid's mouth watered at the smell. "There are wolves. I've seen their tracks."

"We'll die if we don't eat," the woman said. They stood round the fire. It was too cold and wet to sit down. The man was a shaking statue, staring at his shoes and dribbling from his mouth. Even with thick clothing, he was barely there. His wife was just as thin, but she seemed stronger. More present, less close to death.

"And with Lina still out there, we can't just go on," she said. "We lost our other children. Our three boys, two girls, dead and gone . . . " She stared into flames.

"The French?" Winfrid asked.

"Some of them." She stretched her hands out to be warmed. "The things I've seen . . . "

And the things I *have seen*, Winfrid thought. The murders and rapes, the fury and wretchedness, the inhumanity. And sometimes the pity and love. That kept him going. God's love, always, but even more affecting was the love he saw between people. Not everyone was given over to violence. It provided hope.

He prayed that this sad couple might also give him hope.

"What happened?" he asked.

"We were leaving our village," she said. "Four weeks ago."

"More," the man said. Winfrid had not even thought he was

aware, but now he saw that the man's shivering had lessened, and he leaned against his wife. Still looking down at his feet. "Six weeks, maybe seven. Forever."

"Maybe," she said. "They were burning the village. The cattle had been slaughtered. The knights had killed anyone with a weapon or farming tool in their hands, and their blood was up. They wanted more. Some of them stayed . . . in the background. Just killing things. But one of them, the one in charge, he was bigger than them all."

"Bigger than any man," her husband said.

"It just seemed that way," she whispered. "He was taking the girls and raping them. I ran with Lina, crawling through a muddy field, and Eadric here met us a day later on the other side of the woods."

"I saw what else they did," Eadric said. He stared into the weak flames, then knelt and ripped a chunk of meat from one stick. He handed it to his wife, then tore off a scrap for himself. They both started eating, noisily, slurping at running fat and grunting in satisfaction as the hot, chewed meat slipped down their gullets.

Winfrid's hunger turned from pang to pain, and he swayed where he stood. A fat snowflake landed on his nose and remained there, as if he gave off no heat. As if he were dead.

"Ten days, it took, to get this far," the woman said, chewing and swallowing as she spoke. "Meat?"

"Yes, I . . . " Winfrid said. He leaned forward and fell to his knees. Coldness ate through his clothes and surrounded his legs. Heat stretched the skin of his face, and as he reached forward, his hands tingled, burned. He touched the hot meat on one stick, then drew his hand back again.

"Where did she go?" he asked. Their daughter Lina kept them here, and suddenly he wondered how. The singing he might have heard could have been the wind, or perhaps it was this woman's own madness. Or this man's. Neither seemed all there.

"The shadows," the woman said. Her eyes went wide and she stopped chewing, staring off past the fire into the shady woods.

Snow continued to fall, dulling any sound, making even the crackling flames sound weak and distant. "She walked into them and never came back."

"She got lost in the woods?"

"She is not lost," Eadric said, looking up at last. He followed the woman's gaze. "*We* are lost." He started to sob, going to his knees and clasping her clothing all the way, trying to keep himself upright. "We *are lost!*"

"How do you catch rabbits?" Winfrid asked. "Where are your spears? Your snares?"

"We find them dead," the woman said. "Hanging from the trees."

Winfrid stood and backed away from the fire. The remaining meat was blackening beneath the flames, and it would be dry and tough now, hot. Filled with juice and fat. Rabbit, that was all, and he had eaten rabbit a thousand times before. But though hunger squirmed in his stomach and writhed in his bones, he no longer had an appetite.

"God help you," he whispered. Eadric smiled at him then, displaying several teeth and the dark gaps between them, and shreds of meat speckling his tongue. The woman smiled as well. "God help you both, because your daughter is dead, and—"

From somewhere higher up on the hillside, there came singing.

A sweet, light voice rose and fell. Winfrid could not hear the words, but the music they made drove through him like the sharpest blade.

"Lina!" Eadric shouted.

"She sings to us," the woman said. "Every day she sings, and we go to find her, and we never do . . . but one day we will, one day when the snows end and life returns to the land and Lina sings us closer and closer, we'll find her, and in the end everything will all be good."

"Lina!" Eadric shouted again. The singing faded in and out, seeming to shimmer through the falling snow. Flakes danced to the voice.

Eadric ran. There was no warning, no tensing of muscles. One moment he was still clasping his wife's clothing, the next he leapt past Winfrid and darted across the small clearing. He scrambled up the steep slope and soon disappeared among the trees and falling snow. Winfrid watched him go. He breathed lightly because Eadric had come so close, and he had smelled of death.

When Winfrid turned back to the woman, she was also gone. He searched for her footprints in the snow, and then saw movement across the slope as she dashed between trees.

Logs settled on the fire with a shower of sparks. A chunk of meat fell into the flames, spitting and letting off black smoke. The singing drifted in from somewhere far away, and though Winfrid turned left and right, he could not tell which direction it came from. But there was something about the song that terrified him. Though high and light on the surface, and it was sung with a mocking humour, and not with the voice of a little girl.

This voice sounded ageless.

In a land like this, with snow falling and cold seeping through his thick habit and woollen undergarments, a fire would be the safest place. But this one no longer felt safe. It poured sick smoke at the sky, and as he turned to flee he tried to summon a prayer, a plea, to help him on his way. He muttered to God, and then shouted at Him. It seemed that the more he prayed, the closer the silent surroundings crowded in around him.

He stumbled across the slope towards the west, slipping eventually down a steep hillside towards a valley bottom. The singing had ceased, left behind or faded away. He slipped several times, falling onto his back and escaping injury when his bag broke his fall. Everything he owned was in there, the material things at least. His heart contained his true riches; a knowledge of God, and a soul given over to goodness. *I am good*, Winfrid kept telling himself, and in that mantra he found courage. A sense of evil hung dense all around him. It hid behind tree trunks, hunkered down beneath rocks tumbled from the heights an endless time before, danced from snowflake to snowflake, daring him to find it. And though he feared this evil—unknown though it was, and more awful because of that—he also felt secure in his beliefs. The worst could happen to him and God would be there on the other side.

At last he reached a place where he thought he could rest. It was gone midday, the smear of sun in the sky already hidden behind the western hills, and his pounding heart had begun to settle.

A stream gurgled merrily along the valley floor, the flat ground on both banks smoothed by virgin snow. Winfrid crouched beside the water and enjoyed the sound. Better than his own heavy breathing, the crunch of his feet through snow and fallen leaves, his grunts as he'd slipped and fallen. Better than the singing.

"God's voice," he said as the stream ignored him.

"God does not speak."

Winfrid fell onto his behind, hands sinking into the snow to find wet, muddy ground beneath. He clasped at the mud, securing himself to the world.

Across the stream, in a spread of snow unmarred by prints, stood a little girl. She wore a simple dress made of rough, grey material, poorly fitting across her shoulders and dropping almost to her ankles. It was thin and holed. She did not appear cold. Not her body, at least.

But her eyes were ice. Their glimmer was frozen as if at the moment of death, and her pale skin was mottled blue.

"God speaks through me," Winfrid said, and the little girl laughed. It animated her face and shook through her body, but gave her no semblance of true life. *Lina*, he thought. *This must be Lina the singer, and her voice is even more terrible than her song.*

"Your pride pulsates within you," she said. "You take your vow and assume too much."

Winfrid pushed himself to his feet. Mud was wet and slick between his fingers. "And you speak well for a farmer's little girl."

"I'm not little anymore." Her laughter had ceased, but the smile remained. Like a slash in dead flesh.

"Then what are you?"

The girl tilted her head to one side, a wolf observing its prey.

"Your parents mourn you."

She looked him up and down. He felt her gaze upon him, rough beneath his clothing. Wherever she looked, he was colder than ever.

"I'll return to them soon."

"Did they hurt you? Whoever took you, did they . . . do things to you?" he asked, already knowing this was wrong. The French had had no hand in this.

"You don't even know who *they* are."

"Then tell me."

She ignored him, finishing her assessment and then turning to walk away.

"Wait!"

Across the other side of the stream, Lina strode towards the trees. Winfrid could have gone after her. But that would have meant splashing through the icy waters, and if he did that, he would risk freezing if he did not stop to dry his clothes. He had seen plenty of weak, sick people dead from the cold, and he had no desire to lie with snow filling his glazed eyes.

Besides, he could do nothing for her. The way she moved, the disregard, her calmness in this cold brutal landscape, all seemed so unnatural. So unholy. He went to call her again, but then the singing recommenced, and he had the disconcerting sense that it did not come only from her.

Just before she disappeared into the forest, the girl paused and looked back at him. Squinting through the flitting snow, he just made out her mouth moving. It did not seem to match the strange words of the haunting song.

Then she was gone, and the thick mud between Winfrid's fingers was starting to dry and grow hard. It showed that he exuded the heat of life, at least.

Where Lina had stood, there were no marks in the snow.

He believed he was fleeing the song. There was nothing Winfrid wanted more than to lose himself to anyplace where that monstrous girl was not, and as he struggled through the snow, he craved his simple room in the monastery. Away from there, he was lost. Until recently, life at the monastery had been peaceful, calm, and safe, and Winfrid had rarely considered travelling farther than the next village. Now, with so much destruction and murder in the land, with hopelessness almost manifest in the marsh mists and the silent landscapes of snow, he had no idea what dark things were abroad.

Such time might attract horrendous things.

The snow fell heavier. Any hint of the sun was obscured in the uniform grey. Perhaps it was late afternoon, but he could not be sure. The heavy gloom seemed intent on confusing him. The land-scape, too. One patch of woodland looked the same as another, and when a breeze blew up, whisking snow into the air and driving it in drifts against trees and rocks, he lost his way completely. He might have been travelling in circles, but drifting snow covered his tracks.

I should have stayed with her, tried to help her! The child was lost and alone, terrified by her ordeal, and he had probably scared her more than anything. But though guilt inspired such thoughts, truth shoved them aside with a sneer that might have suited the girl's own face. He could not fool himself. Realization that she was something unnatural assuaged the guilt, but in its place was his own harsh, growing fear.

So he hurried on, hoping that he saw no place he recognised, praying that he did not hear that song again. He was leaving Eadric and his wife to some unknown fate, but he could do nothing for them. Even if he knew what their girl had become, he was useless. *God does not speak*, the girl had said, and the memory of her voice caused him to shiver, his vision growing hazy and unsure. He leaned against a tree and closed his eyes, but in memory there was only her.

Staring at him with those dead cold eyes.

"God save me," he muttered, pushing away from the tree and moving on. The snow was deep here, coming almost up to his knees in places, and the long habit grew heavy where snow and ice stuck around its hem.

He struggled on through a dense forest, the stark tree canopy offering little shelter from the snowfall. A while later, as light began to fade and shadows emerged from their daytime hiding places, he found a place to rest.

It was barely an overhang, but the rocky lip of a shallow ravine offered some shelter from the weather, and the snow cover was lighter than elsewhere. He dragged a log into the sheltered area to sit on, then went about building a fire. He carried a flint and kindling in his bag, and was relieved to find it still dry. But to find other wood to burn, he had to root around on the sheer walls of the ravine, reaching up onto narrow ledges to rescue fallen leaves and twigs that had gathered there. Though damp, they would be his best hope for a constant flame.

He hoped the practicalities of survival would divert his mind from what had happened. But he found himself pausing every few moments and cocking his head, listening for the one thing he dreaded hearing. The breeze remained, but it carried only the gentle patter of snowflakes against the rocky wall above him, and the creaking of trees.

God does not speak. The words echoed back at him, however much he cast them aside, however hard he disbelieved them. She had been not only mocking but confident, a certainty in herself that belied her years. *I'm not little anymore*.

It took Winfrid a long time to light the fire, and by the time he had an ember and nursed it into flame, dusk had settled around him.

The growing fire made the night even darker. He welcomed the crackling of the flames, but for the first time in his life he feared what lay beyond. Darkness had rarely troubled him, because he had always been surrounded by safety at the monastery. Even fleeing the French and the devastation they had left in their wake, God had been with him to soothe any doubts about what might lie beyond his nightly fire.

Now he saw glimmering eyes among the trees, heard the creak of snow compacting beneath cautious feet, smelled the carrion rot of creatures stalking the shadows just beyond the reach of his fire's light. He sat close and took comfort from the heat, but he could not sleep. Weary though he was, each time he closed his eyes, something jarred him awake. He hoped it was memory. He feared it was something else.

Winfrid tried to position himself as close to the steep slope as he could, but even then, his back felt exposed. He prayed. He stood and circled the fire, realised that the snow had ceased, looked up at the clearing sky and the stars and moon silvering the landscape.

When the breeze died out and moonlight revealed the deserted woodland around him, he began to settle at last. He ate the last chunk of stale, hard bread from his bag, and drank the final dregs of ale, thankful that the bottle had not been smashed. Thirst and hunger attended, if not sated, he finally closed his eyes to sleep.

The screams shattered his dreams and scattered them across the snow. He stood quickly and staggered as his sleeping legs tingled back to life. Snatching up a burning log from the fire, he turned a full circle, wondering whether he had heard anything at all.

Maybe I just imagined—

Another scream, long and loud, sang in from some distance. It changed to a series of short, sharp cries that seemed to echo from the cleared sky.

"Not wolves, not foxes," he whispered, comforting himself with his voice. "Nothing like that. That's human pain."

He shouldered his bag and started through the woods. Away from the screams, the agonies, and whatever might be causing them. He imagined Lina smiling in the shadows, her childlike shape hidden beneath the trees and as ancient and uncaring as the hills. Guilt pricked at him but he was only a man, a monk who had never raised a hand against another. How could he help?

There was movement ahead of him. Shadows shifting, flitting from one tree to another, and when he paused and stared they grew motionless. He held his breath, heart thumping in his ears. Edging sideways, downhill and away from the shadows, he came to an old trail heading through the trees and down into the valley. He followed, glancing over his shoulder and seeing movement behind and to his right.

Following him.

Winfrid tried not to panic, running at a controlled rate instead of a headlong dash that would wear him out, trip him up, injure him and leave him prone and vulnerable to whatever—

Another scream, and this was much closer, coming from just ahead of him past where several trees had fallen across the trail. He skidded to a halt and pressed in close to the splayed branches, hunkering down so that his habit and cloak gathered around his knees and thighs.

Ducking down lower, he saw beneath one tilted trunk to what lay beyond. His breath froze. His heart stuttered. Vision funnelled so that all he knew, all he saw, was the grotesque, moonlit scene playing out not thirty steps away.

A man was impaled on a tree several feet above the ground. A broken branch protruded from his chest, bloody and glistening, and he was clasping it, trying to pull or push or twist himself away. He writhed and kicked against the tree, every movement bringing fresh pain inspired another scream.

Who put him up there? Winfrid thought, and then Eadric and his wife came into view, running to the tree, reaching up, and for an instant Winfrid believed he was going to see the man saved. It was the natural thought, the only good one, and it lasted less than a heartbeat.

Because he remembered the dead man he had seen hanging from a tree the afternoon before, and what had been done to him.

Eadric tugged at the scraps of clothing the man still wore, ripping them away. The man kicked feebly, and the woman caught his foot, pulled his leg straight, and hacked at it with an axe.

The man screeched.

Eadric sliced at his other leg with a knife, cutting away a chunk of flesh as big as a fist and dropping it into the snow. Blood spattered and sprayed, drawing sickly curves across the ground. Moonlight blackened the blood.

Winfrid wondered how they could both still look so thin, so weak, considering the meat they had been ingesting.

But perhaps the flesh of your own was poison.

"No!" Winfrid shouted, pushing his way through the branches and clambering over the trunks of the fallen trees.

The woman glanced back at him, surprised, but Eadric continued cutting. He worked only on the man's thigh, and already the victim was bleeding out. He cried now rather than screamed, shaking uncontrollably so that Winfrid heard his ribs creak and break against the snapped branch.

"What are you doing?" Winfrid shouted. He ran towards the couple, and the woman turned on him with the axe raised.

"We've got to eat," she said. "Got to stay strong so we can find Lina."

"Lina is gone!" Winfrid said.

"No!" Eadric said, still slicing, dropping gobbets of meat to the ground and wiping blood from his face. "She's still with us. We hear her singing."

"That's not your daughter you hear," Winfrid said. Tears filled his eyes, then anger dried them away.

"Stay out of our business," the woman said.

"Killing people to eat is a work of evil, so it *is* my business."

"We don't kill them. We *find* them."

"Then who—?" Winfrid said, and then the singing began. At his back, perhaps as close as the trees he had just been hiding behind, the song floated across the small clearing and seemed to freeze the scene in place.

In Eadric's and the woman's eyes, delight and disbelief as they looked past Winfrid.

The dying man saw only horror.

Winfrid turned and saw Lina approaching him. Three others were with her, two women and a man, and Winfrid knew that he was in the presence of the unholy, the monstrous. They presented themselves as human—scraps of clothing, pale skin marked with dirt and scars, an air of insolence—but they were clearly something else. Their eyes betrayed that.

"Lina," her mother whispered.

Winfrid went to his knees and began to pray, and Lina stared at him. Her mouth was not quite in time with her song.

They passed him by.

"Lina, we knew, we waited, and you've come back to us," Eadric said.

The singing ceased. Winfrid found his feet again and backed towards the fallen trees. Before him, Lina and the three adults. Beyond them, her desperate and insane parents, hands marred with the dying man's blood, chunks of meat from his wretched body melted into the snow at their feet. The hope in their eyes was grotesque.

But it did not last.

Lina and one of the women took her mother down. The other man and woman pounced on Eadric. Neither of them screamed as the beasts bit hard into their throats, their necks, opening them up and gasping in the sprays of blood that arced into the starlit night.

Winfrid tried to back away further, but his feet would not move, his legs would not carry him. He was as bound to witness this horror as the dying man stuck on the tree. For a second, the two of them locked eyes but then looked away again, the terror drawing their attention.

A new song began. It held nothing of Lina's previous tune, which though unsettling had been light and musical, singing of uncomfortable mysteries best left untouched. This new song was made up of grunts and sighs. The sounds of gulping and swallowing. And then the sickly groans of ecstasy as Lina and the others bit, lapped, and raised their faces to the stars, their bodies squirming in intimate delight as blood flowed across their pale skins and into their heavily toothed mouths.

What monsters are these? Winfrid thought, but he could dwell only on what he saw. It horrified and fascinated. The victims on the ground were thrashing beneath the weight of their attackers, and he caught sight of the mother's face only once. Eyes wide in disbelief. Throat wide and gushing. Her daughter dipped her head down again, seemingly lowering her face for a kiss but then pressing herself into her mother's open neck.

She drank and groaned, and the woman died.

Winfrid still could not move. He had to watch, and he saw the moments when Eadric and the man on the tree perished also. That left him alone with them, and when Lina stood and turned, he thought she was coming for him.

But she paused, only looking his way.

"Because I'm a man of God!" he shouted. "Because He *does* have a voice, and you hear Him in me! That is not pride. That is faith."

"Your blood is weak, your flesh bland," Lina said as she turned her back on him. "Holy man."

She and the others disappeared into the trees, shadows swallowed by the night, and he saw that the truth should have been obvious to him long before. That Eadric and his wife had been fed and nurtured for this moment, eating the human flesh presented to them to make their own that much more . . . delectable.

Winfrid remained there for a while, unable to move, slumped down against the fallen trees. A chill seeped into his bones, though his soul was already colder.

As dawn broke and colour came into the world, most of it was red.

SLEEPER

He should have had a gun. *Everyone* in zombie movies or apocalyptic stories had a gun. Maybe a Magnum for optimum brain splatter. Or a rifle. With a scope, so he could sit up above the treeline and pick them off as they came for him. He didn't care which. He just wished . . .

But Philip was not resourceful, and had never been shooting in his life. The best he could manage was the baseball bat he now had slung over his shoulder. It became heavier with every lonely mile. With each step, he thought he'd have to drop it if he really wanted to carry on. But he couldn't bring himself to lose it. He'd smashed his wife's skull with the bat, and all that was left of her was smeared on the head, a drying cake of black blood and auburn hair.

"I need a gun," he said, wretched, crying. The trees didn't hear. Neither did the rocks. If anything *did* hear, it offered no reply.

He walked higher into the hills, and a warbler sang him on.

"Going into the hills will be best," he says. "There are mines. Deep, dark, easily defended. And they keep stores of food and water down there in case of cave-ins."

"You really believe that?" Rose asks. The sneer is in her voice, if not on her face. Even now, with everything they're hearing on the news and seeing on TV, she finds time to put him down.

"Yeah," Philip says. Feeling uncertain now, as always when she questions him, even if he knows for sure what he's saying is true. That's the hold she has on him. She strangles his certainty and obscures his world.

So they go, even though Rose exudes disapproval.

But when they leave their neighbourhood and start their drive out of Knoxville, they see sights that silence them both, and she scoots over in the seat so that they can touch each other for comfort. It's never the same on TV.

Then in the beautiful foothills south-east of town, the car runs out of fuel. Philip's fault, because he hadn't checked. So they walk, and an hour later they can look downhill and see the car park at the beginning of a scenic walk. People are running and shooting, a car is on fire, and they see more terrible things.

"Up," he says. "That's the only way. Up to the mines."

He's even starting to convince himself.

Two days after he destroyed what his wife had become, close to the most beautiful landscape of hillside, valley and lake he had ever seen, Philip witnessed a group of zombies taking down a woman and her child.

He had not slept for almost sixty hours. By day he walked, and at night he climbed a tree and cowered, licking moisture from leaves, listening, waiting for them to come. Terror kept sleep at bay. That, and Rose staring from beneath her blood-caked hair with dead, accusing eyes.

He heard the mother and son screaming from a distance and ran to see, crazy ideas of saving them terrifying him. With every step the fear bit in, and by the time he caught sight of them scrambling down a rocky outcropping he knew there was nothing he could do.

Useless, he thought, but it was Rose's voice, and it was him she was talking about.

So he hid behind a pile of felled trees and watched. The woman was helping her young son climb down the rugged cliff face, perhaps believing that she could escape them that way. She was correct in assuming that the dead could not climb.

They fell instead. The first one tumbled, cracking his head on an outcropping and spinning past six feet from the boy. The second and third missed as well, but the fourth struck the woman's shoulder. She cried out, twisted, and lost her grip on her son.

Philip closed his eyes as the boy fell, but he could not close his ears.

"Nate! Nate! Nate!" the woman screamed, and whatever she saw below her—hidden from Philip's sight by a fold in the land and more piled logs—must have been awful. It took only five seconds before she let go and fell after her boy.

Philip ran in the other direction. He ran further than he ever had before, hardly stopping for two hours, and by the time he slid to the ground beside a stream and took a drink, he thought he was going to die.

They find the family late that first afternoon.

"We need to stay away from them," Philip says. "Something's wrong."

"One of them's hurt," Rose says. "That's what's wrong."

"So let them call an ambulance!"

Rose does not even answer. They've both tried calling the emergency services and heard the same recorded message.

When Philip fell in love with Rose, it was her compassion that drew him to her. She cared too much, he would tell her, but at the same time he found her selflessness and concern for others incredibly admirable and attractive. He loved her love for other people.

After their wedding, her lack of empathy for him would have struck him as ironic if it weren't so sad. Rose was intelligent and sometimes even superior, and did not suffer fools gladly. And Philip was first to admit that he was a fool.

I can't help it, he'd tell her. *I just don't see the world the way everyone else does.*

"I'm going down there," she says.

"No, don't be stupid!"

"Philip." Spoken with ire.

"I mean it! Look . . . " He grabs her arm, gently, and pulls her down beside him. The family is gathered around a truck with two flat tyres, and Philip and Rose are well hidden up a small embankment, trees and bushes making them part of the land. "Look, Rose. The tall guy there has a gun. He's holding it ready. That's his family he's standing there protecting. The girl on the ground . . . maybe his daughter." They never had children, but Philip thinks he can understand the protectiveness that man must be feeling. He yearned to feel it himself.

"He's not just going to shoot two people coming out of the woods."

"How do you know?" He struggles to keep his voice down. "We haven't got a fucking clue what's happening, and no one else has, either!"

"No need to swear at me."

"I'm not swearing at you! I'm swearing at *everything*. You saw what was happening in town as we left. The smoke. The fires. Those people. You *heard* the *guns*, Rose! And you saw . . . " They both saw things. Terrible things that do not need vocalising again. "The news. What people were saying." He points along the road towards the crippled car. "He'll do anything to protect his family. And that's what *I'm* doing."

Her laugh is almost a spit. A cough of derision. It stings, but does nothing to temper his caution.

"Please—" he says, and Rose shrugs him off and stands.

"Hey! It's okay, we're normal, not like *them*."

The man aims his rifle and freezes into a shooting stance, and Philip can't help watching even as he thinks, *I'm going to see Rose's head blown off, he knows how to shoot, perhaps he's done plenty of shooting today already, and her hair will fan out with the impact and her brains will stain the road.* And deep inside where the most hateful thoughts dwell blooms a tiny spark of relief. With Rose gone, he will only have himself to save.

"I'm a nurse," Rose says. That isn't quite true; she is a care worker, looking after old people in an expensive retirement home in the countryside north of Knoxville. But maybe today it is close enough.

Philip stands slowly and steps out into the road, but he does not advance with his wife. Something is still wrong. The girl lies on the road beside the truck's open rear door, and even from this distance he can see the blood.

"Ask what happened to her," he says, loud enough for Rose alone to hear. She ignores him.

"Got bit!" the man shouts. Perhaps he heard Philip after all. "My little girl got fuckin' bit by that crazy old fuckin' loon from three doors down!" Rose reaches them and kneels, obscuring Philip's view. Those around the prone form move back a little, giving her room.

How long ago? Philip thinks, because he has been reading frantic reports on Twitter. Already a timeline seems to be forming. *More than half an hour? Because that seems to be the longest—*

Someone coughs, and growls. And then a scream. It is such a shocking, chilling cry that Philip closes his eyes and turns away, which means that he only hears the gunshot.

He falls to the ground, dropping the baseball bat he's been carrying since the car ran out of fuel. Presses himself flat to the road. Scoots around so that he can look back towards the truck—

And Rose is rushing back towards him, eyes wide, a bloody smear across her left forearm.

Touched her! Philip thinks, and there are more screams. Close to the car three shapes struggle in the road—the bloody girl and two others. The man with the rifle steps around them, gun raising, lowering, coming up again as he struggles with what to do. The shot must have been accidental, and the bullet had gone nowhere. The next might find wet.

But Philip will not wait to see. He grabs up the bat and reaches for Rose's hand as she runs past him, but she ignores him. Her eyes are frantic. She's terrified, and soon he will ask what she saw.

Soon. Because first they have to escape the screaming and chaos. The bloodied girl is up.

And Rose has blood on *her*. Philip runs after her, watching her movements, listening to her breathing. Waiting for something wrong.

Four days after leaving Knoxville, he found a mine.

It was almost a hundred hours since he'd slept. He'd done his best to avoid anywhere there might be people, or the dead—skirting around small towns, staying off roads, losing himself in the wilds. If he heard voices he ran in the opposite direction. If he heard other things—once there were soft hooting sounds, and then the shuffle of aimless feet—he ran even faster.

He ate little. A hard, dry sandwich found in an abandoned car. Wild strawberries. He drank from streams, and he'd had diarrhoea for almost twenty hours. It seemed that the more he drank, the more thirsty he became.

Hallucinations haunted him. Rose trailed him through the trees, wearing the dress from their wedding five years previously. She had only ever worn it once since, when they'd come home drunk one evening and wanted a dirty fuck. Now it snagged on branches and brambles as she came for him, always walking faster than him, yet never arriving. At least Philip still *knew* they were hallucinations, however awful. Soon, even that would change. Perhaps then would be the time to follow that poor mother from a cliff.

And then the mine.

"There it is," he said quietly. The sound of his voice in the wild silence was already shocking him, but it felt like company. "Down there'll be food and water. And somewhere to hide. But I've got to make sure . . . "

So he found a rock with a slight overhang, from which he could watch the mine entrance, the workings, the buildings and car park surrounding it. The trees to the west were made ghostlike with dust that had been blown that way over the years, the guts of the earth brought up and exposed to the elements. He waited there for an hour, two, and saw no movement.

He closed his eyes to sleep, but sleep would not come.

"Maybe down there," he said. "Down in the dark." But he was already starting to wonder whether he could ever descend from the world. There could *anything* down below. There could be . . .

The time came to move. He staggered down the slope and across the muddy enclosure around the mine entrance, ground churned up by heavy wheels and soaked by the previous night's rain. His boots picked up wet soil, each step heavy. His limbs did not belong to him.

There was a green corrugated structure around the mine shaft itself, and one flap of iron smacked rhythmically against its support.

He thought he heard voices. Paused. Turned this way and that, listening to a gentle breeze passing through telephone wires above him. A soft call, like doves in the distance.

"Rose," he said, looking at the mess on the baseball bat.

Three shapes emerged from out of the darkness.

He tries to convince himself that there's no alternative.

They ran for thirty minutes, desperate to put distance between them and the stricken family. Along trails, across the stark open space of denuded woodland now consisting of stumps, rotting trunks, and a creeping undergrowth that seemed to be doing its best to smother the sad ruin. There was one more gunshot from far behind, and a child's scream, and for a terrible moment Philip thought that Rose might turn and go back. But then he started to wonder.

"Rose?" he asks again. She's sitting on a rock beside a stream. She has one trainer off, foot dangling in the water, but doesn't seem to have the strength to remove the other. She has not spoken for half an hour.

Half an hour, Philip thinks. He holds the bat by his side. She laughed at him when he brought it along. *What are you going to do with that? Fucking idiot.* It was her fear talking, partly. But for years now, he had often seen *fucking idiot* in her eyes when she looked at him.

"Rose?"

Her head is dipping, chin touching her chest. He can't hear her panting anymore.

I should circle around. See her face. See if that's a cut—a bite—*on her arm, or just a smear of blood. It looks like a handprint, but that could be where she grabbed it after she was bitten. Bitten.*

They're saying it's the bites.

Twitter has been alive. Panic has gone electronic. The end of the world, with hashtags.

"Rose?"

She snorts. Coughs. Maybe she's just exhausted. But—

Philip raises the bat and waits for her mocking glance, her dismissive comment, her constant denial of all the good things about him, her emphasising of the bad. Everything that makes her Rose. Yet none of that comes.

So he swings.

The three people were dead. Two were men, one of them with his throat ripped out, the other wearing bib overalls and with a hole where his left eye should have been. He carried a length of hose that he might have been gripping for four days, since he died.

The third was a young woman. She tilted her head to the side and hooted softly, a strangely mournful sound coming from something so dead. She had no face.

Philip swayed. He had no strength to lift the baseball bat when they came. He had a headache from dehydration and exhaustion, and his limbs seemed far away.

Before the battery on his phone ran out, he'd read reports about how the contagion had spread from somewhere deep in the Appalachian mountains, and that the victims' only aim seemed to be spreading the disease. They were fast, he'd read. They ran.

He could do nothing to defend himself now. And as he waited, he wondered whether it would really make any difference if they bit him, or not.

THE GLEEFUL ONES

S tylist stood in the dark and breathed in the scent of rat piss and decay and fear, because this was where he did his greatest work.

The abandoned shop's rear area had once been used for storage, and there were still several cardboard boxes, wet and slumping down, deformed by time. Inside, piles of rotting clothes. A grille across the single window slanted weak moonlight through dust-obscured glass. The room was never quite silent—sharp feet skittered, dust danced, and Stylist's and his quarry's intrusion had altered the space, agitating stale air with their unexpected presence.

"Whaddafu'?"

Stylist could still sense fleeting memories floating on the air. In the poor light, he could see the haze of fine hairs settling. After he was through, the room would be still again. He wondered how long it would be before these settled hairs were stirred once more.

"Wha' . . . what am I . . . ?"

He had never been completely immune to the effect. But familiarity meant that he knew what to expect, and could brace himself. The others—his targets, the scumbags, the pond scum, the clingons attached to society's fat arse—were always caught unawares. Shredded hair from a thousand customers, chopped so fine, blown with Stylist's own miraculous breath, inspiring countless dreams and memories, images and flashbacks. Violent episodes and grunting fucks.

Sensory overload. Unconsciousness. And then . . .

"Where . . . ?" The man tied into the chair froze, looking around at his surroundings. Then he began to struggle, thrashing left and right against the plastic zip-ties, growling, rocking the chair so much that it was in danger of turning over.

Stylist sighed. He placed his left hand on the man's shoulder, and reached around to touch his throat with the scissors in his right hand.

"Now then," he said. "'Let's calm down first, shall we?"

"Fuck you."

"Right." He pressed with the scissors. They were closed, outer surfaces dulled. But he knew that the scumbag knew who he was, and what was happening here. A lot of what he dealt in was fear. Anticipation. Potential. It was very rare that actual pain procured what he desired.

"Wait!"

"Wait?" Stylist echoed. The room seemed to swallow his voice. The air was thickening with fear, and that was good.

The man started chuckling.

That was unexpected. Stylist increased the pressure a little more. The scumbag pressed back against the chair, wincing from what he must believe was an open pair of scissors. But through his terror, that laughter. Maybe he was high on something. SkullFuck was flooding the streets from the reopened ports, but it was usually the real lowlifes who used that. Not someone like this. Someone connected.

"Guy Meloy," Stylist said. "Twenty-seven. Born in Leamington Spa, moved to London ten years ago, string of minor skirmishes with the law."

Meloy snorted, probably at the word "minor". Scumbags like this wore their crimes with pride. But Stylist was getting there.

"Hooked up with the Morris Mob four years ago. Couple of banks, then moved on to posh homes around Kensington and Chelsea. The gang's calling card was to anally rape the woman of the house in front of her husband and children."

"Bitches loved a good butt-fuckin'."

"Right." Stylist slammed his flattened left hand against Meloy's ear. It might not pop his eardrum—odds were even that an impact like that would do any lasting damage—but from the noise he made, it obviously smarted.

"You're gonna fuckin—"

"I'm gonna fuckin' cut your hair," Stylist said. "I'm going to finish what I have to say, pronounce my sentence, and then take out my comb and give you a new hairdo. Because that's what I do. And ... " He leaned in closer, breathing into the man's right ear. "I just *know* you know what that means. You've got friends I've worked on, I'm sure. You've seen."

"You don't scare me," Meloy said, his voice loaded with the lie.

"Oh, I'm not here to scare you. I'll leave that up to Cthulhu Girl, or Downside. That's their territory. My aim has always been self-improvement." He snipped the scissors, their sharp *snick!* ringing through the room. "Now, if I can finish?"

"You'll *be* finished, fucker."

Stylist slapped Meloy's ear again, but he was frowning. Unsettled. Usually by now they'd be begging.

"The Morris Gang disbanded when Morris was killed by The Plumber. Ewww. What a mess that was. Did you ever see what became of your boss? I'm sure you did. The pictures are all over the net. Huh. Plumber. Bless him, he always does enjoy the notoriety. He'll get himself caught and cancelled one day."

"Not before you, hair man."

Stylist decided to ignore the quips. They were bravado, nothing more.

"Since then you've been on your own. If it'd stayed at burglary I'd have probably left you alone, let one of the newer, younger Vees sweep you up."

"The newer Vigilantes can suck my—"

Stylist struck the same ear again. It sounded wet. "Maybe you'd have even avoided anyone's attention for a few more years. But on those raids with the Morris Mob, the rapes became more important to you than the robberies."

"Yeah," Meloy drawled.

"My sentence is rearrangement," Stylist said. He withdrew his comb, wielded the scissors, and made the first cut. He felt the intimate brush of just-snipped hair falling across the back of his hand and then away to the floor. It always felt so alive. Sometimes, he thought he heard it scream.

"Do-gooder," Meloy said. "Weakling. Trim away. Cut away. Leave me like one of them. But you . . . your number's up, hair man. Your name's been called. You and all of you stupid fuckin' Vees who think you're 'normal'. Ha!" Meloy started laughing again as Stylist continued cutting, channelling himself through the comb and scissors, everything he was and had, and everything he wanted for Guy Meloy. He felt the criminal's hair falling away, and even in the darkness he was aware of the shape forming before him. The man's hair was being crafted into an impossible design, bearing the weight of his crimes and creating the gravity of guilt. And from now on, it would always be this way.

But Meloy remained defiant.

"And your family, hair man."

Stylist paused, the silence shorn of scissor whispers.

"*They* know where your family live. Your boy, your girl."

"Who are 'they'?"

Meloy sniggered. Stylist cut some more, lessening the man and making a permanent scar of his hair.

"They look at you and all your friends, and laugh. And . . . plan."

"Who are they?" Stylist asked again. He snicked the scissors close to Meloy's right eye, trimming eyelashes.

"And your wife." Meloy's tone fell, heavy with something other than fear. "Her, with her gorgeous arse just waiting for me to fill—"

Stylist felt a rush of blood, pulsing from his heart and deadening his senses. He shifted his right hand, casually, without effort, and felt a spray of heat across his wrist and forearm.

"Who are they?" he asked yet again.

"Gleeful . . . " Meloy muttered. But then he started gasping in surprise at what had been done.

Stylist took two steps back to avoid the blood, and watched as Meloy bled to death through his nicked carotid artery.

"Damn," he whispered. The dying man's blood was a shadow amongst shadows as it pulsed from the wound, splashing against the wall and dirty flood. Already there came the patter of rat-feet. Meloy tried to speak, but shock had stolen his voice. "Damn." Stylist did not like loss of control. What he did was *defined* by control—careful cutting and combing, forming an idea that would be borne forever by the shape he made of a client's hair—and losing it was not a good sign.

But the scumbag had said that about his wife.

Stylist swept the clippings, tipped them into a small bag he produced from his pocket, turned to go, and he could still hear the sounds of Guy Meloy's slow death behind him. He didn't care. One scumbag or another, it was all a case of extremes.

"I didn't do anything wrong," Stylist said as he emerged into the cool night air. A familiar mantra. A phrase he lived by.

Making his way home through the city, smelling its corruption, sensing its violence, and catching sight of one other fleeting shadow that might or might not have been someone he knew, Stylist was happy to let the inhumanity that dwelled within sweep away the guilt.

Extract from *Once Were Vigilantes*,
by Max Gold, London Council Press

Stylist (active London, England: July 2022-?)—One of the minor Vees, using arcane knowledge to alter the people whose hair he cut through subtle shifts in brain patterns, a slow-release effect loaded into permanent, untouchable hair styles, and tools—scissors, a comb, a brush—whose origins are still unknown. It is believed he also ran a barbershop in London, and while there have been rumours of his identity, there was never a definitive exposure. When The Gleeful Ones came to the fore, it is rumoured that The Stylist either went to ground, or fled the country.

Conflicting reports also suggest that he was one of the first Vees murdered by the Gleeful Ones for disagreeing with their philosophy.

His street was dark and asleep when he arrived. It was almost midnight. Glancing up, he saw the shadow of one of the airships passing slowly and silently overhead, distinguishable from the clouds only by its uniform shape. He slipped into an alley between two abandoned houses and lifted a loose fencing board, crawling through into the dilapidated shed on the other side. Here he removed his mask and boilersuit. Stylist had never been one for elaborate costumes, feeling that Vees who needed to make a statement with how they dressed did not really understand their purpose. He dropped the clothing into a tub, poured in a measure of dry-wash, then crawled back out into the alley.

By the time he stood beneath a streetlight once again, Stylist had become Jason Hamm.

Fifteen houses along the street stood his own home. The lights were out, and inside it was quiet, but for the gentle hum of the TV and games console the kids had left on. Jason tutted, moved across the living room, and then sat heavily on the sofa. Breathing hard.

Feeling blood drying on his wrist and hand. Seeing Meloy's shadow struggling into death, and hearing him saying, *They know where you live. Your boy, your girl. And your wife.*

Jason had always promised himself that the minute his activities threatened his family, he would stop. Throw away his tools, try and forget the thing inside him that fed Stylist, powered his creations. But squeezing his eyes shut now, the truth he had always known forced itself to the fore—that the choice could never be his.

He crept upstairs and showered, then went into his children's room. Holly and Sean still insisted on sleeping in the same bedroom, and while they were young enough, Jason hated to dissuade them. At nine, Holly was three years older than her brother. The time would soon come when they bickered more than played, argued more than laughed. Jason and Janie wanted to grab onto every minute of the present as shield against the future.

Jason sat on the beanbag by the door and, illuminated by the weak nightlight, watched his children sleeping. Holly had her cuddly tiger clasped tightly beneath her arm, and her long hair partly obscured her face. She snored, very softly. Sean had thrown off his covers, as usual. His face glimmered with beads of sweat. He mumbled and twitched. Jason wondered what both of his children were dreaming of, and hoped that it was good. Everything he did was to make their lives safer, and their dreams better. Everything he did was for them.

He stood and kissed them both goodnight. Then he crossed the landing to the smaller room he and Janie used as their bedroom, slipped in between the covers, and snuggled up to her warmth.

"Hmm, where's the cake?" she asked, sighing in some dreamy satisfaction. Jason laughed softly. Her dreams, as well. His family was everything to him, and the thought of any danger befalling them . . .

He touched his wife's long, luscious hair, running it through his fingers, closing his eyes, sensing the power in her hair and knowing that he would never, ever touch it.

He fell asleep surprisingly quickly, and as ever his dreams were sharp.

"Bunch of roses," he said. "Red ones. Thirteen."

"Unlucky for some?" the woman asked.

"Not today." Jason smiled. Florist nodded, glanced past him at the shop doorway, then scanned a CCTV camera display she kept beneath her counter.

"Well?" she asked. "What do you want?" She never had been the friendliest of people.

"I'm not just allowed to visit?"

"Fuck's sake. A barber visiting a florist. Anyone looking for patterns . . . "

"You're just paranoid."

"Huh. You know there're searchers out there. Wanting to expose us, end us."

Jason shrugged, then sniffed a rose. It was beautiful. But Florist could make it un-beautiful. Some of the bouquets she sent out carried aromas to intoxicate, confuse, cripple, wipe memory, or kill. The beauty of her gift was that anyone who suspected her of being something more than she projected would have their suspicions erased. Jason had often believed her to be one of the most dangerous Vees he knew about. Whereas he could play with fate, Florist could deal in memory.

"What do you know about 'gleeful'?"

"Huh?" She continued arranging, trimming, sizing stems. But in a very deliberate way. Her movements had shifted from natural to forced.

"Doesn't matter," Jason said, and he turned to leave.

"Stylist."

He turned back, raising one eyebrow. Using such names in public, in the open, was so foolish that . . . But she had caught his attention. And she held out one yellow rose, aiming at him like some beautiful gun.

"What?"

"There is nothing gleeful," she said. And she lowered the rose and nodded at the door. "Customers." A man and woman entered, laughing over some secret, and Florist's smile lit up the shop as she welcomed them in.

Jason left and walked along the busy street, passing greengrocers and jewellers, betting shops and furniture showrooms. People jostled and bustled. Cars grumbled by, the line of traffic hardly moving any faster than pedestrians.

He looked up at the clear blue sky, empty of airships at the moment. Maybe the Councillors had a conference, in which case they would be parked and floating above the ruins of the Houses of Parliament. Or perhaps there was simply nothing of interest in this suburb of London today.

"Bullshit," Jason muttered. An old woman looked at him suspiciously, and he smiled at her. She shook her head and hurried away. "There's *plenty* of interest here," he said, looking back at Florist's shop and the colourful explosion of blooms spilling across the pavement. His blood was chilled. "Plenty."

Extract from *Once Were Vigilantes,*
by Max Gold, London Council Press

Stylist's modus operandi has been gleaned from several victims, none of whom wish to be named or photographed. All describe a "tingling in their mouth and nose, an explosion of stranger senses and memories, unconsciousness, and then waking somewhere else". Abandoned buildings were his favourite haunt, and it is suspected that he had prepared such sites—there was always a chair present, adequate plastic bindings, and in some cases a mirror in which the victim could view the cutting. The styling would take place (an experience described by separate victims as "odd", "unsettling, like someone trimming my personality", and "seriously fucking whacked, man"). Following the trim, Stylist would collect the hair trimmings using a small pan and brush, and then leave the victims to effect their own

escape. Some remained bound and trapped for many hours or
even days, and on release they were changed people. Lessened.
Criminals mostly, but there are alleged cases of mistaken identity. And of course, there are those whom Stylist murdered.

Later, in the small office and kitchen behind his barbershop, Jason
was in preparation. The hair from a hundred heads, finely chopped,
mixed, breathed upon, and imbued with the breath of the thing
inside that drove him to do what he did, and gave him the means.
It carried memories and dreams, fears and nightmares, and when
sprinkled into someone's face, stunned them with sensory input.
No normal person could withstand the sudden rush of imagery
and remain upright. Many drugs worked on the muscles, but Jason
knew that the brain was the centre of the body. He chopped and
chopped again, mixing and processing until it was unrecognisable
as hair, more as a powder. Dampening it as he went to prevent any
escape to the atmosphere, he then separated the compound into
small, pinch-sized folds of foil. He hid these away in a dozen cracks
between floorboards and brick walling, keeping one in his pocket
as always.

Standing, tapping the foil packet, and wondering what the hell
was going on, the bell above the door chimed him back from Stylist
to Jason Hamm.

He walked through into his barbershop and stopped. Staring. She
was probably used to people staring.

"I'd like a haircut, please," she said, a smile playing at the corner
of her lips. Gorgeous, there was also something about her that
instantly set Jason on edge. She wore tight jeans and a white tank-
top vest. Straight, shoulder-length blazing red hair. Three earrings
in each ear, another in her nose, and tattoos reached from the neck-
line and arms of her top, like a many-limbed thing wanting out.
Jason wondered at the full splendour of the ink.

"This is a barbershop," Jason said. "I'm usually only visited by
men."

"Oh, *barber*!" the woman said, waving the words away. Her smile was sweet, enticing. "You're a hair stylist, aren't you?"

And there it was.

"I can cut your hair if you want," he said.

"I want." She walked to the single barber's chair and lowered herself down, releasing the lever that dropped the chair to the floor. "Oh, whoops," she said. "You'll have to raise me up again."

Jason stood behind the chair and rested his foot on the bar. Pumping, the chair rose in jolts, and each time he pumped the woman's breasts moved beneath her vest. She watched him in the mirror, watching her. The smile never slipped from her lips, but neither did it fully form.

"You cut, I'll talk," she said. "Oh, and don't even think about using any of your stuff on me."

"Who are you?" Jason asked.

She stared at him in the mirror. Now, the smile did drop. "I said *I* talk."

Jason nodded, and started brushing her hair.

"He was a scumbag, but he was useful to me."

Jason knew that she was watching him, so he raised an eyebrow. He could not take his eyes from her burning, blazing hair.

"Meloy."

"Who?"

She sighed. "He's not why I'm here, though. Not really. I'm here because I suspect he might have been a little . . . gleeful with his talk. Before you killed him."

"Killed who?" Jason tried to affect shock, but simply catching her eye in the mirror melted him a little. His face relaxed, and he offered a half-smile. *Okay. Fair enough. So what's the game?*

"Loose talk costs lives, Jason. Meloy lost his, but there are lots, lots more whose value is much higher. If he made you think there might be . . . something going on, then cast that thought from your mind."

He looked at her. Her eyes were green. *They know where they live. Your boy, your girl.* Snip. He trimmed quarter of an inch from the hair above her ears. He heard every hair parting, every one falling. He cut it as Jason Hamm.

"Loose thoughts cost lives, too. And what Meloy might have been hinting at . . . what he might have let slip, if you didn't cut his throat too early . . . " She paused, forcing him to look at her. "Eh? Too early?"

Jason shrugged, giving nothing away.

Snip.

"Well, it wasn't his to let slip. It was *ours* to tell."

"Gleefully?"

She frowned, just slightly, betraying some internal conflict.

"Meloy threatened my family." He smoothed her hair, closed his eyes for an instant, and felt the thing inside that made him *other* move to the fore. He held the hair between his fingers aslant, so that it caught the light and seemed to burn like ancient fire. Opened the scissors. Breathed out the thought, *She will forget who I am and where my family and I live.* Started to—

"Don't you fucking dare." The voice was so different that Stylist dropped the scissors and Jason stepped back in shock. The woman's hair rose around her head as though a strong breeze swept through the still barbershop, and as she stood from the chair, the tattoos on her shoulders and upper arms squirmed awake. They writhed in exotic rhythm, stroking sensuous tendrils across her pale skin.

She turned, lifting the vest up over her head in one fluid movement, exposing the designs splayed across her body. Enticing, hypnotic, the tattoos moved in synch with the woman's flesh as she closed on him and placed a hand on each shoulder.

"You'd try to cut me?" she asked. "You'd try to change me?" She ran one hand through her hair, giving freedom to the thing that was her skin. And . . .

And Jason so wanted to fuck her, there, then, bent over the counter and pressed against the mirrors, bury himself in her and feel her staggering warmth taking him in, and she grinned because she knew exactly what he was thinking.

"I'm Succubus," she said, "and you'll remember me. If you value your life, and the lives of those you love, you *will* remember me. And you will forget Meloy, and his mention of the Gleeful Ones, until the Gleeful Ones come for you."

"Who are you?" Jason asked.

"I told you my name."

"But I've never seen anyone . . . like . . . "

Succubus ran her hands across her chest, the tattoo hazing in and out of focus as though rippled on a pond. Fine tendrils writhed, skin pulsed, Jason's heart hammered.

"The time to hide ourselves has passed," she said. He could feel her heat. "Plans are being laid. You, Stylist, will be called." Her breath smelled of delight, and he so wished to revel in it.

"I don't understand."

"You don't need to." And then she was gone, slinking her vest back on before pulling the door open and exiting onto the street.

Jason reached quickly into his pocket and found the folded foil slip, but it was too late. He took three steps towards the door, shaken by her presence and what she had said and implied, and eager to know more. But it was too late. He pressed his face to the window beside the "open/closed" sign, and the street was full of people ignorant of the miracles in their midst.

And if those same people had known who he was and what he did, they would likely want him dead.

Extract from *Once Were Vigilantes*, by Max Gold, London Council Press

While it is true that some people supported the acts carried out by the Vees, the majority of the general public disliked, feared, or loathed them. Before the Gleeful Ones, there were frequent lynchings of those suspected of being Vigilantes. Most readers will remember the infamous Crow Talker incident, when a man—Nigel Wheeler, from Croydon—was caught allegedly guiding crows to attack pick-pockets in Hyde Park. Tied and beaten by a gang of teenagers, onlookers quickly joined in the persecution. Few can forget the images of Mr Wheeler being strung up on a lamp post, hanged in front of crowds of Londoners and tourists, while the minority calling for mercy and justice were shouted down and hounded from the park. And no one will forget the crows that sat on his head and shoulders as he slowly choked to death.

The Gleeful Ones, and what they did, quickly turned public opinion into Council law. A state of emergency was declared. The war was short. The airships sent down their pronouncements, the Vees were rounded up, the prisons began to fill.

No one has yet written an impartial analysis of the effect of this pogrom on Vees' families.

No one cares.

Jason kept low for the next few days. He remained a barber, a family man, and nothing else. While the thing inside urged him to take his talent out into the night, he resisted. But the urge was beyond his control.

On the sixth day he closed the shop early and went home. He hovered close to the abandoned house, whose garden shed he used as a changing and staging area for his activities. But it was too light to change just yet. And he had his family to think about.

"This thing I do," he said quietly over dinner, but Janie hushed him up.

"Not in front of the kids!"

"Not in front of the kids!" Holly echoed, and little Sean copied her, the two of them turning Janie's admonishment into a chant. Jason waved a hand, smiling, feigning embarrassment. But all the while he wanted to drag Janie aside and tell her what was wrong. *I think it's getting dangerous. I think something's going to happen.*

She had never really understood, and had spent a large part of their marriage trying to ignore what her husband was, and what he could do. Whenever he tried talking about it she cut him off, raising a hand or turning away. She had made his power into something that would always come between them, but could never be discussed.

He had tried, so often. But Stylist would always be an invisible barrier, preventing them from ever truly touching.

With dinner finished and the children hustled upstairs to bathe and prepare for bed, Jason prevented Janie from leaving the kitchen.

"Janie—"

"Nope. Don't want to hear about it."

"But I've got to tell you—"

"No, Jase." She looked him in the eye and stood firm. "You know what I think about . . . that."

"But can't you change?"

"Why should I?"

"Because I think I might."

She blinked, frowned, and seemed about to say something when Sean started crying from upstairs. Holly's raised voice only aggravated him. Water splashed. Someone stomped.

"I've got to sort out our children," Janie said. "I assume tonight you're . . . ?"

"Just for a couple of hours," Jason said. He felt the need more than ever, his power burning inside like a pressure valve that needed venting. Sometimes he went a couple of days without going out as Stylist, but it had never been this long. It felt like he was going cold turkey from his soul.

You speak as if it's a separate conscious thing, Janie had said once, and he had not replied. How could he? He barely knew what it was himself.

"I doubt if I'll be awake when you come in," she said. Jason felt a pang of regret, a stab of rejection, before realising that this might be a good thing. What he had to do might take all night.

Stylist, boiler-suited and masked, stalked from shadow to shadow and left worries behind.

Some worries, at least. Not all. Some worries, like those everyday niggles that plague people on a 9-to-5, or parents, or those whose boundaries are too tight to appreciate the good amongst the bad. But tonight there were other worries, and Stylist carried extra foils of his hair dust. And extra scissors.

He knew where to find Florist. Her shop was a front, and her real home was in a place that no one would ever suspect. Deep in the Docklands, high in a tower of exclusive apartments that were now mostly locked shut and slowly going to rot, Florist hid in clear sight. Hers was one of a dozen apartments lit through the night by soft lighting, and marked as inhabited during the day with open windows and billowing curtains. She had once claimed to Stylist that she believed herself and her abilities to be things of beauty, and to hide them away was a crime. Secrecy was different. Secrecy preserved beauty and gave it the space it needed. Florist was in constant bloom, and now Stylist needed to ask her some questions.

He slipped through the streets without being seen. If he heard voices, he would hide. A shadow was his friend. Once he saw Spite—a once-handsome man who had sliced off his own nose, and who now punished criminals by mutilating them—but Stylist pressed himself into a darkened doorway and watched the angry madman drift by. Beneath his coat would be a dozen knives, razors and machetes, and Stylist had never trusted him.

Madness haunted the Vees. As Jason Hamm, he did not consider himself madder than any average person nowadays, struggling to make ends meet and fight against economic depression, oppression, and the unfair demands of the rich people in power. But to become Stylist—and for any of them to manifest as someone more incredible, and powerful—insanity had to be at work somewhere.

"I don't think about it," he whispered as he watched Spite pass by, and in trying to convince himself, he lied.

And what of Succubus? *The time to hide ourselves has passed.* To exist in her altered state permanently must be . . .

Fascinating. Terrifying.

"Fuck it," Stylist said, and he moved on. The streets were quiet at this time of night, but he kept watch on the places where people might be watching him. Being seen was not a problem, but being attacked was a constant threat.

The door to Florist's apartment block was electronically shut, and he took several seconds to open it. No alarms sounded, at least none that he could hear. Either way, though, he should assume that she knew he was on his way.

Before today, that would have not upset him too much. Never exactly friendly, Florist had however welcomed his occasional visits, counting him as someone she could call a friend. Though private lives were always kept that way, he was convinced that she had no family or lover. She was very much alone.

There was an atrium inside, stairs climbing around its edges. A long, fine filament hung from the clear roof framing twelve storeys up, and its ceramic pendulum hung six inches above the atrium's floor. It moved, ever so slightly. Nothing was ever still.

Stylist took the stairs. He hid his strong core and knotted muscles beneath a camouflage of easily-gained fat, just one small aspect of needing to fit into normality. Most people who saw him assumed he was a middle-aged, slightly out-of-shape barber. His work-outs were hidden even from his family, and twenty-four flights of stairs would suffice for today. To begin with, at least. He had a feeling there would be more.

Outside Florist's penthouse apartment door, he raised one hand to knock. Paused. Pressed his ear to the wood, listening, exhaling slightly to clear his hearing. There was nothing at all from inside, but he had a startling image of Florist standing two inches from him doing exactly the same thing. There was no peephole in the door. No cameras hidden in the hallway's ceiling corners.

He raised his hand again, and the door opened.

"The fuck do you want?" Florist asked.

"Nice to see you, too."

"What is this, a social call? Come to do my hair?"

Stylist glanced at Florist's head. Everyone's hair fascinated him, and he wondered what he would feel were he to run his fingers through her golden locks; what pollens he might release and breathe in; what terrible, wonderful memories each strand might contain.

"No," he said. "It's a . . . working call."

She raised an eyebrow, and glanced around the hallway behind him. But he guessed she already knew they were alone.

"Come in." She turned and walked into her apartment, leaving the door open for him to follow her inside.

Her apartment smelled of roses. He breathed deeply as he stepped inside and closed the door, then caught his breath and felt a momentary panic. Pressing his hand across his mouth and nose, he reached for scissors with his other hand.

Florist glanced back at him from the large, open plan room, and smiled.

"Do you really think I would be so obvious?"

"Only if you had need," Stylist said. He glanced around her home. "I didn't peg you for a minimalist." The room was sparse in the extreme. Wide, tall-ceilinged, it was home to three lonely armchairs and a low glass table. In one wall he saw the telltale lines of a hidden cupboard, within which he guessed were housed entertainment systems.

"It's my clean place," she said, voice softening. "My retreat. Away from all those flowers and plants, and the uneven blooms, the chaos. The air here is filtered and conditioned five times per hour. Almost pure."

"The rose smell?"

Florist half-smiled, shrugged. "I can never let go completely."

"So are you gleeful, Florist?" he asked. Her face dropped. He saw no fear there, and very little surprise. Only regret.

"Oh, Jason." She had never called him by his real name, ever. He didn't even know hers, and for the years they had known each other—a distant friendship, if a friendship at all—he'd believed that they were as much a mystery to each other as to those around them.

"What's going on?" he asked, trying to keep his voice level. He still had not removed his mask. It was his identity out here, his shield. But her use of his name was unpicking it thread by thread. "What's happening? Is something going to change?" He thought of Succubus with her squirming tattoos, and things he had never before seen, or imagined.

"Something?" Florist asked. "No. Everything is going to change." She vanished quickly through an invisible door in the wall, and Stylist followed. She left the way open for him. There were stairs and darkened corridors, and then he smelled something stiflingly familiar—the tang of London. Exhaust fumes and food, refuse and roses. All the smells were London's, but for the last. That was always hers.

Because they were on the apartment's roof now, where Florist's huge greenhouses captured what goodness the sun could force through the clouds of pollution and apathy that hung forever above the city. She was weaving between planting beds, reaching out to stroke leaves and stems and tendrils and flowers with her supple hands, arms shifting as fluidly as kelp in a gentle current.

Stylist followed, a pair of scissors in his right hand, a foil fold of hair dust in his left. *I could be breathing in anything right now*, he thought, and somewhere a fungus head popped with a gentle sigh. Spores and pollen drifted on breezes that had no source.

"Florist!" he called.

"Ellen." She was standing behind him. She had dropped her clothing and stood naked, exposing the fine tracework of stem filaments up her legs and torso, and the intricately veined wonders of her arms and hands. Her head was a bloom waiting to happen. Her eyes were purple. Bees buzzed at her hair, and they drifted away with legs heavy with pollen.

"How did you . . . ?" Stylist asked, but to question this was pointless. She came closer and reached for him, and he lashed out. Whether she believed herself beyond his touch, or never thought he would dare touch her at all, the scissor blade slicing through her hand brought a gasp of shock, and a spray of green blood across the air.

"I'm sorry," Stylist said. But he held up the scissors. "Stay back.

Stay *away*!" He thought she would come at him then, and in her domain he wondered what chance he would have. He raised the foil fold and blew, but Florist closed her eyes and a surge of air passed through the large greenhouse dome. Leaves and flowers and shrubs shivered, and Stylist sensed a thousand dreams and memories carried away on the breeze.

"You'll give my beauties nightmares," she said, and her concern for the plants growing here was palpable. "Please, Jason, don't try anything like that again. You're in deep waters here. Deeper than you know, and if you try and fight against the current . . . " She shrugged, sad.

"What, you care about me?"

"Of course I care. As I would for any child."

"I'm no child."

"But you don't revel in what you have," she said. She came forward again and this time he let her. She touched his shoulders, and her hands felt suddenly very human again.

"I don't want to know," he said, suspecting that she was manipulating him even now. How could she not, when he was in her domain?

"You think it's a curse, not a gift. You carry it like a weight, deep down inside you, and you think of it as something separate. Something unknown and alien that drives you. An invader."

"Because it is," Stylist said, and he probed deep down for the darkness that had always haunted him. It gave him breath when he needed it to touch the hair dust with dreams, and it edged forward through his hands, into the tools he used to style new lives for the bastards he chose to work upon. He felt it, watching and listening with a silent smirk. It was the deepest part of him, and yet so distant he could never hope to understand.

"No," Florist said. "It's more you than this human front you give yourself. Jason Hamm with his wife and children. Jason Hamm with his barber shop, for fuck's sake. You make yourself false, because you can't accept the real truth."

"I can," Stylist said. He gripped his scissors tightly. "I do. I'm a husband and a father, and sometimes . . . sometimes, I have to give this thing free rein."

"And that's when you're truly yourself! I found that out years ago. I had a husband and a baby girl, and they were simply a shield. They were as false to me as that mask you choose to wear is to you. I gave them up, and I've revelled in it ever since." She moved away and regarded him kindly, knowingly. "Stylist, we're pretty fucking far from human."

No, he thought. *I love Janie, and Holly, and Sean. They're my centre. My focus.* But Florist was looking at him now, and in her eyes he saw a point of no return. She saw a choice for him to make, but she did not know him quite well enough.

"And the Gleeful Ones revel in inhumanity?" Stylist asked. "Is that it?"

"You make it sound like such a bad thing."

"And now they're going to expose themselves," he said. "Try and make things different."

"Things have *always* been different," Florist said. "The Gleeful Ones are simply bringing that difference to the masses."

In the distance, a thumping explosion.

"What was that?" he asked. Somewhere, a flare of light filtered through the dome, reflected from shiny leaf surfaces, direction confused.

"The beginning." Florist came forward, naked and alien, and she thought she had him. He had always felt a sense of mockery from her when she addressed him, and perhaps she had always underestimated him. A man who cut hair to change lives. She reached for him, and Stylist snorted and blew.

A million fine particles trapped on his nostril hairs flew towards Florist. Never quite immune to the countless memories and nightmares his hair dust brought, Stylist had at least come to accept them, able to tone them down so that they were little more than echoes. Now, those same dreams and memories screamed.

Florist's eyes went wide. Stylist smiled. And then Florist laughed, and her hand swung around on an arm that seemed to be extending, growing, like a bloom searching for the sun.

The impact sent him sprawling across the ground, skidding into a planting bed where his hands sank in soft, warm soil. It felt almost alive, the touch sickeningly intimate. Plants stroked across the back of his neck and face, and in a panic he batted them away, slashing with his scissors because he thought they were reaching for him. One stem parted, one leaf fell in half. Stylist felt a moment of regret.

"Fucking idiot," Florist muttered from behind him then, and he worked his hands and feet to power himself between plants, dodging between stems until he emerged onto a deserted path.

I'm in her world here, he thought, but he shut down the panic. He ignored the thing inside that was not part of himself—could *never be* part of his real self, whatever Florist said—and thought instead of his family. Janie, with her gorgeous hair that he could not help stroking. Holly and Sean, sweet and small, beautiful human beings with little history and futures waiting to be formed. He wanted to be a part of their future, as much as he had been present in their past. Their lives from now on could not be without him. *I love them all more than this*, he thought, and the dark thing inside him twisted and writhed as if he was slicing it with his sharpest scissors.

Florist grabbed him beneath the arms and lifted, ripping off his mask and flinging him across the dome. Leaves and fronds slapped at his face as he fell. Something scratched across his eye.

"You have to be one of us!" Florist said. "There is no Jason. But if you don't agree, I have to kill you. And . . . I care, Stylist. I always have cared about you."

He picked himself up, gripping the scissors, and he glanced in the keen open blade and saw her reflection forming behind him in a wall of greenery. *She comes from them*, he thought, and he spun around with the scissors held out.

It sounded like shears cutting long grass. Florist's fingers fell away with a spatter of greenish sap. She stared at her hand.

"Sorry," Stylist said. He ran. Bashing between plants, shoving heavy blooms aside, tripping on trailing vines, tendrils stroking around his ankles and seeking beneath his clothing, and every step of the way he heard her calling after him.

"I can't let you!" she said. "I *won't* let you. They won't allow. I'm sorry, Stylist. Goodbye, Jason. If only you'd been willing to look deeper, without fear. If only you could have been Gleeful." And in concert with her sadness, he heard plant noises. The pop of opening buds, the hiss of escaping spores, the groan of branch upon branch. The insides of the dome were more than alive, and the air around him changed colour. Clear, yellow, and then bright red.

Though he held his breath, he looked down at his hands and clothes, and the layers of Florist's stuff coating them.

Soon, he would have to breathe.

Some of what he saw was nightmare, given to him by Florist to wipe him out. Some might have been real. All the way home, Stylist had no idea which was which.

There were monsters in the nighttime streets. London crawled with shapes dragged up from its hidden guts—subterranean things, slicking and leeching along streets. They screeched when they saw him, letting out vicious ululating cries that echoed between the high buildings and drifted away into darker streets. Some of them manifested more fully, as if the sight of him drew them further in from whatever reality they had previously inhabited. They squirmed and groaned their way to solidity, growling through the pain and showing teeth reflected in starlight. Their bites were a billion years old. They came for him, darting across streets from hidden corners, crossing intersections, springing from shop doorways and leaving wet trails on the roads. Stylist dodged them and ran on, scissors grasped in one hand but feeling, for the first time, ineffectual.

The scissors belong to it, *not to me*, he thought, but he could not quite throw them away.

He heard laughter that turned to screaming as he rounded a corner and passed a busy club entrance. A dozen misshapen creatures were piling in towards the laughing screaming woman, and though she herself was monstrous in ways he could not quite place, the things they did were much worse. Limbs and phalluses punctured her, blood flowed in crimson tides, and luminous fluid spurted across the pavement and the club's façade, catching starlight and setting fire to everything.

Stylist should have gone to her aid, but he was not sure how real she might be. The thing inside that drove him in these dark forays seemed to cringe back, driven down by something that surely could not have been fear.

"It's not afraid," he said aloud. "I'm not afraid."

Janie and his children drew him on, and the scent of daffodil fields and bluebell woods accompanied him as he ran. Buildings seemed to move around him, as if shifting independently of the ground he covered. More screams, more shouts, more shadows forming and becoming grotesque.

Stylist shook his head and wondered how much she could have affected him. He snorted to clear the alien spores from his nose, and a cloud of something yellow hazed his vision. The colour was felt rather than seen. Her sweet pollen.

Stylist stripped the trappings of his alien identity as he ran, throwing the bland mask aside, stumbling and falling as he tore off the boilersuit, and he turned a corner onto a large square as Jason Hamm.

The monsters were still there, gathered at the square's far side in one undulating mass. Individuals darted from the crowd and seemed to stretch echoes of presence behind them, joining them to the throng like memory tentacles. He skirted the edge of the square but they saw him, flooding across the pavements smoothed by decades of feet, cawing and calling for his blood, and for that thing inside that made him what he was.

Florist's plea that it was the core of him, not apart from him, had marked the greatest difference between them. Her and her kind—the Gleeful Ones—considered themselves different, and blessed by differences. But Stylist knew the truth. He was a simple man, and whether what he did was a blessing or a curse, he would do every-thing he could to clasp hold of his humanity.

As the shapes stormed across the square towards him he turned to face them, holding his scissors high. He snorted and took deep breaths. He squeezed his eyes closed until he saw stars. And as the shapes came, so they began to change.

By the time they reached him they were people again. Men and women, dressed for a night out but now scared, frightened by something he could not see. He saw hatred and terror in their eyes, though he could get the measure of neither.

As the first woman skidded to a halt ten steps from him and started shouting, a massive explosion rumbled through the air and ground. Stylist crouched to keep his footing and looked to the east. The sky was aflame, and a boiling, blazing mass drifted gracefully down from the heavens, trailing a cloud of fire behind it. Burning shapes fell away and matched its descent. Another explosion bloomed from inside, and for a moment he thought of one of Florists's most beautiful blooms.

Then he saw the ribs and skeleton of what the thing had been, and his blood turned cold.

"Another one!" someone shouted. "Oh God, another, they've done another! How many now? How many?" The voice was rough with the remnants of hallucination, but now Stylist knew that he had almost purged himself of Florist's touch. There were no monsters other than what she had wished him to see.

Or maybe there are, he thought, watching the horrendous burning shape plummet behind distant buildings. The impact was gentle in comparison, but he thought of those hundreds or thousands caught within its fiery embrace.

"What's happening?" he asked.

"Bastard," someone muttered. A man, sneering at him.

"You freaks," a woman said. She was wearing a slight summery dress and high heels, and she carried an empty wine glass.

"I don't understand," Stylist said. "My name's Jason Hamm. I don't know—"

"Don't lie!" the sneering man said. "I saw you throwing your mask away. Trying to hide as a *human*. But you'll run, and hide, and it won't do any good!"

"Like the Nazis—"

"Always knew it would come to this—"

"A war, my father said that's the only way—"

"The Gleeful Ones have begun," Jason said. It was so obvious now. The councillors would be first, blown from the sky by the Vees who craved exposure and control. And what else had they done? What other horrors had been taking place whilst Florist tried to steer him to their cause? The crowd looked shocked and terrified, but angry as well. And perhaps there lay the Vees' first, greatest mistake.

Jason ran. Their fury followed him, but he was faster. All he could wonder on the way home was whether they had known who his Vee was. Everything might depend on that.

Now, more than ever, he needed to hide.

Extract from *Once Were Vigilantes*,
by Max Gold, London Council Press

That first night and the day that followed shocked everyone. Few had any real understanding of how many Vees were out there. While some branches of the police and military were in contact with certain Vees—and no one can or would deny that many worked in cahoots—the numbers were thought to be in the scores. Many had perhaps not even practised their skills (or curses) until that night. It became Gleeful Night. Named by the Gleeful Ones, the name stuck, even after the terrible battles and their eventual defeat, arrest, incarceration, and the executions that followed.

One thousand is a conservative estimate. Some suggest *many* thousands across the globe. For every one caught, a hundred might have escaped.

They're out there now. Hiding. Sleeping. But after what they did—the assassinations, the slaughter, the poisonings and pollution, the explosions and savagery—they cannot expect any form of immunity. And even though many captured Vees profess anger at what the Gleeful Ones perpetuated, there can be no pity.

They're not human. And the Council will never rest until every single one of them has been found.

Jason Hamm reached his street, and many lights were on. It was almost 3 a.m. People were milling in the street, huddled in groups, talking animatedly while they watched the fires to the east. Others were hurrying from somewhere to somewhere else.

Jason looked for shadows that did not belong, and saw so many.

He gripped several opened foil folds in his left hand, scissors in his right. His mask and boilersuit were gone, but if needed he would still be Stylist.

I am always *Stylist!*

The thought was fleeting, and surprising in its intensity. It had come from him, in his own voice, not from the thing inside that he put to sleep each morning in that tumbled-down shed, storing his Vee clothing and implements. He still felt its presence, but it was calm and contemplative now. As if waiting for something.

"I am Jason Hamm," he said. *There is no Jason*, Florist had told him. He dashed along the street towards his house, and several sets of eyes turned his way.

"Jason!" someone called. Ten minutes before, Jason would have heard the voice as an animal, monstrous roar. The shapes of his neighbours would have writhed and seeped as Florist's pollens worked through his system. Now, he found the voice almost comforting because it recognised him as a human being.

"What's happened?" Jason asked.

"Where have you been?" The woman was looking him up and down, and her eyes settled on the scissors in his hand.

"Out," Jason said. He glanced at his house. The upstairs light flickered on—his bedroom. He so wanted to be there now with Janie, but he also needed to know the lie of the land.

Something flickered across the rooftops and he turned, crouched, left hand expertly presenting a foil packet ready to whisk and blow.

"Jason?" the woman asked, uncertain.

"What's happened?" he asked again.

"Three airships," she said. "They say it's Vees. Some of them have made a broadcast, and . . . oh my God."

Jason had seen it as well. The man flowed down the side of a house from the shadowy junction of roofs, moving like thin oil, slinking across the garden and then standing upright, shaking slightly as a ripple passed through his form. He smiled softly at Jason, but there was something in his eyes. Perhaps sadness, or resignation.

"No," Jason said.

"I wasn't sent to ask." The man's voice was slick as blood.

Jason did not wait. With one sweep of his hand and a gush of breath—pushed from deep down by the thing that drove him, shoved out and across the street towards the danger—he cast his dust into the Vee's face.

The man twisted sideways, but then started batting at his head with both hands, as if waving away a swarm of flies. He was living a thousand nightmares, and he screamed. Jason had never met *anyone* who did not scream.

"Jason's a—"

"That guy from number 42 is—"

"Get back, get away—"

"His poor kids, do you think they—?"

For the first time ever, Stylist had no mask or boilersuit when he darted in and slashed the man's neck. A spray of blood caught him across his face. He closed his eyes and turned away, and the man fell with another splash. He seemed to spread across the pavement even as his blood pooled around him.

Stylist turned around when he felt eyes on his back. They were staring, his neighbours and friends. He saw them through the sticky mess of the dying man's blood, dripping from his eyelashes and slick against his cheeks.

"I'm no harm to any of you."

"You're not *human*!" the woman said.

Jason dropped the scissors. He closed his eyes. And for the briefest instant he considered running as far and as fast as he could, leaving his family behind to live whatever life he had left. But the thing inside him rebelled. *They're all you really have*, it said in Stylist's voice, and the voice was Jason's as well. The last thing he could do was give in.

"Stay away from me," he said, and his neighbours cringed back. As he snatched up his scissors and ran for home, Jason looked around at the strange night. There would be more of them, coming for him and for every other Vee who refused their exhortation to reveal themselves. There was a difference between being open with who you were, and using that openness to gain advantage. Gift or curse, Stylist's talents could never be used for self-benefit. Jason had always understood that when Stylist was something separate, and it persisted now that . . .

Now that he was beginning to see the truth. *We're pretty fucking far from human*, Florist had said, and she might have been right.

"There are ways and means," Jason muttered. He opened the front door, entered his home, and closed it gently behind him. As he turned in the hallway Janie was coming down the stairs.

She screamed.

"No, no, no," he said, holding out his hands and seeing the terrible blood across them, feeling it tacky on his face, and he knew it would take more than a calming touch. "Janie!"

"Jason?"

"Wake the kids. We're going."

"What's . . . ? Why . . . ?"

"It's not my blood, Janie," he said. "And I have something to tell you."

They watched the news as they packed. It was easier that way; it meant he didn't have to explain everything to Janie on his own.

The images were startling and shocking. Four airships had now been brought down, and while chaos and violence were rife all across London, three Vees were transmitting messages across all radio and TV stations. One of them was Succubus, and each time he looked at the screen, Jason thought she was speaking only to him. He remembered her exposed tattoos flexing luxuriously as she slipped off her top, and the animal desire she had inspired in him. Her gaze pressed into the heart of him, and he imagined a million other men feeling special.

"They're taking over," Janie said.

"They're trying."

"And you?" she asked. He'd washed most of the blood away, but his heart would not settle. He had never killed a Vee before. He did not like the feeling it invoked—a sense of power, and superiority. *I am Jason Hamm*, he kept thinking, but Stylist haunted every word.

"Me," he said. "Me." He sat on the bed and Janie came to him, holding his hands as he brought them up to his eyes.

"I never liked that other part of you," she whispered. "I always thought it might come between us. I feared it."

"You shouldn't," he said. "It was never another part, Janie. I thought it was, but that was just . . . self-deception. In truth, it was always just me."

"But you changed when you were him. I sensed it in you, and saw it. Sometimes I thought I could smell it, as if you were a different man. Different smells, senses."

"No," he said. "She was right. Florist. But not right in everything." He sighed and stood, hugging his wife close and feeling the heat of her, the slight tremble.

"Where are we going?" Janie asked.

Jason did not answer. When she pulled back to look up into his eyes, he touched her chin and smoothed his other hand across her tangled hair.

"Trust me?" he asked.

She frowned.

Jason flexed his fingers in her hair, and understood at last that being more than human did not mean he had to exclude humanity. He kissed her gently on the lips. "Trust me."

Jason woke his children and took them with him. He held Janie's hand as he guided her through the back garden to the narrow alley that ran behind their houses. Sean and Holly followed obediently. The explosions in the distance seemed not to trouble them. Perhaps they were still half-asleep, or maybe it was simply that they were children.

He considered running, fleeing as far as he could, but decided against it. They had sent that one man against him, but with everything going on tonight, he did not imagine they would send any more. He was not special. And if for some reason they *did* want him that badly, running would offer no defence. On the confused TV reports, the Gleeful Ones were relishing exposure—flyers, tunnellers, fire-makers, thought stealers, and people whose powers could not yet be understood.

So they went to the abandoned house's garden, and into the shed where Jason kept the paraphernalia of Stylist's existence. He had lost the key to the lock with his boilersuit, but he picked it quickly and easily. It fell to the ground with a wet thud, echoing a distant explosion that might have been another airship coming down.

"Are there fireworks, Daddy?" Holly asked.

"There are," he said.

"Can we see them?" Sean asked.

"Soon," Jason said. "Got to do something first. Here, all of you sit on this bench." He sat the three most important people in his life down in the dark, and scanned the gardens and houses around them. *Please no more*, he thought, gripping his scissors. The power thrummed within him, the sensation that was all his own and which made him so different. And using it to slice throats was an abuse of such power. *Please, send no more to find me tonight.* He closed the door and turned back to his family.

"Tomorrow, it won't matter any more," he said.

"What won't, Daddy?" Holly asked.

Jason only smiled. Then he drew a dust sheet from a huge mirror leaning against one wall, pulled the cord on a single, weak light-bulb, and helped Janie up into a rickety kitchen chair.

"It's bedtime, and you're cutting Mummy's hair!" Sean giggled beautifully.

"Not just Mummy's," Jason said. And he set to work.

For a while, he thought he was being watched. It unnerved him. These were paranoid times, and seeing a shape standing out on the hillside, motionless as a statue and staring at the old farmhouse, was more than troubling. He did not mention it to Janie and the kids. That would be unfair. They were under enough stress settling into their new existence, though all three claimed to have fallen in love with the gorgeous Welsh valley. The kids were in a new school, and Janie had taken a job at the local brewery, dealing with all their overseas accounts.

Jason was out of work right now. He'd had enough of cutting hair in the big city. Too many weirdos.

The watcher soon vanished, there one day and gone the next. Jason went to see where he or she had stood, and across the hillside were several patches of strange purple flowers. He found them both beautiful and repulsive. He stomped them into the soil.

They were left alone to come to terms with their new lives.

"They got another one today," Holly said. She had become a quiet, serious girl, fascinated with the Gleeful Ones and what they had done. She sat at their dinner table and twirled her single, long curl around one finger. Both she and Sean had the same curl, and Janie joked that they had inherited it from their father. He'd chuckle and run his hand over his bald head. It was obvious where it had come from—Janie's hair was completely straight, but for the cute curl at her left temple.

"Oh?" Jason asked.

"A flower lady. Florist, they said she called herself."

Jason caught a brief, perfumed aroma, closing his eyes and frowning slightly. It must have been the herbs and berries Janie had used to cook the lamb.

"Was she a Gleeful One?" Sean asked.

"They haven't said yet. 'Spect so."

"I expect so," Jason echoed.

"Good," Janie said. "They'll soon have them all."

Jason nodded and took a mouthful of food.

"Daddy!" Sean said, suddenly excited. "I got an idea of what job you could have! My friend in school, Dylan, well, his dad's a farmer, he's got a big farm in the next valley, and Dylan lives there and wants me to go over one day and go exploring in the . . . Anyway, so, he told me all about what they do there, and there's a job that's perfect for you."

"And what's that, son?"

"A sheep shearer!"

"Ha!" Jason sat back in his chair and rubbed both hands over his head. Barely five p.m., and he could already feel hints of new hair growth.

He would shave one more time before dusk.

THE FLOW

I n many ways, Ruth had never really left. But when she heard about the village being revealed again after six straight years of drought, she knew she had to go back. To see the only place where she had ever belonged. To relive that time when she had become her true self.

To make sure.

She stood high on the hillside and looked down on the distant remains. She'd prepared herself for the emotions this moment might stir within her, but when the time came she was surprised, because she felt nothing. Not sadness or joy, not fear or delight. Perhaps she was too far away to really see.

She moved down the hillside, looking for somewhere to sit for a while. She found a small stone memorial, one of six that had been built around the valley using stones from the old demolished chapel, and sat on the ground beside it. Someone had left a small bunch of flowers there recently. Though the petals were shrivelling and turning brown, they were still pretty. There was a card attached with scrawled writing fading to the elements, but she didn't bother reading it.

From high up, the view across the valley brought back so many memories. She'd spent over twenty years of her life in the little village, most of them happy, the last few much less so, and she'd walked these hillsides many times before. She knew them well. Knew the sweeps and slopes, the streams and small ravines. The places to hide.

"Bloody hell," she said softly, sighing into her cupped hands. It was getting chilly up here, even though the summer was not yet over, and the drought had sucked all but the final few pools of water from what was once a great reservoir. They said it would fill again, given time. They said it was an unusual occurrence, and one which the village's exiled residents should not take advantage of to visit their old homes. It was dangerous, there were sinkholes and quicksands, the walls still standing would become unstable once they started drying out. But there were those who'd already vowed to return, and some who said they were looking for lost things. One old residents' association had promised to remove any remaining structures and rebuild them higher on the hillside, tributes to the drowned village and those who had been forced to move from there. The local news even suggested that there were those searching for a legendary hoard of jewellery that had been left behind.

People would be digging.

And that was why Ruth had to come. She could not allow anyone to go digging. Not after three decades of water had worked at the ground, washed it away here, burying it deeper there. Moving stuff around. Nothing was certain now that the tides of time had receded. After all these years had passed she had a whole new life to protect—a job as business manager of a large building firm, a husband, three great kids. She had respect in her London neighbourhood two hundred miles away. She was growing through her middle age gracefully, and disgrace had no place in her life.

Most of all, she could not let her nightmare become real.

She shivered, but it was little to do with the chill. Standing, leaning back against the stone memorial, she accidentally kicked the bunch of flowers so that it fell over. Petals scattered, and a waft of sweet decay touched her nose.

Mud, must, dampness, the rich smell of muck upturned, her dream is all this, so much more tactile and sensory than is usual in a dream. Many times she wakes and looks around her bedroom, searching for a trace of mud on the sheets or damp footprints on the pale carpet. She laughs at herself afterwards, but for a few seconds after surfacing she is struggling to surface at all. Gerald's hands are clawed around her shoulders, pulling her back down into the nightmare. She has the sense of a rapid, liquid movement beneath him, washing away his rot, flowing. His eyes are starting to open, bloodshot yellow orbs in the dark brown silt, rolling in their sockets as his face breaks surface and his mouth spews a deluge of foul muck. He cannot speak, but that says it all.

And then he rises, and this is when she wakes.

"Fuck's sake!" she said, angry at herself. The dreams never usually bothered her that much anymore, and they were so irregular that she easily forgot about them. Thinking about them now, here in the sunlight of a late Welsh afternoon, was just foolish. She was no fool. "Just concentrate, Ruth!" She shrugged the small rucksack higher on her shoulders and started down into the valley.

The walk down the hillside was surprisingly nostalgic, and while to begin with she did not recognise exact locations, she knew where she was. The lie of the land was familiar, its weight around her, the shape of the sky and the carved ridges separating them. It was as if she'd heaved on an old coat from decades ago and found that it still fit.

She came across the copse of trees where she'd played with her friends when she was very young. They'd built a tree house, and though the structure itself was long gone, she was amazed to see a trace of decayed nails in the old oak's trunk. She stared at these scars for a while, actually remembering tall, dreamy Gareth banging them in with a hammer he'd borrowed from his father. They'd had a picnic that same day—cheese sandwiches, lemonade, bitter apples scrumped from Mrs Machen's garden—then later they'd raced back down the lane into the village. The lane was gone now, overgrown and subsumed into the deep hedgerow between fields. She wondered whether Gareth was gone as well. He and his family had left the village several years before it was flooded to make the new reservoir, having no part in the lengthy legal processes, disputes, and demonstrations, and she hadn't heard of him since. He could be anywhere. Maybe he was dead.

Further down the hillside was a place that inspired a more complex mix of feelings. The old barn had been a ruin even thirty years before, and it was here that she and Gerald had first made love. She had been nineteen, him a couple of years older. He'd brought a blanket and a bottle of cider, and under the blazing sun of a day very like today they had their first experience of each other. At the time it had been nice. It had hurt at first, but she had gone back to the village smiling and happy. It had become Their Place, and they'd ventured there another half-dozen times that summer to make love, becoming more and more daring in their explorations.

The complexity of her feelings were because she only associated this place with good times. Gerald had only ever been loving and gentle here, nice to her, not violent and evil. That had all come later.

"Bastard," she breathed, looking through a tangle of brambles and ferns at what was left of the barn. Only one wall still stood, and it was held up by the undergrowth surrounding it. "You bastard." Ruth was surprised to find tears blurring her vision and she angrily wiped them away.

As she walked further downhill she knew what was to come, but she tried to keep her eyes down, seeing only what was close by. Another field, an overgrown hedge where she had to trample ferns to find the stile, a woodland she could not remember being there, and then she emerged from beneath the shadows of trees and saw the full devastation before her.

The valley was gone, and it took her breath away. In its place were the remnants of the vast reservoir. Thirty feet ahead of her and slightly downhill, the dried reservoir bed began. It stretched right across the valley in every direction, a monochrome splash of nothing upon the rich green palette of the countryside. It was as if someone had come to paint this scene and had yet to finish, leaving only the background tone ready for colours of life, the final scenes, to be painted in. A reservoir, perhaps. Or a village.

Even this close it was all but camouflaged by the layers of silt. It had dried in the sun to a pale grey, though darker patches across the valley floor showed where water was still present. It was the ghost of the place where she had been born and brought up, and which even after so long she still thought of as home.

Despite everything that had happened here, it was still where she belonged.

Ruth started to cry. This time she did not wipe away the tears because they were for all the right reasons. Not Gerald, but everyone and everything else that village had been. Her parents, owners of the small shop for almost fifty years before she and Gerald had taken it over. Her friends, forging a life for themselves in that small community of fifty houses, a school, a chapel, and a corner store. The people whose ancestors had built the village, and whose descendants would only hear about the place on long-forgotten documentaries or obscure YouTube videos. And the village itself, a disorganised collection of buildings that had grown around the small, cheerful stream and the pond that it birthed. Such a happy place now made sad. Sadder still now that it was no longer only in her memory.

With the landscape so altered, it took her a while to figure out where the old shop had stood. It took a little while longer to make out where the coal shed had been.

She hefted the rucksack, heard the clank of metal tools inside, and took her first step out into the grey.

Ruth stood in the space where she used to live and looked around at what was left. There was more than elsewhere. The shop that had been in her family for generations was no longer recognisable, but the layout was still familiar to her. The end wall had fallen, but front and rear walls still stood, and the top third of the fireplace was visible in the other end wall above the silt. There were even the stubs of shelf brackets still evident between stone joints, though the counter behind which she'd stood for several years had rotted to nothing. The doorway behind the counter, leading into the rest of the house, was half an arch.

Silt filled the room, feet deep. It clung to everything, painting it greyer than the vaguest of memories.

Gerald had proposed to her in this room, one evening when she was tidying the shop and locking up for her parents. He had first punched her here, too, close to the doorway. The first *real* punch.

She crouched and ducked through the half-arch, and then she was in the room where she had killed him.

The staircase was gone. The hallway was misshapen, one wall bowed inward to such an extent that she crept carefully back out, certain that it would fall at any moment. She retreated from the remains of the house, and only then did she see the drift of smoothed silt piled against the other side of the wall.

She stared into that space and remembered what she had done.

He has her pushed against the hardwood staircase, bannisters pressing uncomfortably against her back, the stench of booze about him, hair greasy and stringy where it hangs over his once-handsome face, and it's all so unfair. Not in this house. This should always have been her happy place. In a way that's what upsets her more— that he can hurt her here, where her parents were always so kind, where memories were always so fine. He's marring those memories, and she hates him for it. That, and other things.

"You never would," he says, stumbling forward. His confidence is his downfall. She does not lower the knife, and his clumsy strike fails to turn it aside.

Ruth gasped and raised a hand to her mouth as she remembered. Seeing the place brought the memory fresher than ever before, with every smell and sight, every sound of flowing blood and dying breaths.

She sobbed, once, and then gathered herself and stood straight once again. It had been a long time ago. The guilt was a faded thing, mellowed by time in the manner of grief. She had never doubted that she'd done the right thing, but for years afterwards she had beaten herself up about it, in those long quiet times when she was on her own. He'd cast his evil shadow over her even after his death—in guilt, and fear of being found out—and she hated the fucker even more for that.

Now she was here to make sure it remained history.

The coal bunker was close to the back of the house, and the small, heavy stone structure had withstood much of what had been thrown against it. The level of silt inside seemed lower than else-where, as if the ground itself had sunk away beneath the weight.

Sunk into a void, she thought with a shiver. As she shrugged the rucksack from her back, someone watched her.

She stood up straight and looked around. Everything had changed without her noticing. It was suddenly quieter, more still, the landscape holding its breath. Even the sunlight seemed flatter than before, a memory of heat. She felt eyes upon her—skin tin-gling, hairs on the back of her neck standing on end.

"Hello?" she said, but not too loud. Shouting seemed out of place here, as if the remains of the village were sacred.

There was no one. Or if there was, they were intentionally hiding away.

Ruth turned a full circle, seeing no one. But she did see the village as it had been in memory—the heavy bank of trees and bushes at the bottom of her garden, the several houses surrounding hers, the pub, the church spire that had been demolished before the valley was flooded. Some of the bodies in the graveyard had been disin-terred and buried elsewhere, others remained where they had rested for a century or more. The gravestones had all been removed and a layer of gravel and concrete poured over the graves, but nothing could hide the fact that hundreds still lay there.

Hundreds, plus one more that must never be known.

She pieced together the segmented spade, stepped into the roofless coal bunker, and pressed the blade against the dried silt. That first cut into the muddy ground shocked her rigid as—

—the blade opens his skin and slips inside, smooth, meeting little resistance against his hated flesh. Gerald gasps and his eyes go wide. He lashes out at her. She pulls out the knife, shocked at what has happened, terrified at what she has done, and before she can drop it he lunges closer to her, impaling himself again. The metal whispers against flesh, warmth flows across her hand, her husband's expression shifts from shock to pain. "Ow.Ouch!"

She almost laughs.

He slumps a little, tugging the knife and her hand down with him, his clothes lifting so that she can see the pouting, leaking wounds and the blade still clasped tight between his ribs—

—the spade opened the soil in a fine, dry smile. She pulled back a little, staring at the wound she'd placed in the land. It pouted.

And someone *was* watching her, she could feel it across very inch of exposed skin, a creeping awareness that she had felt before but never questioned. Sixth sense, some people called it, but she'd never felt the need to put a name to what she knew.

"Who are you?" she shouted. "Where are you?" Her voice echoed across the barren, monotone landscape, the sound flat as if the greyness had stolen its life.

"Ruth Games," a voice said. She jumped, dropped the spade and turned around, and a man was standing thirty metres from her.

Gerald, it's Gerald, and his eyes will be filled with mud!

But that was ridiculous. She barked a nervous laugh and raised a hand in greeting.

He must have emerged from behind the stone wall standing there, the last remnant of one of the three Franklee Cottages that had once stood along the lane from her home and shop. The wall was clotted with dried mud and shrivelled water plants, and several holes in its upper reach held the rotten remains of roof timbers. "Ruth Games, it really is you."

"Gareth?" she breathed. He seemed taller than he'd ever been, more gaunt, and his rich hair had mostly fallen away, those few fine strands remaining grey as the landscape around them.

He smiled. It should have illuminated his face, but somehow it avoided his eyes.

"It's so good to see you," he said.

"It's been . . . "

"Over thirty years." His smile faded a little, still touching his lips. "Thirty-five? You're looking good."

"For my age," she said, berating herself. Was she really slipping into flirt mode? Here, now? She'd always held a torch for Gareth, even though they'd never been more than teenaged friends. She had often wondered how different her life might have been if she'd tried to turn that torch into a blaze.

"It's strange being back," he said. He walked closer, limping slightly. She was shocked that this slight weakness in him upset her. "Especially as it all looks so familiar."

"Really?" she asked.

"Well . . . " He looked around some more, never focussing on one thing for more than a second or two. Even her. "Well, after so long away I can still see things . . . still remember . . . "

"I found where we built the treehouse."

"Oh, that old thing." Gareth's gaze flickered left and right, and every now and then he looked down at his empty hands.

"Why did you come?" Ruth asked. It suddenly seemed like a very important question.

"I'm looking for something."

"Me too," she said. They stood in silence for a while, surrounded by the washed-out remains of the place they'd both once called home. They had a shared history, and in this ruined village where time was blurred it felt so recent. He'd been tall and effortlessly graceful, a twinkle in his eye that all the village girls liked, imbued with a deep-set kindness that Ruth's mother had once called beautiful.

"Well . . . " this older version of Gareth said. "I'll keep looking.

Others will be here soon, so they reckon. People digging. I want to find it before them."

"Me too," she whispered. She was going to ask what he sought, and why, and what he'd been doing for all those years. But suddenly three decades felt like nothing. It was their time in the village that mattered, back then where they were mere kids, and now, when she was here to protect the memory of her past and however much future she had left.

He smiled, turned, started walking away. But she called him back.

"Gareth!" He turned around again. "This evening, will you sit on the hillside with me? We can watch the sun go down on the village, reminisce. I have wine and some food in my car, and I was going to camp. Just like the old days. Will you?"

"Of course," he said.

She watched him disappear eventually behind hills of dried mud and tumbled walls, and when she started digging again, she no longer felt eyes on her.

It must have been him.

Evening fell quickly in the valley. She was deep, but not deep enough. Her husband and children thought she was in Nottingham at a conference, and what would they think of her now? Digging in filth, seeking a corpse, moving herself closer to a secret that was hers alone? She was sweating, uncomfortable, hungry and thirsty, and knew that she needed to rest. There was a heavy sleeping bag in her rucksack, and the green hillside had never been so inviting.

She was covered in dust, as grey and timeless as the village she had returned to.

But she decided to keep digging. With every three spadefuls she removed from the hole, two more slipped back in when the sides collapsed. The fine, dusty silt was still damp this far down, but also fragile and wont to slump at the slightest disturbance.

They'll dig, she thought. *They'll come to see what they can find, tourists and historians and old residents of the village.* While she was living there, no one had reason to go excavating her garden. Under fifty feet of water, her secret should always have been safe. But now the novelty hunters would come, and the history seekers. She could not risk them finding Gerald down there after all this time, did not want to consider the uproar and the gossip that would ensue. It had been hanging over her forever.

She'd told everyone that Gerald had run away with a student from Cardiff. Those that knew him well had no trouble believing that of him, and those who did not—some of her family, friends, people from other villages—only felt sorry for her. Ruth played the part of the betrayed wife for a while, but then the plans to abandon the village and flood the valley came, and everyone had more important things to think about. Not at all sure she'd got away with it, she shovelled coal, but never let it get so low that she saw the compacted earth floor of the bunker, beneath which lay his shallow grave.

And sometimes she had those dreams.

His foul mouth that had kissed and bitten her, rotten teeth, peeling skin over mummified flesh, the flow of water somewhere deep beneath him, and the soft, susurrant shhhh as he pushed up from below and grit slipped away from his face, his nose, his open eyes . . . and they had always been open, even in his grave. Open, and searching for her.

"Damn it." She kicked a pile of soil and watch it disintegrate, hearing no whispers.

One more time she pressed the spade in, moving soil, searching for her murdered husband before anyone else came and found him. But she went no deeper.

The lush green hillsides called to her. She went, crying, trying to convince herself it was because she had grit in her eye.

She walked back uphill to where she'd parked her car, taking a head torch from her rucksack for the last scramble up the steep slope.

The back seat of the BMW was tempting, but something about sleeping out under the stars attracted her.

There was Gareth, too. She didn't like the idea of him sitting down there waiting for her. She didn't want to disappoint. Hopefully by this time tomorrow she would be on her way home to her normal, safe, secure life, but for now he was her link to a past she enjoyed remembering. A past before Gerald.

I don't know him anymore, she thought, thinking of Gareth's thinning, grey hair and the limp. But though that was true, their old friendship still hung between them. Besides, she could look after herself.

By the time she walked downhill again it was dark, the landscape lit by star and moonlight, her torch splashing her route. She paused several times and turned it off, and the reflection of moonlight from the vast expanse of dried reservoir bed was eerie. It was a silvery colour, dusty, dead. She imagined shapes walking there at night, and she was suddenly pleased that she would have some company.

Gareth called her over when he saw the torch, and she found him standing close to the copse of trees she had visited earlier. He was smiling.

"I found it too," he said, pointing up into the canopy.

"You hammered your thumb," she said. "It might have been the only time I heard you swear."

"Fucking hurt." He sounded so sad.

"I have a bottle of wine," she said. "No tent, but you can have my sleeping mat, I'll just use the sleeping bag. That okay?"

"If that's okay with you, Ruth."

They sat close together, and Gareth spent half an hour building a small fire. They chatted about old times—friends they'd had, incidents, people from the village. Never once did their questions and comments involve anything later than the day Gareth and his family had left the village. They didn't even talk about the compulsory purchase of houses and businesses and the construction of the reservoir. There was no need, because it was not part of a history that linked them.

They passed the bottle back and forth. It grew cold, and they both slipped on warmer clothing. At last their talk brought them closer to the present.

"I hear you married Gerald?"

"Huh. Yeah."

"Nice bloke."

"He was a prick."

"Oh. So what happened?"

"He ran off with a student from Cardiff." It sounded so false, so ridiculous, that she thought Gareth would laugh in her face. But he said nothing. He stared out over the silvery valley. Something seemed to haunt him, shadowing his features and stealing the life from his eyes.

"What is it?" Ruth asked. "What's bothering you so much?"

"This place," he said. "It's just . . . weird. When we left I never thought I'd see it again. And when I heard about the reservoir drying up and the old place resurfacing, I thought it'd be an opportunity. But I wish I hadn't come back."

"Why?"

"It's not the place it used to be." He shrugged. He was stating the obvious.

But later, as Ruth huddled in the sleeping bag and tried to get to sleep, she began to think that he spoke a much deeper truth.

She knew that she was dreaming . . .

Gerald stalked from beneath the trees, laughing, cursing, spitting soil from his mouth. He was wearing the clothes she'd buried him in, his body withered and leathery, eyes rolling in their sockets.

"Stupid bitch," he said, the words he's spewed on her time and again. "Look at you. *Look* at you!" He raised his hand and pointed the knife at her. She'd left it buried in his gut, but now it was in his hand, blade still keen after all these years.

She was trapped in her slapping bag, unable to move, stand, run. She rolled like a butterfly constrained inside its chrysalis. Perhaps with the knife Gerald would free her.

She screamed, because it was so unfair.

It was the first time she had dreamed of him out of the ground. She *knew* that she was dreaming.

But still . . .

She snapped awake, breathing hard, listening for her screams echoing across the landscape. Birds sang. A gentle breeze muttered between the trees.

She struggled quickly from the sleeping bag and looked around, but she was alone on the hillside. Gareth was gone. He'd left her a note rolled in the neck of the empty wine bottle, written on an envelope.

> *Ruth*
> *I'm going home. I realise I won't find what I'm looking for here. Maybe you won't either. Think about it before you go back down there, won't you? I don't like that place anymore. It's not where we used to live and had those great times.*
> *Thanks for remembering them with me. Take care.*
> *Gareth*
> *x*

She felt sad. She did as Gareth had suggested and thought about it.

Then she packed her stuff and walked back down towards the old village.

She saw them from far away. They were the only splash of colour on the landscape. Dread filled her as she approached, but her feet took her rapidly closer, puffing up clouds of dust as she drew nearer to her old, fallen home.

There were maybe eight or nine people gathered there. Others were walking around the rest of the village, and Ruth wished that she'd finished her work yesterday. It would be so much harder today. Digging, retrieving, hiding the remains . . .

Some of them turned to watch her approach. One shape lifted a hand and waved, and for a moment she thought it was Gareth. But this man was much older, shorter, and his other hand clasped an old woman's arm. She seemed ready to drop.

They were gathered around the dangerously leaning wall at the back of her old house. They were looking up.

Her heart hammered. *Turn and go*, she thought. *Get the hell out. Get away.*

Twenty metres from them she circled around, not wishing to approach the house.

"What is it?" she asked. But none of them answered, because moments later she saw.

The shape was huddled on top of the wall, exposed for the world to see. The skeleton sat—clothes rotted to scraps, dark hide visible here and there, shreds of dirty hair stuck to its browned skull—as if it had just finished watching the sunrise. It was hunched down, but not so low that she could not see both of its arms bent inwards, both hands resting around the wood-handled knife protruding from its belly.

"Oh, my God," she whispered. "My God."

"Quite," the old man said.

The slope of silt dried against the wall showed a mess of thin scratch marks, trails perhaps put there by loose skeletal digits. No shoe or footprints. No sign that anyone alive had placed the remains on view.

It seemed to be grinning at her. Staring right at her. *Look at you!*

Ruth turned away. She was going to walk, but she started to stagger. She did not want to attract attention, but she started to run. Out of the village, up the slope to the point where grey turned to green, still she felt those hollowed eyes watching her go, and heard that hate-filled voice mocking her every step of the way.

She fled her past. But eventually it would catch up.

THE PROTECTOR

Even when the words took me away, part of me always remained in the real world. I was desperate to be all the way there, beyond. On the tropical island with pirates and vagabonds, in the dusty west with grizzled cowboys and trackers, stomping through deep Arctic snow with icicled explorers, climbing cliffs above a rainforest, existing in places I had never been or seen but which I could imagine so well. And I tried.

But I was alert to reality and all its terrible sounds, sights and promises.

True escape was a dream, and it was only in dreams that I found any shred of freedom.

I heard the front door open and close, and immediately I was ready for the first signs of sadness. It was always like this. There were things to listen for, like mumbling under his breath or doors and cupboards slamming. Closer, there would be something to smell, too; the tang of alcohol or the warmth of blood if he'd been in another fight. Merely looking for the possible confrontation and grief to come had become too unreliable, because he was good at hiding fury behind a smile.

Mum knew, too. But I think she was too far gone. I had places I could escape to, at least partially. But Mum always remained behind.

I'd once asked her if he'd always been like this. She'd smiled and said she couldn't really remember.

I sat up in bed and glanced at the clock. It was almost midnight. I hadn't heard Mum come upstairs to bed yet, and I wished she wouldn't wait up for him. It was later than usual, so he'd had longer to keep drinking.

I heard my father's first shout. Through my closed door and the old house's heavy walls and floors, it was an incoherent roar, rising and falling like the swell preceding a tidal wave. Mum's voice came next, high and soft and almost not there at all. He raged, she pleaded. In the five minutes before silence descended again, I did not make out one single word. It was as if they communicated in the language of hate and fear, a dialect still relatively unknown to me.

But that could not last. Fear grew richer as the hate grew heavier.

I tried to continue reading. I was a small, weak boy, short for my age and always the last chosen for team sports at school. I wasn't bullied or hated there at all, and I had a few close friends. But when it came to kicking a ball around a field or proving myself physically, I was ignored. I sometimes wondered whether to be derided might be better. At least then they'd acknowledge that I was there.

It had never crossed my mind to confront him, at least not while I was awake.

I heard the stairs creaking. Behind and beneath them, a few heavy sniffs as my mother went about locking up the house.

My door opened.

"What shit you reading?"

"It's called *Wizard and Glass*."

"Wizards!" He almost spat the word, stumbling into my room and knocking the door wide. He stank of booze, sweat, cigarettes, the stench of mysterious adulthood. There was a small cut above his left eye and a graze on his chin. I'd learned long ago not to ask, he'd only say, *You should see the other guy!*, and his pride in violence made me feel sick. Sometimes I imagined him saying, *You should see your mother!*, and my growing hate for him fed on that image.

"It's good, Dad. Part of a series. You should—"

"I should what? Fucking crap." He sat on the end of my bed, sighing heavily as the springs creaked. He was a big, strong man, gone to fat in his middle age but still so powerful. Probably no more than six feet tall, in my eyes he was a giant. "You should be out with mates. Football. That sort of stuff. Girls."

"I've got friends, Dad."

"Girls. Your age, I was fucking them behind the village disco. Janey Dickson, she gave me a blowjob, all my mates watching. I tell you that? About Janey Dickson?"

"Yeah, Dad."

"This . . . this . . . " He reached for the book and I held it protectively against my chest. He glared at me. His nostrils flared. He had never hit me. "Give," he said.

I slowly lowered the book and slipped in the bookmark before closing it.

He grabbed the book and threw it across the room. "Get yourself a life. A life! Not bloody reading. Sitting in bed reading when you should be . . . " He waved a hand at my door, the window.

A ghost passed by the door and I looked up to see Mum's night-dress passing out of sight.

"I need to go to sleep," I said. "Got tests in school tomorrow."

"Tests!" he said. Scoffing. I was never quite sure what he wanted of me. To be more like him, big and brash, a man with rough hands and rougher thoughts. Or, more likely, to be nothing like him at all. I'm not even sure he knew himself.

He staggered when he stood up, slammed my door, stomped into the bathroom. I heard him pissing. He always said a real man pisses into the middle of the water. I always peed on the side.

Laughing to himself, he stumbled across the landing to the bedroom he shared with my mother.

I buried my head beneath the pillow and tried to get to sleep before what came next.

I approach the top of the steep hill at last. It's been a hard climb, made harder still by the weapons I've carried with me—the sword, forged in the deep Northern Caves of Drandor; the spear, once owned by Helgarth the Spite; the heavy spiked club, used to kill the Granmoorian Giant. But I know that they are necessary. Coming up here unarmed would be the same as throwing myself off the mountain.

Strange, winged mammals rise and fall on the currents above me. They're as large as my head with heavily veined wings, colourful duck-like beaks and delicate, long-clawed paws. A few places on the climb I scared them from their burrows, and I passed close enough to one to see the mewling, pink babies nestled inside. I wonder at a parent's instinct that allowed it to leave its young in the face of danger. Perhaps it's a way of seeing how fit they are to survive.

A strong breeze drifts across the steep face of the hillside. The last two hundred feet are a scramble, not quite a climb but steep enough to cause me serious injury if I stumble or fall. I am being very careful. It's not only my life at stake.

At last, summiting the hill and standing on the plateau, I see what no one else has ever witnessed and survived.

There is a forest here, but it is not made of trees. Heavy timber spikes driven deep into the ground bear wretched fruit. Some are still recognisible as people, flesh rotting, hair still clinging onto scalps like the desperate might cling to life. Other spikes bear so many remains, and so old, that the decayed victims have merged into a morass of bone, rotten clothing and shredded skin. The stink is awful. My stomach drops, and my heart cries out as I experience the terror and agony felt across this high, vast plain.

The forest of death continues for as far as I can see. And not too far from me is a flash of pale skin.

There she is. Tied to a spike, and not yet impaled. Still dressed and moving, still alive. The Draze has not finished with her yet.

As if summoned by my thinking its name, the Draze manifests from the endless fields of spikes. It might have been hiding in shadows, or perhaps it was so still that I could not make it out. But once it starts running at me it becomes my whole world.

I glance once at the woman, and she catches my eye. I see no hope there. Only sadness at the prospect of another life lost.

The fight is epic, and heroic, and some time down through the years I suspect they will write songs about what happened on the top of that terrible hill.

I lose a hand, the Draze loses an eye. It tears Helgarth the Spite's spear from my grip and snaps it in half, casting it aside. I lure it close and bury the Drandorian sword in its thigh. The Draze screams in agony and delight. I cry out in rage. The beast steps back and rips the sword from its bone and flesh, throwing it out across the hill and two thousand feet down into the valley below.

I heft the spiked club. It has tasted giant's blood, but never something as large as the Draze, never a being so dripping with evil. And one so confident of success.

The club strikes its abdomen and drives it up, back, and down onto one of its own spike-trees. It cries out in shock and pain as the spike pierces its chest, bursting from its ribcage with a spew of vile blood and a gush of yellow, poisonous fluid. I climb the beast to finish it. It stares into my eyes.

But it sees no mercy there.

The woman is still alive. I go to set her free, wanting to tell her, *They'll write songs about us.* But before I can reach her—

It was snowing. I was too old to build snowmen and throw

snowballs, but Mum and I went outside and did it anyway. The snow was so deep that no cars were coming through the village anymore. We played in the street with neighbours and children. The streetlights were on, casting spheres of light through which the flakes fell fat and heavy.

"Got you!" Mum shouted. The ball had burst against my cheek and was sliding inside my collar, slick and cold against my skin. "Got you a good one then!"

I ducked behind a car and formed a ball. My heart was pummelling and I was sweating inside my jumper and coat, but this was just the best time. The best.

Dad wasn't there, of course. I had vague memories from my childhood of him building a snowman with me, but he'd marched from the house after work that day, having barely been in for fifteen minutes, saying, "I'm going to the pub. Dave's coming over. Don't wait up." Then looking at me he'd said, "Why don't you go and play snowmen, fucking pussy?"

I didn't know what I'd done to upset him. I was almost seventeen then, and some of my mates from school were regulars at my father's favourite pub. The idea of being there with him was horrific.

Mum threw another ball, then leaned back against our garden wall. She looked up into the darkening sky and stuck out her tongue, catching snowflakes. I stood beside her and did the same.

Why don't you leave him? I asked her almost a year before. *Because he needs me*, she'd replied, and I'd never asked again. When those bad times came, I only thought it.

We went inside and changed, and Mum made some hot chocolate. I crashed out on my bed and started reading. It was a Ranulph Fiennes book; I loved reading about adventures, pushing extremes, lucky escapes. Dad still thought it was a pointless pastime, and sometimes he told me I should be learning a trade, getting an apprenticeship with a local builder or plumber instead of studying fucking A levels to move on and get a useless degree. He often sounded bemused at my choices. On occasion, he became angry with me.

He'd never once laid a hand on me. It was Mum who bore the scars of his confusion.

I heard him coming home from way along the street. He was laughing, his friend Dave laughing along with him. They were both drunk, but even though that state always thickened the atmosphere with trepidation, for once I could only hear his good humour. Eight inches of snow had changed the village landscape completely, and perhaps I was hearing the man he could have been, my dad from another existence.

I threw down the book and turned off the light, opening my curtains and staring out at the glowing, otherworldly snowscape. It was beautiful. The sky had cleared and they were forecasting a heavy frost, meaning that the snow would freeze and stay around for some time. The moon was almost full, and I could have sat there and read in its reflected light.

Dad was swaying along the middle of the street. Dave was with him. They were still laughing, their conversation a confusion of unheard words and jokes. Dave headed off down the footpath that led to his small housing estate, and Dad seemed to freeze. Then he bent over, staggered, nearly fell, stood up again, and launched a snowball at Dave's head.

He missed. Dave turned and called him a cheeky fucker, and then the two of them were throwing snowballs at each other, ducking behind cars and slipping on ice. They laughed. They laughed so much they snorted.

I found myself smiling, but sadly. I could not for a second imagine him doing the same with me.

Which was perhaps why I scooped snow from my windowsill and rolled a snowball ready for when he walked in front of the house.

My shot was perfect, a complete bullseye. Something he'd never praise me for.

He started shouting and screaming at me even as he skidded along the driveway, hateful words that made me feel as if I'd swallowed a handful of ice.

From the bathroom I heard my mum, and her small scream was all the more terrible because it wasn't fear. It was resignation.

The tree is under siege. I can see it in the distance as I cross the inimical landscape, sight enhanced by suit sensors, alerts sounding as dangers close in. Every circuit of my suit urges me to turn away, but every human instinct keeps me on course. I override tech and good sense and face the future.

The tree is on a hilltop, alone and regal against the stormy red skies. Its branches are huge and lush, laden with fruit and dense with leaves. It's difficult to tell from such a distance how tall the tree might be—a dozen times my height, or a mile into the sky. But however small or large, it's clear that the assaulting armies care nothing for its uniqueness. They surge at the hill's lower slopes, like a poisonous sea crashing against unknown shores. They fight the tree's defenders, whose cause is hopeless, and I rush across the landscape as their only beacon of hope.

The attackers are small from this distance, difficult to make out. The defenders are saplings, hauled up from their planting points, tendril roots waving at the air. They are far too young to be entering into such a fight. But circumstance dictates the need.

I leap ravines whose bottoms are way out of sight. My suit sends probing beams deep down, and they bounce back to tell me the rents in the planet are crawling with life, seething, pulsing with violence. I cross an area of open swamp, trusting the suit's sensors to guide me from one solid outcropping to another. The swamp's waters are sheened with an oily skin, beneath which lie isolated instances of quiet, contemplative intelligence.

The closer I get to the fight on the hill, the more warnings my suit issues. At first they are standard protocols which it is easy to ignore or put aside. But then the suit's Self makes itself known.

I advise against this course of action.

"I can't just leave it," I say.

The nature of the attackers is uncertain. The source of the tree even more hazy.

"It's beautiful. It's unique. It might be the only one in the universe, and I can't stand by and let it die."

Very well. But don't say I didn't warn you.

"Thank you. Please bring all weapons online."

By the time I leap eighty feet across the river at the foot of the hill, I can feel the potential power in my arms, my hands, and nestled across my suit's faze circuits and nano vents.

It seems the attackers can feel it, too. They turn as one and come my way.

For an hour I fight. The attackers are slow but many, and their constant unrelenting onslaught comes close to overcoming my defences.

They are a strange conglomeration of plant and animal, with stocky bone legs, spindly bodies, and limbs tipped with sharp spikes to pierce and wedge, or saw-like appendages that buzz at the air as they rub them together. Their heads hang low and drip sap, teeth grinding and growling, eyes rolling backwards in their heads whenever they attack.

And attack they do, again and again, wave after wave of them trundling forward across the bodies of their cousins. I blast and burn them, vaporise and hack, shoot and freeze. The suit enables my victory, but it does not come without cost. One foot is trapped beneath a pile of corpses, and their blood is toxic and acidic, eating through the advanced materials and exo-structure to melt away three toes and half of my foot. The suit keeps the pain at bay and seals the damage as best it can.

Beyond, I see the tree gathering its defences. The saplings are delicate, thin things, and where once there were thousands I now see only a dozen remaining. They plant themselves around the tree—the amazing, wondrous tree, as high as the sky and constantly moving, gathering knowledge, seeding it for the future. Its roots fill the world, they *are* the world, and if the attackers had succeeded then another existence would have blinked away to nothing in this endless universe.

At last the fight is won. I work my way up the hillside, exhausted and in shock from my injuries. The suit is glitching.

Three blind mice . . . it says, constantly starting a lullaby that it can never finish.

See how they—

See how they—

I reach the tree at last. The saplings let me by, because in me they recognise their saviour. But just as I reach out my hand to touch the tree's bark, and open my mouth to tell it how I feel—

Mum went to buy a takeaway. She loved having me home from university. This was my third time since I'd left, and she said she always liked a takeaway on the first night. Meant she had more time to talk to me, without having to be busy in the kitchen.

Dad would have gone, but he'd had a couple of drinks. "He's lost," she'd told me on the way home from the station. "Ever since you left. Just . . . lost."

"All right, Dad?" I said. I dropped onto the sofa, fluffing up a couple of cushions and propping them behind my back. The sofa was almost as old as me.

"Suppose," he said. "You?"

"I'm good," I said. I wasn't. I was lost too. It wasn't something I could tell Mum, because everything she'd ever done, everything she'd been through, had been to make things right for me. After all of that, how I could I possibly tell her things were wrong?

The first time I'd come home, I'd expected that being there would make things better. It hadn't.

The second time had been a trial, a tense time filled with explosive outbursts from my father and the familiar silence from my mother.

This third time was the last. After this, I was leaving for a long time. All I had to do was find a way of telling her.

"What're you watching?"

"Some shit."

I watched TV with him. He was right, it *was* some shit about arguing families, one of those soap operas that people seemed to watch searching for an escape. It seemed painfully familiar. A man screamed. A woman shouted. A knife was brandished, a son slept with a sister, a husband went missing.

A man raised his hand. A woman cowered. I caught the flicker of a smirk on my father's face.

"You fuck," I said. I reached across and snatched the TV remote from him, clicking it off. Silence settled across the room. "You complete fuck."

"What'd you say to me?" He turned and looked at me like I was a child, and it was the same way he'd always looked at me. Looking *through* me, as if I was barely there at all. He'd never recognised that I'd grown up, got older, turned from a snivelling kid into a young man. I wasn't sure what he saw when he looked at me, but I was only glad it wasn't himself.

"I hate you," I said. And I smiled. Those three words seemed to pour from my whole body, lightening it almost to the point that I floated up out of the sofa. They freed possibilities that had until now been weighed down with masses I could not identify or dare touch. I'd felt the hate for so long, but actually saying it felt something like growing up.

"You little—"

"I'm *not* little!" I said. I stood, towering over my father where he sat crumpled in his armchair. His arms were tensed, readying to push himself upright.

"Ungrateful shit," he said, standing, sneering, flexing his hands. I could smell the alcohol wafting off him, seeping through his pores and clogging them with hate, the opposite to what I had just experienced.

"I'm very grateful," I said. "To Mum, for everything she's done for me. For everything she's had to put up with, from you. All she's been through with you, you weak, pathetic bully."

He laughed. Once, loud, like a cough. "Great! So you go to

university to study some crap that'll get you nowhere. More fucking books to read. More fucking shit to take in and drown yourself with. Where will that get you, eh? Queer. Fucking queer, are you?"

"Why would I tell you? You don't count for anything in my life."

His fists were clenching again. I heard his knuckles cracking, and I knew for sure that if he came at me he'd beat me, because that's the sort of person he was. I'd never had a fight in my life, not in real life, at least. In my dreams I had saved whole worlds.

He'd beat me down, but I would win by facing up to him. The first time ever. It felt foolish and brave, but there was no going back now.

"If you hurt her again, I'll kill you," I said.

His eyes went wide. Shock punched him. He took one step forward.

The front door opened. "It's bucketing down out there!" Mum called. The scent of Indian food followed her in, and I smiled at her through the living room door. She only paused for a second. But seeing me smiling set her smile in place too, and she moved through to the kitchen. "Come and help me dish up?" she called.

I knew she was asking me. He'd never demean himself by helping her in the kitchen. He had too much important stuff to do.

"I mean it," I said, quieter, stepping in so close that he could smell my breath. "In your sleep, when you're drunk, I'll stick a knife in your eye." I stepped away and threw the remote control at him. It struck his cheek and fell into his chair.

As I walked along the hallway I heard the TV clicking back on. A woman shouted at a man. A man growled back.

"Okay, Son?"

"Yes, Mum," I said. I kissed her cheek and fetched plates from the cupboard.

I walk through the jungle searching for the beast, but there is no beast to be found.

The trees are tall and stretch up out of sight, heavy mist obscuring their canopies. The heat is immense, the life here abundant and rich. Spiders the size of my hand eat small mammals, birds of prey swoop down and pluck the spiders from branches, flying lizards larger than me drift through the mist and pierce the birds with serrated tongues. Life circles, and I am cautious. But I know the way. I have lived here for a long time, and my body is well adapted to this environment. I belong here.

Every now and then I pause and listen. I hear no bellows of the beast. But that's not all I'm searching for. I seek also the song of the blessed one, the giver of life who had made all this and still exists within it. She's here somewhere, I know. The beast hunts her. But already I am starting to wonder.

I have been searching for a long time, but I carry no weapons. That surprises me because it's so unusual. It's almost as if . . .

Around every corner there are new wonders. Sometimes these wonders are brutal and harsh, because that's how life is. Sometimes they are purely beautiful. Weaponless, I cannot recall whether I have cast the weapons aside because they are bloodied and used, or simply because they are no longer required.

Flowing like life through the jungle, time will tell.

CARRIED AWAY ON A SUNBEAM

Rosie says it all began when any sight, sound or trace of the *Sunbeam* was lost forever. I can see why she thinks that, and it makes sense if you believe in ghosts, but I don't. Danzer was haunting me for years before the *Sunbeam* was even a whisper in its creators' minds. Some days, I think she's been there from the day I was born.

I'd been following the progress of the *Sunbeam* expedition—to use a well-worn saying, who on Earth hadn't?—but it had been gone for over four years, and sometimes several days went by when I didn't even think about the ship. We all had our own lives to live, work to undertake, thoughts to have that didn't always revolve around *Sunbeam* and what she might find. We'd been making hay for several days, and the baler kept breaking down. I was elbow-deep in its workings, trying to figure out what was wrong, oil ingrained in a hundred scraps across my hands and arms from where sharp hay-stalks had scratched me.

"Mark!"

I extricated myself and stretched my arms to the sky, fingers

361

locked above my head. Rosie was running across the field, lifting her legs high to avoid the sharp spiky hay stumps. I watched her approach, disappointed that she wasn't carrying a bottle of water. Our car was parked on the dusty lane between fields, and I noticed its door hanging open. That's when I realised something was wrong.

"Mark, the *Sunbeam* . . . " she gasped. She grabbed my hands and held on so tight that I winced.

"What about it?"

"It's gone. No sign. No daily message."

I frowned and glanced up. I always looked to the skies when *Sunbeam* was mentioned, day or night. I could never help myself. It was ridiculous, and Rosie usually laughed when I did it, because the chance of me looking up in the direction of the ship was one in billions.

"So what does that mean?" I asked.

"They're saying it doesn't mean anything. Power outage, some sort of disturbance, a storm, one of a hundred things. But . . . "

"But we've never not heard from it," I said.

"Never," she said. Rosie had been following the whole *Sunbeam* project much closer than me. Of course she had. Her brother Jimmy was on that ship, and though we both knew he was lost to her forever, while the daily communications continued he wasn't really lost. Just gone.

"Come on," I said. "You should have—"

"You left your phone back at the farm."

"Yeah. Sorry." I liked being out of touch, and Rosie was always having a go at me about it. *What if you cut your fucking arm off?* she'd ask, and get angry if I laughed. It was very irresponsible of me, but I was in no rush to change my ways.

We hurried back across the field together, dodging the huge round hay bales. By the time we arrived at the car we'd both cut and scraped our legs, and blood bubbles speckled our skin like rouge jewellery.

The sun was bright, hot and high in the sky. *I'll get back to work after a bit of lunch*, I thought, *get the baler fixed and finish the field.*

But the baler was destined to remain where it was, door open and engine compartment exposed, until morning.

Rosie drove quickly along the lanes, and it only took five minutes to reach the house. We were silent all the way, and it was only when we both jumped from the car and rushed across the dusty yard that I said what neither of us could possibly know.

"I'm sure he's fine."

Rosie offered me a weak smile and I followed her inside. The shadowy interior of the old farmhouse was a welcome relief for my sunburned, sweaty skin, and I could already hear the muttering of the TV.

"I'll just get a drink." I grabbed a couple of bottles from the fridge and followed her into the living room.

A news presenter was talking over a collage of images that virtually everyone on Earth knew so well. The *Sunbeam*, built in orbit and surrounded by various construction craft and structures, so hemmed in that it resembled a spider's victim twirled in a web. *Sunbeam*'s captain, Michelle Gomez, in a still from one of her many transmissions back to the home she would never see again. Schematics, images, the celebrations across the globe when the ship left orbit, all of it was stuff we'd seen countless times before.

Then something we had not seen. Pete Williams of Mission Control, looking so grave-faced that I stopped with a bottle halfway to my lips.

"Every indication is that *Sunbeam* has suffered some sort of cataclysm," he said. "That doesn't mean it's destroyed, or disabled. But it's been two days since the datastream was disrupted, and the ship has failsafes, including four backup cores, and I . . . " He shook his head, and I was sure I could see tears in his eyes.

"Rosie," I said. She hugged me, and I hugged her back, and we both took comfort in each other while something we had always dreaded played out on the TV screen. This time I offered no useless platitudes. Rosie wouldn't appreciate it. Her brother might be dead. Light years away, distances beyond imagining, they had both always known that they were lost to each other forever, and yet dead was more final. Distant, apart, there was still the link of love between them, and she'd often smile when we were talking about him and say, *So far away, always here.*

I heard a voice. It was Danzer. I stiffened a little, then relaxed, because I knew she would wait. She always had before.

After another hug Rosie let go and sat down, and said, "I'd love a coffee, Mark. Really strong. I'm going to carry on watching." I nodded and went out into the kitchen, and Danzer was sitting in the old wooden chair by the fireplace. The fire was rarely lit, the chair never occupied, but it didn't surprise me at all to see her there.

I paused for a moment, as I always did, turning my head this way and that. She wasn't fully present. I could not see through her, and she looked complete, but there was no *solidity* to her. She was like a memory cast onto a scene, as if I'd walked into this room another day, another time.

She smiled at me, and I smiled back. I'd never tried to approach or touch her, because I was always afraid that would make her go away. She was a calming presence, yet I'd always sensed that her being here was a fleeting ability. I didn't want to do anything to upset whatever delicate balance had brought Danzer to me.

"You'll need to replace the oil filter," she said.

"I did that last month." I kept my voice down. Rosie had heard me talking to Danzer a couple of times before—talking to myself, she said, and deep down I knew she was right, even though her saying that made me unreasonably annoyed—but I did my best to keep our brief, strange discussions private. Danzer spoke aloud, but Rosie never heard.

She shrugged, scratching at her chin. "Got to maintain things," she said. "Things need attention. Need to know you're looking after them."

"Oil filter," I said, turning to the sink and filling the kettle.

"Uh-huh."

I plugged the kettle in and switched it on, and when I turned around Danzer was gone. I felt the familiar sense of loss tinged with relief. I knew that she was never really there, and had always known, and after each appearance I stood for a moment looking around the room and wondering who or what I had just seen and heard.

"Oil filter," I muttered. "Right." I made coffee and took our cups in, and sat beside Rosie, and we watched into the evening as coverage of the potential loss of the *Sunbeam* continued. Rosie cried for Jimmy. I'd always thought that he was so far away that alive and dead no longer really mattered, but it never crossed my mind to say that. I could never be so insensitive.

My first memory of Danzer was when my family dog pulled me over and I skinned my knees, and a shard of gravel became stuck in one of the cuts. I must have been five years old. I returned home crying, leading the dog by the lead. Sheena knew she'd done something wrong and she came with her head hanging low, but I loved her too much to be angry with her.

While my mother cleaned my cuts and grazes and gave me a bag of sweets to chew on, and dampened a cotton bud ready to try and tease out the bit of trapped grit, a figure walked in through the open back door. She was short, adult, with long brown hair and a friendly face. She wore a bright blue one-piece suit, and I thought maybe she was a mechanic from the garage in the village square. But I'd never seen her before, and her hands were clean.

"She needs to use tweezers," the stranger said. I stopped chewing for a minute, looking down at my mother where she was bent over, concentrating on working the stone from my knee. The pain wasn't too bad, and even though tears still flowed down my cheeks I was crying silently.

"Is it out?" I asked.

"Not yet, son. Just let me . . . " She leaned in closer and I saw her tongue protruding from the corner of her mouth, something she always did when she was concentrating.

I looked up and the stranger was doing the same. She giggled when she saw me watching. "Tweezers!" she said again.

I glanced down at my mother.

"She can't hear me."

"Why?" I asked. Mum looked up at me, frowned, back to my bloodied knee. It was starting to hurt more now.

"Because I'm Danzer."

"Okay," I said, and Mum looked up at me again.

"You feeling alright, son? You look pale."

"Tweezers," I said.

Mum nodded, stood, then disappeared into the downstairs bathroom. "Just a minute!"

Alone in the kitchen with Danzer, the moment seemed frozen. She stood half-in, half-out of the back door, sun casting her shadow fully into the kitchen. That shadow convinced me I wasn't imagining her, even though everything else suggested to me that she wasn't actually there.

"It wasn't Sheena's fault," Danzer said.

"I know that. She's a good dog."

"Aren't they all?" Danzer leaned down and scratched Sheena behind the ear. The dog seemed not to notice.

"She is a good dog," my mother said as she came back in. She had tweezers in her hand, and she went to work on my knee, and I closed my eyes and actually heard the soft *pap* as the stone left my flesh, and when I opened them again morning sunlight was streaming in through the open door and Danzer was gone.

Mum held up the stone shard for me to examine. "Tweezers!" she said. I couldn't believe how something so small could have hurt so much.

Next morning I checked the baler and found the oil filter clogged with dirt. I took it out and cleaned it as best I could, and once it was replaced the baler started up again. I stood back and listened to the motor whirring. Another problem solved.

It was cooler, and the sun hiding behind a haze of clouds cast a more restrained light and muted colours across the landscape.

Rosie and I had stayed up into the night watching the news on TV until it started repeating itself, which even the most profound, earth-shattering news does when there are so many minutes to fill. They'd brought on various talking heads and so-called experts to discuss *Sunbeam* and what might have happened, and when they started dragging up minor celebrities to offer their take on things we'd flicked the TV off.

Rosie was still back at the farmhouse, but she was getting ready to feed the chickens and collect the day's eggs. Life went on. At various times through the sleepless night she'd pronounced herself certain that Jimmy was dead, or confident that he was alive, and she attributed her confusion to shock and grief. I knew her well enough to know when she wanted to be left alone.

I carried on baling, and the simple comfort of honest physical exertion distracted me from the news. It was always there though, nestled at the back of my mind waiting to seethe into my thoughts. It might have been the biggest news item of my life, and its effects stretched far.

Around mid-morning Rosie walked across the field carrying a flask of coffee and some pastries. She seemed more level, calmer, and we sat with our backs against a roll of hay and poured, drank, ate. The sun had burned through the morning haze and it was hot against my skin. I always used sunscreen, because the denuded atmosphere made continued working outside virtual suicide if you didn't.

I leaned back and thought of infinity. The *Sunbeam* had been gone for over four years, and on the news they said it was over a hundred thousand times more distant from us than the sun. Way beyond the Solar System, somewhere in interstellar space on its way to a distant star, the vast craft carried a hundred million souls and the dreams and hopes of a planet. Those soft dreams, those desperate hopes, were now under threat.

"I just don't know," Rosie said.

"You might never know."

We'd discussed the possibility that the true fate of the *Sunbeam* might be lost to us forever. Broken communications did not necessarily mean a dead ship, and that was something mission control was eager to preach.

"We had two dozen eggs this morning."

"I guess I know what's for lunch, then!"

"Fixed the baler, then."

I nodded, slurped more coffee.

"Oh," Rosie said. She could read me like an open book. Sometimes it frightened me how well she knew me. "Her?" I'd never told Rosie Danzer's name. I wasn't quite sure how I knew it myself. It was such an odd name, I thought I'd probably dreamt it up.

"She was in the kitchen last night."

"Wait, you saw her?"

I blinked, wiped sweat from my forehead. Giving myself time. I'd always been vague about how Danzer communicated with me; the haze of a dream, a flash of inspiration. It was a very private thing. I'd never suggested to anyone that I could see her.

"Seemed to work," I said, nodding at the baler. "Oil filter."

"But you *saw* her?"

"Just a . . . sort of a glimpse."

Rosie chewed thoughtfully. I always liked it when she got her teeth into a problem, worked it through. "Must've been the *Sunbeam*," she said.

"How'd you mean?"

"Yesterday. Traumatic event. News like that kicks reality out from under you, makes you question what you know. It's so huge. Such a shock, when we've been here day in, day out, growing and harvesting, and suddenly something like that happens and it's . . . " She raised her hands, scattering pastry crumbs across her legs. "And I was so affected by it all that you were dealing with that, too. So your childhood friend came along and presented herself to you to help."

"She's not my childhood friend."

"You know what I mean."

I did, and didn't. I'd long since ceased trying to rationalise

Danzer, because nothing I thought about her seemed to change or settle anything.

"I didn't mean to lessen her," Rosie said, and she leaned her head on my shoulder.

"So what are they saying this morning?"

"Pretty much the same as last night. Same interviews, same clips of *Sunbeam* being built, launching. It's disaster on a loop."

"If it even is disaster," I said.

I felt Rosie shrug.

"Come on," I said. "Give me a hand. Let's stay away from the news for a while." I thought she'd object, but maybe the touch of the sun and being out in the fresh air had cleared her head a little. We spent the next few hours working the land, while above us speckled clouds faded from the vast blue sky like dreams dissipating in the dawn.

Danzer came to me a dozen times between when I left school and met Rosie, and several times since. There was no real pattern to her manifestations, except that she always seemed to appear when I needed help with something. It wasn't only tough life-lesson things, either. Once, in my early twenties, I fell off my bike and broke my collarbone. I lay beside the road for a while, then managed to crawl up against the hedge and drag my bike with me. My phone had been smashed in the fall and was useless. It was a quiet country road and early on a Sunday morning, and I had to wait forty minutes until a car came along and I flagged it down for help. Danzer didn't appear to me then. I'd watched and waited for her, hoping she would step from a gateway or wander along the road and suggest how I could help myself. I wonder if that's because I was already doing all the right things.

The time that sticks in my mind happened a few years later, and it took me a while to realise how important it was. It was a moment that changed my life, and an instant that Danzer herself made happen. There's something comforting in that. Maybe a little chilling, too.

I was driving along the main road leading from my family's farm to the local town. Music blaring, windows down, I was singing along to AC/DC at the top of my lungs, loving life even though I knew I was going to be late for a job interview. Tardiness has always been a fault of mine, and I'm not sure where it comes from. I was keen on the position with a local supermarket, but for some reason the fact that I was going to be at least ten minutes late didn't bother me too much. A little more gas, singing a little louder, wouldn't get me there on time, but it made the journey fun.

As I neared the turning for the supermarket, I saw a car parked beside the road. It was up on a jack and a woman stood beside it, looking in despair at not only a flat rear tyre, but a flat front tyre as well. That was tough luck. I saw the look of frustration on her face, then I passed her by, and with a glance in the rearview I indicated for my junction.

Guilt niggled at me. I didn't want to be a knight in shining armour—I was far from that—but I knew she needed help. She'd probably already called for a tow, but the main road was busy and dangerous, and the least I could do was drive her to the local garage.

But I'd passed her by then, and the junction was close, and there were a dozen other people who might stop to help.

As doubt and guilt toyed with me, I became aware of a figure sitting in the passenger seat.

"You could easily turn around," Danzer said. She was there, solid, in her bright blue one-piece suit. Yet the sun shone through her, and if I blinked there was a void where she sat, just for a moment. She was the space between blinks.

"I'm late for my interview."

"You won't be working in that supermarket." She said it with such confidence that I turned to ask her why, and as I lifted my left hand from the wheel—I don't know what I was planning on doing, reaching for her own hand perhaps—she smiled and disappeared from view. One blink to the next, here and gone.

I took the junction, reversed into a gateway, turned around and drove back to the main road.

The woman glared at me when I parked in front of her car. I opened the door and got out.

"Need some help?"

"Do you have two spare wheels for an old Audi?"

"It just so happens . . . " I said, turning to walk around to my car boot. I heard her utter a short sharp laugh.

"Is there a decent local garage?" she asked.

"Morgans," I said. I pulled out my phone. "I can give you their number, or I could drop you around. Only a mile or so into town."

"A lift'd be good," she said. "And if there's a coffee drive-through in the way? I need caffeine."

"Sure," I said. The job interview was forgotten, and I glanced into my car, half-expecting to see Danzer sitting there. Of course, she wasn't. I wouldn't see her again for another six years.

"What's your name?" the woman asked, standing in front of my car.

"Mark."

"Thanks, Mark. I'm Rosie."

It was another three days before mission control confirmed the news. The spokesman Pete Williams said they wanted to be sure before they made their findings public. And their findings were that *Sunbeam* had flown right into the path of a comet's tail. It should never have happened. There were systems to prevent it, failsafes, and the ship's computers should have spotted the danger from five billion miles out, giving them enough time to tweak the vessel's course. But something had gone wrong, and while the spokesman said it might take them weeks to analyse the data to discover just what the fault had been, the result was the same.

It was over in the blink of an eye, he said, and the clip of his sad, staring face, eyes glimmering as he remembered everyone he'd known on board that doomed ship, went around the world. They presented a roll-call of the small crew whose job it was to remain awake and run the ship, thereby caring for the millions of sleeping souls. A dozen images in I realised they were all wearing the same clothing—a blue, one-piece uniform.

Rosie said she'd known Jimmy was gone, but she still became upset all over again. We cracked a bottle of wine and turned off the TV. She lit candles and I built a fire, and we sat together on the sofa and drank and talked long into the night. She worried at an image, turning it again and again—that Jimmy would have been blasted out into space, and might have died breathless and freezing and with only infinity holding him tight. I said if he had died like that, then he had gone further than virtually every human ever. And before I had time to consider, I said, "And he'll be out there forever." I bit my lip, wondering if I'd planted an image that would haunt her. But I knew Rosie so well. She fell silent for a long while, relaxing into my embrace, and after a few minutes she raised her glass and said, "To my floating Jimmy."

We toasted her brother. I threw a log on the fire, while Rosie opened another bottle. Then she started to talk, and most of it was memories of her and her younger brother when they were kids. I let her talk, head back and tiredness sweeping over me, with the fire heating us through and the wine chilling us down. I chuckled here and there, and then she said something that felt like a dream.

"Huh! Jimmy. Rosie and Jim. We were kid's book characters, you know? I used to tease him about that. If he'd been a girl, our folks were going to call him Danzer. What a name, eh? If it even is a name. Who the hell knows."

I froze, then Rosie carried on talking about a family holiday, Jimmy's first bike, and the first time he said he wanted to be a scientist. We were both sleepy, and I wondered if I'd misheard her. I also wondered what it meant if I hadn't.

A little while later she was snoring gently against me. I took her glass in case she spilled it, but though my arm was asleep I didn't want to move. I listened to her peaceful breathing, and before I knew it she was nudging me awake.

"Bed," she said.

"Yeah."

Drunk, almost sleepwalking, we went to bed.

Rosie was nudging me again. I snorted, tried to roll away, dreams and the cool darkness of our bedroom stirring around me.

"Hey!" Another nudge.

"Lemme. No. I'm asleep."

Her hand on my shoulder, shaking, more violent this time. "The fire."

My eyes snapped open. Rosie lay on her side of the bed, cuddled up with knees up to her chest and duvet clutched in tight. She breathed deep, heavy, and I sat up straight, looking around the room.

She was backing away towards the open door. She had never, ever touched me before.

"The fire," she said again as she slipped out onto the landing.

I jumped up and dashed from the room, glancing back once at Rosie's shadow as she slept and dreamed on.

Downstairs the fire was crackling as it ate its way through the remains of the last log. Knots spat, and sparks speckled the rug in front of the fireplace. There were already a few darkened patches where embers simmered. I picked up a cushion and beat them out, then used a poker to spread the remains of the fire in the grate. I put the guard up against it, then sat down on the rug. My breathing was fine and level. I wasn't afraid or shocked, and maybe that was because I was still groggy from sleep.

"Too much wine," Danzer said, exactly as I thought those same words. She was sitting on the sofa, in the same place where Rosie had fallen asleep against my shoulder, and I tensed as if to go and sit beside her. But I didn't think that would work.

She nudged me.

I thought if I stood, she'd probably fade away just like she had before.

She shook me awake!

"Are you real?" I asked.

"I'm so far away, it doesn't really matter."

Then she smiled, and instead of vanishing she sat there with me for a while, until light touched the curtains and a new day dawned.

SEARCHING FOR THE ROOM
YOU CAN NEVER FIND

The door scrapes on grit and something that has been dropped and smashed, and it sounds so much like an angry growl close to my ear that I jump and glance behind me, out across the desolate dust-covered gardens where my footprints to this place are already fading away. It's the gentle breeze that does that, the fine dust. The breath of the world wipes out any trace that I have ever been there. The scraping is the loudest sound I have heard in days, perhaps even weeks, and I freeze in place. I imagine the sound echoing away through this vast old mountain hotel and wonder what it might wake, but that is only fanciful make-believe. In reality I know there's nothing and no one there, or anywhere. Only dust.

Inside, I turn and stare at the large front doors for so long that the hazy sun has moved across the light brown sky by the time I come to my senses. The light has changed and shifted, but it's difficult to tell how much time has passed. I decide to leave the door as it is. I can't bear that noise again, and I can now see that the door ground across the shattered remains of something that might once have been fine china, or bone. It doesn't really matter that it will remain open.

Quick escape, I think, but that's an idea from many months ago, not now. Back then there had been things I needed to consider escaping from quickly.

I turn and head into the large lobby area. It's illuminated by six huge hanging chandeliers, each holding two dozen clear glowing bulbs. It's curious that the power is still on, but I don't dwell on it for too long, because this is a whole new world of mysteries. Three weeks ago I saw a car sitting on flat tyres with its engine still running. There's a spread of tan leather sofas to my left and a long reception desk to the right, with large columns holding up the three-storey roof, mirrors, and paintings reflecting what the gorgeous landscape beyond the windows and doors had once looked like. It's nice to see these paintings, but sad too. It's like looking into my dreams, framed by the limits of recollection. On some of the low tables between the leather sofas, large vases hold the brittle remains of flowers. Petals are fine dried sculptures on the tabletops, waiting for a breath to reduce them to dust. A stack of luggage is piled close to the reception desk, with a laptop bag left carelessly open on top. A trolley stands nearby, empty but for a folded pushchair. On a single lonely chair placed against one of the columns, a book is open face-down. I see the title and it's one I always thought I should read, but I don't pick it up just yet.

There's a fine sheen of dust across everything, just enough to dull the whole scene. I don't mind. Most of what I see now is like this, and that's fine, because there's a place where it isn't so. I've been travelling for some time, so I decide to go and find this place before thinking about anything else—the food I might discover here, the water, the booze, the clothing and blankets and tools and anything else that might help me to continue in this strange new world. Before *all* of that, I go to rediscover the past.

———————

Room 104

Alice tripped as she came to sit back down and she giggled as she went sprawling, left hand sinking into the sand, knees thumping onto the blanket, and despite everything she retained hold of the wine glass in her left hand.

"Didn't spill a drop!" she said, and her giggle turned into a guffaw that ended in a loud snort. From along the beach another couple who'd come to watch the sunset applauded and the woman let out a supportive whoop, and Alice raised her glass to them and said, "I thank you."

I helped her sit, hugging her in close.

"Water's freezing," she said, even though she'd only gone in up to her shins. I'd remained seated on the blanket, nursing a beer in one hand and content to watch her paddling. I'd managed to take a few sly photos with my phone, even though she didn't like having her picture taken. I never really figured that out or understood. I told her she was beautiful, to which she only shrugged.

"Sun's going down," I said, stating the obvious. It seemed to settle the moment and Alice leaned into me, resting her head on my shoulder. I hugged her close, and brought the second blanket up over our legs. The waves shushed up against the shore. A dog barked in the distance, so far along the beach that I could hardly see it against the sand. A few seagulls still whirled overhead, readying to roost.

"Do they just float?" I asked.

"Huh?"

"The seagulls. Do they float around on the sea at night? Roost on the cliffs, or rooftops? Where do they go?"

"Seagull hotel," she said, sipping some more wine. "Turn your brain off. Look."

She was right. Nothing needed to be said, and we sat close to each other and watched as the sun burned its way into the sea, setting the water aflame and bleeding its last across the cloudy skies. The colours started bright and then turned deep, like an oil painting being sketched, layered, and then given depth by an invisible and patient artist. Darkness fell quickly, and soon we'd finished our drinks. The other couple walked past us hand in hand towards the paths leading through the dunes and back into town. We stayed, though, and neither of us needed to say why. Some moments that should last forever just seem to play out that way.

I wake after several hours' sleep. The bed is the most comfortable I've slept in, perhaps ever. I am alone, even though for a while I feel sand between my toes and smell Alice's hair, that brand of shampoo that simply says *Alice* however autumnal-woodland or spring-flowers it claims to be.

Soon those sense memories bleed away like a sunset, and I sit up against the headboard. It's night outside now but the lights are still on, and I see myself reflected in the dark window. I need a shower, and I've already established that the hotel still has running water. As far as I can tell it has everything that makes it a hotel, apart from the staff and guests. I don't know how long it's been since I've had a proper wash. To begin with I was keeping count of the days, and then the weeks, but once I lost track it was difficult to grab hold of them again, and more time dashed past with every blink.

I stare into my own exhausted eyes and lean back down into the pillow, but sleep does not come.

Later, I hear faint voices in the distance, like poor radio reception or a stilted conversation. Perhaps they belong to people back on that faraway beach and they're just an echo from my dream. Or maybe they're ghosts. Either way I don't go to investigate, because I'm sure they are best left alone.

When morning comes I have that shower. It's delightful. The gel smells of pine forests not covered in dust, and I stand beneath the powerful spray until the water swirling down the plughole turns from brown to clear. It feels strange being so clean, and when I look at the filthy clothes scattered on the bathroom floor I can't face pulling them back on. There's a fluffy, heavy robe hanging behind the door, and I slip it on while I'm still wet and go looking for something to eat.

I've been lost in hotels before, especially at night after a few drinks. Once in New York I found myself in a shadow hotel, corridors slightly more run down than I was used to seeing, doors speckled with damp, and when I found my room number the key would not fit. I tried for a long time, but the door was not opening. I checked the room number and tried again, and again. Eventually I found my way back down to reception and the receptionist smiled and said I'd found my way into the *other* hotel, the one not taking guests anymore, and she directed me to my own room. I woke up next day doubting the memory, and I doubt it even more now.

I wander the huge building, with no receptionist to ask the way. It's half an hour or more before I find my way to a large dining room, imbued with the memory of old breakfasts. I walk through to the kitchens and the larders, and there I find shelves and shelves of tinned goods, and in a large walk-in fridge there is bacon and sausages and more food than I could ever eat. I cook on gas rather than over an open fire for the first time in forever, and the food tastes glorious. I eat it at a table at the edge of the dining room, and several times I raise my hand and chuckle as I imagine a waiter or waitress walking over to top up my coffee. I finish the mug, feeling as though I've drunk two or three, and leave the plates to clean up later.

It already feels like it's been a long day. I'm tired again, probably from my long search for the dining room, cooking, and eating such good, rich food. Still in my robe I stroll out of the large dining hall and pass by a staircase. I turn and look up at no one coming down. I venture up the stairs. The corridor on the first floor is identical to the one below, with the same patterned carpet, chequered colour scheme, and subtle light fittings. Between blinks it is pristine, and dust-coated. It reminds me of that long-ago hotel with its shadow self.

Every door is closed but they all have old-fashioned keys in their locks, with heavy wooden fobs engraved with room numbers. I wonder why any hotel would have been left with keys in open doors. Maybe it's simply been waiting for me.

I choose a door at random and inside I immediately feel at home. The room is familiar, as if I've only just left it, even though it is bland and sterile and clean and contains nothing of mine.

The bed is huge. The covers are turned down, and there's a small wrapped chocolate on one of the pillows. It's in the shape of a small bird. I peel it and starting chewing, and the taste accompanies me down.

Room 134

Another beach and a different time, this one was in a small fishing village in Cornwall. We'd had a meal and shared a bottle of wine, and we went for a walk before going to bed to help our food go down. We were both relaxed but far from drunk, and we were the only people on the small sandy beach, as far as I could tell. It was dark and breezy, and waves washed against nearby rocks, throwing up ghostly spray in the moonlight. There was nothing really special about the moment, no more than a thousand others we had spent together and would spend together in the future. Alice hugged me from behind and we watched the sea together.

"Food baby," she said, tightening her arms a little around my stomach. I groaned.

"Shouldn't have had that apple pie and custard."

"Eyes bigger than your belly."

I opened my eyes as wide as I could, and even though she couldn't see I knew that she knew what I was doing.

"I'm looking forward to growing old with you," I said.

"Idiot." She sighed heavily into my neck, and we watched the sea ebb and flow, up onto the beach and back down, a gentle heartbeat indifferent to our own and yet so bound with that moment.

When I wake it's morning again. I stretch in the bed, sit up, and look at the once-glorious views. The curtains are open, and I can't recall whether or not I closed them the night before. Beyond, the landscape is wide and huge and desolate, with mountains in the distance, valleys closer by, the flat sheen of several lakes interrupting the rugged terrain. It is all grey. Dust has made this place its own. I cough as though it's still in my throat, even though this room is sealed and clear. I walk to the windows and run my hands around the edges, testing the seals. I tug at a handle and one casement pops open, and I shove gently until it reaches its limit.

The familiar smell of my past few weeks or months is carried in on the constant, equally familiar breeze.

I realise that I'm naked, and the robe I'd been wearing is on the floor. I go to the wardrobe and there are some clothes in there, trousers and socks and underwear and several shirts. They're tatty but clean, and they're just about my size.

I decide that I have to take some control of my situation. I know there's plenty of food here, and that the power is still on, but if I'm going to remain here for some time—and there's no doubt in my mind, and when I look out at the colour-bleached landscape it's as if I have always been here—I have to check out this huge hotel properly, see what else is here, and make sure . . .

Make sure I'm alone.

It's a strange thought, because I haven't seen another person in so long that I cannot remember what their face looked like, nor the sound of their voice. All I can remember is Alice from my dreams, and how her hair felt against my cheek and the smell of her on my skin. And that's fine. If I'm to remember just one person, it is always going to be Alice.

As I wash and use the bathroom, I hear the distant thump and rumble of water moving through pipes. I turn it off and step from the bathroom, and there's still a sound coming from somewhere. I think it's water hammer, or perhaps a leak, but then it comes closer and is easier to identify.

Footsteps on soft carpet.

I stare at the closed door and the narrow band of light below it, cast there by the corridor lights outside. No shadow interrupts the light, and the footsteps—if that's really what the sound is—soon drift away. Perhaps whatever cast them is too nebulous to affect light, or maybe it was merely sigh of fading waves.

I spend some time walking the corridors of this strange, empty hotel. There's no sign that I am anything other than alone. I peer into several other rooms and one of the larger suites, all empty and perfectly prepared for future guests. I check the ice machines close to the staircases—two machines to each floor, one in each of the two vast wings—and they're humming with chilled delight. The paper cup holders on each machine are full and untouched. I travel up and down in the elevators, examining myself in the mirrors that cast a thousand images of me back and forth, as if seeking enough of me to fill all the rooms. I'm looking older than I remember, more drawn, my eyes not as bright as before as if coated in dust. It's hardly a surprise. I've been out there in the ruined world for longer than I can recall, and I must have seen terrible things.

I find the gym with sauna and jacuzzi, and there's even a small pool, nowhere near large enough to swim in but still warm, rippling from two small vents on the pool floor. There are eight loungers around the poolside, each with folded towels and robes and one of those wrapped bird-shaped chocolates that I found on my pillow the previous evening.

The restaurant is as I left it, one table strewn with yesterday's meal. The bar is large and relaxed with subdued lighting, and soft music is piped in from somewhere through speakers I cannot find. The tunes are innocuous, written for background, and I don't recognise them. I find a computer room for guests, the computers all on but with no internet access. There's a small shop selling essentials and books and a counter of souvenirs from the area. Hidden down a corridor just past the shop is a laundry room. There's no sign of anyone else being here, and no indication that anyone came here since the hotel staff and management left.

It's as if the hotel has been left ready for me.

I take a dip in the pool, bobbing around for an hour or so before sitting in the sauna for a while. The jacuzzi is too violent after such gentleness, so I sit on one of the loungers instead, towel draped over my nakedness even though there's no one here to see. I drift off, then back again. I'm relaxed.

Later I make another meal, this time steak and chips and mushrooms, and as I follow up with apple pie and custard I smile and think of Alice by the sea, and I hear the hush of waves washing onto a distant beach. It sets my eyes drooping. I had intended going to the bar for a nightcap, but I can do that tomorrow, or the day after. I can do that whenever I want.

Room 232

Alice was driving because I'd had a pint with lunch, in a small country pub on the way to the hotel where we were going to spend a long weekend walking, eating, drinking, just being with each other. The roads were less busy now that we'd left the dual carriageway, and the route winding up into the hills revealed more and more of the glorious views all around. I felt bad because I could take them in, while Alice had to concentrate on the twisting road, the stone walls protecting us from sheer drops, and the potholed surface. A bike race came from the opposite direction, and soon they were sweeping past us heading downhill while our little car continued to climb. Their focus and effort impressed me. Sometimes it was single riders, while others rode in small groups. All of them showed the sweat and pain of the climb they'd just made up to the high pass where our hotel sat, and I wondered how many had glanced at that hotel and thought about stopping for a drink.

"Maybe we can go for a ride," Alice said.

"On our balcony?" I asked, wriggling my eyebrows even though she was concentrating on the road.

"You." She changed gear and we turned a corner, and the moment became special. Alice driving. Me relaxed in the passenger seat. Her hands on the wheel, the way the light played across her skin as the car shifted direction, as if she was guiding the sun and conducting its rays.

"Love you," I said, and she waited a while before saying it back. In that while, everything between us was calm and perfect. I knew she felt it as well. Calm, and perfect.

The drive went on for another half an hour, but it was that moment that stuck with me, pinned to the memory-scape of our life together. Sometimes it happens like that. Most memories hang from bigger moments, but it's the smaller ones that hold no real import at the time that sometimes persist. Her voice when she returned, "Love you too." Her hands on the wheel, steering the sun. Those forgotten moments that turn out to mean so much.

I wake to the sound of people walking past my room. They're talking in low voices as if to not disturb me, and there's a *whoosh . . . whoosh* that might be heavy feet dragging along the carpet, or perhaps the memory of bike wheels whisking past. I lie motionless in bed until they've passed me by, though it's difficult to tell when silence falls again.

I sit up in bed and look around the room. *My room*, I think, but that idea doesn't sit quite right. I stayed in different rooms the previous two nights, and though they were both quite similar to this one—though not identical, because this is an upmarket place with different colour schemes and furnishings in each room, even though the corridors all appear to be the same—I know that they were elsewhere. I'm not even sure I can remember their numbers, but I'm equally certain that does not matter.

I go to the door, looking through the fisheye and seeing nobody outside, touching my ear to the wood and hearing nothing. I probably imagined the noises as I rose from sleep.

Washed and dressed, I leave the room and head outside, closing the door behind me. I know I probably won't see inside that room again. There's something quite exciting about choosing a different room each night. It feels a little like exploring.

I head along the corridor, searching for a staircase that will take me down to the ground floor and the dining room. I have a raging hunger every morning which I don't recall from my time outside, beyond the comforts and safety of this huge, empty hotel. I pass by a painting on the wall and pause, backtrack, and stare. It's a beautiful image of a bird, small with a red flash across its head and speckled brown wings that could never be called dull. I've seen this bird before. Elsewhere in the hotel, probably, but somewhere else as well. I frown. It looks . . . out of place. It's the first time I've thought that since I've been here. The painting style might be called old-fashioned, the sort of image that would have looked more at home in a quaint old pub in the countryside, whereas the rest of the hotel is decidedly modern. Some of the artwork I've seen is of the *I could have done that* sort. Alice and I had always argued about that, in a good-natured way. *Then why didn't you?* she'd ask.

I could most definitely not have painted this bird. I step back and it's almost lifelike, so much so that I half-expect it to turn its head towards me, then alight from the wall and flit off along the corridor.

The bird remains motionless, and I head off in search of breakfast.

That afternoon I sit at the bar and drink good whiskey and cry a little, because I don't know where Alice is, I don't know where anyone is, and the front door I left open three days before has let in a haze of dust that has covered the entire reception area, dulling the paintings that hang there, all of which now seem to be of that red-crested bird. The whiskey goes down well, though, and after a few more tears I'm happier. The bar remains empty but I no longer feel alone. I wonder at all the people who have drunk here, breathed this air, and sat where I am sitting. After another couple of whiskeys it's almost as if they are here with me. I hear chatter and laughter, and shadows start to move in my peripheral vision. Perhaps it's the dust-laden breeze drifting through from the reception area, but I like to think not. I raise a glass to them all and take another sip, and somehow, later, I find my way to bed.

Room 352

Alice and I sat on our hotel room balcony. The view was beautiful. We were consumed by the glow of recent lovemaking, a relaxed heat, and we were both nursing a glass of red. We sat close together, arms touching. The sun was sinking towards the mountains and already spreading its colours across snow-speckled peaks, and we were silent as we waited for it to dip beneath the horizon. We had no doubt that it would set the clouds afire in a staggering display all for us.

Even before the bird came I knew this was one of those special moments. Then the bird fluttered up from the garden and landed on the balcony's handrail, and Alice's slight gasp stuck in my memory, and I saw her tense from the corner of my eye as the bird sat there, head jerking left, right, left again as it checked us out. It had a red stripe across its head and speckled brown wings, a light chest with darker markings.

"What is it?" I asked.

"Never seen it before," she said.

I tried to hold onto that moment but it flew away with the bird. It was the last day I saw Alice alive.

We spent the rest of that beautiful day together, and it was the longest, most profound great moment I ever experienced. You know what I mean. These moments punctuate life, and often there's no real reason or cause why they stick in your mind. They're imbued with the sense that all is well and always will be, your heart is pure happiness, and they are perfect moments in a life that is otherwise by necessity imperfect. You breathe them in and give thanks, and then they're gone and often it's difficult to remember the exact feeling, only that the feeling was there.

That was it. That was my last time. That night during our sleep we left each other, and I wake in another impersonal hotel room with a painting of that bird on the wall above the dressing table, and I cry because I know Alice has gone forever. Even though I have these perfect moments, she has gone.

I find peace, however, when I spend the rest of that day walking the hotel. It's difficult to see how many floors there are, and how many rooms there are on each, but I aim to visit every single one, until the dust from the open front doors sweeps in and dulls this place from my mind forever.

STORY NOTES

In Stone (*Dark Cities*, 2017, Titan Books Ed. Christopher Golden)

The brief for this anthology was something like "scary, haunting stories set in an urban environment". Having spent twenty years of my life living in Newport, South Wales, I had plenty of inspiration! This story drew very heavily on times in my late teens and early twenties when I used to go into Newport drinking with friends. Even back then we weren't really fans of nightclubs (apart from the epic Metro's on a Tuesday evening which was Heavy Metal Night! There are many stories to tell about that, probably enough to fill another collection). Instead, we usually favoured a handful of pubs where we could have a few beers and a chat, and invariably we were on our way home before midnight. This story is set *after* midnight. The streets and alleys, the shadowy places and the hollow, haunted breaths through dark streets, all have a very particular place in my memory, and whilst writing I realised I was plumbing all the little fears I always had about the urban environment. Because sometimes, Newport didn't feel particularly safe. It wasn't often I'd walk home alone, but when I did it was quickly, via routes I knew. Places I didn't know might hide anything. Urban legends whispered in smoky, dimly lit pubs resurfaced then, muttering back at you from deep shadows where rats scampered and claws scratched. The city at night was an altered place with different rules, and this story was a way to invite past me to take a step into that domain.

Trick of the Light (*House of Fear*, 2011, Solaris Ed. Jonathan Oliver)

I've written plenty of ghost stories, but this might have been my first actual haunted house tale. I wasn't sure I could do it to begin with—haunted house stories seem to have a particular set of rules I wasn't certain I'd be able to follow and also come up with something original—but I let the writing flow, and managed to not worry about rules much at all, and I came up with something I was very pleased with. It's a gentle story, and sad, and *quieter* than much of my fiction (quietness is something I seem to be embracing more and more in my writing as I get older, and maybe that's just age, or maybe experience. Whatever, I welcome it). I can't remember an awful lot about the writing of this story—that tends to happen a lot, as I usually just launch in with an idea or a character and see where the story takes me. For me, short stories are very rarely planned. In this case, I believe I started with a place.

Clown's Kiss (*Blurring The Lines*, 2015, Cohesion Press Ed. Marty Young)

I'm not an orderly person. I have a mess of files and folders on my computer for short stories. Short Stories Completed. Short Stories Bits & Pieces. Current Short Stories. There are duplications, partial files, ideas scattered all over the place, and often when I open a file I haven't touched for five years, or sometimes fifteen years, it's to see one line. That was the case with this: "It was the day the clowns moved in next door." That single line no longer starts the story, but as is so often the case it was my way in, a line that conjured an image or a series of images that expanded and grew into something more. I've never been someone who's afraid of clowns, but I had fun writing this story and trying to unsettle or frighten those people who are. It was also written as I was edging into middle age, and this might be one of the first stories I've written from an elderly person's point of view. Maybe that fear of clowns comes as you get older. See more weird things you can't explain. Like that old, tumbled-down house in the village that no one ever talks about . . .

Relics (*Streets of Shadows*, 2014, Alliteration Ink Ed. Maurice Broaddus & Jerry Gordon)

Well, not all my short fiction is quiet. This story begins with the line, "I know where you can buy a dragon's cock." Sometimes a single line is how a story starts for me, and when this line popped into my head I knew I had an interesting starting point that might open up into a whole new world. And when Maurice Broaddus and Jerry Gordon approached me to write a story for their urban horror & magic anthology, I grabbed onto that first line—that dragon's cock, if you will—and decided to see where the flight might take me. An adventure which, I have to admit, the producers and writers of *Game of Thrones* really missed out on. The result was *Relics*. And this is one of those occasions where a random thought—one line in this case—can lead to something much bigger. Because the short story *Relics* was the inspiration for my novel of the same name, and that novel became a trilogy. Sometimes that's the way things go! One day over a beer I'll tell you about how writing the novelisation of *30 Days of Night* led to me and Chris Golden joking about "vampire Polar bears", and how that resulted in us writing a trilogy of novels, which were then optioned by 20th Century Fox and they hired us to write the script! That story could only have ended better if they'd made the film, but as so often happens in Hollywood that didn't come to pass. But I digress! *Relics* . . . yes, enjoy this adventure into London's dark, sometimes furry and scaled underbelly.

Sole Survivors (*Scaremongrel*, 2015, Pigeonhole Ed. Anna Jean Hughes)

I met Anna Jean Hughes when she edited my novel *Coldbrook* for Arrow/Hammer. A couple of years later I was in London, and met Anna for a beer at Paddington station where she told me she was employed by a new venture, the excellent Pigeonhole. She asked me to write her a story, and *Sole Survivors* was the result. I can remember very specifically where the seed for this tale was planted. In 2010, 33 miners were trapped in a mine collapse in Chile. The world watched as efforts were made to rescue them, and after a couple of months they were pulled out, one by one, into the glare of sunlight and media attention. And because I'm a writer and I muse upon stuff like this, I remember thinking, *What if 33 were trapped but 34 were rescued?* It's an intriguing idea and I did nothing with it for a while. But no idea is ever wasted, and when Anna asked me for a story the concept expanded and winnowed itself into *Sole Survivors*. I'm very fond of this story and I've revisited it several times, thinking about how it might be a novel or a movie, or perhaps even a TV series. Maybe one day.

Skin & Bone (*The Doll Collection*, 2015, Tor Ed. Ellen Datlow)

When Ellen Datlow asked me to write a story for her new anthology which at the time she was just calling "the doll collection" and which became—because of course it absolutely had to—*The Doll*

Collection, I knew at once that I didn't want to write a story about a haunted doll. Or even, a doll. Instead I had a good think about what dolls are, where they come from, and what it is about humans that makes us want to build representations of ourselves. Is it ego? Superstition? Art? Sometimes all three combine, but sometimes it's something else entirely. Maybe race memory.

Strings (*Adam's Ladder*, 2017, Written Backwards Ed. Michael Bailey & Darren Speegle)

The idea for the great anthology *Adam's Ladder* was to examine how humanity might evolve in the near future, whether by our own hands, nature's input, or something more mysterious. Now, I'll get it out there up-front that I'm no scientist. Even so, I'm fascinated by science and often inspired by it—the weirder and more exotic, the better—and I've often spent time researching various scientific subjects to give my writing at least a sheen of realism (multiverse theory for *Coldbrook*, nanotech for my novella *The Origin of Truth*). With *Strings* I'll admit that I let the idea of research slip a little and just went with it, looking for the horror in what we might find when we start trying to better ourselves with science, altering our destiny, our evolution, or even our own realities. Sometimes, Here Be Monsters.

Strange Currents (*Innsmouth Nightmares*, 2015, PS Publishing Ed. Lois H Gresh)

This is one of those stories I can't remember an awful lot about. It happens. Sometimes they come with a splash and a hit, and they're usually the ones I remember. Sometimes they're a worker, a tale that is more dream-like than a memory of something solid that really happened. So yes, someone in a lifeboat (and it's not the first time I've started a story this way), strange shapes in the ocean beneath and around him, and the hope—and perhaps the fear—that he is about to be saved.

A Man Walking His Dog (*Phantoms*, 2018, Titan Books Ed. Marie O'Regan)

I should write a companion story to this called, "A Jogger". You know what I mean. Bodies found in woodland by a man walking his dog or a jogger, and it's too obvious to write a story about that man or that jogger actually being the murderer, isn't it? This was a fun, quite gentle, sad story to write, exploring my love of dogs and the countryside, and it's partly inspired by an incident that happened close to me, the discovery of the body of a man who'd gone missing from a nearby village. He was found in woodland just off my local canal towpath, after having been missing for several days. I honestly can't remember how he was found or by whom, but knowing the canal as well as I do I suspect it probably *was* a jogger or someone walking their dog. There's a bench in place there now with a plaque dedicated to the dead man, it's well-kept and well-used, and it's such a sad monument to someone's life. So this story is partly inspired by that, but it's also about getting older, and maybe even accepting more strangeness into your life. I'm in my early fifties now, and my agent has noticed that I'm writing more and more about the processes of ageing, and the effects it has upon us. It's not something I do consciously, but I guess it's natural.

Embers (*Nightmare Magazine*, 2014, Ed. John Joseph Adams)

I guess in some ways this is another story about ageing, but it's also about ghosts from the past, and revisiting old haunts, and old memories of happier times. It's one of those stories that is informed by a couple of separate ideas or inspirations—that happens a lot, and it'll often bring a cool, staid idea alight. Part of this tale is about me and my cousin Andy tearing it up in our childhood village, having adventures, scrumping apples, getting sunburnt, riding our bikes and causing trouble, and having the sort of fun that just seems to stick with you, and is the sort of fun you don't seem to have enough of as you get older. I don't know why that is—maybe it's the power of nostalgia giving memories that tantalising gleam—but I honestly think that even at the time we knew what was happening. Each day stretched out before us, each week was an eternity, and the six-week summer holiday lasted forever. I still have a sense of returning home whenever I revisit that village, even though I haven't actually lived there in over forty years. Another aspect to the story is more local—the several pillboxes scattered around the countryside where I live now*. They always interest me, probably because of their age and intended use. It's as if they are automatically inhabited by ghosts simply because of these factors. "Embers" is another gentle ghost story. Or is it? I'm not even sure myself.

(*Tens of thousands of pillboxes were built during WW2, constructed from bricks and concrete and intended to form lines of disruption in case of a German invasion. Thrown up quickly, thousands still remain to this day).

Flotsam (*The 2nd Spectral Book of Horror Stories*, 2015, Spectral Ed. Mark Morris)

I write about grief and loss a lot, but never really understood it until my mother died. This story is about loss, and also the mysteries of the sea. I love the ocean, enjoy swimming in it, but there's always the tingle of fear and doubt about what else is in the water with you. I'm also fascinated with the idea of messages in bottles, and how long they can bob about on the sea, carried by strange currents around the globe until they're delivered, eventually, into the hands of the person they were always intended for.

Into The Death Zone (*Slices Of Flesh*, 2012,
Dark Moon Books Ed. Stan Swanson)

Since I've been more into outdoor exercise, I've become more and more interested in extreme adventuring such as climbing Everest. There was even a brief time a few years ago when I thought about how great it would be to have a go at it myself! But that idea was never serious and didn't last too long, and I certainly don't want to add to the problems of mountaineering tourism. And one of those problems is . . . a lot more dead mountaineers. I've read plenty of books about mountaineering and watched documentaries, and I've always found it shocking and haunting that there are still scores of bodies up on Everest. Many of them are in inaccessible areas, so it's too dangerous to bring them down. Some even provide navigation points for those climbing the mountain. Just a few years ago there was news of a team's efforts to bring down some of these bodies, and I instantly saw a story in that. This is a very short story, but it's one of my favourites, and it's gathered together in this book with "Embers" and "Flotsam" because it has that same ambiguous haunting tone that I love so much.

Emergence (*New Fears* 2, 2018, Titan Books Ed. Mark Morris)

This is another story influenced by the area where I live. I'm lucky enough to live close to Abergavenny in Monmouthshire, and all around us is gorgeous countryside. One of my favourite local mountains to walk and run (and occasionally cycle) around is the Blorenge. There's an easy way up this mountain, and a hard way, and sometimes I'll run, walk and crawl up the hard way, trying to beat my previous times and always with the gorgeous views at the top as reward. Halfway up the woodland ascent there's an old brick tunnel built into the hillside. It doesn't go far, at least not that I can see—I've never been far inside to check, because it's very old and looks pretty damn precarious. But I just can't imagine why it was built where it is, and what might once have been on the other side! Well, actually I can imagine . . . and that's where "Emergence" came from.

Land of Many Seasons (*The Dreaming Isle*, 2018, Unsung Stories Ed. Dan Coxon)

This is another story set on the Blorenge mountain, and another tale of ambiguous hauntings, beautiful countryside, and a painter falling in love with that enticing place. If you've read this far in the book or story notes you'll have gathered that I love the countryside over the urban sprawl any day of the week, and more often than not my fiction reflects that. The Blorenge really is a lovely place, and those culverts and brick tunnels really do exist. There are also leftover mine workings, and places on the mountain where it can sometimes feel no one has ever been. Who knows what else is up there?

The Lonely Wood (*Letters To Lovecraft*, 2014, Stone Skin Press Ed. Jesse Bullington)

This was an interesting anthology concept from writer and editor Jesse Bullington (check out his brilliant novel *The Sad Tale of The Brothers Grossbart*). We were asked to read Lovecraft's essay "Supernatural Horror in Literature" and pull a quote that might inspire and inform a short story. This resulted in a very varied anthology, and my piece was inspired by this quote:

> "But the sensitive are always with us, and sometimes a curious streak of fancy invades an obscure corner of the very hardest head; so that no amount of rationalisation, reform, or Freudian analysis can quite annul the thrill of the chimney-corner whisper or the lonely wood."

In this tale I take a trip to St Paul's Cathedral and play with belief and doubt, and what happens when the two collide.

In The Dust (*The New Dead*, 2010, St Martin's Press Ed. Christopher Golden)

I love zombies. One of my favourite novels I've written is *Cold-brook*, a multiverse zombie apocalypse novel which I'm currently working on developing as a TV series, in collaboration with a good friend of mine. Wouldn't that be lovely? So, when Chris Golden asked me to write a zombie tale for his anthology *The New Dead*, of course I jumped at the chance. "In The Dust" is set in my local town of Usk, and it plays around with the whole zombie tropes—when the plague happened, how it ended, how far it spread. My characters are desperate and contained, struggling to survive and wondering whether they even should. I wrote the story over a long weekend in a cottage in Wales with a few other writers, and some mornings after the night before we resembled those shambling, pale creatures. You can't beat a good zombie story, and *The New Dead* is full of them.

May The End Be Good (*Seize The Night*, 2015, Gallery Books, Ed. Christopher Golden)

I've been tinkering for a while with a trilogy of historical fantasy novels collectively called *The Lords of Stone*, each set in one of the Norman castles built in efforts to quell the Welsh uprisings after William the Conqueror's invasion of 1066. I like the idea, have written a good portion of the first novel, but it's one of those projects I drift away from. I'll get back to it one day and hopefully finish the first novel . . . but in the meantime there's this story, inspired by a famous and desperate quote of the time following the Harrying of the North. An unknown monk said,

"Things went ever from bad to worse. When God wills, may the end be good." My idea for the trilogy is that in those awful times of plague, famine and pestilence, there were plenty of opportunities for unknown creatures to exist in the land and prey on the helpless. This story was written for a vampire anthology, and the theme seemed to fit well with the period I was researching. It's one of the grimmest stories I've written. I love it.

Sleeper (*Appalachian Undead*, 2012, Apex Publications Ed. Eugene Johnson)

Back to *Coldbrook*, and zombies. I set that novel in the Appalachians, even though I'd never visited. I did a lot of research about the place and I was told by a few readers that I'd carried it off OK. So I was pleased when I was asked to contribute to *Appalachian Undead*! Perfect . . . a zombie antho set in Appalachia. It was almost as if it was meant to be.

The Gleeful Ones (*Barbers & Beauties*, 2013, Hummingbird House Press, Ed. Michael Knost & Nancy Eden Siegel)

I never thought I'd write a superhero story. I'm still not sure I have. That's how odd this one is. This is also a great example of how a particularly narrow theme can make your imagination work harder. "Write a story set in or around a barbershop" I was asked. Anyone who knows me will realise I haven't visited a barber's in several decades, and I think that probably helped me think laterally on this one. And so of course I wrote something about maybe-superheroes and killers and plenty of other weirdness. Like the first story in this collection "In Stone", I took inspiration from the city of Newport where I used to live, trying to capture that edgy feel of potential danger that the nighttime streets of the city centre sometimes exude. This one stands out as one of the stranger stories I've written, and

I love it because of that. Sometimes focussing the mind on a tight theme really works wonders!

The Flow (*Terror Tales of Wales*, 2014, Gray Friar Press, Ed. Paul Finch)

I've always been fascinated at the idea of villages emptied of people and belongings and flooded to make new reservoirs. Who isn't? Not only are these places that once thrived and bustled now empty of humanity—like the best of post-apocalyptic fiction set in empty towns—they're also in an utterly changed and alien environment. I love the idea of walls still standing, roofs still on, and the phantoms of previous inhabitants wandering those watery rooms. Wales has several such places, and when my mate Paul Finch asked for a story from me for his excellent *Terror Tales Of . . .* series, this was the first idea that appealed to me about Wales. I combined it with another favourite theme of mine—going home. Of course, in a horror story it's never quite obvious what you're returning home to, and whether past sins might still be rich and raw, however long they've been forgotten or drowned from your memory.

The Protector (*Peel Back the Skin*, 2016, Grey Matter Press Ed. Anthony Rivera & Sharon Lawson)

This was a tough one to write. As a writer it's my job to put myself in other people's shoes, and to experience and even try to understand things I've never experienced, and have trouble understanding. I tried that here with a story about domestic abuse. But really it's about something deeper—the power of the imagination, strength of character, the ability of a child to adapt and change, and survive. I think it's a pretty powerful story, and ultimately upbeat. And while it has monsters and beasts and bloodied victims and fantastical terrors, its real horror is much closer to home. I'm lucky that I've never experienced anything like this story, but even so it was very difficult to write and live with for a while. I was glad when it was finished.

Carried Away on a Sunbeam (original to this collection)

This is one of two original stories I wrote for this collection. I'm fascinated with the idea of generation ships—huge vessels laden with millions of sleeping people, built to travel for hundreds of miles through space in the search for a new home for humanity. My novella *Rime* (also from PS Publishing) is set aboard one such ship, and I've also tinkered with the idea of a TV series toying with a similar idea. For this story I decided to remain on Earth and spend some time in the lives of two people left behind. It's an upbeat story in many ways, and though the ending is ambiguous—sit down with me over a pint one day and we'll talk about it, but I can't guarantee I know exactly what this story or its ending really means—I'm very satisfied with how it turned out.

Searching For The Room You Can Never Find (original to this collection)

This story came from a couple of places, and it shows how sometimes a couple of ideas, often decades apart, will meld to form an idea. First, an experience I had in a convention in New York maybe fifteen years ago (I think it might have been when I was a guest at the World Horror Convention, or perhaps one of the Stokercons I attended in NY). I'd had a few drinks and decided to head back to my hotel room. The hotel lobby was quiet, and I ventured along corridors and up staircases until I found my floor, and saw room numbers on the wall signs. I tracked along to my room, and already I was noticing that the corridor seemed . . . tatty. I hadn't noticed this previously. Strange. So, I tried getting into my room but the key wasn't working. I tried again. Concentrating. But nope, no joy.

I wasn't drunk. Squiffy maybe, so I concentrated harder, still unable to open the door. I headed back along the corridor to the staircase, frustrated that I'd have to go all the way back to reception to check my key. Once I arrived there and explained my predicament, the receptionist smiled and said, "Oh you've been to our shadow hotel, it's being upgraded so no one's staying there right now." *Shadow hotel*, I thought, and that was really bloody weird. I went to my room—directed by the receptionist this time—and that strange experience really stuck with me. Much more recently, an episode of *Black Summer* (a great zombie series on Netflix) featured an abandoned ski lodge which seemed untouched by the flesh-eating apocalypse. These two ideas collided, and this story was the result. It follows a recent gentler pattern in my work, and I'm very pleased with where it went, even though as with the previous story I'm not *quite* sure where that was.

Story Credits

"In Stone" (*Dark Cities*, 2017, Titan Books Ed. Christopher Golden)

"Trick of the Light" (*House of Fear*, 2011, Solaris Ed. Jonathan Oliver)

"Clown's Kiss" (*Blurring The Lines*, 2015, Cohesion Press Ed. Marty Young)

"Relics" (*Streets of Shadows*, 2014, Alliteration Ink Ed. Maurice Broaddus & Jerry Gordon)

"Sole Survivors" (*Scaremongrel*, 2015, Pigeonhole Ed. Anna Jean Hughes)

"Skin & Bone" (*The Doll Collection*, 2015, Tor Ed. Ellen Datlow)

"Strings" (*Adam's Ladder*, 2017, Written Backwards Ed. Michael Bailey & Darren Speegle)

"Strange Currents" (*Innsmouth Nightmares*, 2015, PS Publishing Ed. Lois H Gresh)

"A Man Walking His Dog" (*Phantoms*, 2018, Titan Books Ed. Marie O'Regan)

"Embers" (*Nightmare* Magazine, 2014, Ed. John Joseph Adams)

"Flotsam" (*The 2nd Spectral Book of Horror Stories*, 2015, Spectral Ed. Mark Morris)

"Into the Death Zone" (*Slices of Flesh*, 2012, Dark Moon Books Ed. Stan Swanson)

"Emergence" (*New Fears 2*, 2018, Titan Books Ed. Mark Morris)

"Land Of Many Seasons" (*The Dreaming Isle*, 2018, Unsung Stories Ed. Dan Coxon)

"The Lonely Wood" (*Letters to Lovecraft*, 2014, Stone Skin Press Ed. Jesse Bullington)

"In The Dust" (*The New Dead*, 2010, St Martin's Press Ed. Christopher Golden)

"May the End Be Good" (*Seize the Night*, 2015, Gallery Books, Ed. Christopher Golden)

"Sleeper" (*Appalachian Undead*, 2012, Apex Publications Ed. Eugene Johnson)

"The Gleeful Ones" (*Barbers & Beauties*, 2013, Hummingbird House Press, Ed. Michael Knost & Nancy Eden Siegel)

"The Flow" (*Terror Tales of Wales*, 2014, Gray Friar Press, Ed. Paul Finch)

"The Protector" (*Peel Back the Skin*, 2016, Grey Matter Press Ed. Anthony Rivera & Sharon Lawson)

"Carried Away on A Sunbeam" (Original to this collection)

"Searching For the Room You Can Never Find" (Original to this collection)